PENGUIN BOOKS

TWO IS LONELY

Lynne Reid Banks, who is the daughter of a Scots doctor and an Irish actress, was born in London and was evacuated to the Canadian prairies during the war. On her return to England she studied for the stage at R.A.D.A. and then had several years' experience with repertory companies all over the country. The first play she wrote was produced by several 'rep' companies and later performed on B.B.C. television. She wrote and had published other plays, one having been put on in a London 'little theatre', and many performed on radio and television. She was one of the first women reporters on British television. She worked for I.T.N. for seven years – from its inception until 1961 – initially as a reporter and later as a scriptwriter.

Her first novel, *The L-Shaped Room*, appeared in 1960 and was made into a successful film. She published *An End to Running* in 1962, *Children at the Gate* in 1968, her fourth novel *The Backward Shadow* (a sequel to *The L-Shaped Room*) in 1970 and *Two is Lonely* (the concluding book of the trilogy of *The L-Shaped Room*) in 1974. She has also written *One More River*, *Sarah and After*, *The Adventures of King Midas*, *The Farthest-Away Mountain* and *My Darling Villain* for young adults and children; *Dark Quartet: The Story of the Brontës*, its sequel *Path to the Silent Country*, *Defy the Wilderness* and *The Warning Bell*.

After leaving I.T.N. she went to live in Israel (the scene of several of her novels) where she married a sculptor. She and her husband lived on a kibbutz in Galilee for eight and a half years and have three sons. They now live in London.

TWO IS LONELY

Lynne Reid Banks

PENGUIN BOOKS

Penguin Books Ltd, Harmondsworth, Middlesex, England
Viking Penguin Inc., 40 West 23rd Street, New York, New York 10010, U.S.A.
Penguin Books Australia Ltd, Ringwood, Victoria, Australia
Penguin Books Canada Ltd, 2801 John Street, Markham, Ontario, Canada L3R 1B4
Penguin Books (N.Z.) Ltd, 182–190 Wairau Road, Auckland 10, New Zealand

First published by Chatto & Windus 1974
Published in Penguin Books 1976
Reprinted 1976, 1977, 1978, 1979, 1981, 1982, 1983, 1985

—

Copyright © Lynne Reid Banks, 1974
All rights reserved

—

Made and printed in Great Britain by
Hazell Watson & Viney Limited,
Member of the BPCC Group,
Aylesbury, Bucks
Set in Monotype Fournier

PART ONE
ANDY

Chapter 1

IT HAD been an awful night and I came to in the morning, with the deepest physical reluctance, to find the alarm clock hatefully clamouring and my head and mouth and limbs giving me unmistakable messages of woe and protest as if I'd been on the worst sort of binge.

I hit the button on the clock so hard I knocked the thing off the bedside table, and heard the noisy ticking stop with the ringing as it hit the floor. I cursed hard, hating the world and everybody in it, and rolled over on my face. My eyes were sealed shut with tiredness; the morning sunlight streaming in over the downs was an affront. My mouth felt dry and my fingers swollen. The idea of getting up to face life and house-cleaning and shop-keeping and being a mother, after being a mother the whole damned night when I should have been asleep, just seemed too bloody, bloody much.

It had been most nights now for weeks. Get David to bed at nine, and myself – exhausted from the day and from the night before and the days and nights before that – at ten thirty; two hours' sleep, and then – the urgent, frightened, imperious cry: 'Mummy! Mummy!' If I didn't respond, he would come into my room and into my bed. Once I had been so tired I hadn't woken up sufficiently to take him back, coax him, sit with him, and do all the right and proper bookthings; he had slept curled up next to me the whole night, and in my sleep I had wrapped my arms around him and held him close to me, a warm, alive, male presence against my breasts and stomach and thighs, moving a little sometimes in sleeping contentment, and I, befuddled, dreamt he was Toby and woke up in the morning with a sense of horror and shame, as if I'd debauched him ... This feeling rebounded in anger against him and there was an awful scene, far more shameful to me and harmful to him than the physical companionship of the night ... But I was tired. The tiredness was

5

to blame. How can you go on, night after night, being patient, being kind, playing games he wants to play which are not really games but frightening manifestations of some deep inner disorder that you are afraid to let yourself guess at – wondering when, if ever, it is going to pass, what you can do about it, how to find out what is really the matter when he won't tell you . . . Does he know? Do you really want to know? Because whose fault can it be but yours, who else can you blame – except the child himself, and you do blame him sometimes when the strain becomes too much – 'David, you're just putting it on, all this! I'm not coming in to you any more, you can yell as much as you like, you're a big boy and this is all nonsense—' And stopping at the look of mulish bewilderment on the small, loved face.

But even these basic considerations fade as the weeks go on; all you ask yourself then is, how can I go on, how can I stop myself hating the child for keeping me awake? Even the whys no longer seem to matter, only the how-longs have weight, because it's like torture, it's a constant rubbing friction on a relationship. The exhaustion, the bewilderment, the shame, made me short-tempered even during the day; my work suffered, my friends suffered, my child suffered. I suffered.

I'd taken him, first to a doctor who, after examining not David but me, prescribed a mild sleeping draught for him which I was afraid of but which in desperation I finally tried – unsuccessfully; then to a psychiatrist. The psychiatrist did examine him. She took several sessions over it. Then she examined me.

'Has he ever asked about his father?'

'At one time he used to ask a great deal, but that was – oh, three years ago. Now, he never mentions him.'

'Doesn't he notice that he's different from other children in this respect?'

'His closest friend – my partner's daughter – is also fatherless. That helps him not to feel too isolated.'

'In what way is she fatherless?'

'He died.'

'Does David know that his father is still living?'

'Yes.'

'And you say he never mentions him?'

'Never.'

'But you realize he must think about him.'

'I've had no indications of it. Why should he hide his thoughts from me about that? He's quite frank about everything else.'

'Miss Graham, no doubt he gathered from your reaction when he was talking about it and asking questions that the subject made you uncomfortable.'

'But it doesn't.'

She said nothing to that. Whenever she said nothing, I came to take it as a sign that she thought I was fooling myself – or trying to fool her. At first it used to annoy me, but later, when I went over our conversations, I realized that she was very often right – certainly in this instance.

'Does he tell you why he is afraid to sleep at night?'

'He's never told me he's afraid to sleep. He just says he doesn't want to sleep, or he can't.'

'That's a child's way of saying he's afraid.'

'But why has this come about only recently? Until he was six, he slept perfectly well.'

'Until a child is six, he hardly realizes he's different from other children. Even the Thalidomide children were mentally and spiritually quite happy and satisfied until around that age.'

This violent comparison shocked me, as it was meant to.

'David's a normal child.'

'During the day, he is. But night time for a child is rather like strong drinks for an adult. It brings truths to the surface which are otherwise kept hidden.'

'But hundreds of children – thousands—'

'Manage with only one parent? Oh yes. And some manage very well. And others don't.'

'Then you're convinced that this – wakefulness of David's is the result of his coming to realize that other children have fathers and that he hasn't?'

She looked at me for a moment. She was a very unusual-looking woman, with a face like a caricature of a cat – high quizzical eyebrows, small snub nose, wide mouth like a cupid's bow enormously attenuated at the ends, and short black hair clubbed into a youthful fringe. But she was over fifty, and the effect of the girlish hairdo was a little bizarre. However, she had the 'right' type of personality for a psychologist. She wasn't a Freudian. I'd made sure of that first. All they do (Jo had told me, having been to one in her youth) is to sit and listen. I wanted practical advice. But getting it in this way was something a bit more than I could readily take. It wasn't so much what she said as the things she left me to figure out by myself from her silences, her mildly-raised eyebrows, her sudden, wry pursing of the lips, when the long corners would draw in suddenly and she would put the forefingers of both hands up to the place where her eyebrows joined. She seemed to be trying to conceal from me some impulse to frown in dismay or disapproval – no, disapproval is the wrong word; *pity* for what she saw me revealing, and which she could interpret. This sudden movement of the hands and mouth always put me on the alert to what I had just said.

'Have you never thought of marrying?'

I laughed a bit. 'I hear there are unmarried women who don't think of marrying,' I said, 'but I've never known any personally.'

'And in seven years, you've never met anyone . . . ?'

It was I who was silent now. In seven years I had met several men. But the simple fact was that they were all – including Pietro with whom my relationship was strangely simple, and now Andy, with whom it was strangely complex – overshadowed by the two who pre-dated the birth of David: Terry, his father, and Toby.

Terry, looked back upon, seemed like a shadow, some *deus ex machina* who had set upon me like a legendary shower of rain and impregnated me on the solitary occasion of our mis-mating. He was no more solid in my memory than that, and I thought about him as little as possible, which was very little indeed. My only thoughts connected with him were watermarked with fear, fear that he would one day get so fed up with his barren second marriage that he would really set about finding us and would batten on to us – or even only on to David – laying claim to him in some way and upsetting us both beyond calculation.

Since the telephone conversation I had had with him several years before, I had had no contact with him, and yet from time to time, sinisterly as it seemed to me for I was anxious only to avoid all thought of him, he was brought to my attention. One day when I was leafing through a film magazine in the local launderette I had been thrown into confusion by suddenly coming upon a photo of Terry, a Terry somehow indefinably altered, not merely by years. I had sat there gazing at it numbly. 'Terence Boyden, ex-rep actor who for the past seven years has neglected show business for the world of publishing, returns with a new smile [a *new* smile?] and, so he tells us, a film contract only waiting for his signature ...' I peered closer. Yes, it was new. The crooked front teeth were gone, replaced by artificial-looking straight ones ... and some trick of the photographer's light had invested his head with a sort of halo. He no longer looked quite male, or even quite human ... I shivered and threw the thing down, grimacing, so that the woman at the next washing-machine opened her mouth to ask what was the matter ...

And Toby?

I had told the psychiatrist the basic facts about Terry, but I had not mentioned Toby. Not mentioning Toby had become a deeply-ingrained habit with me over the past five years. Since Dottie's departure for America, which more or less coincided with Toby's marriage, I had shut him up inside me where he occasionally fought to get out like an imprisoned genie. But he was safer in than out. I did not talk about him, even to Jo, my friend and partner. It had been bad enough, Dottie knowing. Now there was no one left in my life who knew, except John, and John, with his mysterious dark-continent insight, also seldom mentioned him.

I sighed heavily. 'Yes, I've met men ... quite a few. Never the right one, somehow.'

'Right for whom?' the psychiatrist asked.

'For me, of course ...'

Her fingers flew up and made a steeple under the sudden ridges between her eyebrows.

'No, really!' I protested. 'A woman must choose a husband for herself, surely?'

She didn't answer.

At the end of the counselling, she said: 'David needs a father. He needs one very badly.'

I asked the question I feared to ask. 'Will – will this terrible night-waking go on, then, until – I get married?'

'Oh no! It can't. You might never marry. He can't keep it up in-

9

definitely – physically, he must be getting tired, as you are. Besides, it's a phase. But it's a phase which, because of its very painfulness, is useful. You see you couldn't just ignore it, as you may have done other signs and symptoms in the past. The point is that while it lasts, you must try to come to terms with his lack. And do something about it. Because one morning you'll wake up after sleeping all through the night, and you may think to yourself, "Thank God, it's over, he's cured", only of course he won't be cured at all, it will just have gone to another place where it may not be so obvious but may be eating holes in him just the same. And later on he may eat even bigger holes in you than he is at the moment. Because everything that's wrong in his life has to be your fault.'

'You mean, it must seem so to him?'

She drew in the corners of her mouth, then spread them again quickly in a smile.

'He's a very bright child, you know,' she said as she shook my hand.

'I know. It's something to be very grateful for.'

But she didn't answer that, either, directly; she only said, 'Well, that depends how you look at it.' Only then did it seem to me that she had said, 'He's a very bright child, you know,' as if she'd been saying, 'Look out.'

And now here I was, still lying half-comatose at 8 a.m. swallowing down gall and wormwood with my weariness, dreading the moment when I would hear him pattering along the wooden corridor in his bare feet, the moment when he would leap on top of me expecting his morning romp or at the very least a cuddle and a cheerful face. I had a million things to do, and not the slightest will or energy to do any of them.

And I'd broken the god-damned alarm clock. I groaned aloud and turned my head sullenly towards the window. Without raising myself, since the bed was right against it, I could look out into the spring countryside.

I was so tired that the tiredness opened up a gaping chasm into the depths of my mind, where unnamable fears lay blackly, slimily writhing. I didn't look, of course, but I knew they were visible – I could feel them moving there in my brain, going look-at-us, look-at-us. Suddenly I jerked upright and forced my attention on to the beauty outside the window. Green, with a backdrop of soft purplish hills, hedges that the farmers hadn't yet cut down to make room for another yard of crops. No motorway, no blocks of flats or factories or building developments of any kind; not even an airport whose flight path led over my cottage. Not so much as a pylon. So much to love, so much to be grateful for ... I felt the tears coming, tears not of gratitude but of loneliness and terror. It was day, and now David would be himself, he would go riding his pony with Amanda and laugh and be naughty and hug me or fight with me; he would eat with good appetite and I would look at his sturdy eight-year-old figure and be comforted; I would congratulate myself, I might even get smug again and think 'Alone I did it!' – exult in him as my sole accomplishment. And then night would fall.

What if I'd been fooling myself all the time, all through the years of effort? And if I'd harmed David, if my life with David had been based on a mistake – if *that* achievement was nullified by an inner canker, what of my personal victory? Oh, but I already knew the hollowness of that. Not all the time; sometimes I could kid myself about that too, and think I was happy and fulfilled. But not when I was tired, or depressed, and not in the cold darkness of the night when David was forcing me to be awake and aware of, instead of hiding in the merciful oblivion which had protected me before. To wake alone at night to a recurrent challenge – ineluctable physical and emotional demands – how it brought it home, the solitariness of a task meant to be shared!

And now I heard him coming. It had been a worse-than-usual night to which he had paid minimal tribute by sleeping in – not the four hours I would have slept if left to myself, but twenty minutes longer than usual. Now, with a child's quick-recovery potential which even a healthy 36-year-old woman can only gape at with bitter envy, he was fully awake and ready for his day, untrammelled and (apparently) untroubled. His feet came thud, thudding up the carpetless stairs, and I heard the whirr of the spinning-wheel on the landing as he spun it. His morning ritual. ('Has he any obsessive habits?' 'Yes, he spins the spinning-wheel every time he passes, and won't throw out his gum till he's chewed it at least a hundred times.') And now, his head round the door.

And instantly, if temporarily, all the black anxiety and guilt and anger and even the weariness fell away, because of the dearness of him, the perfection. Small, dark, neat head; horizontal eyebrows cornering downwards at the outer ends, huge brown eyes, a smile of devastating potential . . . No, not quite perfect, for there were the two crooked teeth exactly where Terry's had been. Lovely well-developed little body. Athletic, by God . . . There at last was something to thank Terry for. My own school memories are still blotted by run-off races where I couldn't even beat the slowest, fattest child in the class to get into the relay team . . . I could never quite believe in David's ability to climb trees and run and ride – and jump, which he now did straight on to my stomach with both feet.

'O W! God! Get off!'

He fell down on top of me and we wrestled briefly.

'Can we go over to Amm's today, Mummy?'

'You can, on your bike, if you keep to the side of the lane and are very careful.'

'Aren't you coming?'

I hesitated. I could easily tell him it was my day at the shop; he never kept track. Then, when he'd gone out for the day, I could catch up on some sleep. But the lie wouldn't come out this time, though minor lies were not always beyond me.

'I'm pretty bushed, David – after last night.'

I hadn't meant to reproach him. If there was one thing that woman had taught me, it was that he couldn't help it. In any case, it was useless. His reaction was always the same when I brought up the nights during the days. He frowned slightly, moved away from me a little, and changed the subject.

'Amm and I could go out on our ponies, and leave you a map with a cross where you had to meet us with the picnic. Oh, Mummy, do let's!'

He lay on me, belly to belly with the bedclothes between us, his face poised eagerly a few inches from mine. I felt his slight but formidable weight on me and I trembled suddenly.

'You cold, Mummy?'

'No . . . Get off, darling, will you? I must get up now.'

'And will you come today?'

'Okay then.'

'YIKE!'

'Only darling, I must, *must* have a nap this afternoon. Will you promise to play quietly?'

'Promise. Or I'll stay over at Amm's if you like.'

'Well, we'll see. Now go and get dressed, and don't forget your teeth.'

'Why don't you wear pyjamas in bed, Mummy?'

'Because I prefer a nightie.'

'Amm wears a nightie but she says it gets up under her chin and leaves her bottom bare.'

'Oh do dry up about bottoms, David! You're obsessed.'

'What's obsessed?'

'When you think about a thing far more than it needs to be thought about.'

David dawdled on the bed and watched me getting dressed.

'Why do you do everything behind your dressing-gown, Mummy? Amm says Auntie Jo goes around the house with nothing on in the mornings.'

'Do you want me to go around with nothing on?'

He considered. 'No, but not to hide, either.'

'I'm not exactly hiding. I'm just being modest.'

'What's modest?'

'Keeping covered what ought to be kept covered.'

'That's hiding.'

'Oh dear – perhaps it is. Well, that's how I am. If you want a bare Mummy rushing around the place, you'd better move in with Auntie Jo.'

David rolled over on his back with a snort of laughter.

'Bet she wouldn't rush around bare if I was there!'

'No, I bet not too. Why's that, do you suppose?'

'Because I'm a boy, I should think.'

'Exactly.'

'But Amm and I see each other's bo – I mean, bare.'

'David, honestly, you know there's a difference between a little girl and a woman.'

'Yes. Bosoms.'

This word had its inevitable effect of reducing him to such a helpless condition that he fell off the bed.

'Oh come off it, for goodness' sake! Go and dress yourself.'

Eventually I had to hike him to his feet and propel him through the door, hicupping, and he tottered off to his own room crying 'Bottoms! – and Bosoms! Alive, alive-o!' I went downstairs and got the breakfast ready. While the eggs were poaching I went out into the hall and phoned Jo.

'Hi—'

'Hi, Jane, don't stop me, duck, I'm on the verge of being late.'

'Never mind, Georgie's always there to open up.'

'The employer should be there first, you know that. Besides, we've got that consignment from Brum to unpack.'

'I did it before I left last night.'

'Oh really? You *are* good, thanks. Listen, what about the kids today? Any plans?'

I told her David's.

'Can you face it?' she asked. 'What of the night?'

'Unspeakable – don't even ask.'

'Poor, poor you.'

'My eyes aren't properly open yet. Never mind. A breath of fresh air'll do me good, and after lunch I thought I might leave David at your place and get some kip – would that be all right?'

A slight pause. Jo was never happy about the kids being left alone. 'Why don't you sneak up and kip on my bed? Then you'd be around if they needed you.'

'That's a thought. Right, I'll do that then.'

'What about supper? Shall I bring home fish and chips?'

'Yes – I can't face cooking.'

'Don't blame you. You must be buggered.'

'That's an understatement.'

'I'll be back by 5.30. If you're asleep I won't wake you. I'll feed the kids and, if you like—' I knew what she was going to say and I knew why she'd stopped herself. In the good old days, David often used to sleep at Jo's house with Amm. But you can't do that, even to your best friend, especially when she's the kind of sleeper that even the alarm-clock doesn't always wake. 'Well,' she broke off, 'maybe not. Though we might give it a try one night; you never know; maybe he wouldn't wake up if he knew you weren't going to be able to come.'

'You don't know how he is at night. I'd be afraid to risk it. He might go into hysterics or something . . .'

'It's hard to imagine . . .'

For Jo, perhaps; but she'd only ever seen David's daytime self.

While David ate breakfast, I prepared the picnic to his instructions and incidentally swallowed three cups of very strong black coffee. After that I went upstairs, undressed again and had a cool bath. Then I made the beds and tidied up and washed the breakfast things, and by that time I felt a great deal better and David was literally dancing with impatience.

'Mummy, come *on*! It's nearly ten o'clock. It won't be worth going–'

'Take it easy. I asked Auntie Jo to tell Amm to catch the ponies and saddle up – they'll be ready to start when we get there.'

'If we ever do.'

Just as we were leaving the cottage, the phone rang. David nearly burst into tears.

'Oh, leave it, Mummy! Please leave it!'

But it's against my nature to leave a phone to ring.

'You open the gate and unlock the garage door. I won't be a moment.'

'Good morning,' said a voice I knew.

'Andy. Hallo.'

Anything? Something, undoubtedly. A feeling as if the skin of my face were being lifted. A slight breathlessness. I was given to these acute moments of self-analysis. I wanted to retain my objectivity, and this seemed one way.

'I'm phoning in the hope of persuading you to spend the day with me.'

'Oh, I'm sorry, I can't.'

'It's not your shop-day. I've been counting.'

'When it's not my shop-day, it's my children's day.'

'Are you taking them out?'

'They're going riding and I'm meeting them with a picnic.'

'Sounds fun. Couldn't I come? I'll bring my own grub.'

I hesitated. 'But I don't know where we'll be meeting. They set the place always.'

'Well today you set it, and make it somewhere near the site.'

'Well – all right. Let's say one o'clock.'

'Good. I'll expect you.'

He hung up without goodbyes as he always did. His curtness was

15

not a lack of manners; it was more as if he rationed himself for words, as if he were determined not to allow himself to waste any. His movements, too, were almost nervily direct and contained. Sometimes when we were together I longed to stroke him, soothe him somehow, make him relax with me ... I thought if he relaxed physically, if he were not always so *stiff*, so spare and squared-off and unsprawling, I might get that mouth of his open and some words out of it which would let me know what the hell was going on in his head. His speech was quite stark in its lack of frills; like his blueprints – like his buildings, as a matter of fact – his sentences came out in clean pre-fabricated neatly-finished shapes – geometrical. He never stumbled or withdrew anything or repeated himself. It put me off him, and yet, perversely, attracted me. There was more there; I knew it. Shut away, but there. That hidden human being I could sense, huddled inside those hard straight lines of certainty, order and purpose made me wonder bemusedly from time to time whether it was possible that I could love him.

Often I was quite sure I couldn't. How can one love a man who never reaches out to you, never offers you any part of himself or, for that matter, invites you to give any of yourself to him? Anyway, he was often pompous. Once he'd said, while we were having what ought to have been a cosy drink together in the Swan, 'Geometry is founded in natural laws, and so are we. We unearthed the laws of form and numbers, dug them out of the world like ore. They're impregnated with us, and we're impregnated with them.' I choked on my beer. Who the hell, I wanted to say, can find a warm, on-coming answer to a remark like that? And the insane thing was that even while this mini-lecture was in progress, I got a strong intuitive feeling that he was trying to *woo* me. His hand, a traitor to its orders I felt sure, suddenly shot out at the end of his speech and enclosed mine, a hand as warm and male and desirous as his words were remote and didactic and impersonal.

This was, and had been during the whole two months I had known him, the pattern. During his dry, often witty but never forthcoming comments over a dinner-table, his eyes, his hands, his whole inner self would be *yearning* towards me in a way that had me utterly confused. Every instinct I had told me that he loved me and wanted me, and often it was hard to tell whether what I felt for him was an answering, concealed desire, or merely a burning curiosity bordering on exasperation.

Physically he had attracted me from the first time I saw him, leaning against a gate with his large black Rover parked in the lane right in my way. When I honked, he'd turned in my direction with an expression of thinly-veiled annoyance as if I'd interrupted a mood of cogitation.

'Could you please let me get by?' I asked politely, leaning out of my own car window.

'Oh,' he said, straightening reluctantly from his gate, 'sorry.'

As he took the few steps to the Rover, I saw he was tall, square, solid – the antithesis of Toby; middle-aged, middle-class, well-dressed, square-featured, brown-haired, clean-shaven. I liked his looks; I liked his *bulk*. I've always seemed to fall in love with thin (Terry) or small (Toby) men; and a man like that who looked like a bulwark could not but appeal, other things being equal.

He drove ahead of me to a lay-by, where he drew in, and then leant across to roll down his offside window and ask, 'Are you local?'

I pulled up level with him. 'Yes. I live in a cottage over there. Why?'

'Only that we'll be neighbours.'

'Oh really? Where are you going to live, then?'

'Back there, where you first saw me.'

'But there isn't a house anywhere near there.'

'I know I'm going to build one.'

Oh, God. Bulldozers, builders, noise, despoilation. I suppose it showed in my face (every bloody thing does, apparently) because he grinned a bit ruefully and said, 'Sorry. But it won't last long, the upheaval I mean, and after that I'll let nature take over again. It'll all look very green and unscarred by the time I've settled in – I'll bury the house in trees – you'll hardly know I'm there.'

Our eyes met for about two seconds and something in me registered: *possible*. Later I asked Jo about him. She knew at once who he was.

'His name's Felix Andrews. He's an architect, quite successful I believe. Moving out of the Smoke and going to build his own country house. He's bought quite a large acreage from George Downing, over the other side of the wood.'

'Yes, I know, that lovely open bit where the children can ride. Has he got planning permission?' I asked unkindly.

'Must have, surely. What's he like?'

This question meant, Is he a possibility for either of us? And I answered it: 'Nice, early forties, but of course he must be married.'

However, Jo knew all about that too, trust her. 'No, he's not, not any more. He must have been, at one time, because he's got a grown-up son—'

'Doesn't necessarily figure, as we know—'

'Come on, we're not all like you.' I may say that after seven years of the closest ties, she only just knew me well enough to get away with that kind of remark, even though I'd asked for it. 'He's probably a widower. Anyway, according to the grapevine he's building this house for himself and his-son-at-weekends, sort of thing. It won't be very big. Meanwhile he'll be down in the district a lot, supervising the building. He's staying at the Swan.'

'With the Davies?'

'Yes. It was Alf who told me all about him.'

Alf Davies, who, with his buxom wife Dora, ran the Swan Inn, had once been my employer. They had a daughter about the same age as David, called Eleanor, known to Jo and I as Little Nell because she was so precisely the opposite of that pathetic waif – a fat little blonde replica of her mother, rosy-cheeked, good-natured, lolly-sucking, over-dressed and spoilt rotten as the only offspring of besotted parents (well, Dora wasn't all that besotted, and frequently redressed the balance with a good clout on her ample bottom when Alf wasn't looking). Naturally she was the butt of contempt of all her school-fellows, including my son, whom I could reduce to howls of outrage by reminding him that he had often, as a baby, shared a bed with her. I had a number of photos, taken by Alf with a flash, to prove it.

Alf, having despaired of the large family he had hoped to raise, had turned the slack of his overflowing energy to being the village gossip and matchmaker. Dora, un-cooperative in the matter of child-bearing, was more keen on Alf's substitute enthusiasm, and, to hear them tell it, they had already 'brought together' several couples towards whose children they adopted a possessive attachment even when they were not invited to be god-parents. They both took a special interest in me, of course, and I couldn't help wondering whether all this information, filtered through Jo in Alf's typically elephantine idea of discretion, might not be directly aimed at promoting a match between me and this stranger.

'I couldn't marry a Felix, could you?' I asked unguardedly, following in a completely unserious way this train of thought.

Jo looked at me sharply. 'Hey! Was he as attractive as that?'

'Oh, don't talk cock.' (Dottie's style, not mine; I was startled to hear myself say it, especially to Jo. I only use male swear-words under high pressure. I hadn't realized, till I said that, that I felt under pressure then.)

I had next encountered Felix Andrews in the saloon bar of the Swan when Jo and I went in there some days later to pick up our kids, who were in the Davies' living-room behind the pub attending Eleanor's eighth birthday party. This occasion held sufficient hedonistic promise to overcome their everyday distaste for the hostess. I had thought this highly hypocritical and had tried to dissuade David from going, but he just looked at me as if I'd gone daft.

'But Mummy, it's her *birthday*! I mean, it's a *party*, with games, and presents, and special food, and a *conjuror*.'

'Well, I hope you'll take her something very nice, to make up for all your beastliness to her.'

'Oh yes ... Mummy, will you ...?'

'No, I won't! Out with the old money-box, my lad, a personal sacrifice is called for.'

Now I listened through the pub noises for the lighter, shriller sounds of happy children at play, but hearing half-pitched shrieks instead I raised my eyebrows questioningly at Alf, who looked harassed.

'Just a little *contra tomps*, I expect. With twenty-two of them in there, you can't expect much peace and quiet.' He listened a moment, then his face changed. 'My Gawd, it's Nelly! What are they doing to her?' And he dashed through the dividing door, leaving the bar unattended.

Several customers came in just then, and for old-time's sake I ducked under the bar and began to serve them. Jo said, 'Oh, come on, ducky, you don't have to do that, he'll be right back,' in a slightly put-out tone, but I was enjoying myself and the jokes of two old-timers who knew me from my first year in the village when I'd acted bar-maid for Alf out of necessity. Now, when I had lived down my dubious fame as an unmarried mother and become a respectable shop-proprietor and – so to speak – village matron, it was amusing, and fun, to find I could still pull pints neatly and hadn't forgotten my skills.

Suddenly I caught sight of Felix Andrews. I became selfconscious, and stupidly, snobbishly, wished myself on my own side of the bar. However, I had to brazen it out now, so I went up to him.

'What would you like?'

He was staring at me. 'Hallo. Do you work here?'

I was relieved to get the chance to explain at once, and I did. He smiled. Did I detect relief there, too? We're all snobs at heart, we English, all of us. And yet the feminine machinery went into automatic motion, because I immediately registered his relief as a compliment. Why else should he care if I was a bar-maid? What sort of list would I be struck off, if I were? He held my eyes, once again, a fraction too long for perfect casualness. I turned away quickly to serve someone else, and left it to Alf to find out what Felix Andrews wanted to drink.

The party, Alf informed us (all smiles now, having discovered that his Nelly had worsted her persecutor with a fat-handed blow to the ear) was going like a bomb, but was at the present-giving last stage. Our young would soon be available for us to take home. Meantime we might as well have a noggin – I think he was about to say 'on the house' but then he caught the eye of the architect and, divining his intention by instinct, bit back the words and waited. Sure enough, he came across to us. Seen like that in isolation, crossing a room towards us, he was easy to appraise as a good-looking, confident man. Jo straightened herself and I sensed her favourable reaction, even before she knew who he was.

'My name's Felix Andrews,' he said. 'May I buy you both a drink?'

Jo accepted for both of us. Odd, how often I felt the age-difference between us, not in any loss of sympathy or understanding, but in a sharp and fleeting feeling every now and then that we were basically of different generations. She had passed some subtle, fortyish bourn into what I can only term middle-age, however lightly it sat upon her, while I was still – well, not exactly young, but *not* yet middle-aged. I wondered if it had anything to do with the change of life, which Jo was now passing through. It was something I viewed with horror and dread, though paradoxically I didn't (yet) fear growing old. It wasn't so much a matter of losing my youthful looks, smooth skin, and so on. I just hated the idea that I wouldn't be able to have any more children. The opposite was true of Jo. She reckoned she'd been lucky to fit in even one child, marrying as late as she had, and Amanda seemed to satisfy such maternal instincts as she had quite amply. But she had been a beauty; she had had quite a few lovers and many admirers. I couldn't escape the conclusion sometimes, listening to her talk about her days in the theatre, that it was the admiration more than the love which had been important to her, and that was no doubt why she had never married until at 37 she suddenly woke up and realized that what mattered now was to secure herself against the time when she would not be a beautiful but not very talented actress any longer. Happily she got love, and admiration too, from Ted, and the baby was more like a gift to him than a satisfaction of any basic need of her own nature.

Now that her looks had begun to fade – her hair no longer bright blonde of its own volition, her delicately-boned face beginning to look a tiny bit simian with wrinkles under her ever-more-careful make-up – she couldn't help mourning the beauty she was losing. I who had no beauty to lose, only youngness, sympathized deeply, though for the first time I could see that the lack of beauty could be an advantage.

We sat down together at a table with our drinks, and began to exchange polite pleasantries. Jo asked all the questions to which she already knew the answers. Felix Andrews didn't hide the fact that his work was the most important thing in his life; I liked him for that, though I kept wondering where his son came in – he didn't mention him. He did, however, say that his wife had died four years before.

Quite soon Alf beckoned us. The party was over. We said good-bye to Felix Andrews, shaking hands with him. I felt the unmistakable current of his maleness running into my hand, and I smelt his male smell. Later, Jo was to say, 'I should say only about two per cent female hormones in that one.' Jo has a basic animal quality which reacts instinctively to the male and female animal in people she meets. I thought (though I did not say so because I knew Jo was watching me and suddenly about this I didn't want to be watched too closely) 'Yes, there's a very male animal there which is looking for a mate.' I was a little frightened by the purely physical *frisson* this thought gave me.

'We'll be hearing from him, I expect,' I said casually.

'You will, you mean,' she promptly replied. She fixed her sharp bright blue eyes on me. 'Interested?'

'Don't know yet,' I answered as shortly as friendship allowed . . .

Chapter 2

'MUMMY!'

I started guiltily, wondering how long I'd been standing there, my hand on the phone, brooding. I was always brooding these days. David kept having occasion to say sharply, 'Your eyes have gone dead again.' It hurt me to realize how much more often my withdrawn thoughts were with Toby than with Andy . . . Today, for instance, I had been awake (more or less) and functioning for two hours and until I heard his voice and got my face-lift I had not thought about Andy actively. This did not conform to previous love-patterns. As I walked out to the car I did a quick memory-recce – had I thought either of Toby? No. Somehow that made it all right. Toby and Andy were for ever paired in my mind, like racing figures, or like weights on either arm of a scale; I watched them always and minutely to see who was getting ahead, cursed my folly, and continued to do it.

The post van came bumping up the lane, and the postman handed me my letters through the window. 'Sorry I'm late, mum,' he said. (He knew I was not entitled to more than a 'miss', but he had long ago granted me the 'madam' as a courtesy.) 'Mr Broughton's boy left the gate open and his cows were all over the place. Had to back up and tell him, and then we had to chase 'em back. Took best part of half an hour. I wouldn't like to be that lad when his dad catches hold of him.'

And our anachronism gave me a cheery wave and went bumping away out of sight round the hedgerow. I watched him go. Soon he would go for good. His route along this country lane had already received its doom in the form of the accursed word 'uneconomic'.

It was a bare ten minutes by car to Jo's house. It was much larger than the cottage and elegance itself by comparison – Jo's urbanism had only given way to the claims of the simple life on condition that it was not permitted to become too simple. Jo's husband, Ted Barclay, had left her a tidy fortune, part of which she had invested in my – now our – handcrafts shop in the village, but a large part of which she had used to buy and equip this house. She had not my retrogressive prejudices against television, for instance, and possessed two, one a colour set, and her daughter Amanda – slightly David's senior, being already five months past her eighth birthday – had all the toys and clothes that were good for her, or even, as I sometimes thought, more. My son, being somewhat of a hedonist, sometimes seemed to prefer Amm's house to his own as a place of recreation, for which it was hard not to blame him. But since the advent of the ponies last Christmas a lot of problems were solved: the indoor attractions of the respective homes had faded into a common denominator of pallidness by comparison with the main interest of their joint lives.

There the ponies stood, already saddled and hitched by their reins to the paddock-gate, David's little fat roan shaking the hair out of his eyes and Amanda's undeniably more slender and handsome chestnut cropping the hedge. Their names, taken from a series of children's books which had once been all the rage, were Bee and Ant. Amanda, immaculately got up for riding, including a hard hat and a proper vented hacking jacket, her blonde pigtail turned up and tied with a neat black velvet bow, was sitting on the gate, switching the early flies off Ant's ears with her crop, and looking rather bad-tempered. When she saw us coming she jumped down and began opening the gate.

'Where have you been?' she asked peevishly as we got out and David ran to Bee to give him his lump of sugar. 'I thought you were never coming!' She spoke to David and not to me, seizing this opportunity to set the tone of the day with a little mild bullying; it was part of their relationship and she was the leader and the boss, but as her bossing rolled straight off him, I didn't object. Besides, she was remarkably self-confident and dependable for her age. She had all her mother's will-power, and a dollop of Ted's sound practical business-sense; she knew as if by instinct what risks were too great and which were worth taking, and if by any chance she were too rash, David's native caution ('My child is cautious, yours is timid, hers is a coward') prevented him from following blindly into it. They made a good team. Sometimes nowadays when they were allowed to go off riding by themselves and I got imaginative about stones rolling under hooves and low-hanging branches I would find myself thinking, 'Oh, he'll be all right with Amm,' as if she were his nanny.

They were already mounting. Amanda trotted Ant briskly up to the car and handed me a scrap of paper through the window.

'Here's the map, Aunt Jane,' she said competently. 'The picnic place is marked with an x like we did that other time. It'll be a nice game for you to find it.'

'Thank you, dear,' I said drily, 'but I'm not in the game-playing vein today.' I glanced at the map – dashingly but quite clearly delineating the main highways and byways of the district – fetched a felt pen out of my glove-compartment and set a large red x of my own in the middle of a field. '*That* is where we shall be meeting for lunch. One o'clock sharp. You can borrow my old watch,' I said smartly as she opened her mouth to protest. That closed it again.

David naturally set up a jealous caterwaul.

'Why can't I keep it, Mummy?'

'Because it's a ladies' watch, and also because I don't trust you to remember you've got it.' The watch and map were handed over. Amanda looked doubtfully at the latter.

'That takes us a long way from where I'd planned,' she objected.

'Bad luck. No show up, no eat.' I put the old station-wagon into gear. 'Take very good care of yourselves now, and make quite sure what's growing in the fields before you ride across them.'

'Oh, Auntie! We know every field for miles.'

'Yes, and every field knows you, and so does every farmer. We don't want any more trouble with Mr Broughton and his baby wheat, thank you.'

The children waved to me and jogged off down the lane, their black hats bobbing. I turned into Jo's expansive drive and sat quite motionless for a few minutes, listening to the quiet and smelling the air and feeling the spring breeze touching my cheek and neck, staring half-awarely at the winter jasmine and crocuses in the flower-beds on either side of Jo's white front door. Though my senses were engaged, the whole operation rested me. After a bit I heaved a deep sigh – tasting the horsey odour, too tangible for mere smelling, on the back of my tongue – and reached for my letters which I'd thrust into my coat pocket. Nothing but business, no doubt – but then suddenly I stiffened with interest. It was a letter from Dottie! With the photos, of course. I hadn't expected it yet, it was only a few days since she'd phoned me in the very middle of the night (I'd left David's bedside to answer the phone, thinking it must be a wrong number) – and there came Dottie's voice semi-circling the globe: 'To Dorothy a daughter! I've done it, I've done it I tell you! It's here beside me. Well, say something! – My God, doesn't it hurt like hell, though? Doesn't it hurt, Jane? Why did you never tell me how much it hurts?'

'Darling, it's marvellous, I'm so glad—'

'You've no business to be glad it hurt! Bill says—' (Oceanic roarings mingled with the pips.)

'What did Bill say?'

'He says it couldn't have done, he says they gave me the latest injection that paralyses you from the neck down and leaves you laughing, but I was yelling so loud I didn't know I'd had it.'

'What, the baby?'

'No, the injection!' she bawled over the increasingly bad line.

'So what's she like?'

'Just a minute, I'll look—'

'A minute costs three pounds—'

'We can afford it, love, we're doing great these days. Listen, I've looked, and – Jane? – sorry, thought we'd been cut off – she's beautiful! I didn't notice before. She's got nicer since she was born, more peaceful. She's not mauve now.'

'How old is she?'

'Let's see – about half-an-hour.'

'Good God, why aren't you sleeping?'

'It's that damned coffee they gave me afterwards instead of tea.

Really, there are some things about America I'll never get used to.'

And now here were the first photos, the first maternal letter. I looked at them – efficient flash-snaps of her sitting up in bed, her hair longer, softer, pinned up with a few wisps escaping, not the crisp streaky short bob she'd always worn; no make-up; looking older but prettier, in a bed-jacket very like the one she'd bought me when I nearly miscarried with David. I hardly looked at the baby, which was just a baby. I looked at Dottie, her thin, vigorous arms veiled in the lacy woollen sleeves, her hands curved in that peculiarly possessive, graceful position against the shawl, her head tilted on the neck, bent at an almost unnatural angle to look down into the baby's face with a smile at once fatuous and sublime ... The lines of her age were marked in necklaces around the base of her throat. She was a year older than me and this was her first baby.

I did not entirely like looking at the photos. As I stared, I found my hands and neck and arms and head imitating that position from memory. I had not forgotten the sensation. Despite all the suppressing I'd been doing for eight years, I now had to acknowledge that I had not reconciled myself to never having it again. I didn't read the letter just then. I looked through the windscreen at the mellow umber bricks of Jo's house with the yellow stars of jasmine picked out against them and thought, 'I must marry. Why don't I marry? There is something wrong with David and it comes from this, that I haven't married, and maybe that's because there is something wrong with me.'

I shook myself together and looked at my new watch. It was a present. From Andy. He'd bought it for my birthday because I'd told him no watches ever kept time on me, and he said, 'Your time is out of tune. I shall buy you watches one after another until I find one that matches your metabolism.' Then he looked at my old watch and said, 'Do you wear this in bed?' and when I said yes, he said, 'You must not wear the new one in bed. I know what happens. It's not your electrical magnetism at all. You sleep with your head on your arm, and you dribble.' 'I do WHAT!' I cried in outrage, though it burst upon me in the same instant that what he said was true. 'We will say no more about it. Unlike some men, I have no objection to an occasional dribble. Leave your watch on your bedside table. Suffice it to say that if it goes wrong, I shall know why.' Looking at it now, I laughed aloud, a silly, half-humiliated laugh. How could such a ridiculous conversation contrive to be, and remain in the mind, so intimate, so sensual, so titillating?

I had two hours before I was due to meet the children. Time enough to go home and do the house, or go shopping, or to our shop to do some accounts, or again home to wash my hair, or write some letters . . . Instead of doing any of these useful and necessary things, I climbed into the back of the station-wagon, unrolled the mattress I kept there for David, spread a horsey-smelling rug over myself, and gave myself permission to sleep.

Need it be said that I couldn't? The three cups of coffee had done their work too well. After ten minutes I rolled over on to my back and lay, wide awake, staring at the underside of the car roof. Random thoughts – or what used to be so called until the psychiatric small-change of our era taught the least brilliant of us that no such thing as a random thought exists – trailed their coats through my weary, artificially wakeful brain. I tried an experiment. I made a windscreen wiper – very realistic, with a slight squeak – and sent it back and forth across the screen behind my eyes until it was quite blank. Every little drop of thought that splashed against the screen, the wiper wiped away. It took some time, but in the end I got it – total blackness. Then I held that as long as I could and waited to see what 'random' thought was strong enough to burst open on the empty screen first.

When I realized it was going to be Toby, I fought it; the windscreen wiper went mad, squeaking back and forth frantically, but his face remorselessly materialized, and at last, like sleep overtaking me, the effort spent itself and I let the thought take me over.

It was nearly seven years since I'd seen Toby. After his marriage to Melissa (whose nickname, Whistler, aggravated my bitterness towards her by its overtones of cheerfulness) I took very good care to keep clear of any situation in which I might possibly meet him – or her. If the man you love is lured away from you by some un-principled syren, I suppose it may be legitimate to share the blame with her; but when you have no one at all to blame but yourself, it is much harder, and takes much longer, to rid yourself of the bile of bitterness and regret.

I could have had him – or so he told me, at the last ghastly meeting. If, instead of removing myself from what I regarded as my millstone position around his neck, I had just stayed around, after David was born – if only (in his words) I had 'insisted a little' at the right time . . . But I hadn't thought it was fair to him, especially considering that David was not his child. How ludicrously *faux naïve* that sounded now. But at the time I was filled with idiotic concepts which have no place in the love-game at all if one is playing to win. I suppose the underlying truth was, I never doubted that he was basically mine, that we would be together in the end, and that I could afford the moral luxuries of fairness, consideration and his needs as a budding writer, etc., etc., since our marvellous, unassailable love would inevitably survive all manner of neglects and absences which might endanger any of the frailer varieties of human affection. Idiot that I was . . . So while I, filled with self-conscious nobility of spirit, was learning the invaluable lessons of independence in the country cottage I'd inherited from my dear dead aunt Addy, Whistler was capturing Toby with the help of extreme youth, unconcealed need, and above all, proximity.

If I had by any chance been flattering myself that my few months of solitude in the cottage had really taken me far along the thorny road to true independence, those months following Toby's marriage would have taught me otherwise. I fell flat on my silly face emotionally, and if Dottie, and the shop, and later Jo had not been around, I would surely just have gone quietly to pieces. I had learnt to do without a man in my life, but I had never learnt to be completely alone – I'd never had to. At the worst, there was always David: not much of a companion in infancy, it's true, but a being, someone alive to talk to and look after whose needs had called up whatever strength I had and kept me more or less on the rails.

And of course, I mustn't overlook the therapeutic effect of John.

John was a constant in my life. He was not often around, living as he did in London and being involved in the twilit mysteries of his sub-culture world of jazz, pot, and so on, which he did not attempt to share with me. In the same way my business life was a closed book to him; he disliked Jo, believing (correctly, I fear) that she bore some subterranean prejudice against his colour, and in any case nothing could have interested him less than the shop, apart from some of the more vivid objects to be seen there.

But he and David adored each other. He was the one male presence woven like a bright if intermittent thread through David's entire life from babyhood; what cared he for John's black skin or for his unacknowledged lack of masculinity? As for the almost childlike simplicity of John's nature, this merely drew the two of them closer together.

More by some kind of primitive instinct than because of anything I'd ever told him directly, John knew that I had never wholly shaken Toby off. Though we never talked about this, I believe his intuition about it sprang from empathy, for he too, had loved Toby, in a manner not entirely different from mine. At the time of Toby's marriage, John had quietly stopped seeing him. He said it was because he loved me best and didn't want to hurt me by seeing Toby when I couldn't; I believed this, but added the silent rider that he wanted also to spare himself much the same sort of pain.

Once, however, an isolated incident occurred which John reported to me in full. It had happened around Christmas of the year before. John came down for Christmas as he invariably did – it would not have been the same for either me or David without him, and I sometimes thought he enjoyed it more than either of us – and while we were filling David's stocking, in the early hours of Christmas morning, John told me that Toby had recently brought his wife to the night-spot where John played guitar with his all-black combo.

With John it was useless even to try to hide my feelings or pretend, so I was free to ask him outright all my questions. How did he look? How did they seem together? What did they say, to him and to each other? He answered everything quite simply and exactly in the way I needed, seeming as he did so to provide me with a glimpse of the inner situation which only his deep-seeing instinctual eye could perceive.

'They not right together, Janie. Sat there all night with their hands lockin' together on the table, but like two people drownin', never lookin' at each other, never lettin' go of each other, hardly talkin'. They only talk to me, when I got my break and sit with 'em and we had drinks. This little Whistler, she very sweet, I have to tell you. You don't hate her, do you?' I shook my head, busy wrapping a yellow sugar pig, and thus not having to look at him. 'That's

good, because ain't no harm in her, except she's too young for bein'
a good wife for Toby. Was hard to find what to talk about after
such a long time we ain't seen each other, and Toby don't seem like
Toby, he different, far away, lookin' at me like he's all the time
rememberin' . . . He only come really alive when I asked about their
kids. They got these two little girls – is this hurtin' too much?'

I frowned and shook my head again. It was hurting like hell as a
matter of fact, but it was a pain I didn't want to forgo.

'They showed me pictures. Pretty little things, like black kids
except they white of course, curly hair and full lips and little round
faces, and big eyes, only too serious, like they know already what's
comin' to 'em . . . No, Jane, I ain't wrong. It can't last. I see it in the
way their hands gripped together and the way they burst into talkin'
when a third person comes, like they had nobody to open up to
except some stranger. She all of a sudden sparklin' and laughin' too
much and even kind of jokin' about Toby, criticizin' him to me before his face, but it was wrong somehow. Not that she don't love
him; but she's got things to say against him, and she's so young she
got to get someone on her side, even a big spade she never saw in
her life before. Say, this is great!' He broke off for a few moments
to play with a toy monkey; you squeezed a rubber bulb and it
played a drum.

'Go on,' I said.

'Then she go off to the ladies, and Toby sittin' there quiet and
starin' at the band although he ain't listenin', and suddenly he looks
in my face and says, "Do you ever see her, Johnny?" And I knew
he means you.'

He had the toy in his huge hands and he turned his back on me so
I wouldn't feel him watching for my reaction. I found myself sitting
down on the sofa, breathing deeply, and wrapping paper silent in
my hands.

'I tell him I see you often and you're well and David is well and
your business is goin' good. I tell him you're alone. I knew what he
wanted so I tell him. Why make him ask? And he sit there starin' at
me like he wants to say something and can't, and then he says, "It's
the kids. What will happen to them? We can't go on much longer,
but it's a question of the kids." Then, after a bit, just as she's comin'
back, squeezing between the tables in her beautiful rich dress, wavin'

to us with like this fixed sort of smile, he watches her comin' and says under his breath, "I feel like *her* father, too, sometimes."'

It was mainly due to this renewal of belief in the underground tie between Toby and me that I swopped trips with Jo and sent her to Paris in my place in February. After what John had told me, it would have been quite impossible to go to bed with Pietro even once more without a sense of unequivocal betrayal.

It occurred to me that Toby was too fair to expect me to have lived like a nun all these years (although I practically had). Just the same, it filled me with irrational dismay to imagine a renewed relationship with Toby now that I had slept with another man, one whom I couldn't even claim to have loved – at least, not in any sense congruent with the emotional touchstone lodged in my memory with Toby's name on it, like a grave which now promised (or threatened) to give up its dead.

It may seem quite absurd that a woman of my age should have found it so difficult to forgive herself for one solitary affair in six years, and a pretty unintense one at that. But I was labouring under the kind of puritanical conditioning which is harder to break out of than a steel chrysalis. I was brought up to think that you shouldn't have affairs, or at least as few as possible, and that each one represented a moral defeat. Of course nobody thinks that nowadays. I don't *think* it myself, but apparently I still feel it. Dottie thought you could have as many as you liked, providing they were all part of 'the search'. To her, each affair was a sort of dry-run for marriage, and, other things being equal, you had no cause to reproach yourself, after or during, as long as you had gone into it with what she loftily called 'serious intentions'. The problematic emergence of the fact that the man's intentions were less weighty might be a burden on your heart, sooner or later, but not on your conscience.

My father's variation of middle-class morality, however, had hamstrung me to a greater degree. The fact that he not only had me convent-educated but actually turned me out of the house when my first fumbling attempts at a sexual relationship, in my mid-twenties, resulted in the conception of David, illustrates this. I had fondly supposed that motherhood, independence and Toby had liberated me; they evidently hadn't. Possibly the shock of getting pregnant at the first go-off, not to mention all the trials and heartaches that followed, had served to reinforce my subconscious conviction that all sexual pleasure has a heavy price. Though how much could even the most punitive fates impose as a fine for dear, Gallic, no-strings Pietro?

He began as one of those oh-be-joyful things that men can be heard declaring have nothing to do with their everyday lives – and no more had it, in its way. I was in Paris on shop business, in about 1963, when I made the discovery that just once in my life I actually was liberated enough to bump into a man painting Notre Dame (a picture of it, not the spire itself), talk to him casually for a while, go for a friendly drink with him in the gay, euphoric, live-for-the-moment atmosphere of the Place du Tertre; on from there to a fabulous eight-course lunch – and finish up in his big brass bed amid a stench of turps at four o'clock in the afternoon.

We didn't, as I recall, rise from it until late at night, when only renewed hunger drove us forth. We ate onion soup and drank a carafe of wine with a bunch of his cronies, who all kidded us in a matey, ribald fashion unthinkable in England; after which brief, revitalizing interlude we went laughing, singing and dancing through the sex-lined streets of Montmartre and up those endless steps, back to bed.

And that was that. Next morning we kissed a fond farewell over huge bowls of fragrant coffee, croissants and peaches he'd gone out early to buy. He rolled up one of his pictures and jammed it through the umbrella-loop of my suitcase, and took his canvases and easel back to the Left Bank, while I went waltzing off to do my buying in a state of unutterable, if astonished, physical fulfilment. It was only when I returned to sane, sober, sexless Surrey that I paused to ask myself just what the hell I had thought I was doing.

And answer came there none. Just a gently fading sense of what I can only call luxury. It had nothing to do with Toby, nor, as a matter of fact, with me, really. It was just isolated and innocent and lovely. Which only goes to show that Dottie and I don't work on the same moral precepts at all.

I revisited Paris and Pietro four more times, and each time it followed the same pattern. I looked forward to it, bought frivolous new clothes for it, worried for fear he might be gone or married or changed or that I might have grown too old to attract him. In the event he was always there, always sweet and welcoming and amorous, and always I returned after two or three enchanted days with mild reluctance to manless reality.

But this could only continue so long as Toby was not part of that reality. The merest hint that he was, or might be, was enough to germinate the guilt which had lain doggo for four years. So this last time Jo, puzzled but uncomplaining, went to Paris, where everything naturally went wrong – she came home after a wasted week of cancelled meetings and pouring rain with a rotten cold, saying sourly that I must be a witch.

And then one fine Sunday morning I opened a paper and saw Toby's photo grinning at me over a caption which said: 'Toby Cohen, whose fourth novel *Oh Lord How Long?* came out last month to rave reviews, is being sued for divorce by his wife Melissa. The suit is not defended. The couple, married seven years, have two daughters, Rachel, 6, and Clarissa, 4.' I hadn't let myself realize till that moment that during the whole time he'd been married I had been waiting – so secretly I hadn't even let myself know it – for the marriage to crash.

This, if true, could scarcely enhance my image of myself. Because what humane woman could wish upon another the horrible disaster of a broken marriage at the age of 24? Not to mention the children. But there was the private grin exposed, the private pain set down in terse print, and all I'd been hiding from myself was stripped away at one stroke, like a bear's huge paw exposing a bone.

From that moment on, I lived in hourly expectation of hearing from Toby. I realized it was unreasonable, unrealistic, absurd ... Seven years without a word, after all ... yet with every mail delivery, every ring of the phone, buried expectation crystallized into illogical but absolute certainty. Time after time I was disappointed.

All I had to go on was a brief conversation over the phone with Billie. Billie Lee was a sort of friend, or rather acquaintance of mine, and my only only real remaining link with Toby. Not that I had been much in touch with her over the years, but she was the literary agent who handled my aunt's book, which was still selling; she was also Toby's agent. Furthermore she happened to be – well – Whistler's mother. She had never been happy about the marriage, and perhaps the greatest irony of my life had been her coming to *me* for advice about whether to let Whistler marry Toby . . .

She now told me Whistler had come home to her with the two little girls, but that she, Billie, didn't know how long the arrangement could last. Whistler was taking the divorce very badly, and most of the work of looking after the children fell upon Billie, who simply hadn't the time – 'Nor, frankly,' she'd added with characteristic tartness, 'the inclination. I'm not the grandmotherly type exactly. To tell the truth, I think they'd be better off with their father, but then I suppose he'd never get any books written – which, both as his agent and his mother-in-law, I would naturally deplore.'

I didn't dare ask her about Toby, but I felt obscurely angry with her for not realizing how badly I needed to know. I went through the days with a sensation of continually holding my breath. This feeling was aggravated whenever I was with Andy, which seemed to be surprisingly often. I say surprisingly; it wouldn't have surprised me at first, when I had felt this definite current of interest between us; but the relationship did not seem to develop along any of the normal channels. When I tried to analyse it, it seemed to me that he was behaving as if there were some agreement between us that we had already thrashed out – almost, I sometimes thought from his possessive behaviour when we were together, an agreement to marry. He even made old remarks from time to time which bore this fantastic theory out – oblique references to the future, a future by inference already mapped out but in fact not overtly spoken about between us, ever. My whole mind centred on Toby, or rather, divided between him and David, I floated along with Andy, meeting him, going out with him, allowing his comforting male presence to cushion me, and didn't ask too many questions. My tiredness contributed to this . . . If he had made the least demand on me physically, apart from holding my hand or my arm, I would have been brought back quite sharply and positively from my limbo. Perhaps he sensed this . . . Anyway, he became simply a man who was always there, and as such somewhat surreptitiously gained a certain undeniable emotional value. Apart from John, who hardly counted in that sphere, he was the only man I had ever known of whom this could be said. By some obscure variation on Parkinson's Law, simply by virtue of being constantly and dependably around, my emotional life (if it could be termed that) spread out to include him, and he became, for all his peculiarities of temperament, speech and manner, a fundamental part of the picture of my life – how essential a part, I dimly supposed, I would only find out if and when he was no longer there.

Chapter 3

THE huge open field on which David and Amanda had used to ride was now a shambles of planks, metal rods, piles of large hollow grey bricks, heaps of sand and gravel, and a large noisy concrete-mixer, among a lot of other unbucolic objects. The flat irregular foundation lay in the middle like a lifeless concrete lake. The friendly gate had been taken off its hinges and part of the venerable hedge torn out to facilitate the entrance of lorries and other vehicles. Of the cluster of trees which, from time immemorial, had stood against the elements in the middle, only three remained; the rest had been bull-dozed out or chopped down. Some of these sad dead giants had not yet been carted away, and lay on their sides in distant corners, the slowly rotting corpses of beauty and antiquity.

I looked at it all with a sorrow and regret I could hardly explain or conceal. Andy, coming to meet me, saw my eyes on the raped hedge, the desecrated ground and the murdered trees, and turned me quietly towards him with both hands.

'My dear Jane,' he said gently. 'I'm a fool. I shouldn't have let you see this.'

'But I knew.'

'Knowing is one thing; seeing, another.' The workmen were all around us and he dropped his hands, but he held me with his eyes. 'Forgive me for doing it, and forgive me for showing it to you. I can see it's hurt you. You shan't come again until it's finished, until the ground is healed. But just today I needed you to be here.'

That word 'needed' sprang alive and armed into my mind, lit up like a sudden warning sign. He had never used it before in connection with me. John and Toby between them had taught me that this word is not to be ignored or despised in relations between men and women. Unless I were quite sure (which I wasn't) that I didn't want Andy, this was a turning-point which I must take the greatest care of. It was where I had gone wrong before.

I pushed the sadness away and smiled at him. 'Why? What's going to happen?'

'Wait and see.'

He sat me down on a portable bench the workmen used for their tea-breaks and disappeared into a little prefab, re-emerging after a few moments with the foreman, who blew a whistle (I hadn't known foremen dared to do that any more, but I suppose it's all right when it signals a break) and all the men downed tools and gathered round. Andy had gone to the car, and now came back with a large basket, from which he took several bottles and enough glasses for everyone. The foreman brought a table out of the prefab and the drinks were arranged on it.

Then the foreman cleared his throat. 'Now then, men. Mr Andrews wants us to lay the foundation stone today in a little ceremony, and then, as you see, he wants us all to have a drink with him.'

The men, who'd obviously been briefed beforehand, trooped off to one corner of the irregularly shaped foundations, and we followed. Andy put his hand between my elbow and my side; I felt it warm there, through my spring coat. It was the way he usually walked with me. He had never kissed me. This restraint – and it was restraint, as my blood told me very loudly every time we were together – not merely puzzled but alarmed me. The longer he went on not kissing me, of course, the more I wanted him to, and the more I felt him wanting to: I could feel our mutual desire to kiss building up in both of us like a head of steam, and sometimes the force of it in myself frightened me. What would happen when . . . ? The lightest touch, like now on my arm through my coat, produced a most exaggerated reaction.

The ceremony was brief, but oddly touching; perhaps I was touched chiefly because I could see Andy was, and I was beginning, in spite of myself, to share his reactions to things. Two of the men lifted up a big slab of stone, and another man spread fresh cement on another slab almost flush with the ground. Andy took hold of one end of the stone himself and the foreman took the other, and together they lugged it until it was directly above the cemented slab; then they carefully lowered it into place. Andy took a builder's trowel and tapped the top corners, and then scraped off the residual cement that had oozed out like butter from the stone sandwich. The men clapped politely. Andy stood back from the stone and looked at me. He had no hat on; his brown hair had fallen across his face. He grinned like a boy. Suddenly he handed me the trowel.

'Hold it upside down and tap the corners gently,' he ordered.

I did what I was told. I very nearly always found myself doing what he told me. But this time, as I carried out this small, apparently meaningless action, I was abruptly overtaken by the feeling that by doing it I was committing myself; something was being shared, accepted, promised. After tapping two corners, I gave the trowel back.

'You haven't finished.'

I shook my head. He looked at me, frowned slightly, and slowly took the trowel from me and tapped the other two corners again himself. The men were watching, smiling knowingly. I stared at the stone, wondering to myself: 'What does this mean? They understand something. Andy is one of them, and this ceremony means something to all of them that I know nothing about.' I noticed there was engraving on the stone. The date:

MAY 14TH, 1967

Afterwards the slight tension broke and we all walked back to the table where I was invited to dispense drinks. Most of the men were locals; I had served drinks to some of them when I was Alf's assistant at the Swan. Yet none of them gave me a teasing wink or referred to it in any way. Instead they responded with polite thanks, and one of them called me 'ma'am'. The courtesy was not strained; the mere fact that I was a woman and was handing them a drink would have ensured no less. But the 'Ma'am' was more than my ordinary position in the village would entitle me to, or had ever been accorded me before, except by kind Mr Rudge. It made me feel faintly uncomfortable. Did they already regard me – perhaps because of the little ceremony in which Andy had arbitrarily involved me – as the 'squire's lady'?

'Now,' said Andy, 'what about going into the village for a bite of lunch? I've ordered it.'

'Oh, but I can't. I told you this morning. I'm on duty with the kids – I'm meeting them here. Can't think why they haven't got here yet.' I looked round, searching the softly-curving green horizon on all sides for the sight of domed velvet caps and pointed pony-ears.

'Hell, I'd forgotten that! I could have brought the champagne here, and a "pack-lunch" as Chris always used to call it at school.'

I registered the mention of his son – not quite the first, but so nearly as to make it almost sinister in its rarity.

'But *I've* brought a picnic. No champagne, of course, but plenty for all of us. Why champagne, anyway?' I thought to ask as an afterthought.

'I always drink champagne on special occasions.'

'And is this one?' I asked innocently.

'Isn't it?'

'The foundation stone of your house?'

'Not only.'

'You are such a cryptic fellow, aren't you?'

I looked sideways at his secretive, quietly smiling face. This situation, in which so much was felt and so little said, suddenly seemed to me intolerable and unnatural. Full of feminine curiosity, I longed to know about *him* – his marriage, his odd estrangement from his son, and most of all, needless to say, his plans for the future. Why for example had his new house been delayed several months because of radical revisions to the original plans? When I had asked him what the changes were, he retreated into his 'Wait and see' routine, which gave me the half-excited, half-uneasy conviction that they somehow concerned me. This was the first indication I had had that he wanted to marry me, and there had been others since, coming to a climax with this morning's ceremony and the mention of champagne. But if so, why, why didn't he say something? Was he simply taking it for granted, without a word, without a kiss, that it was all settled? Quite impossible, surely. And yet he had this quality of inwardness, entirely incomprehensible to an extrovert like me. Our relationship developed under cover of small talk, where I could neither watch it nor be sure of it but could follow its progress only by emotional instinct.

He knew very little about me. He didn't even know – or if he did, not from me – that David was illegitimate. I hated him not knowing, though I suppose, not without some deep intuitive uneasiness, that in this day and age if he really cared for me it would not make very much difference. Several times I had trembled on the brink of telling him; but something always kept me silent.

It began to rain. Instantly I stopped thinking about Andy and began worrying seriously about the children.

'They're half an hour overdue . . . I wish they'd come.'

'Let's sit in one of our cars.'

We sat in his. As always, a car interior provided a private-feeling haven, warm, safe and intimate. I am never surprised by the number of indiscretions which occur in cars, despite the physical contortions which must be necessary. Instinctively I huddled close to Andy's warm male bulk as the rain began to lash down in earnest against the windscreen.

'Could you run the wipers so I can watch for them?'

He turned them on. 'Would you like me to cruise around the lanes and look for them?'

'No, we'd better wait here.'

He took my hand and tucked it, with his, into his deep coat pocket.

'You're cold.'

'Just my skin . . . The wine's keeping me warm inside.'

'Do you think wine was the wrong thing? Most of the men left theirs.'

'Beer might have been better.'

'Damn. Thoughtless of me.'

'Thoughtlessness is hardly one of your faults.'

He smiled at me. I drew my breath in a deep sigh. He was wildly attractive to me now. What kept us apart? Not just unspoken words. It struck me suddenly, as his eyes withdrew from me in an uncharacteristically nervous little movement, that he might – *sense* Toby.

'Why don't we ever talk?' I brought out abruptly.

He glanced at me sharply, then away through the windscreen at the glossy lane, the wet hedges. The windscreen-wipers swept to and fro, to and fro, as my mental ones had that morning.

'Too much to say, I suppose. Where to begin?'

'You behave like a man with a past,' I said with half a laugh.

'Aren't we all that?' He squeezed my hand. 'Oh, nothing villainous. Just . . . I'd like you to know *everything*, to share me like a Siamese twin, but there's no way. And the compromise between total sharing and inevitably partial communication by word of mouth is hard to embark on.'

'But as it *is* inevitable—'

Now it was he who sighed. 'I know. Of course I know. Did you ever read that novel about future mutant humans who could read each other's thoughts and send mental pictures to each other? It struck me *that's* what one needs to create a proper love-relationship, nothing less than that – direct, mind-to-mind communication. Instead of filtering it all through mere *words* . . . Words are like condoms in that connection. The communication penetrates, but it can't produce a true conception in the other person. That can only happen through some kind of spiritual meeting which takes ages to develop, and I sometimes think words are actually a barrier to that kind of coming together.'

I sat silent. There was truth in it.

'But I want to talk,' I said at last. 'Feelings, moods, impulses can be transmitted in the way you mean, between two people who—' I hesitated, conventionally afraid to be the first to say it – 'who love each other enough. But there are the facts. Since we can't read each other's thoughts, and frankly I prefer it that way, there's only the one other method of conveying all that's happened to us in our lives up to now. After all, half our lives are over, we've lived them apart from each other. It's not enough to say, as it were, "Well, here we are, whatever's happened to us till now has added up to you being as you are and me as I am, and if we like what we seem to be, that's good enough." Sooner or later we have to – simply – tell each other things.'

'Can't we take each other on trust?'

I thought about this for some time, as deeply as possible while half my mind was wondering where on earth the kids were and reflecting how wet they must be. Eventually I answered, 'I don't know. Is it just plain curiosity that makes me want to know about you, your family, your marriage, your son and so on? Could I repress it as something unworthy or unnecessary? Maybe I could . . .

though it would be against my nature, and it would be there, like Bluebeard's cupboard, tickling my imagination, always . . . But even if I could take you on trust, you'd be very silly to take me.'

He smiled at me, almost mockingly. 'Now *you* talk like someone with a past.'

'Well . . . I am.'

He raised his eyebrows in mock interest and surprise but, despite the joking quality of his expression, I sensed something else – a sudden doubt, a sudden unease.

'And must you tell me all about it?'

'That depends.'

'On what?'

'On – well. On what this morning's little ceremony really meant.'

Now the mock-surprise became entirely genuine and disconcerted. 'Well, really! It means exactly what you must *know* it means. If you are not perfectly clear in your mind about that, then my theories about wordless communion must be just so much old cod's-wallop.'

A faint clip-clop behind us made me swing round. Amanda, her black riding-hat shining on her bent head so that it looked like the head of a seal, was trotting round the bend on her sodden pony. There was no sign at all of David.

I was out of the car in a moment and running through the rain to meet her.

'Amanda! Where's David?' I asked as I splashed to a halt and grabbed the bridle.

'He fell off, the silly clot. He's crying back there and he won't get up. I said I'd come and get you—'

'Get into the back of the station-wagon. How far away is he? Far enough to drive?'

'Oh no, he's in that field back there, you can't get there in a car. Here, take Ant.'

'No, thanks, I'd rather run . . . Andy, will you come?'

I was in a cold panic as I dashed round the corner, through a gate (which Amanda had inexcusably left open, and which I even less excusably did too) and up a steepish slope which was already streaming with muddy water. I hadn't worn my boots for once and the stream overflowed my shoes immediately. Andy was ahead of me by now. I saw him disappear over the brow of the hill as I struggled and slipped, and then I heard Bee whinny just out of sight. My mind was full of broken arms, legs and collar-bones . . . At least it could be no worse on this soft ground.

In fact it was a good deal better. When I panted up to the far gate, there was David, covered with mud and muck, his limbs straight and sound and not a scratch on him that I could see, sniffing sheepishly and trying ineffectually to brush the mud off his jodhpurs. He was steadfastly refusing to answer Andy's questions about where, or if, he was hurt, and he likewise refused to meet my frightened, but already suspicious, eyes.

'Are you hurt or aren't you?' I almost yelled, wanting to shake him. I'd seen this syndrome before. Fall, shock, minor discomfort, disproportionate howls, filling me with never-failing terror of mortal injuries – and then, anti-climax, chagrin and sulks. Usually he pretended for quite a while he *was* hurt, just to save face, but perhaps he was growing up, or just learning that it wouldn't wash, because after a hesitation he shook his head.

I felt unaccountably more furious than usual. I really had been frightened, and besides, my shoes were full of muddy water and I'd torn my tights and snagged my best skirt on a bramble.

'Damn it all, then why didn't you remount and ride back instead of sitting there boo-hooing like a baby?'

David sniffed and hung his head. 'I thought I'd broken my shoulder,' he muttered. Then he looked up and added more spiritedly, 'It was all that stupid Amanda's fault, pushing through the gate like that and making Bee buck.'

'It's a very nasty feeling, falling off a bucking pony,' Andy put in unexpectedly. I stared at him, with some indignation at first, but then suddenly I felt rather sheepish myself, and a bit jealous too, because David was rewarding his defender with a look of gratitude and warmth which I might have earned myself by the expenditure of a trace of maternal sympathy.

'Oh well . . . Come on, let's go back and eat, before Amm scoffs all the chicken.'

As we walked back together down the slithery hill, with David between us and Bee breathing heavily on us from behind, I reflected that satisfaction, and not resentment, would be a more appropriate reaction to Andy's sudden intervention on David's side. He had, in the past, stood aside quite passively during any parental exchanges, hands in pockets, jingling his keys embarrassedly and staring in a different direction. Such a stance proclaimed louder than words, 'Nothing to do with me.' Today's *volte-face* presupposed a new attitude, one which would be essential for him soon to adopt towards David's and my tight little ménage, if . . .

We picnicked, uncomfortably but quite happily, in my station-wagon, us in the front, the kids muddying up the rugs in the back. Andy disappeared in the direction of the site and returned with half a bottle of Mâcon which the men had spurned. There's nothing like wine for transmogrifying an ordinary picnic into a festive occasion.

'Shades of Glyndebourne,' I mumbled indistinctly through a mouthful of cold roast chicken.

'You've obviously never done Glyndebourne,' said Andy. 'A very far cry, I assure you. We'll go this summer – I'll book tomorrow.'

'Cor.'

'You don't want to,' he realized affrontedly.

'It's on account of not liking opera much. Now, if you started muttering about Chichester or the Edinburgh Festival . . .'

'H'm. I see we have indeed a great deal to learn about each other, much of it evidently seriously to your discredit.'

'You mean, my philistinism about everything but the theatre?'

'Never mind.' He patted me avuncularly on the head. 'I'll strive to overlook it, if I fail to correct it.'

'Ta ever so,' I said drily. 'It must be nice to be so culturally enlightened.'

'Oh, it is, it is! All my own work, too.'

I had to turn my face to the window to hide the sudden flush that came over it. It was at moments like this, when we were fooling around, that I felt the abrupt, incongruous onset of desire. I suppose it was my body's response to my mind's delight that we shared the same silly sense of humour. But in any case I often seemed to want him when we were eating. Food and sex, or rather the appetite for them, are very closely linked in me. I love food. I love the sight of it growing – in fields, on trees, on the hoof. I love seeing shops and markets full of it, clean and rich in all its natural colour and promise – even pictures in cookery books bring out the beast in me. I love buying it and preparing it in such a way that it will tempt all the senses and do credit to the good wholesome earth that produced it. And of course I love eating, and watching people I love eat. After all, there is a close parallel between the actions of eating and making love. Both are so sensual; both involve touching and smelling and tasting, handling and biting, caressing with the lips and tongue. And both are so natural, so satisfying, so much more exciting in proportion to how strong your appetite is, how long you've waited, and how well you've earned it . . .

'What are your plans for now?'

'What? Oh. I thought I'd do some shopping in the village and drop into the shop on the way back, and then make tea for the kids.'

'What will they do meanwhile?'

'Ride home to Jo's, have a bath and change. I hope.'

'Did you get that, David?' asked Andy over his shoulder in an unwontedly sergeant-major tone.

'What?' asked David unwarily, looking up from his meal.

'Ride home. Bath. Change of gear. I quote your mother.'

'Oh, okay,' he said in a casual tone which told me it was already out of the other ear and floating off into the ether.

'Amanda, have you finished eating?'

'Not quite. Super cake, auntie.'

'Well, the rain's stopped, so you can take your cake and start for home. Did you hear the bit about having a bath?'

'Okay. Then can we watch Dr Who?'

'Must you? Oh, all right then. I'll be back before then anyhow.'

I thought David looked a little relieved. The Daleks with their throaty extermination threats have never commended themselves as strongly to him as to the tough-minded, unimaginative Amanda.

'And what about me?' put in Andy plaintively.

'No fun for you, pottering about the shops . . .'

'Oh I don't know. I could carry your parcels.'

'What a thrill for you. Would you really?'

'Speak now while you see me.'

'I've spoken.'

The children had been carrying on a subdued quarrel in the back for some moments, and now David's voice rose resentfully.

'Well, look who's talking. You know we're not allowed to jump yet, but you—'

Before he could finish, Amm had flung herself on top of him, chicken-leg and all, and began banging his head very roughly on the floor.

'You bloody little tell-tale!' she shouted.

'*Amanda!*' I cried, though it was not the first time. Casual swearing seems to be a habit neither Jo nor I can break ourselves of, and of course the kids pick it up. As we've often said, it's our fault and you can't blame them, but it really does give you a jolt to hear little children saying 'bugger' and 'Jesus' and we do try to stop both them and ourselves.

'Well, he is, auntie! He promised not to tell!'

'OW!'

My fingers itched to pull her off, but they're pretty evenly matched and it galled me to have to rescue him from a mere girl (not that Amm could ever be accurately described as 'mere').

'Enough, Amanda! Why is it such a secret, anyway?'

Amanda reluctantly desisted, picked up her horse-hairy cake which had gone flying, and said sulkily, 'It's too silly, but Mummy says we have to learn jumping from Mr Rogers first.'

'Oh. Yes. Quite right. Well, go on, get off home. And David, don't cry, for God's sake.'

I was a bit over-impatient with him, first for telling tales which I've begged him not to do, second for letting Amanda beat him, but most of all, perhaps, for not being the one who had done the forbidden, daring thing. It was hard to understand myself at moments like this. I didn't want a ruffian; I was much happier to share my life with someone quiet, thoughtful and gentle. But I was constantly, not always consciously, anxious about the lack of positive maleness for which I felt myself responsible. I had so much wanted a boy; and now that he had left sexless babyhood behind I longed for the masculinity which had so long been lacking in my life, even if it were at one generation's remove ... But it's only now, much later, that I'm able to admit it to myself. It was too dangerous to face then, in that situation; his timidity, his slight effeminacy were not only worrying, they were a source of potential and actual guilt, for who does not know that out of such situations the majority of unmale men emerge, crippled for life by their devoted, unmitigated mothers?

The children remounted their steaming ponies and trotted off, and Andy and I drove together to the village. We decided to go to the shop first. Outside I paused, as always, to look at the windows through the eye of a discriminating passer-by. The frontage needed a new coat of paint, but in a way that slight shabbiness made it blend better with the other, more elderly and conservative shops in the high street – at least till you looked in the window.

For four years after Dottie's departure I strove unavailingly to achieve, in my window and shop-dressings, that originality and vital spark unique to her. But recently, her parting words had finally sunk in. '*Us and Them* is yours now. You must make it your own, and you won't do that by copying me.' Perhaps it took four years to get me over the feeling that it could really never be anybody's but hers, since she had done all the work of starting it – the whole inspiration and impetus had been hers from the beginning. I often wondered if I really could have kept going, if Jo hadn't come along.

Anyway, it was Jo's and mine now, not Dottie's. Inevitably, perhaps, we had departed to some extent from her original *idées fixes*. She would never allow anything into the shop which had not been hand-made. But simply in order to keep ourselves supplied we'd had to begin stocking factory glass, and I could never be quite sure of the pedigree of some of the other stuff we got from abroad, the wood and so on – some of it looked a bit too perfect to me; but unlike Dottie, I was prepared to wink an eye if it were beautiful.

So our windows – two of them now – didn't have quite the look of rough-hewn craftsmanship they'd had under Dottie's dominion. Nor were the displays ever as good. Dottie used to have themes for her windows, sketching designs for them first and working on them for hours down to the last detail. I, on the other hand, based my windows on more commercial considerations.

'That's a well-stacked bit of Anglo-American trade relations,' Andy suddenly remarked. A splendidly large American lady swathed in mink was just coming out of the shop, with a uniformed driver, no less, behind her bearing a splendidly large parcel swathed in our wrapping paper. Jo stood in the doorway, beamingly seeing her out.

'I do wish sometimes you weren't quite so successful,' said Andy grimly.

'Why on earth do you wish that?'

'I wish you were starving and destitute.'

I stared at him. I realized I knew him better than I had thought, because quite suddenly I knew that this odd and apparently joking remark was virtually a declaration.

On an impulse of escape, I started to climb out of the car. 'We'd better start at the supermarket—' I began, but he unexpectedly laid a brusque hand on my arm and pulled me back.

'We're not going shopping today after all,' he said.

He put the car into second and it jerked forward. I didn't argue. At the Swan, he stopped.

'Don't get out. I'm going to fetch the champagne.'

'Oh, don't let's – let's leave it for another time—'

'No, I want it now.'

I sat still, suddenly chilled and apprehensive. He returned with the bottle of champagne still dripping ice-water, wrapped it in some newspaper and gave it to me to nurse. The coldness of it soon seeped through to my arms as we drove out of the village the way we had come. I began to shiver, mostly from some unidentifiable fright.

It was still raining and the men had not returned to the building site. We sat there in the Rover in silence for some time, both staring fixedly through the weeping windscreen, breathing heavily, until I suddenly said 'If this goes on much longer I shall scream.'

Andy gave me a startled look, grabbed the bottle, and prised out the cork. It thwacked against the roof, ricochetted off and caught me a stinging blow on the temple. 'Sorry,' said Andy, not sounding in the least sorry. He clambered out and ran through the rain to the hut, returning at once with two glasses. The champagne, which he had left standing on the floor, had fizzed out, and somehow in the brief interval he had forgotten it was there and knocked it over with his foot as he got in again.

'Oh *pisspots*!' he roared, grabbing it.

I exploded.

'What's your trouble?' he barked irritably.

'*Pisspots* . . .' I shrieked, rolling about helplessly. 'Is that the worst word you know?'

47

'It's the worst I ever use, and I have to be driven almost berserk before I give vent to that. What the *hell* is so funny?'

'Pisspots...' I croaked, wiping tears from my eyes.

'Oh here, for God's sake, drink what's left of this and get hold of yourself!'

I gulped down some champagne so fast that more tears came. If I get even a little drunk, I thought wildly, or if he does, God knows what'll happen with him in this weird mood and me so tired and uncontrollable... We drank in silence and then Andy said, 'Damn the stuff, I feel like chucking the bottle through the windscreen.'

I tossed off the last of mine and said nothing. I felt boneless and rather hysterical.

'Today's gone all wrong,' he said with an effort.

'I'm sorry,' I said, and I was, because I knew what he meant and yet I felt heartlessly that he hadn't really deserved it to go any better when he kept alternately shutting me out and expecting me to get *in* by some process of osmosis. Sitting there beside the ruined field, hugging our empty glasses, we had one of those moments of cold isolation, the cruel feeling of oceans rushing through the abyss between us. Each man his own island . . . Suddenly he reached across the gulf and gripped my hand. His eyes had a look of desperation as he pulled me, with entirely uncharacteristic roughness, towards him.

'Damn it, what's the matter?'

'Nothing. We're two separate people. Words are the only bridge, and you won't use it.'

He stared into my eyes, his teeth set tight, and then he kissed me – the kiss so long wanted and so long deferred. That first kiss, which one always remembers, was, unlike subsequent ones, empty of the tenderness I had taken for granted, clumsy, almost brutal. But I loved that kiss, because it gave me what had always been lacking before – a sensation of communicated need.

I have been wrong about need for half of my life. My father needed me, and I him, and neither of us would ever admit it until the time for a father-child relationship had passed. Toby and I needed each other, and again you'd have thought it was some kind of deadly sin which we would both have died rather than give way to. Only when I had David did I begin to learn that needing another human being, and responding to that need, mutually, is rewarding

48

and not degrading, that it builds a relationship instead of corroding it. Independence had been my watchword, and I'd spent years striving to achieve it. I had put independence first, and triumphed in a victory almost perfectly Pyrrhic over my heart and David's life.

And now here was Andy, another independence-seeker, even more of an addict than I was, for he sought to be independent even of shared thoughts. His unwillingness to communicate in words was nothing but an evasion; a desire for 'perfection or nothing' is actually only a way of avoiding reality. Yet now he kissed me as a child kisses, despairingly, without finesse, simply as a way of breaking down barriers. It did nothing to arouse me sexually; but every other part of me responded to it. I had not known at all that this, not the other, was what I wanted most from him; the open avowal, not of love or desire, but his need to be with me as two people alone need to be together, to meet, to touch, to be as close as it's possible to be for as long as a life geared to separate entities allows.

When the kiss finished we were close together, our arms round each other, and he searched my face for a second from a distance of three inches and then, with a sudden shake of his head, he tried to pull away. But I wouldn't let him. I tightened my arms round his neck and held him.

'Let go, Jane. I'm hating this! I'm making such a mess of it.' He twisted his head free and tried to get out of the car. But this time it was I who stopped him.

'Where do you think you're going? You've lifted a corner of the veil and now look at you, you're in a panic! What are you planning for us that can possibly happen, the way you're going on? Does everything have to go exactly to plan before you'll kindly agree to keep moving forwards?'

He stared at me aghast.

'Why are you so angry?' he asked. 'Not because I kissed you – so badly.'

'Of course not, you idiot. I needed that maladroit kiss more than I've needed anything for a long time. I think I've doubted if you were a human being at all. How can you be so self-contained? I'm not like that, I can't love anyone like that. Not having to say things – that's god-like. It's a life-companion I want, not a communicated soul-process!'

'Oh Christ I am a bloody idiot. Come here. Come here.'

After a while we changed cars. We lay on the horsey rugs surrounded by the shattered remains of the children's picnic lunch and swigged down the remains of the champagne straight from the bottle. In between swigs, we kissed and cuddled (if that is not a completely outdated word and concept) and when we'd drunk it all Andy said,

'There now, I'm drunk and that apparently was what I needed to break down my inhibitions and let me say it. I love you. I love you *madly*. I do *love* you. Blast it, but it doesn't mean what I want it to! You see I'm right, words are *empty*, they're like this bottle, you tip them over the person you're trying to make understand something and nothing comes out, not a damn thing.'

'You're quite wrong, it's dripping all over my hair.'

'*Dripping*. That's it. It drips meaning, when it should pour, it should deluge and drench you with my feeling . . .' He threw the bottle down and rolled on top of me. 'Jane, shall we do it here and now? Would that help to make it real? Oh hell—' A car swished by so close I could see the driver, and Andy almost leapt off me. 'It takes more than half a bottle of champagne to rid me of my inhibitions against making love in public. Sorry. You'll have to take a rain-check on that one . . . The smell of horses doesn't exactly help either . . . You'd never guess from all this what a vigorous lover I can be, given the right circumstances . . .' He sat for a moment, staring out of the back window, and then turned to look down at me. 'Having said it, I want to hear it from you,' he said in an altered tone.

A long moment passed.

All this – the first genuine physical contact, especially the recent sensation of his deliciously big, heavy body pressing mine down on to the unyielding floorboards, not to mention the champagne which had evidently been freely adulterated with powdered rhinoceros horn – had aroused me almost beyond the point of reason, fairness or honesty. The words he wanted seemed true, simply because to say them would express some part of what my body was feeling, but more because they would open the way to the sexual relationship which was now, at this moment in time, more important to me than anything else.

But I had not forgotten Toby, and because of him this happy

moment with Andy, which could have been so simple and have led to all my problems being solved, was suddenly rendered ambiguous – not spoilt, but unclear, out of focus, vitiated by doubts. To give him his straightforward loveword would have been to tell a lie; and lies, while they may well be safe and even necessary further on in a relationship, are not tolerable at the beginning.

He was waiting, a frown deepening on his face.

'You do love me, don't you?' he asked sharply.

'I want to,' I said slowly. 'Only it's a lot more complicated than you think.'

'You want to?' he repeated, blinking and looking around him as if becoming suddenly sober. 'But of course, that's not enough.'

'Of course it's not. But it's only the beginning. Now you've put your foot on the bridge, the word-bridge, we may only have to walk across it towards each other.'

'You mean talk.'

'Talk, and kiss.'

He turned away, putting his head down on his arms and knees. 'I don't want to kiss any more,' he said. 'You can't have it both ways.'

I sighed heavily, aware abruptly of my wet feet and my weariness. 'Oh Andy! Come on then. Let's go home.'

Chapter 4

As I came into the shop next morning, Georgie, our assistant, looked up from a packing-case which had been delivered the day before and said, 'Look here, Miss Graham, one of these little animals has a crack in it.'

'Good girl, Georgie,' I said warmly, and she smiled. She had long, straight, reddish hair cut in a box-fringe which, in accordance with teenage fashion, fell into her eyes; her mini-skirt just covered essentials, and in her boots she looked like a principal boy in a pantomime, except that she wore no make-up. The whole effect was very nice, but gave a frivolous impression which was entirely misleading. Our Georgie was no hippie, but a serious girl with her eye on a career, first with us, and later, I guessed, in London.

We worked together for a while, I in silence (I had a lot on my mind), Georgie chatting endlessly and rather soothingly, like the gentle continuous splashing of a small busy waterfall. Suddenly she broke off to say, 'Oh, by the way, Miss, there's a letter came for you, quite a nice fat one.' And she went into the back and returned with a long envelope with my shop address typewritten on it and a London postmark.

I actually left it sitting on the table for ten minutes while I arranged a shelf – it was getting on for nine and, besides, I thought it was just some business letter. Personal letters had never come to the shop. Then everything was ready to open and I still had a few minutes in hand. I sent Georgie into the back office to make a phone-call, and leant against the big pine refectory table we use for the fabric displays and disinterestedly tore the letter open.

It was from Billie – one sheet of it. The rest of the bulk was a second, folded, envelope, addressed to her, with a foreign stamp on it. Also typewritten. But this time the type was familiar. I knew that machine with its jumping s and its crooked t . . . knew it and remembered it from long ago.

Billie had written:

My dear Jane,

After some thought I've decided to send this letter on to you. I've had it some time. Really couldn't make up my mind before. Hope you understand why. There seemed to be some element of maternal disloyalty somewhere.

To put you in the picture, Melissa is living in a flat by herself, or at least only with Carrie, who's four now. As you'll see from the enclosed, Rachel is with Toby. We were all desperately against this, not of course because of Toby but because of where he insisted on going. But he said he was entitled to one of them no matter where he decided to live, so finally we settled on Rachel, who, though only six, seems a tough little customer and absolutely devoted to her father, more than to Melissa. Fair enough I suppose, but with the situation over there being what it unhappily is just now, we are nearly worried to death for their safety. We miss her desperately. And I at least miss Toby too.

I won't go on, since Toby's letter tells all the rest. He hasn't written to me since this, but Melissa hears quite regularly. I gather his letters to her are really no more than reports on Rachel, and she writes the same way to him about Carrie.

Your aunt's book has gone into its fourth printing both here and in America. Whoever would have thought it, after those notices? It must be what we call word-of-mouth publicity. Well-deserved.

Hope to see you sometime.

All the best my dear,

Billie

I must admit I only completed this after I had ripped open and read through Toby's letter twice. The stamp on it was Israeli. Even at that crucial moment I earmarked it for David – it was a beauty, with a bird on it in mosaic.

Dearest Billie,

I'm sorry this is only my first letter, and I'm going to make it a long one because it'll probably be my last for ages. I seem to be suffering from a writing block which even extends to letters. Don't worry, I'll get over it. But it may take some time.

W. will have told you that we arrived safely, and about the difficulties I had getting myself into a kibbutz because of having Rachel in tow. It meant I counted neither as an unencumbered volunteer nor as a family wanting to settle. I think I only got in here at last because of what they call here 'protectsia', which means pull – one of the many anonymous bureaucrats I encountered in my search for a home had read my books. No one in the kibbutz he sent me to ever has, and no-one here gives a damn about me as a writer – very good for reducing the ego. Here I am a working hand, and it's been made pretty clear to me that I have to work for two. I was only accepted on condition that I stay at least a year. Otherwise they wouldn't take Rachel into the children's house. You can understand it – too disruptive for the others to have kids coming and going. Continuity and lack of change and upheaval seems to be a built-in part of the system. Well, I approve. Poor kid, she's had enough upsets to be getting on with.

I thought it would be terribly difficult for her to make the transition to a children's house, but it turned out only to be hard for me. After a week of sleeping in my little room with me, and playing with children her own age during the day, she voluntarily moved over to sleep there. She hardly glanced at me when the time came to say goodnight. I slept there for a week on a campbed, as is customary, but she didn't wake up once. I was glad, of course, but I felt a bit hurt, I must say! However, she makes it clear, during our curtailed time together in the afternoons, that I'm still important to her. I comfort myself with the realization that, wherever I lived, I wouldn't be able to see much of her during the day,

53

and here we're allowed to put them to bed at night, which isn't the case in every kibbutz. Having sixteen other lots of parents around at the same time necessarily detracts from what I had thought was essential privacy, but one gets used to it.

She misses W. She misses Carrie. She misses you. Sometimes I feel a bastard. What am I talking about? I feel a bastard the whole bloody time. I know I didn't succeed in making you understand why I had to come here. But W. understood, I think. You know we'd often talked about coming together. Oh well – water under the bridge.

I won't bore you about the work. I've done three months on irrigation. It's not bad, though it often means very long hours. There's been a drought ... There's something satisfying about it. Two mornings a week I'm let off to teach English and learn Hebrew. The latter is easier than the former! I had heard Hebrew was not so much difficult as impossible, but some sort of ancestral memory must be operating for me here – I feel as if I were simply being reminded of a language merely forgotten. The teaching is ghastly, I haven't the patience. I find myself behaving like the old-type Englishman, when they don't understand, I shout! I think I'll be taken off it soon – I hope so. Now you'll be asking, what about writing? Sorry chum, there just ain't none. At the end of the day I'm so buggered I just lie around. I can't even claim the heat as an excuse – it's *cold*! Maybe as I get used to manual work ... Or maybe not. I feel as if something packed up in me when W. and I split up and I lost Carrie. Or maybe that's just an excuse too.

Now to the point of all this, which I've been nerving myself for. I nerved myself to say it to you, face to face, before I left, but as is obvious, I 'copped out' as the local American draft-dodgers say. I know you never really wanted W. to marry me, and you were right, as we now know. What I want to say is, that it was good of you to be so fair and even-handed through the years, dealing with our infantile brawls and reconciliations as if W. and I were equally your children. I never blamed W. for behaving like a kid – that's all she was when I let myself marry her. But you always treated me with the same tolerance and warmth and restraint as you did her, and with far less reason. I don't think one could find such an objective, unbiased mother-in-law in a long day's march, and I think, after all that's happened, it's something of a marvel that you're still prepared to be friends with me and handle my stuff as always. It's a pity there isn't more to handle. If there ever is again, I mean if the block breaks and I start to write again, it'll be because you made me into a real, serious, working writer, and I liked myself that way. That part at least I could still respect, even while I was bitching up my marriage and your daughter's stability. It's ironic, isn't it?

I'll be keeping in touch with W. to let her know how R. is, and to hear about Carrie. I don't know when I'll see any of you again. There's something here that I have to find out, in connection with myself –no more or less than whether I belong here. If I don't, I shall come back to England. I feel very alien here in some ways – in others, more at home than I ever did at home (England is still home for the moment.) Let me know at once if enough money stops coming in to keep W. and Carrie – I don't need any here, so they can have the lot. If you manage to flog *How Long* for a film, that should keep them ticking over nicely for a while.

Meanwhile there's just one other thing. I know you're in touch with Jane Graham from time to time. I suppose you know I haven't been, since before I married W. With that Yiddish horse-sense you specialize in, you probably know why, better than I do. I just knew it was dangerous. The minute I was free I let myself start thinking about her again. I won't go into it, but I had the strongest possible urge to go and see her. The reason I didn't was because I'd decided to come out here, and I thought, if I saw Jane even once, I wouldn't come. And if I hadn't come, I'd never have known whatever it is I need to know – and, oddly, I don't think the broken-marriage scars would ever have healed. (Here, they will, though so slowly I sometimes doubt it.) Jane once said something to me about how she didn't want to bring me her need, she wanted us to be two whole people when we came together. This stuck. I don't know if I was whole then, but I'm not now. (I have to keep quiet about *all* this here; the Israelis at once begin to suspect you if they think you're treating their country as a hospital to heal yourself in. They naturally only want people who are looking for ways to contribute, not for alms or wound-patches or miracle cures for themselves. It all has to be done quietly and inwardly; but then that's the only kind of cure that works in the true sense anyway.)

So if you see Jane, give her my love, but tell her she'd better not wait. I know she is waiting, in some way or other. Tell her this will take some time. And remind her that I'm a Jew, more of a one that either of us realized. She once said 'So what?' The answer is, 'So everything.' If there's one thing in this damned world that's harder to be than a Jew, it's the goyishe wife of one. Even being true-Jew didn't help W. to be married to me.

Love from me and Rachel,
Toby

Despite having agreed with Jo that Georgie wasn't experienced enough to be left alone, I left her alone that morning. I got into the car and sat in it for a long time, just trying to approach the meaning of the letter. Then I did something odd. I went home and put slacks on, and drove to Jo's place. It had started to rain; the ponies were still out in the paddock, placidly cropping. I parked the car and knocked on the playroom window, through which I could see David and Amanda doing a jig-saw on the floor. David looked up, grinned with delight, and ran over.

'Darling,' I said in a flat voice which told me, if not him, how close I was to tears, 'if you're not going out on him, may I ride Bee for a bit?'

David looked comically astonished. 'Mummy! You? Have you gone bonkers?'

'May I?'

'Of course. Mind out though, his back's all slippery from the rain. Put a blanket on under the saddle. Where are you going?'

'Just around.'

'But why?' he shouted as I retreated.

'I feel like it,' I called back without turning.

I hadn't finished saddling up Bee when Jo came running out with a mackintosh draped over her head. My heart sank. Explanations . . .

'What does on? Have you shut up shop?'

'No. Georgie's there. We won't have much on today with this weather. She'll manage.'

'Are you crying?'

'Not yet.'

'Ducky! What's up?'

'I have to think. I feel like a ride.'

'I'll saddle up Ant and come with you.'

'No! Please don't.'

She said no more, but watched me tighten the girth and clumsily mount. 'Here,' she said, 'take this mack at least. What about a hat?'

'Haven't got one. Never mind. Go on indoors, you'll get soaked.'

'There's a headscarf in the pocket.'

I put this on, grateful for the chill wet drops on my face. My throat was aching and I wanted desperately to be alone.

'Take care. Don't ride too fast on this mud.'

'I won't.'

I kicked Bee and he walked sedately off down the lane, shaking the water off his ears. Amanda's mongrel followed a little way, but returned to Jo's whistle. I could sense Jo was still standing there at the gate of the paddock, watching me out of sight.

That ride is a blur in my memory, as if I was drunk when I took it – I remember only a few isolated moments in it, though it was well past lunchtime by the time I got back, soaked to the skin but feeling much calmer.

I remember spending quite a long time on the site of the new house. I hadn't looked at it carefully the day before, and the blueprints, which I had seen some time ago – prior to the alterations which I now knew for certain had been made to accommodate me and David – had not made much impression. The foundations were laid, and the men were at work on the walls, though they had knocked off when I was there because of the rain, so I had the place to myself. The living-area, as delineated by the foundations, was roughly Y-shaped, with the three trees which Andy had been able to spare growing in between the fork at the top. One of these trees was an oak, somewhat stunted, which spread out gnarled branches quite close to the ground. Andy had mentioned it once, and had called it 'David's climbing tree'. I remember dismounting and standing, with the wide arms of concrete almost encompassing me, my hand on the lowest branch of this tree, simply asking myself: is this going to be the sort of house, designed by the sort of man, you could live with? The answer could only be yes.

Then I scrambled up on Bee's back again and we went jogging off through more quiet lanes, and I touched the letter in my inner pocket and thought, with a wild unrealism no longer characteristic of the sensible, practical woman I had assiduously turned myself into: If I sell my interest in the shop to Jo, rent the cottage, take David out there, find him . . . I shook the rain out of my eyes with a sudden sharp, irritated movement. Ludicrous! People don't do things like that, certainly not people like me. Israel indeed! Where was it, even? Those little sketch-maps in the papers merely accentuate one's geographical ignorance, personally I can hardly tell which is sea and which is land. I certainly doubted if I could put my finger straight on to the place on a map. The only association I could rake up regarding it merely linked it in my mind with Vietnam and Ireland – a vague impression of intermittent military outbursts, a recurrent, superficial reaction on my part amounting to no more than a passing 'They're at it again' whenever it was mentioned on the news – as, now I stopped to think about it, it seemed to have been rather often lately. And now Toby was there somewhere with his daughter, and no matter whether I married Andy or not, I would never be able to hear the word Israel without a clutching at the heart for fear that stupid 'incidents' might endanger them. But if that were true, what right had I to marry Andy? Or anyone?

At this point I remember hauling Bee to a halt under a tree and standing there for a long time, while the rain ran down inside my collar. I was in the dark shade of the tree, but it was the backward shadow which made me shiver repeatedly. A strong, strange, growing guilt stirred inside me, not its first stirring by any means, but now it was not merely moving in its sleep but beginning to wake, like the mythical kraken of the deeps. Something had happened recently which had set up a chain-reaction of disturbance. David and I had been at the breakfast table, and I had been wondering, for the hundredth time, whether Andy knew about David's birth or not, and rehearsing in my mind how I would tell him. Suddenly David startled me almost out of my wits by announcing through a mouthful of Fruti-Fort:

'I saw Daddy yesterday.'

I nearly dropped my coffee-cup. '*What?*'

'Not him himself. I'm not even sure it was him. But it looked like that photo you showed me once.'

'What did?'

'A picture in a magazine of Auntie Jo's. Full of film-actors and junk. I don't mean Daddy's junk, if it was Daddy.' He went back to his food with a slight frown.

'What was he doing – in the picture?'

'Nothing. Just smiling. He's got a nice smile, hasn't he?'

He had your smile, I thought, before he got his teeth fixed. Well, it was only a matter of time. I had been half-expecting it from the moment I read that Terry had gone out of publishing and back to acting. Sensible of him to pick films, where his tall good looks would count and his weak voice-projection and rather smudgy-round-the-edges personality wouldn't. Or maybe I was just being a bitch? I actually had nothing against him any more, except the nagging fear that he'd run us to earth one day and upset David. I knew he wanted to. If he'd been a more determined or ruthless sort of person (or even just a bit cleverer) he'd have found us long ago. But after all, he was married, and, I had inferred, to a rather difficult sort of woman. When I'd spoken to him on the phone he had not been too frightened of the consequences to be prepared to come at once to see what he was pleased to call 'my son' (with whom he had had nothing at all to do since he'd conceived him); on the other hand, he *had* been unwilling to tell his wife of David's existence, even when she was blaming him for their childlessness. It sounded like a pretty uneasy ménage, just the sort that provides a breeding-ground for those 'double life' situations you sometimes hear about, secret weekends and so on to start with, and then something approaching bigamy. Terry was not imaginative or far-sighted enough to anticipate any such thing, but I was, and even though David was wringing my heart with his pitiful little efforts to equip himself with a paternal identity, I had had to be very firm.

I'd thought about it a lot after I'd hung up the phone without giving an address. What it came to was that I felt it was better for David to have no father at all than to have Terry. Was this not taking a very personal view? After all, he hadn't behaved *that* badly, I mean he had wanted to help financially and so on. He'd even asked me to marry him, though we both knew he'd have died if I'd said yes. In fact he wasn't a bad sort at all – just weak. Two-dimensional, like the photo with the nice smile David had now unluckily stumbled on. Fancy him remembering that face, after nearly four years! The picture *I'd* shown him was years older than that, too, taken when Terry and I were in rep together.

I decided to be quite casual and let it, if it would, float by on the tide. But later on, while he was waiting for Amanda to come over, he brought it up again.

'Can I see that photo again, Mummy?'

'Which one, darling?' (Oh God.)

'You know, the one you showed me of Daddy.'

'I don't know if I've still got it.'

A pause; then, in a rather shocked voice: 'You wouldn't get rid of it, would you? You said it was the only one you'd got.'

That sent me upstairs in thoughtful and disquieted silence to look for it. Of course I hadn't got rid of it. One doesn't. I took it down and put it wordlessly into his hands.

'Oh yes, that's him all right,' he said. He looked at it a long time – too long. 'He's got a lot older, of course, and he's different somehow. Is he in a play here?'

'Yes.'

'I thought so, because of his clothes. Is that you?' he noticed suddenly. I admitted it was. 'You look pretty in that long dress. Is he a good actor?'

'I think he was rather, then. Of course for a long time he wasn't acting. He's only just started again.'

'Under the picture I saw in this mag, it said he was going to be in a new film. They're making it at a place called Elm Tree. Can we go and see it, Mummy?'

'What's it called?'

'I can't remember. It's not made yet. I don't think. But can we, when it comes to Dorking?'

'Films take quite a while to make. You'll have forgotten all about it by then, I expect.'

He looked at me, his brown eyes surprised. 'Oh no, I won't forget. How could I? Daddy's going to be in it.'

'David,' I heard myself suddenly saying. 'Why do you call him Daddy?'

'Well, he is, isn't he?'

'No,' I said, more sharply than I'd intended. He looked at me questioningly.

'You told me he was.'

'Listen, David.' How to do this? To do it or not to do it? 'You remember ages ago you asked me how babies get into their mummies and I told you about the father's seed going in and starting the egg growing?' He nodded. 'Well, that's all that a man has to do to be the father of a child. It's a very easy thing, a very small thing. It doesn't take long, and it doesn't cost him anything. He gets pleasure from it. Then the baby grows and is born and he's the father of it. But he's not – don't you see, David, a Daddy is something else. Daddy is what you call a man who's been around while you were growing up, a man who looked after you and played with you, who worked to buy your food and – and that sort of thing. And who took care of your mother. Now that man—' I pointed to the picture – 'he's your father. He's the one who started you growing. But that's all he did. You can't really call him Daddy, darling, I don't think.'

David looked at me while I said all this, and then looked away and fiddled with the rug for a while and then he asked his questions.

Number one: 'So can I call John Daddy?'

'No, darling. He's not around enough. Anyway he wouldn't like it. The man you call Daddy has really got to be married to me.'

Number two: 'If you married *him*' (pointing to the picture) 'then couldn't I call him Daddy?'

'But I'm not going to marry him, David.'

'Why not?'

'Because I don't love him.' As I said this I shrank inwardly, sending up a prayer of gratitude that the question I deserved would not come yet, because he was too young to ask it. But I underestimated him.

'Then why did you let him start me inside you?'

Honest – be honest, it's the only possible way. 'I made a mistake, and so did he. We thought we did love each other.'

Long, long pause. I hoped with all my heart that the inquisition was over for this time. But it wasn't.

'Then I'll never have a Daddy.'

'Why not?'

'You said, the man who plays with you while you're growing up.'

'Well, you're not grown up yet.'

'Can I still have one?'

'Yes,' I said. I gazed at him – my beloved son. 'And you will.'

'Who?'

'Someone who'll be good for you.'

'You mean I can choose?' he shouted excitedly.

'No, I don't mean that! I'm the one who's got to marry him.'

But he didn't hear.

'I choose Daddy! I choose Daddy!' he shouted, jumping up and waving the picture about. Then I suppose he saw my face, because he stopped and said, 'Or if you *really* don't like him, couldn't I choose John?'

I grabbed the bull by the horns. 'What about Uncle Andy?'

We looked at each other. He'd calmed right down and looked suddenly sober and solemn and quite grown up. He silently laid the photo face-down on the table and came and sat beside me on the floor.

'I don't know,' he said.

'Do you like him?'

'Yes...'

'But?'

'He's rather old.'

'Not really, David. He's only forty-four.'

'I think that's bloody old.'

'David! Anyway, it isn't.'

'How old is—' He indicated the photo.

'About my age, I think.'

'Much younger than Uncle Andy.'

'David, stop thinking about that. I might as well tell you, your father's married to someone else.'

To my utter consternation and horror, he burst into tears, pulled away from me and ran up to his room. I followed him, and found him on his bed, crying bitterly.

'Darling, do stop – I'm sorry, I shouldn't have told you that—'

'Bloody bugger! I hate him now!'

Shocked, I gathered him against me. 'Dearest, you mustn't! You're not old enough yet to understand. No, David, listen. He's not at all what you think. Why shouldn't he marry? We decided not to marry each other because of not loving each other enough, so then he had to try to find somebody he did love enough, just like I'm doing – like everyone's doing, David. Men and women shouldn't live alone. I wouldn't have wanted him to – please don't cry, my sweetheart, please don't!'

Slowly he stopped. Boy-like, he pulled out of my arms as soon as he felt a little better, and lay on his front, fiddling with the counterpane and occasionally catching his breath in an after-sob. I sat there staring at him. Some strong unpleasant feeling was growing up in me, familiar and yet strange. It was the kraken of guilt, and its familiar aspect was tied to its stirrings every time David screamed for me in the night, every time the psychiatrist's piquant expression turned my facile replies to her questions inward and gave me a sharp stabbing glimpse of the monster. The strangeness was this sudden new manifestation of David's lack. His night-wakings were due to a subconscious yearning; but this – this rational conversation, this overt wrestling with his situation, these wild furious tears, all showed that he couldn't hide it from himself much longer. And when he awoke fully to the implications of his situation, how then would he regard me? How would I be able to regard myself? Sitting there on the bed with my hand resting lightly on David's still-trembling back, I felt fear running right down to the end of my spine in a tingling wave, like the shock before pain.

Astride the wet pony two weeks later I suffered the same sensation again, remembering it. I had never known what real shame meant, in connection with David, except once, when I found out that Toby was going to marry someone else. For though Toby wasn't his father, I'd always mentally filled the gap with him. That was when I realized for the first time what it means, in terms of guilt, to have brought a fatherless child into the world. It wasn't the fact of illegitimacy, it was fatherlessness. But one can't live with guilt. The feeling faded as I struggled to my feet again emotionally, determined, in what now seemed to me a blindness or arrogance and selfishness, to manage on my own.

I had really contrived to convince myself that if I 'managed' to bring David up, that's to say, if I managed financially, if I managed to give him enough love, to lead a reasonably 'moral' life and in all ways do my best for him, that that would be enough; that I would have earned the right to pat myself on the back and tell myself I'd succeeded. Success in such a loaded enterprise is bound to be entirely relative. But now I felt that even if I provided David with a 'daddy' the next day, it would still be too late to remedy the wrong I had already done him. Did that wrong not begin even earlier than eight years ago?

My mind went back to a day when I sat in the office of a Harley Street gynaecologist, long before the days of the Abortion Act, and heard him ask me for a hundred guineas to rid me of the trifling inconvenience who was now a person in his own right frightening me out of my wits. I remember his bland mouth saying, 'What about the young man – the happy father? Doesn't want to know, I suppose?' Didn't want to know? Who could say? Didn't get told, anyhow. I had been too proud. All right, forgive yourself that, David wasn't real to you then. Another memory: James, my ex-employer, coming to see me in the L-shaped room: 'Why don't you let him know, Jane? Write to him. Tell him. You ought at least to give him a chance . . .' And my answer, the touchstone of the whole thing: 'Nobody ever thinks what it would be like for me to go to him wailing: "I'm in trouble! I'm going to have a baby!"' And *I* never thought what it would be like for the baby.

I must marry. As Bee plodded slowly home, this was the thought uppermost in my mind. But there were many just impediments. The fiery river of feeling that rushed through me each time I re-read Toby's letter was an impediment of daunting proportions. And there were others. The word-bridge had been slung across the abyss between Andy and me, but we had yet to test it with the full weight of confidence.

Chapter 5

ANDY came down on that Friday and took me out to dinner.

I knew it was going to be an important occasion, and I felt extra-ordinarily jumpy as I dressed; when the bell rang a sudden uneasiness close to nausea took hold of me. As soon as I opened the door I was unbalanced still further by the fact that he was wearing a dinner-jacket, which I had never seen him in before. It dismayed me somehow, because I particularly needed to feel at ease with him that evening and in formal wear he had a towny aloofness.

To make matters worse he had brought me, of all things, an orchid, complete with ribbon and cellophane box. I thanked him, warmly and hypocritically, but was relieved when he laughed aloud and said, 'I can see you hate it. Here, give it back.' He stuck it into a little vase on the mantelpiece.

'There. Let it wither as a reminder that you are not to be wooed as other women are wooed. I shall not repeat my mistake.' He took my hands and said something nice about my dress.

'It's all wrong to go with your splendour.'

'Was that a mistake too? Funny how I always overdo my symbolics. When we've had dinner I shall come back here and remove my jacket – oh hell, no, I can't. Even I can't make love in braces.'

'Those could come off too.'

He stared at me, his face so full of different expressions it looked blank.

'That might carry my love-making a little forrader than I'd anticipated tonight,' he said seriously. 'However, let's not plan too far ahead. We have a bridge to cross before we reach the point of removing our braces, I think.'

Georgie arrived at that moment to baby-sit (I was safe in going out and leaving David provided I was home by about midnight – nothing ever happened before then). She looked very pretty in her frayed jeans, love-beads and squaw's headband. She greeted us and went straight upstairs to David, only pausing to ask when I wanted him in bed.

'Eight sharp, and no stay of execution. Remind him about the gymkhana the day after tomorrow, for which he needs to rest up.'

'Oh, that won't work. Even *I'm* not old enough to look more than one day ahead.'

She disappeared round the spinning-wheel. When I turned back to Andy, I was surprised to see a look of interest bordering on calculation on his face.

'How old?' he asked.

'Seventeen,' I said. 'W H Y?'

He laughed. 'Oh, come off it! Either I'm past that stage, or I haven't reached it yet. No, it's for my son I always feel speculative when I see something pretty and promising of that generation.'

Had he dropped this pebble deliberately, as I was sure he had done before, to watch the ripples of curiosity break frustratingly against my sides? But this time I let myself ask.

'Tell me about him.'

'Yes, I'm going to. I've been gearing myself all day. Only after dinner.'

'At.'

'After.'

But it turned out to be 'at' after all, because he took me to a place where the food was so good that as soon as we began on the paté maison and found it really was maison and not tinned, I knew I'd have to take firm action to stop it developing into a Tom Jones kind of meal in which every shared bite is a sensual exchange. So I said again, 'Come on, now. Chris.'

He dropped his eyes from my face and attended desultorily to his paté for a few moments in silence, and then he sighed heavily and said, 'With your natural acuity I suppose you've already gleaned that we're not entirely satisfied with each other.'

'Well, yes. What's the trouble?'

'That can't be told in a word. Well, or perhaps it can – at the moment the word is pot. Or is it hash? I never know the difference. But that wouldn't matter so much. Before that it was filial contempt, which is older, and underlying it all is something even older than that, which I believe was ancient when the devil adopted it as one of his cardinal vices.'

'Which one?' I asked, intrigued.

'Sloth.'

'You mean he's a drop-out?'

'It's such a long time since he was *in* ... Let's see. At fifteen he was still in, a very good school and doing admirably. But by the time he was sixteen he'd been expelled for pot-smoking. He was the first boy it ever happened to there – not the last, of course, but the first: a distinction which he chooses to regard as an honour. Since then he has done *nothing*. I mean, of course, nothing that anyone of my generation would count as constructive labour. The very notion of work fairly bowls him over with mirth.'

'How does he live? Do you keep him?'

'I did, for a while. But after he turned 18, I turned nasty. Since he evidently regarded me as a senile old idiot, in so far as he looked upon me as a human being at all, I failed to see why I should go on giving him money. I was also, at that time, a prey to the naïve idea that since in my day you had to have money to live on, it must still be so, and that if I stopped giving him any he'd have to come back into the world of reality in order to eat.'

'Was that naïve?'

'Oh yes. Because first of all, to these kids food is of minor importance. You can buy a five-pound bag of lentils in the Portobello Road for virtually nothing, and porridge oats, also by the sack; soupbones are often free, and if you grovel round the markets after the stalls have packed up you can scavenge all sorts of semi-edible produce sufficient to maintain your scraggy, underfleshed carcass. And if food doesn't matter much, clothes and a decent place to live don't matter a damn, of course. My son, or rather his scruffy remains, currently shares a pad, which is a flat in an all-but-derelict house, with a varying number of young males and females, virtually indistinguishable from each other. I've seen it. Once. I'd really rather not describe it to you. I believe there are worse places; I mean their lavatory does work and they use it, but apart from that it's hard to imagine anything much more squalid. In those chaotic rooms, or in the park, or in the streets, or at night in an assortment of cafés and coffee bars, they hang around together, smoke, talk gibberish, and copulate in various bizarre combinations. This last they dare to call "making love", but I don't allow Chris to use that expression in front of me. I now feel that I, as a representative of a dying generation which did and do make love, have a sort of sacred duty to guard even our terminology from corruption. They do their own things; let them call them by their own names.'

I noticed he had stopped eating, and a very stiff look about him gave me the impression he would be trembling if he were not holding himself rigid.

'Let's talk about it later,' I suggested, somehow alarmed into cowardice.

He ignored this, sighed again, and went on: 'Of course I've tried to discuss the whole mysterious business with him. We can't really reach each other. I don't think anyone of my age *can* reach anyone of his, and in any case, as you know, I'm not much good at words.'

'But you're good at feelings. How do you feel about him?'

He looked at me sadly, 'I love him, but I detest him. I can't bear the way he looks, his long shaggy hair, his ragged "gear", his unshaven face which once shone with intelligence and which now merely beams with a sort of self-conscious, vacuous, all-embracing benignity. Oh yes, it even embraces me, and it maddens me, because in actual fact he despises me and everything I represent.'

'Yet there's a room in your new house for him.'

'Which is not to say I shall be sorry if he never uses it.'

'Do you expect him to?'

He shrugged. 'Who knows? I haven't set eyes on him for three months.'

Staggered, I asked: 'Then how do you know he's all right?'

After a longish pause, during which he abandoned his efforts to eat and lit a cigarette, he said, 'I have a spy. The house where he *lives* – to lend him a piece of my terminology – has one flat left in it which is still inhabited by a real person, a woman called Mrs Wax. I don't know how she can stand it there, but she's right up on the top floor with two intervening doors which can lock. I went up to see her once, and in a remarkably short conversation – she's not clever but she understood my situation extraordinarily well – we arranged that she should telephone me once a week to let me know that she'd seen him and that he was all right. I offered her a fee for this service, but she refused it. Her own son, it seems, has burst from the pubertal chrysalis as a Skin-head.'

'But I still don't understand. How *do* they manage for money?'

'They con it, which is to say they beg it off anybody who'll give it to them, using their wits or whatever means, fair or foul, come to hand.'

'Foul? You mean stealing?'

'God, I hope not! By foul, I really meant degrading.' After a moment or two he went on: 'And they busk. The latest thing is playing a guitar in the underground. It so happens that Chris plays pretty well, and frankly I wouldn't mind that so much. It's better than conning – at least he's doing something to earn the coins that are tossed at him. But he only resorts to that when easier methods have failed. He has a philosophy, so-called, which he kindly explained to me once. Do you remember the flower-children?'

'They're still going on, aren't they?'

'Are they? Well, with him it's water.'

'*Water?*'

'Yes. It has a weird rationale of its own, the whole thing. Let me see now, if I've got it right. Water is the most vital substance in the world. Our bodies are 80 per cent or something water. Without water nothing will grow. *With* water things grow even without earth. Water can keep us alive, or kill us. Water is great, clean, pure, natural. Water is the force of life. Water is omnipotent. Water is God.' He shifted his position and took another deep breath to keep his voice calm. 'Well, now. So, says my son, let's look at water and see how it behaves. Let us, if you can credit it, *emulate* water. Water toils not, neither doth it spin, but Old Man River, he just keeps rollin' along. Without effort or force of its own, just by its own weight and the pull of gravity it provides motive-power for humanity. And it always takes the easy way. It resists all efforts to force it to flow uphill or to do anything except take the line of least resistance.'

'Go on – it's clever.'

'Oh, he's not stupid. He's worked out all this phoney nonsense, and he's started a kind of cult of his own, of which he's the un-challenged leader, with the help of the good brain he inherited from me.'

'What does the cult practise?'

'Getting wet, chiefly. Not washing, you understand. Just dipping.'

'How?'

'Once a day they all jump into the Serpentine – kind of ritual baths. Clothes and all, of course, which upsets the police, but when there's a guard on the Serpentine they go off to Trafalgar Square and jump in the fountains, or wade into the Round Pond or the pond on Hampstead Heath, or, at a pinch, into the river, though they object to that because the Establishment has polluted it.'

'Has he ever been to jail?'

'Oh, my dear Jane! Lots of times. A night here, a night there. The police all know him and his gang. They never resist arrest, they're never abusive. Just dripping wet. They drip all over the floors of the police-stations. Because of that they often don't bother to arrest them, they just chase them out of whatever body of water they happen to be in and threaten them with mayhem if they ever catch them again.'

The mental picture made it hard for me not to smile.

'Go on,' said Andy with sudden bitterness. 'Have a good laugh. You wait till David's old enough to become a neo-Troglodyte or something.'

'I must say, though,' I said, 'that jumping into cold lakes every day and being lugged off to jail and all that, hardly seems consistent with taking the line of least resistance in life. It takes not only a lot of energy and determination, but hardiness as well.'

'They claim that water attracts them and that it would take greater energy to keep away from it.' He looked at the ceiling for a moment and then leant suddenly across the table at me. 'Jane, what do you think of it all? How would you cope with it? He's nearly nineteen, for Christ's sake!'

'Well, I don't know if it's as awful as you seem to think. I've heard of much crazier things. It sounds to me just like another youth-cult, rather more harmless and better-thought-out than most. Everything depends on what kind of person he really is, under the fad, which must surely be a phase. I mean, is he really bone idle as you suggest, and simply rationalizing it and having a bit of fun at the same time, or is he a genuine rebel against society?'

'If you mean, is there some sort of ethic behind it all, pacifism or anarchy or something of the sort, the answer's no. Chris wouldn't be caught dead banning the bomb, it's much too much like work and far too un-exclusive – he's a bit of a snob in his own warped way, not about class but about intellect. He actually puts people through a sort of Mensa test before he lets them join his soggy company.' He sat back with his face grim. 'No, there's very little snap, crackle or pop about our product. He just lies there. Immersed.'

'Nevertheless, I'd like to meet him.'

He brightened a little. 'Would you really?' Then he lapsed into gloom again. 'Oh, it'd be fatal. Put you right off me. It must. None of us can escape this deep-rooted belief that parents are to blame for their children's aberrations. One look at Chris would put a fast blight on any notion you might have of being the mother of my next.'

I gave a startled laugh.

'You don't want to,' he said, just as he had about Glyndebourne.

'Well – I've nothing against it in theory – but I'm thirty-six—'

'So what?'

'And there's David to consider.'

'Ah yes. David.' We'd both finished eating and he was holding my hand on the table-cloth. 'We've talked about my failure as a parent, now let's talk about yours.'

This startled me considerably more. 'Have I failed?'

'Failure of some degree is the natural concomitant of parenthood,' he said. 'How far you've failed, of course, is for you to say. I've never met a parent with the face to claim he'd actually succeeded, and I don't see how anyone in your situation could claim it.'

Cautiously I asked, 'How do you mean, my situation?'

'Not remarrying. Your failure to provide David with a new father is surely a considerable black mark against you. I wasn't widowed until Chris was fourteen, but I blame myself heartily for not remarrying almost at once. The fact that at this moment I'm thanking God I didn't,' he added, smiling tenderly at me, 'doesn't exonerate me. I was too selfish to even attempt to marry one of the several pleasant women I knew who would have made Chris a very adequate mother and possibly, I say possibly, obviated all that subsequently overtook him.'

When I am very nervous, I don't bite my nails, but I push them between my front teeth and kind of nibble the edges. I did this now. It is not a pretty habit and it makes a maddening clicking noise. Andy drew my hand away from my mouth somewhat sharply.

'Don't do that. What's the matter?'

'Are you by any chance under the impression that I'm a widow?'

'That's what I was told.'

'Told? Who by?'

'Alf Davies, as a matter of fact.'

'*Alf Davies* told you I was a widow?'

'I hope you didn't mind. I wasn't checking up, not consciously anyway, only he got me in a corner, ages ago, and spent an hour telling me what a marvellous brave woman you were—'

'Hold hard. I want to think.'

I tried to, and drank some wine to help the process, but my mind stayed a painful blank. Why couldn't Alf have kept quiet? At the same time I felt tender towards him for trying to help and protect me, in his elephantine way . . . Andy was waiting patiently.

'All right, well, here it comes,' I got out at last. 'I've never been married. David's a bastard.'

Just as, long ago, I had thrown the fact of my pregnancy at my father's head in the most crude and brutal words I could think of, now the same warp in my nature made me do it again to Andy, against whom I had nothing except the word 'failure' which, in connection with David, I could not tolerate.

Andy was gazing at me with a blank look which seemed to me to mask an emotion I could only classify as incredulity. But he quickly if only partially recovered, and said, in an almost normal

71

voice, 'Poor you. Well. It doesn't matter.' But I would have to have been blind not to see that it mattered very much indeed.

'You're shocked.'

After a moment's hesitation he said, 'Yes . . .'

'Go on.'

'On where?'

'Don't you have to explain why, in this day and age, such a very common predicament should shock a man like you?'

'No,' he said quietly, 'I think not.'

There was a long silence, which grew more and more unendurable until I said, much more harshly than I'd intended, but my voice is always the first part of me to get out of control, 'If you don't say something soon, I shall bloody well get up and go home.'

His eyes came back to me from far distances, slowly. They had changed. They were always hard to read, but impossible now, so I put my own unilateral interpretation on what I saw there.

'You're not just shocked, you're appalled. I don't understand you! Have I changed in the last ten minutes? I'm not a tart, you know—'

His hand, still on mine, but lifelessly, returned to life suddenly and clenched mine so hard I stopped speaking with a jerk and a grimace.

'That'll do,' he said in a sharp undertone. He began to stand up. 'Let's go home and talk there.'

'No,' I said, entirely against my own will, for I wanted nothing more than to get to my own little sanctum as quickly as possible before this menacing conversation could develop further. 'I haven't finished my dinner.' With a trembling hand I pulled the menu towards me and affected to be studying it. I couldn't read a word of it. Let him take you home, what the hell's the matter with you? a voice inside me urged quite clearly, but I couldn't move.

Andy gently removed the shuddering menu from my hands, beckoned the waiter and ordered two ices and coffees.

'Sorry, darling,' he then said quite steadily. 'I, too, needed a quick think. I'm afraid my silence put you needlessly on the defensive.'

'Needlessly?' I was so terrified of bursting into tears that my voice still sounded unnaturally shrill.

'Quite needlessly.'

'That's not how it looked to me.'

'How did it look to you?'

'As if you thought I should never have gone to bed with anyone before you.'

He looked disappointed. 'No, no, Jane. Don't take me up all wrong. I should hope you've been to bed, if not with many men, at least on very many occasions. What shocked me was that you'd be – well, irresponsible enough to have a baby for whom you couldn't supply a father.'

'You mean I should have aborted him?'

'That's more than any man dare have an opinion on.'

'I agree with you.'

'But having decided to allow him to be born, how could you let him reach the age of eight with the crippling handicap of fatherlessness on him?'

This conversation was having an inwardly shattering effect on me. Its whole tenor was so exactly in line with my recent self-questioning, underlining and reinforcing my doubts to such a degree that I felt every sentence of Andy's was hacking away at the underpinning of my life. I found myself in a posture of self-defence which I was ill-equipped to back up with conviction.

'I think the word "crippling" is a pretty outrageous exaggeration. I've done everything possible for him—'

'I don't doubt that for a moment. The real question is, is that enough, could it ever be enough, no matter what you did?'

'What more could I have done?'

'Got married. For my sake I'm glad you didn't, but undoubtedly from David's point of view, you should have done.'

'Indeed! To whom, may I ask?'

'Don't tell me you've had no offers.'

I thought of Dottie's acerbic remark, 'Offers! Every female with her glands fully functioning gets offers – of a sort.' 'You mean, just anybody?'

'I'm quite certain, knowing you, that "just anybody" would never have got as far as asking you.' I was silent, thinking of my 'offers' – Terry ('I suppose you don't want to marry me?') Toby ('Would you like to – I mean shall we?') Pietro ('Stay a little longer. Maybe in a few years we could get married") . . . Not to mention the few in between who, as Andy correctly assumed, hadn't been allowed to reach the point.

'Supposing I told you that I had the chance to marry David's father, but refused him because I didn't love him and he didn't love me. Would you say I'd done the right thing or the wrong thing?'

'Oh, the wrong thing. Unless you actively loathed each other.'

'How can you say that marrying a man just to give David a father would have been right, in the practical sense of being good for him in the long run? What if we'd been unhappy together, as I'm sure we would have been, since we had no respect for each other? Would that really have been better for David than me struggling along alone?'

'Well, it might. The child psychologists, the domestic court judges and so on generally agree that almost any mother is better than none, and I think the same about fathers. The parental equation should have two figures in it. That's what nature lays down as the norm. You may say that a reasonably happy home with one parent is better than a moderately unhappy home with two, but to me that's like saying that one strong arm on a human body is better than two weak ones. We're meant to have two arms, and if they're not strong we can work to develop them, but a body with only one arm, however good, is not whole. It's crippled. The owner may get along perfectly well, he may cope, he may succeed in overcoming the handicap – but he is not and never can be normal.'

'You're saying that David isn't normal.'

'Well, is he?'

I tried to meet his eyes with self-confident defiance, but David's distorted night-face got in the way and I failed.

'Does it show?'

'No, not obviously. I mean, I don't think anyone who met him casually would realize anything was wrong. But you must remember that I've been watching him very carefully.'

'I didn't know that. You've always seemed to hold yourself aloof from him, and from him-and-me.'

'Jane, darling, he's going to be my son.'

'That,' I said, 'is by no means settled.'

The ices arrived and made a very necessary hiatus in the tension.

We fiddled with them dutifully and I even got a spoonful as far as my mouth, where I discovered its slippery coldness was most soothing (my mouth always dries up under stress) and began spooning it in hungrily.

'I suppose you think,' said Andy, also gobbling his ice, 'that for a man who hasn't yet issued a formal proposal, I'm taking a lot of liberties.'

'Yes. In what way is David not normal?'

'The question is, how much it matters if one is "normal" in that sense or not. I'm not saying for a moment that he isn't a fine boy, or that he won't grow up to be a fine adult. I think that's up to you – and me, if you'll let me help.' He glanced at me. 'I wouldn't take him on if I thought he was past the point of no return. One failure as a father is quite enough for any man.'

'Look. What if I had been a widow?'

'The situation for David would have been in effect the same, and yet not. Because sooner or later he's going to have to know that you *could* have given him a father. Or, you must let him assume that his father rejected him. If a father dies, he can't be hated or blamed. If a mother loses her husband in death, her child can't say or feel that it's her fault somehow that he's not part of a normal family. Children blame their parents for all their lacks and miseries anyway, but David has you really on the hip.'

It was like listening to a voice which I'd been ruthlessly stifling ever since he was about three, and reacting to men like a starveling reacts to the sight of food. All that time I had been suppressing anxiety; and since he had begun waking up at night, I had been tamping down great lumps of raw fear. I had not dared to know what it all meant. Now here it came, and from outside, from a man who was saying it all out of a desire to launch our relationship on a footing of total honesty; but it was hardly to be borne. Andy's quiet, reasonable voice was waking the kraken from its long uneasy sleep.

I got up hastily from the table and walked as fast as I could to the ladies' room. Luckily it was empty. There was a chair there beside the dressing-table and I crouched down on it, my body curled up, my hands pressed to my face.

After a while I stood up to wash my face in cold water. While I

75

was doing this, another woman came in. She stood beside me at the other basin and began washing her hands. She glanced at me in the mirror, glanced quickly away again, then let her eyes return to me. I tried not to notice her, but her being there broke some inner barrier I had thrown up against the tears and they began again. I saw she was going to speak to me, and turned my back, praying she would not ask 'Is anything the matter?'

'Is there anything I can do?'

I shook my head. She sighed, dried her hands, and went out.

I felt a furious anger, and a deep panic. Being with Andy now would be worse than being alone with myself in the moments of my most frightening self-perception. But the anger helped to give me courage. Why should I let Andy or his remorseless truth, which I recognized, take eight years of very reasonable achievement away from me? The word 'cripple' rang and rang in my head like a discordant bell. But that was a lie. A temporary psychological limp is one thing. But 'crippled' implies 'for life'.

I'd come in without my bag and couldn't even repair my makeup. I washed my face again carefully, stared at the neon light for a few minutes in a futile effort to lessen the redness, then in a sudden mood of defiance gathered myself together and went out.

Andy was walking about outside in the hall, carrying our coats. When he saw me he came to me at once, took my arm without looking at me directly, and led me out to the car.

It was a beautiful spring night. A full moon flooded the countryside, enhancing everything that was lovely and natural by day, disguising what wasn't with its mysterious silvery outlines. I wound down the window on my side and leaned on the frame, my head on my arm; the rushing wind of our passage cooled and calmed me. Also, Andy's presence beside me was not the agitant I had thought it would be. I thought quietly, in the exhausted aftermath of emotion, that I must love him quite a lot to have accepted this punishment at his hands and for my resentment and rage at it to have died away so quickly.

When he stopped the car in a moonlit field, I put my hand out to him and he met it half-way with both his and kissed it.

'I'm sorry I hurt you. I love you so very much. This is what always happens when the talking starts . . .'

He held my hand against his face. After a moment, still without looking at him, I said, 'I don't think I've done so badly.'

'Surely you realize I don't undervalue you, as a mother or any other way.'

'But I'm so afraid for him. I'm afraid you're right, that I've done him serious damage – irreversable damage—'

'Every mother fears that, every time she makes the smallest mistake—'

'But this is different—'

'Of course it is,' he said. 'Of course it is.'

Perversely I was glad he was not backtracking or pretending to belittle the dangers to David which had so shocked him in the first place. I was ashamed to realize how, under all my superficial uneasiness about telling him, I had been counting on Andy to receive the information with unquestioning sympathy, even, heaven help us, admiration. In other words, with a complete suspension of moral judgement of any sort. I was glad he had taken up an attitude, no matter how painful to me it was. In my present state of self-doubt, I would not have trusted him ever again if he hadn't.

'I love you,' he said again, and added, 'now you've started me saying it, I can't seem to stop. But the important thing to make you realize is that I love David. I hope it's unnecessary to tell you that I don't care a damn about his being a bastard, as you rather childishly insisted on calling him. It would come very oddly from me to care about that, being one myself.' I turned to him in amazement, but he warded me off. 'No, no, enough revelations for one evening. I'll spill that lot of beans another time. I only mention it now to reassure you that David might mean more to me, not less, because of that aspect of his life. That being said,' he went on, leaning close to me in the uncanny witch-light, 'would the moment be appropriate to put in a formal offer of marriage?'

Chapter 6

THE next evening I drove David over to Jo's and we helped them catch and saddle the ponies, and then we stood together in the middle of the paddock and 'drilled' the pair of them round and round, periodically shouting 'Trot, please!' 'Canter, please!' in deep, horsey voices, like the judges at tomorrow's gymkhana. We had also been ordered to criticize their riding rigorously, but the first tentative attempt by her mother to check Amanda's over-assertive bounce had resulted in tears and cries of 'I wasn't! That's how Mr Rogers told us to do it!' So after that we had brief intervals in which to talk.

'What's up with you this morning?' Jo asked.

'Andy proposed to me last night.'

'To judge by your happy bridal face, you thereupon politely declined.'

'I had to.'

'Do tell, how long are you going on like this? – WALK, PLEASE. I don't see that you'll ever get a better chance than Andy.'

I said nothing.

'Still, presumably you've left your options open. I mean, you didn't boot him out on his ear?'

'No.'

'So what? Not the old you-must-give-me-time-to-think bit?'

'Something like that,' I admitted.

'Well I dunno,' she said glumly. 'I give you up.' It was typical of her that she asked no obvious questions. I ordered an S-turn to set the show-riders going round the other way, and then apparently changed the subject.

'Jo, I wanted to ask you . . . Could there be any shop-reason to go to Israel?'

'*Israel?* Even if there were, I wouldn't go there now.'

'Why not?'

'What do you want to go to Israel for, of all places?'

'There's someone there I want to see.'

'What's his name?'

78

'Toby Cohen.'

'Have I heard about him?'

'I think I mentioned him to you once, ages ago.' I paused and added, 'Maybe you know the name. He writes novels.'

'Oh yes! Didn't he write *A Hole in the Wall*? I liked that very much. Here, wait a minute . . .' she said suddenly. 'The girl in it – what was her name—'

'Greta—'

'That's it! I remember as I read it thinking she reminded me of you. Well. Am I on the right track?'

'Mummy, we've been walking round and round for AGES, you're not watching!'

'Sorry, love – from a walk to a canter – shorten reins – NOW. Oh, very good, Miss Barclay!'

'David, you're still trotting.'

'Bee's so damn *fat*.'

'Whack her on the rump,' suggested the successful Amanda, cantering round and lapping him.

'All right, back to trot – Amanda reverse – meet at the top and go in pairs down the middle. So you want to go to Israel to see him. Before you can decide about Andy.'

'Yes.'

'Ah ha. But surely you'd be mad to go just now?'

'Why not?'

Jo stared at me, hands on small hips, comically amazed.

'My dear old duck, where *do* you live? Don't you listen to the news? There's going to be a war out there at any moment.'

I watched David and Amanda trotting sedately down the field towards us and then stepped aside to let them pass. I drew in a deep breath as they went by, and realized I hadn't breathed for about a minute.

'What sort of a war?'

'A fairly murderous sort, to hear the B.B.C. tell it. Egyptian tanks massing by the hundreds in Sinai, U.N. pulling out at any moment to let them have a go at each other . . . Oh Jesus, don't look like that! Do you care that much? Listen, you can't go just now, what about David if anything broke out and you couldn't get back? It'd be completely—'

'Selfish—'

'Irresponsible, I was about to say. Same thing.'

'Yes.' I was silent for some moments, and then said, 'But Toby's got his little daughter out there. Surely he won't keep her there if things are really dangerous.'

'Well, listen to the news a few times, watch the preparations going on every night on telly. They're going to massacre each other. I mean, I don't care much, one way or the other, let them have it out and settle it, I say – better than going on for another twenty years snapping and snarling at each other. But then I don't know anyone out there on either side, or I might feel different.'

I looked at my watch. There'd be a news bulletin in a few minutes. 'Will you hold the fort out here?'

'Sure . . . Jane, listen . . .'

'What?'

'If you decide to go, you might look at some of the embroidery and filigree silver stuff the Yemenite immigrants do. I hear it's very nice. Only it'd have to be better than the tat they flog in the Israel Shop in London. None of those nasty green metal vases and olive-wood holy land camels . . .'

I sat in Jo's double-ended living-room and listened to the news on the radio. As I listened, with my blood chilling at every sentence, I felt bemused that I hadn't heard a word about all this before. After all, I have a radio too – but I seldom turn it on except for concerts and the occasional play, and as for newspapers I always start in the middle and work back towards the front page, but lately I'd hardly ever got there somehow. This is part of the penalty – or beauty – of country life. Everything around you is so peaceful that it seems no wars can exist anywhere – at least, none that concern you. Now a dark shadow of alarm fell over my self-contained little world, for I saw that Toby and Rachel, wherever in Israel they might be, were in appalling danger.

I found an atlas among Amanda's school books and for the first time since my own schooldays had a close look at the Middle East. What I saw terrified me. Israel lay like a pointed thorn, a gnome's dagger, sticking into the side of a vast hostile territory. The tip of my finger, anxiously probing the map, covered Israel, while my whole fist hardly extinguished the furthest borders of her enemies. 'It's hopeless!' I thought. 'An absurdity. Why doesn't he come home?'

80

And then I suddenly thought that perhaps he had. That letter, so recent to me, was written some time ago. Probably he'd returned even before this crisis started. The strain of not knowing was so great that it overcame all my inhibitions. I picked up Jo's phone on the spot and rang Billie's home number.

'Hallo? Billie? It's Jane Graham.'

'Hallo, my dear! I've been meaning to get in touch. You got my letter?'

'Yes. Listen, Billie. Is he back?'

'Of course you're worried. My dear, so are we. You can imagine. I mean it's bad enough him being out there, but Rachel—! I don't know how many telegrams I've sent already telling him to bring her home, or if he must stay himself, to send her. All I get in reply is "All quiet here, don't worry".'

'You mean he's not coming back?'

'It doesn't look like it.' Was I deceived, or was there a note of satisfaction in her voice?

'But why not? I don't understand – there's going to be a *war*.'

'Well, that's not absolutely certain yet, though things look very bad of course. Very bad.'

'So why doesn't he come, Billie? For God's sake?'

'Hard to explain.'

'But *you* understand,' I said slowly.

'Oh yes. He's a Jew, after all. And he's a man. And I doubt if there are many Jewish men of army age in the world at this moment who aren't a little troubled in their minds as to where they ought to be. I'm a woman, and I'm nearly fifty, and I've never been noticeably Jewish in anything but looks, yet even I . . .' There was an oddly emotional silence, which I broke into impatiently.

'But the child!'

'Oh God, yes, he should send Rachel home, I've told him that, and Melissa's nearly out of her mind. Melissa phoned him at the kibbutz. She begged him. Do you know what he said? He said that nobody's sending their children out, and he can't be the first and only one. When she didn't accept that, he said that he was fairly sure that there wouldn't be a war, and that if there were, he was even surer that the Israelis would win it.'

'They can't possibly. I mean look at the map. They can't possibly.'

'We must hope you're wrong about that,' she said with a sudden slight coldness.

'Oh Billie, stop that! I know you're a Jew and you probably believe deep down that God'll protect his people and all that, but just look at the population figures. They're outnumbered something like 40 to one. No country can survive against odds like that.'

There was a pause and then Billie said in a strange withdrawn tone, 'Toby says they can, and Toby's there. Everything about that country happened at odds-on.'

'Can't Melissa go over herself and bring Rachel back ? Take the matter out of Toby's hands ?'

'She would, she wants to. But I won't let her.'

'Why not ?'

After another pause, she said, 'Because I'm afraid that if she went out there she wouldn't come back either.'

I almost physically threw up my hands. 'Good grief, is she crazy too ?'

'It's what I'd do myself.' She laughed a little. 'All we Jews are a bit crazy just now. Haven't you seen the fund-raising rallies on TV ? Tight-fisted, hard-headed businessmen giving millions away at the drop of a yarmulka.' She laughed again, exultantly, and suddenly said, 'We'll beat them, Jane – we'll beat them, with or without God, you'll see.'

I made a sound of exasperation.

'Billie, listen to me. I know you'll say it's none of my business—'

'Oh no I won't,' she said, sounding quite sober and calm again.

'I can't go into it all now, but I simply have to see Toby. I can't move, somehow, in any direction until I've seen him. Now what if—' I hesitated only a moment, but it was too complicated to think out, so I went on impulsively – 'what if I went out there, very soon, I mean in the next few days. On my own private business with him. Is there anything you want me to say or do about Rachel ?'

There was a long silence, so long that I asked if she were still there.

'Yes, I'm here. I'm thinking. You won't be going for a day or two anyway, will you ?'

'No,' I said, suddenly getting frightened. Was I really going then ?

'So I'll maybe talk to Melissa and let you know.'

'You're going to tell Melissa about me?'

'My dear, don't you think she knows all about you? She once told me you were breaking up her marriage by remote control.' And on that stunning note, she said goodbye.

Chapter 7

'LET me come with you, Mummy! Please, please let me come! I won't be in the way, Mummy, please, don't leave me behind—'

I was sitting on a bank of damp velvet turf under an oak tree. David, small, compact in his riding clothes, clutching his little crop, jodhpur'd legs bent into a crouch as if he were about to jump on top of me and pin me to the ground, was standing in front of me. His usually alert but placid face was twisted into a flaming mask of passionate beseeching.

Behind him I could see the crowds and the railing round the show-ring, hear the prrrmph of horses sneezing in the damp air. It was a cloudy day. The children, the mothers and fathers and baby brothers and sisters, were bundled up in tweeds and flannels. Picnics were mostly being eaten in cars, which were dotted everywhere among the trees of the large paddock where the gymkhana was being held. There was a tent for refreshments which was used for every outdoor community occasion; it leaked, and had done for years, usually straight into the cups of tea, but it was not yet actually raining, so everybody was cheerful and all the kids and ponies and family dogs and relations were having a good time.

David had begun the day well by coming in third in the junior riding class. His first rosette, a beautiful yellow-streamered symbol of triumph, now fluttered from Bee's bridle. He had been so excited (the more so, perhaps, since Amanda had not been placed and it was the first time he had ever beaten her in anything) that I had had to put a hand on his shoulder after about five minutes of bouncing to restrain him from exhausting all the energy he would need – as I explained – to get a red or even a blue rosette in subsequent events.

Now it was the turn of the 12–16-year-olds, and for three or four events David and Amm had nothing to do except watch, groom their ponies, eat sandwiches and mess around with their contemporaries. Only Amm wasn't feeling her usual ebullient self after her humiliation and David, on the other hand, was in such wonderful spirits that they hardly matched; so David came and sat with me under the oak tree where I'd established myself with the picnic basket, preferring damp outdoors to cramped car, and ate a snack and talked excitedly on and on about his win while I remained silent and preoccupied by my own gnawing inward concerns.

I decided that this would be the moment to tell David I was going abroad. I didn't know whether to expect any trouble about it. I'd been away several times before, on business trips, and the arrangement was a standing one – David went to Jo's and slept in Amanda's room and had a wonderful time. It was half his home anyway, Jo was like the closest sort of aunt, and Amm was his sister in all but fact; his routine was scarcely disturbed, and if he'd missed me (which he sometimes had) it was not too intensely or for long, since I'd never been away longer than a week at a time.

Of course this had been before his 'nights' started. Nevertheless his abrupt and violent reaction to my casual announcement this time caught me completely off-balance.

'Darling, what is it? You've never wanted to come before.'

'I want to this time. I don't want to stay with Amm, I want to come with you. I won't let you go if you don't take me, I won't let you!' His tone was almost hysterical. I reached up, caught him round the waist, and pulled him down on to the grass between my knees.

'I don't understand this, David. What's different about this time?'

His body was rigid in my arms, as it had been the other day when he had had the outburst about Terry. He turned his face away, struggling not to cry.

'You've spoilt everything,' he said in a hard little voice I didn't recognize. 'I was happy and you've spoilt it. I don't want you to go.' He tried to pull away from me, but I held him.

'Listen, I'm going on business. It's not a treat or a holiday, like when we all went to Spain. I wouldn't know what to do with you,

84

David. I can't take you, you'd be bored and miserable while I was seeing people.'

'I could come with you. I could sit quiet and wait for you. Then when you'd done all the business we could see things. Israel's where Jesus was born and all that, isn't it?' The sulky tone was muted now, and the pleading note had come back. He looked at me from under his eyelids. His expression mixed desperation with a kind of craftiness. 'I'd learn a lot,' he said slyly. 'I could write some good news-pieces.' He knows I greatly approve of the emphasis on free writing in his school.

For a moment I let myself play with the idea. But that morning's news bulletin was still fresh in my mind. The Americans were holding the Israelis back at the moment from launching what I'd already, in 24 hours of belated interest, learnt to call 'a pre-emptive strike'. A sort of calm had fallen on the situation – some commentators were calling it a false calm, others seemed genuinely optimistic that a war could still be avoided.

'Listen though, David—'

No. Mustn't tell him there's any danger. That's all he needs. I looked at his face, and it was not the face I knew. The desperation, the terror on it were estranging; it was his night-face, not his day-face, and here in the open air, surrounded by the thumping normality of tweeds, ponies and picnics, it struck a note of eerie unreality, as if his own personality were somehow becoming twisted. I had felt this sometimes, terrifyingly, in the nights. But this was different. Was his unreachable, not-normal night-self beginning to encroach on the days? I suddenly clutched him against me in a spasm of anxiety.

'All right, I won't go,' I said out of a dry mouth.

He didn't answer. But his arms went round my waist and he squeezed with his full strength, straining his head and body against me. Then he disengaged himself and jumped up.

'Aunty Jo can go instead. We'll have Amm to stay with us. We'll be extremely good, Mummy. I promise.'

He looked down at me a moment, flushed, his breath coming in noisy gasps. Then he ran off hard towards the show-ring.

I sat still for a few minutes, shaken by something I didn't quite understand. I had reversed my strongest intention on a whim of

David's. Ten minutes ago I wouldn't have believed anything could change my mind about going. I thought it was something I really had to do. But David, by one change of expression, by one note in his voice higher on the falsetto scale than usual, had swayed me, set me into reverse. This had never happened before.

Before, I had always made decisions to the basis of what *I* wanted to do. Usually I wanted to do what I thought would be best for David, so there was no conflict. But undeniably, I had never before made a sacrifice for him.

I thought of Addy, my great-aunt, who had left me the cottage. Addy never made sacrifices. It was against her principles. But then, she had never had children of her own. I had always admired her way, believing with her that sacrifices, in the end, undermine and destroy a relationship. But now I saw it was not so simple. I would have needed a streak of utter ruthlessness to have denied David's imperative appeal.

But what of my own needs? Balked of the chance to see Toby, the desire to do so was immediately trebled.

I got up slowly and stiffly and wove in and out of the parked cars till I got to Jo's. It was a station-wagon like mine, only a lot grander and more comfortable. The back of it was quite caravan-like. Amanda, looking depressed to the point of sulks, and Jo were sitting in there propped up by numerous harem-cushions feasting off cold roast duck and game-chips. Jo saw me coming and waved a bottle of wine at me invitingly. Then her smile altered and she got out quickly and came to meet me.

'Now what? You look like the kiss of death.'

'Kids . . .' I said hopelessly, spreading my hands.

'Are you telling me? I could personally do David in for beating Amanda, even though from a strictly objective point of view I know it's the best thing that could have happened . . .' She watched me with narrowed eyes. 'Well, what? Has he said you mustn't go?'

I nodded, feeling vaguely ashamed. Jo was a strong believer in not letting children rule one's life. I feared she'd think me very malleable and weak-kneed for giving in to him. But, not unusually, Jo surprised me.

'As it so happens, he's a hundred per cent right on this occasion, though probably for all the wrong reasons. I also think you mustn't

86

go. Children have queer instincts. Maybe he senses you'd be taking risks. Risks you've no right to take, as I think I mentioned.' She paused, and then added, 'You're all he has.'

I said nothing, staring bleakly out through the grey, waterlogged air. 'But what shall I do?' I muttered after a moment. 'I'm in such a mess. I don't know what to do next.'

'For a start, come in and have a drink.'

'No, thanks, not just now.'

'Like that, is it?'

It was seven years since Jo had encountered a problem towards the solution of which a drink was not the first natural step. Though neither of us ever got drunk, this was true of me, too – a drink, usually of wine, calmed me, helped me to get the problem into perspective. But when things were very bad, the taking of this first step seemed to trivialize rather than help. It had been like that for Jo when Ted died – for months she hadn't drunk anything. 'I have to feel all of this,' she had said. 'I owe it to him.' I felt that now, though my trouble was not grief. I simply felt this was a turning-point so fundamental that drinking as an aid to a decision was somehow belittling and insulting.

I wandered off by myself through the sparse crowds. For a while I stood by the ring and watched the senior jumping. I love watching horses jump. The lyrical tension as their great bodies spring away from gravity and arc over the seemingly impassable barriers gives me a repetitive sensation of swiftly winding-up tension and relief, tension and relief, which excites me. There is something sexual in it. The muscles down there draw tight like a suture and then relax again as the swift flight ends, the bunching hindquarters hit and bounce off the ground, projecting the horse on towards the next encounter, the next moment of take-off. My breath came sharply as one particularly lithe and lovely bay horse, his coat contriving to gleam even in this dull light, swept around the ring in a clear round. His tail switched continuously, giving his performance a careless air, as if the effort of clearing those chest-high obstructions was no effort at all, as if he were truly able to fly.

I was almost in tears when his round was finished. I don't know why. He made it look so easy. He and his rider were so beautiful – flawless really. I craved the satisfaction of that flying feeling, that splendid muscular triumph which was a matter of the heart and spirit as well.

My hand gripped the rough, wet rail, I knew very well what I really wanted. And there was Andy, ready and aching to give it to me. Toby was like a warp in my soul, looming large beyond all that was natural or reasonable, a barrier I couldn't leap. An aberration, a neurosis. If only I had done what I wanted to do eight years ago, grabbed him, sunk my grapples into him, fettered him to me, to us, for ever. The gnawing regret, the guilt at letting him go to wreck Melissa's life, to beget children of a broken home – it all, in some moments of despair like this one, seemed to be my fault. And David – *he* was my fault, all, all my fault. On one hand I hadn't been selfish enough, on the other – ever since Toby – I had been too selfish.

That night, after David was in bed, I felt so desperate that for the first time I telephoned Andy in London.

'What is it, darling?' he asked.

'I've got to talk to you.'

'Do you want me to come now?'

I hesitated. 'It's so late—'

'Never mind. I was coming down tomorrow anyway. Hang on, I'll be there in about an hour.'

I didn't see how this was possible, but he was. He must have driven like a fool all the way. He'd brought a bottle of vodka, but it was, like the orchid, the wrong thing. I just wanted him.

'I don't want to drink anything just now, Andy. I only need to talk.' He put the bottle aside without taking any himself, and followed me into the living-room. It was untidier than usual, with shop-papers scattered about with a lot of books I'd been trying to read. He sat down with me on the sofa.

'Let's have it now. All of it.'

After struggling for a while, I temporized, unfairly perhaps. 'What you said the other night makes it hard to talk to you.'

'I know. But I can't soften any of that, or take it back. That's not to say I don't regret having said it,' he added.

'So why did you?'

'Trying to be honest, I suppose.' After a pause he said, 'Though, now I think about it, it's obvious I've lied to you, by silence, all the time.'

88

'Do you mean, by not telling me about Chris until I asked?'

'That, among other things.'

'What other things?'

'My origins, my marriage.'

'Andy—' I began, then stopped. We were holding hands and staring into the fire. It's odd to live so much of your life in one house. This sofa, this fireplace, the rug in front of it, had witnessed so many crucial moments in my life. The very locale we were in threw shadows on us from my past. Toby and I had once lain kissing in the firelight – and long before, I had sat on this same, then bright and new, cretonne upholstery and read Addy's magical book and felt new life of all sorts moving inside me. I suddenly gave a laugh. 'What?' asked Andy.

'Nothing, really. I was just thinking. I was once almost raped on that rug.'

'Good grief! Is that what you got me down here to tell me?'

'Of all the things that have happened in this room, that was probably the most unpleasant and the least important.'

'What were you going to say before?'

'Something about how I feel about you.' He turned towards me with a look of hunger which seemed to fall on me like a net. A look of shameless need – the kind I had spent my adult life trying not to show to men. And yet here was a man showing it to me, and it was, for all its inevitable fettering qualities, more like a gift than a stone to hang around my neck.

'Yes,' I said, looking from one of his grey eyes to the other, 'I do love you, in a way—'

'In what way?' he interrupted almost harshly.

'That's what I have to find out.'

I leant and kissed his mouth and strangely remembered the story of Mary Tudor who felt a baby 'leap in her womb' on the day of her marriage when none was there to leap. It did feel as if some living thing was quivering in spasms inside me, and this was before he said on a gasp of controlled breath after the kiss: 'We must get it all straightened up soon so that we can start having a child together.'

I sat back, our hands still locked.

'There's a lot to straighten.'

'Yes. Come on.'

'But you were going to tell me about your marriage—'

'It can wait. All that need matter to you about that, anyway, is that I loved her with all myself and that something went out of me when she died which I thought could never be put back. But I've found out I was wrong. It's only important to you – my marriage, I mean – because it proves I am an exclusive lover. I haven't loved anybody since Liz. I haven't slept with anybody since Liz. But it's all there, saved up, and I know I'm capable of lavishing it on you in a way that may possibly surprise you.'

'I doubt the surprise,' I remarked, amazed at the simulated casualness in my tone when my blood was clamouring for this love to begin on the instant, my famished sexuality tugging unavailingly at the strange imprisoning strings of my spirit. I obliged myself to stand up and move to the pile of books I had been trying, earlier, to concentrate on. Several of them were Toby's novels. I picked up one of these – his second and least successful – and put it, back uppermost, into Andy's hands. Toby's photograph stared up at him, a patent publicity shot of him posed by his typewriter looking sideways at the camera. But it caught something of the essence of him, the gentleness, the wit, the immature quality which made women of all ages – and men too, if they were like John – reach out towards him instinctively, sensing his vulnerability.

Andy looked up at me, puzzled, then looked down more closely at the photo. He turned the novel over to see the title.

'I've read this,' he said flatly, and then after a while, 'Is this him?'

'Yes.'

'I knew there was someone.'

'I haven't set eyes on him for seven years.'

'Good God.'

'I know it seems extraordinary.'

'No, not really. Most of the great novels of the past contained some indication of the human power to sustain unfed love . . . It's only recently we've decided that since it's hard, *ipso facto* we must be incapable of it.' He turned the book over again and stared at Toby. 'Jewish,' he said.

'Yes.'

'None of my best friends are Jews.'

'What do you mean?' I asked with some trepidation.

'I was just making a stupid remark. I hardly know any Jews. Perhaps this present incident will turn me into a fully-fledged anti-semite, who knows?' He smiled grimly and put the book on the table. 'Come on, let's get it over with.'

'It's hard to begin.'

'Do you love him?'

'That's what I don't know.'

'*Did* you love him?'

'Oh yes.'

'Just talk. I'm listening.'

I talked. I must have talked for nearly an hour. I told him about the L-shaped room and what Toby had meant by way of getting me through that time. In the end, I even told him the damning truth – that I could have had him as a husband, as a father for David, had I only been able or willing to pounce and pin down.

'And you've been regretting this incapacity ever since?'

I said nothing, looking at our hands, linked together. Impossible not to notice that, though the hands were still in physical contact, our spirits were now separated, withdrawn, as it were, up our arms and into our heads and memories. His instinctual honesty made him take his hand away from me, his natural kindness made him cover the gesture by lighting his pipe. This took some time.

He leaned his head back and blew smoke at the low cottage ceiling.

'So what now?' he said calmly, but before I could answer he jerked suddenly to his feet and strode to the window. The abrupt change from apparent calm to violent movement startled me.

'What is it?'

'I'm jealous,' he said in a muffled voice after a moment. 'Christ, what a hideous feeling! I'm quite blind with it.' After a pause during which I watched him uneasily over the back of the sofa, he added, 'I've never experienced anything like this before. I didn't think it was in me.' And in an unfamiliar, harsh, strained voice: 'Damn it all, it's torture!'

'I know, and it's so degrading.'

'Yes!' he agreed, turning, almost as if he were enthusiastic at finding he had even this vile emotion in common with me. Then his face grew hard again. 'You learnt the horror of it from *him*. When

91

he married.' I nodded. 'This whole thing is beyond me!' he exclaimed. 'How can it be possible that I am wishing with all my soul
at this moment that it was *I* who'd aroused this nightmare feeling in
you?'

His voice and his control broke and he seemed to stumble forward towards me. I felt his hands on me, gripping to and beyond
the point of real pain; but it was his face I minded – it was all
different: distorted, angry and unloving. He clutched me against
him almost viciously and shouted, 'Don't go on loving him! You
can't, I feel so strongly for you it must be answered, it can't be left
to go stale!' He kissed me, if you could call that a kiss – it was more
like hitting me on the mouth, and I winced back. 'Oh God, dearest!
I'm sorry! Forgive me. I'm not like this. I feel mad. How can you
love someone else?' He had let me go and was stroking and fondling
my face and arms, where he had bruised me, almost frantically,
caressing me with his own face, rubbing his cheeks and lips against
me. Somehow, still holding me, but more gently now, he came
round the sofa and our bodies met, not in a conventional embrace,
but in little rubbings and strokings, until we lay huddled up, our
arms finally round each other and our lips together.

Eight years make a lot of difference. When you're young, your
body states its demands and it all seems much simpler, even when
you are rather mixed up mentally about sex. You accede or you
don't, and you face the consequences later. You don't *know* enough
for a relationship to be really complicated. But at 36, with the body's
demands as imperative as ever, all your experience, all your imagination, all your knowledge of yourself and other people and what can
happen, give even the lightest gesture and contact a depth and a
dimension beyond anything you could have conceived of ten years
earlier. What's a kiss, in your twenties? What is the act of love? A
climax of what has led up to it, with the double-doors of every next
minute blankly closed just ahead of you, like those thrilling rides at
the fair when your little self-contained go-cart-for-two careers
round bends and down chutes and up hills, bursting through the
swing doors by the force of its owh velocity, with its twin occupants,
locked together in mutual excitement, screaming and gasping at the
delicious jolts and shocks, dives and swoopings . . . You don't even
have breath to anticipate what might be round the next corner, nor

do you bother to try. A climb, a downward dash, a throat-catching wheel round a curve – more doors just ahead – crash! This moment, this, this, only this very instant of sensation counts!

But you grow older, and you learn that beyond those doors lies Afterwards; your this-moment's actions are only a trigger for the future. This insight so colours the moment that sometimes its sensations of pleasure, or otherwise, are numbed by foreknowledge, or apprehension, or conjecture. So, as I lay in Andy's arms, almost obliterated mentally by the force of sheer physical experience, I was aware simultaneously of the shadow – Dottie's backward shadow of the future, thrown back upon now. I knew this was the moment when my physical doubts could be resolved. I had only to shift my position a little bit, accommodatingly, and the metaphorical, and physical, doors would be thrust apart, the next vital inevitable step into the following stage in my life and our relationship taken. But what then? Intimacy, dependency, vulnerability; need, exposed and acknowledged; the physical link forged, with all its associated mental, emotional and domestic sub-links wrapping whole chains of commitment around us.

Lying there, listening to the inner calls, I could almost envy 'the moderns', those shallow, playful, on-again-off-again lovers who lie down together, 'have it off' as the saying goes, get up, dress, kiss (perhaps) in tender or indifferent farewell, and turning their backs on each other, walk away. Unfettered, uninvolved, guiltless. Un-remembering, even. With them, the double doors close behind as well as in front; most of them seem to do it so often (I heard a young man on television only the other day claim with great good cheer to have had sex with a hundred and twenty-two girls and thirty men) that it must be impossible to add even a fleeting sketch to their gallery of remembered love-portraits. Even when I was living with Toby, our encounters in bed were so relatively few that I retain some recollection of nearly all of them. Naturally that would be impossible with a more prolonged relationship; but at least then, a total picture would be formed to which each act of love would add a detail. No, senseless to envy them. It was only for a moment when, with Andy's hand at last on my breast, and my whole lower body on fire with a clean, lovely lust, I craved a divorce from my mind and my imaginings of future complexities. I longed for the simplicity of total, unambiguous surrender, which I could only make if I knew that there would be no repercussion when the rapture was over.

In the end, though, it did happen. The surrender was not, could not be, unconditional, but the terms were within my own brain and involved, I hoped, only myself in penalties and forfeitures. *He* must not be called on to pay my guilt-bills, or solve my personal problems which this act of ecstatic capitulation would give rise to.

My last thought before the white-out was, 'My wretched soul was filched at birth by the Puritans'. For how else to explain why the bliss was not flawless? Andy's ways in love were marvellous – violent and tender by turns, as if his beast were in bondage and the bonds kept yielding a little, straining here and there to breaking-point, but always, in the end, just holding. Generosity made them hold, and a will for my pleasure, and his own innate belief in self-control as a way of life and an oblique spur to the delights of sensuality. In the happy aftermath, before my mind or body had recovered strength to start niggling, I lazily recalled Huxley's metaphor of the hose-pipe. Pierced along its length, it dribbles forth a dozen ineffectual trickling fountains; held in, contained, the water shoots out of the nozzle in a powerful jet. How could I have envied them, even for a second, those poor young dissipators of the flesh? The barren years I had spent without love were, of course, a grotesque misuse of my body; but in the moment of breaking fast, the power of released feeling was almost unendurably intense, and this – surely? – was the way it should be. I no longer begrudged the aching years, while acknowledging them to have been an exaggeration. They had led inexorably to this, this overbearing physical sensation, this feeling of my own bonds bursting gloriously asunder. Flawed, because I was not certain of loving him, and he was certain of my uncertainty, so his loving was perhaps too fierce, as if forcing the issues of the spirit aside with an assault on the flesh. Because of this, his first words afterwards were, inevitably but heart-wrenchingly, an apology.

'Dearest – I'm sorry.'

'Don't!'

'I should have waited—'

'I didn't want you to. Don't be all pardon-me-for-living, Andy! There's a limit to self-control. Don't spoil it. Don't abuse yourself. If you do, I shall start on myself, and then where shall we be?'

I had both arms round him and was cradling his big, spent body, which lay upon me heavily and still-sensuously. There was such luxury in this, these moments when I lay under his weight, my breathing enforcedly shallow, my head still light, my own limbs too exhausted to lift. I had felt the weight of smaller men before; I liked this crushing pressure of a bigger body. The physical burden of it evolved mysteriously into its own antithesis, no burden at all but a lightening, as if gravity had gone into reverse and I were sucked upwards against him, as if we might both float away, upwards into space and worldlessness, guiltlessness, problemlessness ...

Toby was nowhere.

I didn't realize it clearly, but there was an empty place somewhere inside me which was generally filled with pain and anxiety and regret. It was as if Andy's act of love upon my body had had the effect of electrical shock treatment, which knocks a hole in your mind or your memory. I felt Toby at that moment only as an absence of hurt, something blown hollow which I didn't want refilled.

I stroked Andy's sleeping face and his brown hair. I was drowsy but still wakeful, waiting for gravity to reassert itself, waiting for the gnawing anxieties, the guilty naggings to begin. They didn't.

I fell asleep too. Our bodies were still moistly, limply joined.

I awoke with a violent start some time later. David was calling.

It was horrible to be interrupted by maternal duty at such a moment. My instinctive desire to get to David had me shoving Andy off with such ruthless haste that he came to with a shout of almost animal protest.

I was fumbling with my clothes – we hadn't undressed properly – and groping for my shoes in pitch darkness, the fire having long since gone out. Eventually, with David's calls changing to screams of 'Mum-mee! Mum-meee!' I was obliged to turn on the light, which half-blinded us and brought us back to the outside, other-than-us world with the rudest sort of jar.

'Hell's teeth! What's going on?' muttered Andy. 'Is the house on fire?'

'No, nothing, it's all right. It's just David.' I found my shoes and struggled into them, a strange guilty panic making my fingers numb and shaky.

'Is it something serious?'

'Yes. No. It's something not unusual. Look, just go back to

95

sleep if you can. I'll be down—' I wanted to say 'soon' but I knew it might not be soon. 'I'll be down,' I repeated with a final inflection. My eyes were still dazzled and it was hard to see him, sitting there on the sofa, rumpled and dismayed, the dignity of love and sleep destroyed at a stroke. I felt sorry for him and for myself, and for us, the us that we had recently entered into and which David – symbolically? – had ruptured.

I ran upstairs, quickly but unsteadily. My body felt strange, not yet entirely or exclusively my possession again. The inevitable stickiness reminded me with crude vehemence of what had happened, like a hard finger poking me in the chest – 'Now you've done it. Now you're for it.' I burst into David's room and flung myself down beside him.

'David, darling, it's all right, stop now, Mummy's here. Don't cry, love, shhh, don't cry.'

He clung to me.

'Mummy! I had a bad dream!'

'What was it? Tell me.'

'I dreamt you went away and after you'd *promised*! Aunty Jo came and told me, like a joke, that you'd gone. She said Jesus had taken you to his country.'

I felt an irrelevant giggle coming. Jesus wants me for an Israeli sunbeam . . .

'Well, love, if that's all . . . You see, I'm still here, and Jesus doesn't seem to be bothering with me much. Now, suppose you settle down and go to sleep—'

'No! I want you to stay with me!'

I stifled a sigh. I wanted to be a woman tonight; being forced to be a mother was doubly burdensome. I felt a hardness, a brutality creeping over me, a permanent, lurking element in my nature which sometimes, at moments of weakness, overpowers me and leads me to be cruel. On such occasions I hear myself saying, 'Oh don't be such a baby! Now I've had enough of this.' But the proximity of love met the creeping tide of ice and melted it. I gathered him in my arms. 'I'll stay a little while. Give me a kiss.'

He kissed my lips with a child's unselfconscious, but not entirely sexless, passion. 'I love you, Mummy,' he said. And then added, in a totally different, rather querulous voice, 'You do smell funny.'

I blushed to my finger tips. Fortunately the room was dark.

'That's not a very nice thing to say.'

'Well, but you do.' I could actually hear him sniffing me like a dog, and I stiffened and drew away. 'Phew, it's awful,' he said.

I was so embarrassed my lips went cold. 'Well, in that case, I'll go,' I said.

He clutched me.

'No, no, it's okay, I didn't mean to be rude! Sit with me till I fall asleep.'

I got a chair and sat at a little distance from the bed.

'Sing to me.'

'What shall I sing?' At least he was himself; there was no unreachable, shouting little animal in the room, as on some nights, kicking and threshing when I tried to hold him. He was not frightening like this, merely normally troublesome.

'Sing about "The water is wide".'

'"The water is wide, I can not get o'er, and neither have I wings to fly . . ."' When I got down to "But when love is old, it groweth cold, and fades away like the morning dew" I was, as always with this song, caught up in its strange, disjointed mood of melancholy. David had dropped off, I was free to go down to Andy, but instead I sat there for a few minutes, quietly holding his hand, trying to think and succeeding merely in feeling – body-feelings at that, not brain-feelings. A sensation of simultaneous lightness and heaviness, pleasure and discomfort. The smell David had noticed was all about me, pungent and animal and rawly exciting, making me think of clods of rich earth and the red blood of childbirth, the aroma of meat roasted outdoors, of sweat and of milk on a baby's breath. I felt part of life again. I stood up, to feel my own body better, all the length and weight of it standing on my legs.

I knew suddenly that this time I regretted nothing. I had no shame or alarm about it. I had wanted Andy, I had needed his body, desired him in a word, and all at once it seemed no error ('sin' was the word that came, from my convent-tainted childhood, but I shunned it) to allow the fulfilment of desire to be a stepping-stone to a complete love. Why *must* the mental and spiritual aspects precede the physical? And it was, as I might have known it would be had I been a little more worldly and wise, its own justification. It had clarified my tangled emotions as only bringing to the boil can clarify certain food-stuffs. Now it was not necessary even to ask myself, 'Do I love him?' Our relationship was a challenging and creative one, not just without the answer, but without the question.

Chapter 8

I WOKE up early the next morning, with a conviction that everything had changed.

To begin with, I was not tired at all. I felt rested in a way that, as a rule, not even the longest sleep rests me. Andy had been beside me when I had gone to sleep the night before, but I didn't have to reach over to know he had gone. I hadn't even had to make a discreet remark as we cuddled down together at three a.m. or whatever, about the necessity of his removing himself before David could possibly catch him in my bed in the morning. I just trusted him to wake up and go, and he had gone, so quietly that I had not even stirred in my blissful, altered slumbers.

I piled up the pillows behind me and sat up in bed. The window was wide open on a pellucid May morning. I took a deep breath and my head began to spin as if I were inhaling some intoxicating gas, but of an unknown variety, of which you could die joyfully with the earth's wildest and most magical scents passing into your head with the beneficent anaesthesia. It was strange. Life had radically altered for me in the night; this morning the whole texture of my emotions and my senses had changed, I felt happy and relaxed and every aspect of every substance around me seemed to have sprung a new dimension. Yet I was thinking of death, a death-through-pleasure that carried no overtones of fear or darkness . . . Again I breathed, feasting my eyes on the bluish hills; at the line of tall soldierly poplars erect against the sky, my eyes stopped, and I suddenly threw my head back and laughed. 'Everything reminds me of sex . . .'

And now I understood one of the major elements in my euphoric state. It was not merely the aftermath of love. It was the unexpected absence of guilt. The events of the night before were all edged with bright colours. When had the rainbow of sensual delights so out-lined my actions before, obliterating the sub-conscious grey and khaki bogies of my conditioning? Only once before...

I hadn't wanted to find Toby back in his niche this morning. Yet there he was. And now the complications must begin. Because clearly no single action, except suicide, can eradicate and unravel all the twists and knots of one's past life. The hole blasted in memory fills up again, like a child's well dug beside the sea.

I sighed, tasting the May-morning nectar on the back of my tongue, but now it was not bliss unalloyed. Yet what had happened last night I didn't even begin to regret. That it would happen again was all that I cared to hope for. The poplar-tree and what it sym-bolized were arrows pointing straight towards a solution for me and David. I gave myself over to dreams for a few minutes while the thrushes and blackbirds sang loud enough to drown any thought less ephemeral than blatant fantasy.

'Mummy...'

It was a very tentative opening, compared to the usual boisterous entrance. I turned into reality, and saw him, a small pyjama'd figure, drooping in the doorway.

'What, darling? Don't you feel well?'

'Are you going to Israel?'

'No. You asked me not to, and I said I wouldn't.'

I expected a lightening change to joy and triumph, the rush and feet-first leap on to my stomach. But still he stood there, watching me from under his eyelashes.

'But you wanted to.'

'Yes, well... We can't always do what we want.'

'But it was important?' he persisted.

'David, what is this now? You got your own way, and I'm not complaining. Let's leave it at that.'

'I just thought... if you really wanted to go...'

'You mean, you've changed your mind?'

He dropped his eyes and dug his bare big toe into the varnished floorboard.

'No, but...'

Conscience? Newly-awakened social-sense? He was a good child and thoughtful of me as often as any child is, but this *volte-face*, if really caused by an ability to put himself in my place, represented something quite new, and, surely? – premature. I couldn't avoid suspicions of an ulterior motive somewhere.

'David, come here.'

He straightened from the door-jamb and shuffled over to the bed. I hauled him, a dead weight, up beside me. His body certainly didn't have the feel of one in which the spiritual yeast of a heroic unselfishness is at work.

'What's at the bottom of this? Let's have it.'

'Nothing. I was just thinking. If you really had to go, I shouldn't stop you.'

'Has somebody been talking to you?' I couldn't imagine who; it just smelled all wrong, somehow.

'No, Mummy!' A certain irritation in his tone was now evident. My suspicions were becoming too obvious for him to miss.

I lifted his head and peered into his bottle-brown eyes; my own were narrowed. He met them for about two seconds, and then pulled his head away.

'Let me get this straight. You're now telling me that you wouldn't after all mind too badly if I went to Israel for two weeks? Without you?'

He nodded.

'H'm,' I said. 'I think I'll have to think it out again.'

David smiled faintly, still without looking at me.

I got out of bed and dressed. David sat playing with the cord of his pyjamas, occasionally glancing at me out of the corners of his eyes. I tried to appear calm, but my mind was in a ferment. I'd put the idea of Israel, if not Toby, firmly behind me; since last night this had seemed the proper location for it. But now the idea of clearing the whole affair up, of laying the ghost once and for all, seemed acutely desirable, and, suddenly, possible.

We ate breakfast in unwonted silence. We kept eyeing each other. I tried to make conversation.

'Have you any plans for today?'

'No . . .'

'I mean, are you going to Amm's or is she coming here?'

'Amm didn't say anything yesterday. I think she was cross.'

'Oh? Why?'

'Because I won a rosette, and she didn't,' he said, with but a trace of what I would call normal human relish.

'Well, nevertheless, you'll have to get together somewhere. It's my shop-day.'

David said nothing, and picked at his toast. The phone rang. We both jumped, me the highest because I knew it was Andy. Was there an element of guilt in the jump? But as I hurried to answer it, I decided that my asking myself that question that was not a symptom of my former condition, but merely an afterpain.

'Hallo?'

'How are you feeling about last night?' he asked without preamble.

'Glorious.'

'Are you sure? No remorseful anguishings?'

'Not one,' I replied.

'Thank God for that!' he exclaimed, in evidently genuine relief. 'So we're on, then?'

'"On"?'

'Yes. I mean, are we on, for a clandestine affair with a view to marriage?'

I couldn't help laughing.

'No, don't answer, I'm feeling very flip this morning. Lightheaded. Not my usual sober self at all. I want to save the latter part of my proposition for a more suitable moment. In any case, prior to that we have matters to discuss.'

'What matters?'

'The past and its possible effect on the future.'

'Oh.'

This brought about a very accountable silence.

'In that connection,' Andy went on, 'I have a perhaps rather surprising suggestion to make. Is this a good moment?'

'Not really. What about lunch?'

'I'm in London.'

'Oh! I didn't realize.'

'I left you at five a.m., not knowing when the postman made his rounds and might find my car in his way, and arrived at my office, considerably startling the cleaners, at half-past six. I may add I haven't done a stroke of work since. All I've done is drink coffee and indulge in euphoric brooding, if that's not a contradiction in terms . . . May I make my suggestion, because I want you to be thinking about it?.'

I glanced uneasily over my shoulder at David, who, from the set of his head which I could just see through the open kitchen door, was listening. 'Go ahead.'

'Where exactly is this chap of yours that was?'

'You mean—' I gathered my wits. I could suddenly see Andy and Toby pointing at each other like rockets on a collision course. I desperately wanted to keep them separated – the moral and mental confusion that would result from those two vital elements of my life overlapping didn't bear contemplation.

Andy seemed to read my mind, even at sixty miles' distance along a telephone wire. 'It's all right, I don't want to meet him. I want *you* to.'

I swallowed. 'But why? Wouldn't that be—'

'Risky? Possibly. But I'm a very superstitious bloke. I believe in ghosts. I was haunted by one for years. A very benign and loving ghost, but a ghost nevertheless. You laid her, bless you both, and now I have to help you lay yours.'

My own thoughts, echoes . . . Andy, Andy! I said his name aloud, twice, as it had come into my mind.

'What is it?'

'You are not only superstitious, you're psychic.'

'So Liz used to say . . .'

'Mummy—'

David had come up behind me.

'What, David?'

'Who are you talking to?' A bit whiney.

'Uncle Andy.'

'Well, do hurry and finish, it's boring.'

'Go out and play in the garden. I'm just coming.'

'Oh . . .' He turned rebelliously and shuffled off. My conscience smote me, albeit only a slap on the wrist.

'I must go . . . what was the suggestion?'

'You haven't answered my question yet. Where is he?'

'In Israel, of all places.'

'Oh, crumbs! Of all places, indeed! Why not Vietnam? Or the Yemen? Somewhere quiet and peaceful?'

'Why? Don't tell me you were going to suggest I go there?'

'I was. Now I'll have to think about it some more.'

'And I have to go.'

'I'll ring you lunchtime. Get some sandwiches and put them by the phone. We'll have lunch together.'

'All right.'

'Goodbye then, darling,' he said, for the first time.

'Goodbye.'

'Jane!'

'Yes?'

'Have you been wondering all morning how you lived without it all these years?'

'Yes.'

'When can we do it again?'

'Next time you come.'

'That'll be tonight, then.'

'Another five-o'clock up?'

'I'll take the train and nap on the way.'

'So how will you get away from here at the crack of dawn, with no car?'

'Leave it at the station. I'll be there at eight tonight. Be thinking.'

'Even though it's Israel?'

He hesitated. 'Yes.'

'All right. I'll think.'

He hung up. I leant against the wall, still listening to the dead echoes along the line.

One way and another, I was late for work, and Georgie was already bustling around folding post-weekend dustsheets.

'Nice weekend, Miss?' she asked me cheerfully.

'Lovely, thank you.'

'How was the gymkhana?'

'Splendid. David won a yellow rosette.'

'Fantastic!'

'What about you?'

'I went away with my boyfriend.'

'Oh?'

'On a walking trip,' she elaborated. 'Shropshire.'

'Nice?'

'Oh, it was okay, I suppose,' she said. 'I'm getting a bit cheesed with him, though. All this *walking* . . . Do you know what he gave me for my birthday? Boots. Oh, not like *these*! Hideous brown walking boots with cleat-things like a footballer. I was so disappointed I nearly choked! *And* he collects rocks. It's a bit much. Yesterday we were trudging along a narrow path, you had to watch your feet all the time, and he was leading, and every few minutes I'd run into his *behind*. He kept bending over suddenly to pick up a rock. I mean, it was so *jerky*, banging into him all the time. And when his knapsack got full, he expected me to fill mine up with his ruddy rocks, too! I drew the line at that. I was having enough trouble dragging myself along by then, and he got narked and muttered about poor sports. I think I'll drop him,' she finished cheerfully.

'Good men are hard to find,' I remarked sententiously. I wasn't really listening.

'What's good about him?'

'Well, I don't know, what is?'

She paused for a moment between the fabrics and the ceramics, her weight on one barely-adolescent hip, musing. 'He's *quite* good in bed,' she said judiciously. 'But then that's the least you can expect, isn't it, from an athlete?'

I turned and looked at her. I knew she'd said it on purpose to shock me. But the shocking point to me was the implication that athletic prowess was the first prerequisite for a satisfactory sexual performance.

'How many boys have you been to bed with, Georgie?' I asked curiously. It was not a question I would ever even indirectly put to any woman of my own age, but somehow these kids not only didn't seem to mind, they positively invited nosiness.

'Oh, only three or four,' she said airily.

'Good Lord, don't you even know which?'

She looked a trifle sheepish. 'Well, it's only two, actually.' The sheepishness, I saw, was due, not to having exaggerated, but to having had only two, actually. 'The first couple of boyfriends I had, when I was fifteen or so, didn't seem to know the scene at all.'

'Which frustrated you to the point of neurosis, no doubt.'

'Sarky.'

'Well, honestly! Fifteen!'

'You're way behind the times, Miss.'

'Evidently.' We arranged things in silence for a bit. I thought, how ironic that I was being prim and uptight about Georgie, this morning of all mornings. But now I was more intrigued than shocked. After all, fond as I was of her, she wasn't my responsibility. I could afford to regard her in the impersonal light of sociological enquiry.

'Do you mind if I ask what you mean by being good in bed?'

She looked at me with her eyebrows up so high they disappeared into her fringe.

'Oh, you *know*,' she said. 'Making sure you get a bang too.'

'And is that purely a muscular matter?'

She giggled, doubling over like a child, with her booted toes turned in.

'Well, I mean, if they know how to do it, and go on long enough . . .'

'And this one does?'

'In a *way*. I mean, I nearly always come with him. The only thing is, I've begun to wonder lately if I'm not making it happen more myself.'

'Eh?'

'In my head, I mean. I make all sorts of things go on in my head, and I think that does the trick as much as what he's doing downstairs.' She polished a piece of glass slowly and thoughtfully. 'Take last night, for instance. He was working away, puffing like a steam-engine, but I was upstairs in my head almost the whole time. And when the bang came, it was as if I popped down there to feel it and then straight away came up into my head again. And I wanted to push him off, as if he hadn't any business being there, as if I'd rather be by myself.'

'And is that called love, nowadays?' I asked, remembering Andy's dismissive remarks about his son's crowd and their misnomers.

'Oh, I don't call it love,' she said, sounding very definite. 'Surely love must be something different. I mean, I wouldn't get annoyed with him so often if I was in love, would I? I think of it as a kind of rehearsal.' She ruminated a bit longer and then said, 'Older men are more my type really. Like your gentleman. He turns me on much more than Dennis.'

'You don't reckon much to a difference of thirty years or so?'

'I don't think about that. I just get turned on when I look at him. He must be super, I should think.' For a ghastly moment I thought she was going to ask me outright; I think she wanted to, but she caught my eye and stopped herself. 'But I don't suppose he'd get much out of it with someone my age. Men like that expect you to know all the tricks. But how can you ever learn them from kids like Dennis?' She sighed heavily. 'Maybe I could find an older man who'd take me on, like a professor, and teach me. I could go straight into the intermediate class,' she added with another infectious giggle.

I couldn't help joining in. 'Oh Georgie,' I said. 'You are a one.'

'So are you, Miss,' she returned disconcertingly. What kind of a one did she have in mind, I wondered? How did I look in Georgie's surprisingly unromantic, clear-seeing eyes? Middle aged in body and attitudes, undoubtedly. And yet presumably not 'past it', her usual dismissal of most adult women over the age of thirty or so. I reflected for the hundredth time that morning on the rich sensations of the night, and felt myself blessed with youthfulness. Autumnal fruit I might be, but I felt fairly bursting with juice this morning, and longing to have Andy sink his teeth into me; I had a sudden vision of myself as an orange, changed it because of the bitter peel to an apple, but that was altogether too chilly and English, so eventually I let myself be a mango. (Peaches are good, they spill juice liberally and hotly into the mouth when bitten, but they're too furry.) Mangoes have a tough skin – symbol of resistance – but they are plump with exotic rich syrup, it runs down the chin, over the fingers; they need to be sucked, you cannot eat them daintily or with restraint. Of course, they're a bit stringy in the middle . . .

'What's up, Miss? You sound as if you're crying.'

'I'm just quietly having hysterics,' I replied, wiping my eyes. 'Take no notice.'

'Is it me that's so funny?'

'No, *no*, Georgie. It's me. I was taking a leaf out of your book and having a fantasy in my head, and it got a bit out of hand.'

She stared at me, her funny little bird's head cocked. 'Fancy someone like you doing that!' she said.

'Someone my age, do you mean?'

'Maybe I do.' She worked for a few minutes and then said, 'Nice, really. Makes you feel there's not such a hurry-up.'

'Georgie, darling, you've got buckets and buckets of time.'

'Yes, well, that's not the impression you get, is it?'

Jo rang, mid-morning.

'Listen, duck. About this Israel project. Are you quite sure it's off? Because, by the weirdest coincidence, I've had some bumf through the post from the trade department at their Embassy about some stuff we might be very interested in. It's hand-made silver jewellery, none of your musty old filigree, I've gone off that since I saw these photos. It's dead modern and absolutely smashing. knuckle-duster rings and necklaces like horse-collars – I think we could do a bomb with them. What I was thinking was, if you were out there you could try and get some special stuff made, exclusive to us. I was thinking specifically of silver belts. Belts are coming back in a big way next season, and I'm gone on the idea of hand-wrought, real silver belts, unique designs, like an up-to-date version of those lovely Victorian chatelaine belts we used to pick up in junk-shops just after the war ...' She was chattering on at such a rate, as always when she was fired by a new idea, that I couldn't get a word in for five minutes. Finally I fairly yelled, 'Will you shut up a minute? I've got something to tell you.'

'What?'

'I don't think I want to go to Israel now. Everything's changed.'

After a long pause, during which I could almost hear Jo's acute intuitive mechanism clicking away like a computer, she asked:

'Overnight?'

'Yes.'

'Indeed, indeed, indeed? Well well well well well.'

'Oh, all right! Enjoy yourself.'

'My dear old duck, if you think I'm ragging you, you couldn't be more wrong. I'm merely adjusting myself.' Another pause. 'Look, in a way I've been expecting this, but I still can't quite fit it into the sweet complex pattern of our joint lives all in the twinkling of an eye. Give me a few hours to brood. Maybe *I'll* end up by going to Sunny Israel and stopping a bullet, who knows? Wish you'd never mentioned the bloody place.' I felt a little dismayed by the vehemence of her tone.

'Well, I—' I began.

'No, no, no, take no notice of me. I'm all nigged this morning. The lousy kids have been getting on my wick. They won't talk to each other, if you don't mind ... It's Amanda's doing. That a daughter of mine should be such a sore loser really gets up my back.'

'Oh, don't let it upset you, Jo. It's so natural.'

'I know, I know. And it's natural for me to want to hit her for it.' Suddenly I could hear muffled screams coming over the wire. 'Oh Jesus! They've broken the silence now, all right. I'd better go and wrench them apart.'

We normally stayed open at lunchtime but today I decided to shut up shop and 'have lunch with Andy'. I sent Georgie off with strict instructions not to come back in under an hour, exposed the 'Closed' side of our sign, and retreated with my sandwiches into the back office. Sharp at one, the phone rang.

'Darling? Listen, I'm afraid something's happened and I can't make it tonight. Christ, I'm so furious! I'm so damn disappointed. I feel like a thwarted baby, I could drum my heels and scream.'

'Me, too!' I answered feelingly. The mango grew wrinkled and dried-up and suddenly a big black bird came swooping down and carried it off in his talons. 'Andy.'

'What, love?'

'Nothing – only I do so want to see you, and I had a stupid little mental picture when you said you couldn't come which scared me...'

'Oh, my sweet, I'm so sorry! It's that wretched son of mine. You know that woman I told you about, who lives in the same house and keeps an eye on him? Well, she rang me up just now and said she hasn't seen him for over three weeks. Instead of being grateful to her, I gave her a rocket for not calling me before. Is it possible I still care about him enough to be as panic-stricken as I suddenly am? So much so that I'd even ditch you?'

I tried to make a feeble joke. 'Whatever Chris's cult may say to the contrary, blood is thicker than water.'

'Neatly put, my love ... Oh God, do you suppose he's drowned himself during one of his ritual immersions?'

'Oh, come on. Surely you'd have heard if anything serious had happened.'

'I doubt it very much. It would be utterly out of character for him to carry the least shred of identification.'

'Mug-shots?' I suggested tentatively. 'You said he'd been in jail.'

'But you don't think he gives his real name?'

'Perhaps he's just trying to protect you.'

He gave a hollow laugh. 'No, dear. Such a thought would never cross his mind.'

'Well, so what are you going to do?'

'A bit of private investigating, initially. I know some of the places he frequents. If I don't get any leads, I suppose I'll have to go to the police.'

'If I were you, I'd go to them first. He's probably doing another of his spots of "time".'

'You seem to think it's all a bit of fun and games,' he said with a sudden sharpness which alarmed me.

'Of course I don't! I just feel absolutely certain, somehow, that nothing has happened to him. After all, why should it? He's probably taken off somewhere. All the kids do it these days. Maybe he's on the guru-trail to India, or cattleboating off to Cuba . . . Some place where there's more water, perhaps,' I added inspirationally. But he took this the wrong way too.

'I see you can't take him seriously even when you're trying to.'

'Oh Lord, I'm sorry—'

'Not that I blame you. He's quite bizarre, no doubt about that. Perhaps you're right, and flippancy and puns are the only mature reaction.'

'Darling—'

'I'm clearly schizoid about him. Not to be wondered at, I suppose.' After a pause, he added soberly, 'He really was a most lovely little boy. I'll show you photos.'

I was silent. Something in his tone as he said this last deprived me of the insulated status of an outsider, for I too was a compulsive child-snapper; I had albums and boxes of snaps of David from babyhood upward, and could all too easily imagine how I would feel, comparing those untrammelled baby likenesses to something grown wild-haired and shallow-minded, grubby-footed and foul-mouthed, slack-willed and dead-eyed like the young men (and girls) who had begun to accumulate in the village cafés, or whom I encountered slouching down Tottenham Court Road or strumming guitars, very badly, in stuffy station waiting-rooms – lost, adrift, disenchanted with everything, or perhaps all too enchanted, long beyond arm's reach of real life, or so it seemed to me. To see that sort of shadow engulf your child must be a sort of hell on earth, especially if he blames you for it, or you are forced to blame yourself. The only recourse might well be a cynical indifference, strong enough feigned to convince, first and foremost, yourself. But the love that would underlie it – that would take some killing. Andy, clearly, had not even made a convincing first assault on his.

He finally roused himself on the other end of the line.

'Darling, this won't do. I'm depressing you. Look, I'll ring you tonight. Forgive me if I go now? My heart really isn't in anything just this minute except finding out where he is. Does that sound inexcusable, under the present circumstances? Ours, I mean.'

'No. Do, please, forget about everything else for the moment until your mind's at rest.'

'Thank you.'

He hung up.

The eight-years difference again. Eight years ago I would certainly have wept, and without really knowing why – because he had 'failed' me, because I had 'failed' him; out of exasperation, out of frustration, out of physical emptiness. Now I sat dry-eyed and ate my sandwiches because I knew I'd be hungry later, during work, if I didn't; but I felt very grim, and every now and then as I was chewing I would clench my teeth against something very like a sharp pain.

Was this to be my eternal pattern? One-night love-stands, with my partner then whisked away by a malignant, punitive, anti-sex fate in the morning? Thus with Terry; our long-awaited, utterly misperformed night of so-called love had ended with him putting me on to a French inter-village bus the next morning with a peck on the cheek and averted eyes. Toby . . . and a preposterous press-party the following day which sundered us, as it turned out, for weeks. Pietro, if he counted . . . but he was meant to be a one-nighter. And now this. Christ, what bloody lousy stinking luck I had, to be sure!

Childishness. I wasn't thinking of Chris at all, except to curse him, or even of Andy's poor, plagued paternity. Nor of a father for David. Nor of anyone but me. But then sex is such an ego-rouser when it's over. Nothing makes you more conscious of your own body's unique importance, your self as the centre of the universe. Only the presence of the giver of sex counter-balances this in any way at all.

Quite abruptly, perhaps because Andy and all that attended upon him were suddenly too much for me, Toby was back. I knew it before it was quite clear in my mind, because my hand had reached out to turn on the radio. Every impulse towards the news media these days had its roots in concern for Toby and Rachel.

But now, perhaps not oddly, the simple gesture had undertones. I held the knob tensely, the rest of my body slumping with a sudden weary acceptance. This was what I had feared last night. Before, it had been my right to love and care about Toby. Now, concern for him could only seem like unfaithfulness to Andy.

Anyway I'd missed the news, so the ambivalence of listening was obviated. It was Jo who, phoning again a few minutes later, told me that things appeared to be calming down a bit over there.

'Everyone seems to be holding fire. It'll probably blow over. Hell, surely the Americans won't let anything dire happen? Their Sixth Fleet is bobbing about there, and I'm dead sure the Admiral must have at least a grandma in the Bronx who'd sit *shiva* for him if he let the Arabs get away with anything. Oh, *do* go!'

'Jo, you don't understand.'

'Well, no, possibly not, in view of the fact that you've never actually poured out your heart to me on the subject of this mythical yid of yours. But have you stopped to consider that one look at him now, after all these years of separate development, may scotch the affair for good and all? In which case you could settle down with Andy with an easy heart. It isn't easy *now*, is it, Jane? Come on, be honest.'

I admitted it was accursedly uneasy.

'And the principal obstacle is sitting over there in Sunny Israel amid all that silver jewellery and olive-wood and leather . . . Did I tell you about their *leather*?' And she was off on another shpeel. My mind wandered. Pressure from all sides upon me to go. Even the tides of war drew back, robbing me of another impediment.

'Have you talked to David?' I interrupted.

'Yes. Well, he talked to me, as a matter of fact. It's odd, but he seems to actually want you to go now.'

'Odd's the word – don't you think?'

'He's growing up. Realizing you've got your own life to live.'

'At age seven? Allow me to doubt it.'

'He's on the verge of eight, and he's extremely mature for his age.'

'No, he's not.'

'Intelligent, then.'

'That's something else again.'

'Well, what do you think's the explanation?'

'I'm still wondering. All occasions are conspiring together just a little too patly for my entire liking.'

'If you imply by that that we're all part of a plot to drive you off into the wilderness, you're crazy. True, I wouldn't have re-opened the subject if David hadn't let me know he'd reconsidered . . .'

'Look. *You* want me to go. David inexplicably wants me to go. Even Andy thinks it would be a good idea . . .'

'Does he indeed! Well, isn't that extremely interesting. Knowing the object of the exercise, I assume?'

'Of course.'

'A remarkable gentleman. Go on.'

'—And I've just been thinking that if and when I let Toby's mother-in-law know that I'm dallying with the idea, *she'll* join the team as well. She'll want me to bring Rachel back from the jaws of hell single-handed. I wonder,' I added on an afterthought, 'what John would think?'

'Ah, your witch-doctor.' Jo always called him that, and oddly it never struck me as being an inappropriate soubriquet for him. 'That's quite an idea. Why not have him consult the entrails for you? I know you reckon plenty to his native wisdom, if that's not a racialist expression these days. Let him be the deciding factor.'

'I don't know about that. But I think I might as well talk to him about it. He might have a new angle on the whole business.'

He certainly did.

I invited him down for the night, something I didn't do often for a number of reasons. One of them was village gossip, which, if it lights like a swarm of blowflies upon the conjunction of white male with white female alone under one roof overnight, buzzes out in density and intensity into a swarm of worker-wasps if the male happens to be black. Another was the fact that John didn't like the country much. 'Not my scene,' he would say, sniffing the pure air uneasily. His big hands, capable of immense delicacy and precision when handling the strings of a guitar or a semi-visible measure of spice for a dish he was cooking, became as bunches of bananas when he tried to come to grips with a flower. But the thing he disliked most was the quiet.

'Janie,' he said, standing in the middle of the garden and shaking his enormous head. 'How you stand it, all this no-noise? It scares me. Like in a horror-film when something going to jump out.'

'But the whole air's full of sounds,' I objected. 'Listen to the birds.'

'Ugh!' he exclaimed with an involuntary shudder. 'I meant, proper, *natural* noise. People-noise,' he elaborated for the benefit of my raised eyebrows. I said no more. When I reflected on the solid wall of decibels with which he was customarily surrounded, specifically in the night-spot where he played, I could not be too astonished and he found my country garden with its amiable twitterings and hummings disorientating.

'My head going to burst, like up in outer space,' he said. 'Let's go in quick and put on the radio.'

We carried in his 'luggage', consisting of one loudly-striped zip-bag, a huge bunch of wilting flowers, a hospital-type basket of exotic fruit and a whole paper carry-all of bits and pieces for David.

'Where that boy?' he roared as soon as he got indoors.

'Out riding.' His face fell. He adored David. 'Oh, don't look like that. He wouldn't have gone if he'd known you were coming. He'll be back at lunchtime and till then I want you to myself. We've got a lot to talk about.'

'That's right.' He encircled me with his massive arm, and his smile broke out again, a vast, dazzling crescent, like the moon lying on its back. His hug had much in common with that of an anaconda, except that it was inspired by the purest affection. 'I love you, Janie! Much too long we're not together.'

We went into the kitchen and John made a beeline for the radio, which he switched on full-blast to a record programme. I let him have his fix of ear-pressure while I made some coffee, and then, very firmly, I turned it down.

'Hey!' he howled in outrage.

'Ten minutes of your row, ten minutes of my quiet,' I said ruthlessly. 'I've got to talk to you.'

'I can listen with it loud.'

'But I can't think. Sit down and don't loom. It's like talking to a tree.' He folded himself into a kitchen chair and his mug of coffee disappeared between his hands. The steam rose out of them without any apparent source.

'You really look like a witch-doctor with the steam coming out of your hands like that,' I said.

'Hey, listen, you stop calling me that. I don't know no magic. I wish I did.'

'It's Jo who calls you that, not me.'

'Yes, well, she's a funny lady. Prejudice.'

'Oh, rot! She's very fond of you.'

'Sure. In spite of. Not because of.'

'I'm sure you're wrong, but never mind that now. It's me I want to talk about.'

'Go ahead, Janie, or your ten minutes'll be finished.' He made twitching movements of his fingers, as if they were moving of their own accord to switch up the volume again.

'It's about Toby.'

'Naturally.'

'Well, that's one point. I don't think there's anything natural about it, after all this time.'

'What that mean? – that you stop from loving just because you don't see each other for a while?'

'"A while" is not seven years.'

He reached over and grasped my hand. 'But you the faithful type, Janie.'

'Oh, John, don't! Listen to me. You've never really grown out of the L-shaped room, and the relationship the three of us had there. You hated Toby getting married as much as I did, because you resented anything that destroyed our threesome, the whole atmosphere of that time. Me going on with this – this obsession about

Toby, that fits in, it suits you, it helps to keep your illusion that nothing very much has changed.' He looked bewildered, as well he might. 'John, listen—' I began again.

'I listenin'. But I ain't followin'.'

'All right, I'll put it another way. I don't know how you manage without being married, or – or anything like that. How *do* you?' I broke off to ask.

'I dunno. Not too easy. I don't really want to be married, I can't see it somehow; I never met no girl I could love, 'cepting you, and that's different. I always knew you belonged to Toby.'

I dropped my eyes because of the question that had come into them. John could sometimes read my mind. He did it now.

'Sometimes,' he said very quietly, 'some – some john turns me on. You know what I mean.' I nodded. He pressed my hand convulsively. 'But I hate that feeling. I wouldn't never do nothing about it.'

'Why?'

'*Why?* You tellin' me you think that's okay – two men?'

'If that's the way they are.'

'It ain't the way I am. Not if I can help it.'

'But that means you'll never – have anybody.'

'Better nobody than that. That's horrible. Not natural.'

After a moment's silence, he said, 'I ain't never spoke about it even, to anyone but you. Only lately I let myself know it – that I had feelin's that way. I guess I been stupid. I guess you—' He stopped, and then went on with difficulty, 'I guess you knew it all along.'

I frowned and didn't answer.

'Did Toby – sure, I know he must've.'

'What does it matter?'

He shook his head. 'I just can't understand why it didn't make him sick, me being like that.'

'Of course it didn't. Not everybody feels like you about it.'

'Maybe other – fags – don't,' he said stumblingly. 'But a man like Toby, a woman like you, who's normal, how can you look at a big black freak like me and not get sick to your stomachs?'

'Oh, shut up! Now you are being stupid! Don't you know we loved you, as a friend and because of the sort of *person* you were?

115

That's what counts. The whole shooting-match isn't sex, you know.'

'Ten minutes is up,' he said abruptly, and turned up the radio to full deafening volume, like a barrier between us.

I felt this was his way of ringing the bell between bouts of self-exposure. That had been primarily his round and he needed to retreat to his noise-corner and have a rest. So I patted his hand and went out of the kitchen and did something about his flowers till his ten minutes was up. On the dot, I heard the radio go right off and his voice call, 'Come on back. Your turn.'

I sat down again in the same place, opposite him.

'To get back to me and Toby,' I began without preamble. 'You know he's divorced. And he's gone off to Israel with one of his daughters.'

'To the land of the Bible,' said John sentimentally.

'To the land of bombs and bullets,' I retorted. 'There's going to be a war over there, very likely.' John's face changed and he sat up. 'Well, that's a relative side-issue at the moment. The main point of this discussion is that I think I've fallen in love with somebody else, and I want—'

I became aware that John had drawn his hands away from me and was staring at me in horror and disbelief.

'Now don't look at me like that,' I said, trying to keep my voice light. 'It's been *seven years*, Johnny! Seven years of living alone, raising my child alone, dealing with all my problems and worries alone. I don't see the least virtue in being "the faithful type" all that time. Believe me, if it had been within my power to shake myself completely free of Toby when he got married, I would have done it, and been a whole lot healthier and happier because of it.'

'What's happiness got to do with it? Lovin' got nothing to do with being happy, necessarily.'

'Is that so? You must allow me to disagree. Love should have everything to do with happiness, and health, and fulfilment. Love, in the words of the old song, makes the world go round. And my world has been very still for a very long time. Maybe *I* never grew out of the L-shaped room, either.'

'And maybe, just maybe, Toby never did, too. Have you thought of that? 'Cause of that, maybe his marriage don't work out. It had magic, that little room. Strong magic. John-the-witch-doctor say so.' But he wasn't smiling. 'That room keep us in its power, all these years. All the time we wanting, with part of our secret selves, to get back to it.'

'Yeah, the L-shaped womb! Now stop that, will you? I know what you're up to. You're trying to turn me back to that time, you're trying to pretend nothing's changed and that I didn't say I loved another man who was no part of our little L-shaped triangle.'

He gazed at me steadily.

'Who is this john? He better be something special.'

'He is.' I told him very briefly about Andy. His only overt re-action was to say that Felix was a funny name. I didn't tell him any details of our relationship. I only tried to make it clear, against a barricade of almost tangible unwillingness to listen or accept, that I wanted to marry him and sever myself from Toby for ever. Only when honesty compelled me to add, '—at least, I think that's what I want,' did John return to me fully.

Having claimed his complete attention with this piece of emotional ambiguity, I then proceeded to outline my immediate dilemma, to whit, should I or should I not go to Israel? His face, protected by its black skin, presented to me in that moment a strange ambivalent mask. It bore no detectable expression; his narrow eyes with their yellow whites gazed at me unblinkingly from inside the mask but they seemed unfocused, withdrawn to some dark unknowable inner region within the huge black headpiece nature had placed on his shoulders for his ritual dance through this world. These tribal images were impossible to avoid at such moments. Not for the first time I sensed an unbridgeable division between us, though our hands were linked on the table in the simplest, least complicated, and in effect purest love of my life. It was not the difference in race so much as our stemming, way back, from cultures so diverse that we might have belonged to alien species. My question to myself was not, 'What is he thinking about?' but 'By what process, unattain-able and incomprehensible to me, is he arriving at some conclusion?' In the long silence before he spoke, I knew I would act on whatever he said next. Why? Perhaps because I felt and had always felt that John was nearer to some well-spring, some root-source of know-ledge both basic and primitive – primitive in its meaning of undisturbed, primordial, aboriginal. Something lost to us so-called cultivated races, or fatally blunted, like our sense of smell, only usable now for trivialities like perfume, a surface thing – its original function, of providing us with vital information, lost.

At last he stirred, shifting his huge shoulders in a little shiver, as if waking from sleep, and the mask became living skin again, the eyes seeming to come forward and fill their rims.

'We go to Israel,' he said cheerfully. 'You and me both.'

INTERLUDE

CHRIS

Chapter 1

THE little ferry showed its rounded stern to Piraeus docks and began to chug out to sea.

John looked over his shoulder uneasily.

'Plenty of fuzz back there,' he muttered. 'What they all doing, standing around lookin' at us like they'd like to fling us all in jail?'

I laughed. 'Oh, didn't I tell you? There was a coup here about a month ago.'

'A what?'

'A coup. A military take-over.'

'What for?'

'I don't know at all. Ask a Greek.'

John looked round the boat obediently, and made a move towards one of the sailors. I grabbed him back.

'On second thoughts, you'd better not.'

'Why? I want to know.'

'I'm not sure the Greeks know themselves.'

'I don't get it.'

'Don't worry about it. We won't be here long enough.'

'I sure don't want to get mixed up with any military,' John said fervently.

'They won't bother you. You're a tourist. They want your money.'

'Yours, you mean.'

'Some of it's yours.'

'You sure you don't mind me comin' along, specially with you having to pay for most of me?' he asked for the hundredth time.

'On the contrary, I'm eternally grateful to you for coming. I'd be finding this whole double enterprise far too frightening on my own.'

'I findin' it frightenin' with two of us.'

'You mean, the fuzz?'

'Them too.'

'Why are you nervous of the police, John? I bet you've never crossed the law in your whole life.'

'I smoke pot,' he said after some thought. 'That's not legal, for some reason I can't understand.'

'Well, don't start puffing it in some Greek copper's face, and you'll be all right.' But he was jumpy. 'What else?'

'I don't like aeroplanes,' he burst out. 'And I don't like boats. I even don't like trains, though I'm more used to them. Why it has to be so *far*?'

'One would think,' I said, impatiently I fear, because he'd been increasing my nervousness all the way from Surrey to Greece, 'that you'd never travelled in your life. How did you get to England?'

'Get to England?' he asked blankly.

'Yes, from wherever you came from originally.' Quite suddenly it struck me as extraordinary that I didn't know where this was.

He stared at me a moment, then laughed so loudly several people turned to look at us.

'I don't come from nowhere,' he said. 'I come from London, same as everybody. I never been out of it except to visit you and play at some country-house dances.'

'Then why is your English so strange?'

'Who, mine? Don't I talk like anyone?'

'No, you talk like an African who never went to school.'

'Well, that's 'cause I am an African who never went to school,' he said laughing again. 'Mama came from Africa, and she wasn't exactly educated. And after she died, I was raised in a – you know, an orphan's home. Was mostly black kids there, and our person who mostly looked after us, Granny Baker, she was black too. Best, kindest woman I ever knew. She never been to school, so she told us. Life been my school, she used to say. We didn't get much schoolin' either. It was just after that big war they had, there was lots of black and half-black kids left over from the American soldiers, younger than me, of course, and I kind of helped look after them. There was a teacher come there, teached us to read, write a bit, sums and like that, but we didn't pay no attention to him much, specially not me, bein' bigger than the others, I felt so silly sittin' in lessons with 'em . . . All that whole time, I remember like if you could remember something from before you was born. You want to know when it all began to be real, what I think of as my birthday? One day Granny Baker took a bunch of us to a cinema, only it wasn't a film, it was a band. A lot of the kids was so disappointed they started in to stamp and whistle, but after a bit the band played loud and their sound was so good, man, it just forced all those wild ignorant kids to keep quiet and listen. There was one kid who played sax, and boy, he sent me. Way, way out! Out into space, into dreams, into real life. I found myself out in that shitty old street among all the litter and traffic noises. Granny Baker was shakin' me with one hand and dryin' my eyes with the other. "What's the matter with you, boy?" she says. "You never heard real music before?" I just shook my head and cried some more. Couldn't stop. I thought she'd make me go home. But she said, "Get stirred up all you want, only don't cry loud or you spoil the music." And she took me back in and let me hear the rest.'

I tore my eyes from his face and looked out to sea. The coast of mainland Greece was shrinking behind us, its white buildings brilliant under the high sun.

'You didn't need school anyway,' I said. 'You know everything that counts. You knew I was pregnant before anybody.'

'Anybody knows things like that,' he said with a shrug. 'I seen girls get pregnant at thirteen when they still playin' in the playgrounds . . . That's all crap, all that instinct stuff, I want to know real things, *facts*. Too late now, and maybe I never had the brain anyhow.' He contemplated the blue Adriatic with greater calm than I had seen in him since we left England. 'Look at that deep-down water . . . think of all the fish down there. And all that white, where our boat churn it up, like whipped cream . . .' He turned his face up to the tinted sky, and snuffed the air. 'This maybe ain't so bad,' he said consideringly. 'Better than the country. The smell ain't so dainty.'

This was undoubtedly true. It was a strong odour combining Greek ozone, Greek boat, sweaty Greek sailors, bilge, and a lot of stinking rubbish the cook was just tipping overboard below us.

'Plenty of noise for you, too,' I pointed out encouragingly.

'Yeah!' he said, brightening up even further. 'Let's count the noises. Engines . . . nice. Throbby, rhythmical. Goes right through you.'

'Swish of water.'

'Like the wire-drums. And what's with the birds?'

'Fighting for the bits of thrown-out food. Rowdy buggers, aren't they?'

'Don't swear,' he reproved me sharply.

'Sailors' curses.'

'Footsteps runnin'.'

'Baby crying.'

'Ah, and there! Some angel just turned on his transistor,' John exclaimed with a look of rapture.

By the time we had rounded off the list with the deafening shriek of the hooter, John was feeling in much better spirits.

'Well, Janie,' he said, turning his back to the sea and leaning comfortably against the rail, 'What our plans? How we going to find this little boy who got lost from his daddy?'

'He's no little boy, he's nineteen.'

'Never mind his size, how we find him?'

'Don't ask me.'

We walked round to the bow. Somewhere ahead of us lay Hydra, an island among other islands, and somewhere upon Hydra was Chris, the water-boy, now presumably in his element, literally, or at least surrounded by it. And I had to find him. That was my mission impossible, to be accomplished before I would feel free to return to Athens and get on a plane for Israel.

'Is it too much to ask of you?' Andy had said, his arms, twenty-four hours and a thousand miles away, around me. To his ever-lasting surprise, he'd received a post-card from his son. The picture showed an unbelievably picturesque waterfront scene, with white buildings tumbling down a hill, a little church spire, toy fishing-boats and nets, a foreground of lawn-green sea. 'If *I* go, it'll all go to hell, the whole thing. He'll naturally see me in the role of a heavy father, come to dry him off and drag him back to Home and Duty. Alas, I've played the part so often he'd be perfectly justified. But in this instance, all I want to know is that he's all right.'

'But the postcard tells you that much.' I didn't want to object to going, at least not openly. This was, after all, almost literally the first favour he'd ever asked of me. It was not within the bounds of love or reason that I should refuse. But, in point of fact, I quailed from the very idea of it; it did indeed seem too much to ask.

'That's true,' Andy had said soberly. 'So I can't be being honest. Let's see, what do I really want?' He stroked up and down my nose with his thumb several times reflectively. 'First of all, I want first-hand news of him. That's not unnatural, surely? I want to know how he's looking, where he's sleeping – no, not with whom, I really have learnt to regard that as his own business. I want to know if he's happy, if he's – well, if anything is changing.'

'You mean, if he's growing out of it.'

'Do I mean that? Probably. He once told me not to hope we'd ever reach an understanding, he said we never could. But it's a hope that dies hard in fathers. However, there's also something else.' He held my face where he could look into it. 'I was too much of a coward even to want to show him to you as he was when I last saw him,' he said. 'You and I are close enough, if only in age, to share a feeling of automatic – repugnance – for any young human being whose appearance is so singularly unwholesome. But,' he went on, leaving me with a heavy sigh to wander round the room, 'Merrie England is hardly the place where unwashed, underfed, untrimmed young bodies show to their best advantage. If they have any. I suppose I suffer from a typical envious Englishman's convic-tion that everything somehow looks more palatable under a hotter sun, starting with human flesh. After all, in Greece he can't go dirty; he'll spend most of his time legitimately immersed in the scouring brine of his favourite element. His face can't look pasty, and his hair, guru-length and tangled though it doubtless still is, *must* look better for its daily dipping and sun-bleaching. When he was little he used to go quite blond in summer . . .'

There was a long silence. Then he came back to me again.

'I'm only trying, fumblingly, to say, Jane, that since you will have to come face to face with him sometime, it might as well be in the kindly, mellow light of the Greek Islands, rather than in a cold grey London slum.'

'Yes, yes, I quite see all that,' I said. 'What I'm still not clear about is what exactly I'm supposed to do about him if I find him.'

'Would it be too much to ask you to tell him you're going to be his step-mother?'

'Yes, it bloody well would!' I answered feelingly. 'On all counts. In the first place, that is absolutely your job. In the second . . .'

'In the second,' he interrupted. 'Yes, don't go on. I know full well what the second place is.' He stopped wandering and returned to me, holding me against him with his arms round me as far as they would go. 'Am I mad?' he muttered against my neck. 'To let you go on this fool's errand? Better to grab you while you're three-quarters willing. Three-quarters of you is better than the none I may have when you've seen this other bastard again . . . What if you never come back?' He held my face between hard hands and peered into it with desperate intensity, as if it were a crystal ball.

'Oh, surely I will!'

'How can I be sure, when you're not? And I'd have only my idiot self to blame.'

It was a fraught evening altogether. He was so tormented and I so nervous, unable to pay attention, even to my packing. As it grew later and later I knew I'd be dead-beat in the morning, when I'd have to get up at the crack for Andy to drive me to the airport. But we couldn't seem to get off to bed, and when we did, the knowledge that we were actually alone in the house (David was already at Jo's) and that we would not be together again for weeks, plus all sorts of other undercurrent pressures neither of us cared to examine too closely, caused us to make love frenetically most of the rest of the night.

'It's like the Irishman,' muttered Andy exhaustedly at one point.

'What Irishman?' I asked, considerably startled.

'The one in the joke. Confession. Priest asks him if he's been sleeping with a woman, and he admits he did doze off once or twice . . .'

What little sleep I had was jumpy with dreams. Jo had promised to ring me in the night, should anything happen with David, but dawn broke and she hadn't. I could hardly believe it; the first night away from me for months and he hadn't woken up . . . At six a.m., just as we were leaving, I couldn't stop myself from ringing to check.

'It's okay, you didn't wake me,' Jo said as soon as she picked up the phone. 'I knew you'd phone. Ducky, believe it or not – absolutely nowt. Slept like a log the whole night, never even rolled over. It's going to be fine, I feel sure of it. Now take care of yourself. Two weeks and home, come what may – sooner if there's trouble. *Please*, love, don't give me heart-failure.'

'I'll try not to. And you're quite sure you can cope?'

'*Yes*. I've said so. Now go, or you'll be late. Good luck, happy landings. Have you got the sketches? Sorry, of course you have.' (Her faith was mis-placed, and so were the sketches for the silversmiths, which I'd entirely forgotten, but I found them.) 'Off you go, then. *Sholem Aleichem!*' She'd hung up, and my last link with David was broken.

Chapter 2

THE trip to Hydra seemed to last for hours. We had neglected to buy any food for the journey, and by the time we arrived the sea-air had aggravated our appetites to the point of rapaciousness. Hunger is an excellent counter-irritant; the mere prospect of something delicious to eat kicked all other considerations from my mind. All I could think of by the time we jumped ashore was that the Adriatic is full of lobsters, and that the Greeks are reputed to make the best mayonnaise in the world.

John, however, was made of sterner stuff.

'Where we start looking?' he asked briskly as soon as we stood on solid ground.

'Over there,' I said, pointing, after a quick look round.

'That café? What makes you think he's there?'

'Well, we have to start somewhere,' I said sententiously.

'He's not here,' John announced a few minutes later. 'Nobody here.'

This was unarguably true. But the long tables inside the little tavern, and the round ones outside, were laid for lunch; the walls were covered with fishing-nets and other bits of bogus tat, but the smells issuing from the back kitchen were genuine.

'What you sittin' down for? Don't you see he ain't here?'

'He may come in at any moment.'

'Janie, what's the matter with you?'

'I'm famished, that's what's the matter with me. Aren't you?'

'Sure I am, but shouldn't we—'

'John, you're altogether too conscientious. How can you walk out on that delectable, peppery, herby smell? Nothing is going to happen to Chris Andrews in the next hour that hasn't happened to him already.'

'Janie,' said John sorrowfully, sitting down opposite me, 'you are nothing but the slave of your stomach.'

I changed my mind about the lobster when they brought it, still alive and clacking its dark-green claws beseechingly, for me to inspect before they plunged it into its boiling tomb. I had the moussaka instead.

'John, why aren't we vegetarians?'

'Because we like meat,' he said promptly, tucking into his own savoury carnivorous mess with relish.

'Is that good enough?'

'It is for me,' he said. 'This animal I'm eating don't know what hit it. After I'm dead, somebody want to eat me, he's welcome.'

'Chris is a vegetarian,' I remarked moodily. 'When he eats at all. Macrobiotic, probably.'

'Never mind his eatin' habits. You know what he looks like?' He looked out at the broad cobbled walk, full of tourists of every race and condition. 'Seems to me there's enough hippies out there to eat all the green stuff on this island.'

Right outside the tavern, a whole group of them had come drifting along, some standing around, others sitting on the harbour's edge with their feet dangling over the water. They all had long hair, of course, wore jeans with elaborate if shabby tops, and loads of ornaments – ceramic pendants on leather thongs, love-beads, and every conceivable symbol from Ban-the-Bomb to Stars of David. One girl had a bit of driftwood hung round her neck, and another a white stone with a hole in it. A lot of them wore buttons, which I later had a chance to study, bearing ribald or ideological or just plain fatuous slogans – 'Down with Oxfam, Feed Twiggy' being a good example of the latter.

'Maybe he's one of those?' John suggested hopefully.

I took out a small packet of snapshots with which Andy had provided me. Not that he expected them to help much, for they all dated back to Chris's pre-drop-out days. Although Andy had insisted on my bringing them all (no doubt as an antidote to the poisonous effect of the present-day reality, should I encounter it) only one of them might prove of any practical value.

It was a frontal close-up of Chris as a schoolboy, forelocked and solemn-eyed, upon which, in a mood of tight-lipped exasperation, his father had done some graffiti work with a fountain-pen. The devout, typically English look had been obliterated by a furiously-scratched moustache, straggly beard, and curls resembling a full-bottomed wig. As a last resentful touch, Andy had been moved to give him a cock-eye and then attempt to rectify it, with ghastly results. The finished effect was of a rather degenerate one-eyed pirate of the late eighteenth century, upon whom the neat white collar, old school tie and blazer looked distinctly bizarre.

I studied the face before me and tried to peer into the faces on the dockside, but the sun dazzled me. I passed the ravaged snapshot to John.

At first he laughed, then he stopped. 'Who did this other part?'

'His father.'

John shook his head. 'He sure is mad at him,' he said soberly. 'No daddy should be that mad. You sit. I'll go look.'

He stood up and strolled casually outside. I was a little worried for fear he would start peering, gimlet-eyed, into their faces one by one, which would certainly have aroused their irritation. The thought had crossed my mind that the hippies on the island might constitute a colony of some sort, and that this branch of the fraternity might be able to lead me to Chris if I could only win their confidence. I didn't want them antagonized.

But I needn't have worried. John strolled to the water's edge and stood, his hands slotted into the back pockets of his jeans (only the fingers fitted in), rocking on his sandalled feet and gazing out over the glittering blue water as if entranced. No one, the hippies least of all, could have guessed he had the slightest interest in them. I sudenly realized that, apart from happening to possess the only black skin among them, and having shorter hair (though it was beginning to develop into a passable Afro), he might have been one of them. The casual, flamboyant style of dress had been his long before it has become the trademark of rebellion among the young, and he wore it, unlike many of the rebels, with an absolute lack of self-consciousness.

I noticed one girl nudge another, and soon John's broad back was the focus of interested glances. He rocked and gazed and ignored them. I saw that within the group a movement had developed, which gathered momentum, advocating an approach. Several of the boys were urging several girls to go and speak to him, while the girls, reluctant, were in turn urging the boys.

The climax of this by-play was somewhat more than even John had bargained for. One boy, losing his temper with a girl who had given him rather too vehement a push, drew back his elbows and delivered a shove to both her shoulders which sent her reeling backwards. She lost her balance completely, fell against John (who appeared to be at forward rock) – and the next moment John and the girl had disappeared. A shriek, a loud splash and a considerable body of seawater which shot up above the harbour's edge indicated that they had reached their joint destination.

We all leapt to our feet. One local party leapt so precipitously that they overturned their table. Screams of excitement demolished the tranquillity. By the time I reached the water's edge, approximately four seconds later, every able-bodied Greek, Frenchman, Italian, not to speak of red-blooded Britons and Americans, had crowded to the brink, there to shove and point and exclaim and shout advice and generally imperil each other for the sake of a few moments' diversion.

John's head was bobbing about among the fishing-smacks and debris like a shiny black balloon with a face painted on it. He was holding the girl by the scruff of the neck, grinning with triumph, apparently unaware that he was throttling her with her own string of love-beads. She was gargling and threshing and looking as if she might expire at any moment, when a fellow-hippie, who, for the sheer lark of the thing, had jumped in after them, saw her predicament, sliced through the water to her side, and snatched her out of John's massive grasp.

'Here!' I heard John bellow protestingly. 'She's mine! I saved her!'

'You're choking her, you silly nit!' replied the other tersely.

John lost no time in retaliating. A vast black hand, with arm, emerged like the neck of the Loch Ness monster from the surface, and planted itself squarely on the head of the lifesaver. Down he went in an eruption of agitated bubbles. The crowd shrieked with gleeful horror. The girl, finding herself released, swam calmly to the wall and was hauled out by her friends.

'It's great, swimming with your clothes on,' she remarked, wringing out her hair.

I decided the time had come to intervene. 'John!' I yelled above the general hubbub. 'Let him go! Get off him!'

He turned his head towards me. 'What you say, Janie?' He yelled happily. I realized with dismay that the noise had gone to his head like strong drink. Everyone was screaming at him by now, and he was beaming with enjoyment. I cupped my hands to my mouth and fairly bawled: 'Let – him – go!'

John looked around rather vaguely; I could see his glance travel down the length of his arm, clearly visible in the transparent water, to the struggling figure pinioned at the end of it. He seemed to realize the situation and hastily drew it back, whereupon the bedraggled and half-drowned hippie shot to the surface, leaping half out of the water like a dolphin with the force of his desire for air.

At this moment I became aware of some pushing going on behind me, and suddenly I was roughly shoved aside as two unexpectedly efficient-looking uniformed policemen came upon the scene. They began shouting and gesticulating in Greek, and all the hippies (about three by then) who had opted for an illicit dip came hurriedly to order and ashore. John came too. The 'fuzz' grabbed them, one in each hand, and began marching them off in a very businesslike fashion, but were instantly surrounded by the others who began explaining, mainly in English, what had happened.

'This is the only one you should arrest!' shouted John's victim, pointing at him. 'He bloody nearly drowned me, the big black bastard!'

A horrified silence fell among the other hippies. The policemen, bewildered by all the racket, had stopped too, and for a moment you could again hear the lapping of the water and the humming of insects.

The girl who had first fallen in laid her hand on John's arm.

'He didn't mean that,' she said gently, looking up at him with enormous tender eyes out of a wet, fawn-like face. 'Black is *beautiful*.' She said it with such immense sincerity and feeling that she affected the whole crowd, not to mention John, who probably wouldn't have taken offence anyway.

'That's okay,' he said cheerfully. He spread his hands before the furious hippie. 'I'm sorry. I didn't mean no harm. I just kind of forgot I was holding you.'

His apology was so obviously sincere and ingenuous that his opponent was completely disconcerted.

'Then please excuse what I said,' he mumbled. The others were still staring at him in shocked and silent reproach. He glanced round at them, blushed crimson, and suddenly broke away and began to run.

His friends turned to watch him. Not one of them called him back. The policemen went into a hasty huddle, and evidently decided the whole incident, which threatened to involve a great deal of tedious translation and statement-taking, was not worth pursuing. They shrugged their shoulders eloquently, and were just about to withdraw when one of them, discovering his uniform was thoroughly damp down the front, uttered a Grecian expletive and, grabbing the first hippie who came to hand, pointed to his hair and made threatening sheering motions, like the dreaded Scissor-man in Strewelpeter. His swarthy colleague seemed to agree, and they went snip-snap, snip-snap several times, very menacingly, at all the hippies before making their way grumblingly to a distant wharfside café to cool their feelings with glasses of retsina.

'What the hell were they being so aggressive about?' asked one of the men who had received snip-snapping fingers right under his nose.

'I think that was the local equivalent of "get yer 'air cut",' commented one elderly Englishman, who looked as if he echoed the sentiment.

The crowd dissolved into the noontime glitter. I dissolved too, back to the remains of my lunch. I felt this was the most discreet thing I could do. I left John with the others, aware that the incident had made him almost one of them.

I saw no more of him for four hours.

I spent the interim doing nothing at all constructive, other than trying to rest my state of mind. To be precise, I sat in the sun on the wharf, watching the play of sunlight on the sea and the gentle, breathing motion of the fishing boats, half-hypnotized. I had used this therapy in the past – staring out of the back window of the shop at the solitary tree in the yard, or, more happily, sitting in my own back garden minutely observing the barely-detectable opening process of an evening primrose. The semi-conscious play of the senses sharpens some part of the mind which works involuntarily, like the digestion, and, also like the digestion, works better when the body is inactive. This idle afternoon in Hydra did more for me than the whole frenetic week that preceded it. By the time I saw John's tall figure bouncing down the whitewashed steps which led up the steep hill, something, somewhere, had fallen into a kind of pattern of acceptance. I had hardly been thinking about Andy so far as I knew, but he quietly rose to the still surface of my thoughts, smiling and saying, 'It'll be all right.' The visit to Israel became a sort of academic portal I had to pass through to reach safety and certainty which lay on the other side. Knowing it lay there, I felt as contented as if I had reached it already.

John came loping up to me, panting and grinning, and threw his extraordinary length down in a chair at my side. I had moved out of the café into one of the outside tables, but apart from that I had hardly stirred. My coffee-cup, thrice refilled by an amiable and un-impatient waiter, sat in front of me, plus a bottle of white wine, half-empty, and a glass.

'Have a glass of wine,' I said, feeling somnolent and too lazy as yet to hear the news he was clearly bursting with.

'Wine? Great, I love wine. And I earned it! You want to hear?'

He gulped the wine, and choked.

'What's this awful stuff?'

'Retsina.'

'I don't like it.'

'Think of it as pine-wine. Then you'll like it.'

John pushed it firmly from him. 'I think of it as toothpaste-wine,' he said. 'It smells like what they put down the gents in Leicester Square. Anyhow, who wants to drink a pine-tree? Give me some old-type grape-juice wine.'

I signalled the waiter. Laughing had woken me up.

'Come on, then – tell.'

'Well, I found him.'

I straightened. This was news indeed, and far more then I had dared to hope for.

'What! Where?'

'I mean, I found where he is. Only he wasn't there just then. He gone swimmin' off the rocks. We went there too – they took me – Janie,' he broke off, 'you want to know something? They're *great*, them kids, them hippies. Just great. I thought they'd be like the kind we get in the club where I play, which is mainly just street-sweepin's, don't have nothing' in their heads, just pop and sex and maybe a bit of politics some of 'em, all the tearin'-down kind of politics, nothin' buildin'. But these lot's different altogether. Didn't you see it? They're against plenty, but they're for, as well. You know what they for?'

'Love or something, isn't it?' I asked, with a sardonic note in my voice because I was now impatient to hear about Chris.

John stopped short and stared at me. 'I don't get you,' he said in a hurt, puzzled tone. 'The way you said that . . . like you thought believin' in love was funny or stupid somehow.'

'Oh, John . . .' So often he did this, putting me in a position of feeling I'd been cynical and derisive about something that we both, actually, felt the same way about. It was always hard to match John's utter simplicity and lack of worldly veneer about basic subjects. Words which had been lost to the language through becoming embedded in layers of irony fell from John's lips new-coined, without apology or quotation-marks.

'I didn't mean it as it sounded,' I said. 'Tell me about Chris.'

'Well, they took me to their bathing-place, but it took a long time to get there. They don't swim where the other visitors go. They found this place of their own where no one else disturb them. They camp there on the rocks; got a little shelter they built there, but mostly they sleep out in the open, all together, like children. They told me they don't need to be private from each other, only from other people. They like to be with nothin' on when it's just them. It was beautiful, Jane. All them young bodies, lyin' in the sun, jumping into the sea, playin' and laughin' and lovin' each other. Soon as we got there, we stripped off too, and went swimmin'. I never swam

132

before with nothin' on. Come to think of it,' he said with a sudden frown, 'I don't seem to remember I ever went swimmin' before at all.'

'So how come you didn't drown when you fell into the harbour?'

'Dunno,' he said sunnily. 'I suppose I'm just a natural for this water-cult thing Chris is the head of. You know about it?' I said rather grimly that I did. I was suddenly nervous of asking him if he didn't think the whole thing was idiotic. I could see they'd got to him. His hair was still damp, his face shining with excitement and pleasure; I could see the salt riming his jaw and his eyebrows.

'Don't you feel all itchy?' I asked, feeling that I must find some disadvantage to swimming or I should be landed with an opponent instead of an ally before I knew where I was.

'Yeah,' he said, scratching luxuriously. 'It's great, you feel you still got the sea all over you, even after you dry.' He tossed back another glass of wine. 'Ah!' he said, smacking his lips and throwing back his head. The Greek sun fell on his upturned face. He looked, in his relaxation and contentment, like some Moorish demi-deity, satiated in all his moral senses and yet somehow sublime.

I shook his shoulder.

'John!'

'Yeah, Janie,' he murmured with his eyes still closed.

'So tell me! Did you see him or didn't you?'

'I told you already, he wasn't there. They said he'd gone for a long swim. Maybe he went right round the island. Jesus, I'm starved!' He sat upright and beckoned the waiter. He would have been too unconfident to do that five hours ago.

'What do you *mean*, round the island? Do you know how far that is?'

'Nope. But I expect he does. Don't worry, Janie, he'll come back. He's their boy, they all waitin' for him. He often goes off like that, they said. He likes to get in communion with the sea. For that you got to go far, far out, away from the land and from all people. You got a hamburger?' he asked the waiter.

'Of course he hasn't, where do you think you are? The Fulham Road?' I asked testily. But to my chagrin the waiter grinned accommodatingly and left us.

'They got everything here,' said my black Neptune exultantly.

'Maybe you'd like to settle down here, and be a water-hippie,' I remarked, trying to keep the bitterness to a minimum.

Sarcasm was always quite lost on John. 'You know, that's not a bad idea. Who needs London, all that pollution and all them horrible people? I never dreamed . . .' He looked around him at the glittering prospect of turquoise, blue and white, all as pristine as if it had been created that morning. 'No cars,' he murmured. 'It's hard to believe there's places in the world that ain't spoilt by cars.'

'But think of the *silence*,' I said viciously.

'Oh sure, it's too quiet *here*,' said John. 'But I'd be with *them*. They make loads of noise. They got guitars, they play and sing their own music, they shout and laugh . . . They let me play one of their guitars . . . they said I play great. They like me,' he added simply. 'They like black people and they like me specially, they said.' He reached behind him and got his own guitar, which of course he had brought, out of its case, and began to strum. Was I imagining it, or was it a vaguely Greek air, reminiscent of Zorba? I seemed to see John fading away from me into a haze.

I grabbed his wrist. 'John, now will you stop this nonsense? You've got a job to go back to, you know you only got a couple of weeks' leave from the club—'

'Sod the club,' said John dreamily, fading faster than ever.

'But what about Chris? What about Toby?'

The mention of Toby's name brought him back a little; his spiritual outline became quite clear to me for the moment.

'Toby,' he repeated thoughtfully, and the strumming, which, to my irritation, had begun to collect a crowd, ceased. 'Yeah, I was forgettin' Toby. Well, but maybe I could drop off here on the way back from the old Promised Land, after we seen him. Because, Jane, I got a feeling that here is my promised land, right here with them kids.'

I was actually on the verge of saying something really spiteful, like 'Especially that good-looking creep who called you a black bastard, I bet you'd just love going swimming in the raw with *him*,' but thank God I curbed my nasty tongue that time. John hadn't a clue what I could be like when a black mood was on me. Perhaps that was the secret of our untrammelled friendship – that, and there being no sex about it. I thought to myself then, sitting there watching John being happy and not helping me, that if there had been even a trace of sensuality in our relationship, if I had been the least bit attracted to him as a man, I would not have been able to restrain myself from assaulting him with words. Loving friendship, when it exists, which God knows is very seldom, filters out the venom and bitchery from one's nature.

Sarcasm, however, is something else again.

'John,' I said. 'I'm sorry to interrupt your reverie, but did you come to some arrangement? Are we going to see him, if and when he returns from his aquatic amblings?'

He looked me straight in the eyes, that look of his that comes from another time and place. 'Jane,' he said slowly. 'I don't always understand you.' It was the nearest he ever came to reproaching me.

'While you've been doing the water-sprite bit, I've been sitting here cooling my heels for four hours waiting for news. And now I'm just asking. Are we going to see him, or not?'

'What time is it?'

I looked at my watch, which of course had gone wrong. 'Must be about five or so.'

'Then he's back,' he said.

I rose to my feet and gathered our belongings together. 'We'll drop these at the hotel,' I said. 'Then you can take me to your leader.'

'What about my hamburger?'

'Sod your hamburger,' I retorted.

Chapter 3

THE sun was sinking into a sea the exact colour of pink jade as we rounded the last headland and came into sight of the hippies' bathing place. It had been a hard but rewarding walk, with the sea never out of sight, but I couldn't fully enjoy its panoply of colours because I was too busy watching my feet. The rocky paths were steep and none too well defined once we got beyond the outskirts of the town; but the evening air was almost intolerably sweet, so laden with sharp and balmy scents that it seemed irksome to have to exhale between deep intakes of breath . . . I felt like a drunkard who resents the necessary pauses to replenish his glass. My eyes, scanning the path or the rough inclines ahead of my feet, wandered delightedly over the rocks. I never knew lichen could be orange; the pale rock-surface made an ideal background for the tufts of flowers and strange intricate patterns of thorns.

And always, when we grew tired after a long gradient, there was the sea. We could stop and rest our legs and our eyes and savour the salt tang amid the richer, more cloying land-perfumes. I knew what John felt about the place, apart from the hippies.

At last, from a height, we saw the bright scattered colours of the encampment below us like a rag-bag emptied out upon the rocks. John seized my hand and nearly crushed it to a pulp.

'Janie! I love—'

He did not finish. I looked up at his face, alight with rapture, the sweat on it shining pinkly in the reflected sunset. Clearly, he felt unable to set limits on what he loved at that moment.

We made our way carefully down to the encampment below. The sudden Mediterranean darkness was falling swiftly now, and a fire of driftwood had been lit, round which the hippies were sitting. Their music and talk came up to us with the sweet flakey woodsmoke. I shivered abruptly. At any moment now I would be face to face with this boy, who might one day be my stepson. It was a fateful occasion, and I, for all my broodings and the quiet hours I had spent in the town, was unprepared. Once again I had been sending out my thoughts in a random but basically selfish direction. They had returned to me bringing a probably false message of hope and security, but suddenly my own future showed me a new facet, complicated intolerably by an extraneous responsibility for a human being I had never seen and about whom I had heard nothing that was not negative and disconcerting. I was still holding John's hand, and I clutched it convulsively.

As so often before, John intuitively understood. 'Don't worry, Janie,' he said, his voice like soft soot pouring through the twilight. 'He'll be like the others. Even better. He'll be different than his daddy thinks. What do daddies know?'

The circle round the fire shifted slightly as we approached. One figure stood up and came towards us. He was tall and very thin, with narrow shoulders like a boy of twelve and thin, under-developed shanks. He wore ragged shorts and Japanese sandals, and a medallion of some sort round his neck which glinted from the middle of his hairless chest like a huge eye in the last of the light. His hair, stiff with salt, fell straight and solid to his shoulders. His skin was brown and he had a soft blond beard.

Behind all this, the baby-face of the photograph was still there, the blue eyes, the snub nose, the ingenuous English schoolboy look. He looked about as degenerate as David.

When he spoke to me, his voice was very gentle, and had his class and schooling and background indelibly stamped upon it.

'Hallo,' he said. 'You wanted to see me?'

'Yes,' I said, staring at him in helpless fascination.

'Come and join us. I'm sorry I wasn't here before.'

I was just about to ask if we could talk alone, when I thought better of it. Half-cowardice, perhaps, but the other half an instinctive feeling that I would like to get to know him a little first. I was somewhat dazed, dismayed almost, to realize that my first impressions had been favourable. Expecting the pirate-exterior, the defiant, rebellious manner, this slender, vulnerable figure in the twilight had disarmed me. I had to get adjusted to the possibility that I might like him better than his father did.

We joined the circle round the fire, and John unslung his guitar from his back and began to tune up. He was immediately surrounded by a press of people, leaving the sea side of the fire almost un-tenanted. Chris picked up a piece of bleached driftwood from a pile they'd collected, and began to smooth it with his hands. He wasn't just stroking its dry, satiny surface, but poking his fingers into the little holes, running his nails along the cracks as if exploring it.

'Aren't you cold?' I asked him. A little wind was blowing up the rocks from the sea, ruffling his hair on his naked shoulders.

He smiled and shook his head. 'I don't feel the cold much,' he said.

He must have been aware that I was watching him, but he seemed quite unselfconsciously absorbed in his piece of wood.

'Seems a pity to burn it,' he said. 'It's such a lovely shape.'

He lifted it to his nose and smelt it, then licked it.

'Taste,' he said, offering it to me.

I put my tongue to it. Smoothness and sea-flavour.

'Like seaweed,' he said. 'It's more sea-y than the sea.'

'Is the sea more sea-y here than in England?'

He looked up at me quickly. 'That's a funny question. The sea's the same everywhere.'

'How can you say that? The sea has as many aspects as the human race.' He went on staring at me. 'You might as well say there's no difference between an Englishman and a Greek.'

'There isn't,' he said.

'Or between men and women.'

'There isn't,' he said. 'They're a slightly different shape, of course, like the sea is a different colour here than, say, at Brighton. But these sort of differences just mislead you if you take any notice of them. There's no essential difference at all. The sea tastes the same everywhere, unless it's polluted, and human beings do, too.'

'How do you know if a person is polluted?' I asked, intrigued.

'Same as with water. He tastes dirty.'

'How do you taste – a person?'

He shrugged his vestigal shoulders, still occupied with the wood. 'Lots of ways. Sometimes with your tongue, the way you taste anything else. You can find out a lot about people from kissing and licking them. But that's fairly primitive. The best way is to taste their minds.'

'By talking?'

'Talking and *not* talking.'

My eyes wouldn't leave his face, now lit only by the flickering firelight.

'Like now, do you mean?' He didn't answer. 'Are you tasting me?'

He chuckled quietly, without looking at me.

We were silent. I kept looking at him. Partly I was fascinated, and partly I wanted him to look at me; but he took no notice. He was absorbed in the wood, and the fire, and the sea, at which he threw tender glances every so often over his shoulder as if to re-assure himself that it was still there, however steeped in blackness; only the faintest, almost luminous glow on the surface of the water, and the soft swish of the swell against the rocks below us, confirmed its presence now.

138

John was playing, but very softly. Chris lay back on the rocks and stared up at the sky, now beginning to boil with stars. I sat still, watching him, letting his face grow into my knowledge and become part of all that I was familiar with and accepted. It was not difficult in any way.

'I like you,' he said at last. 'You don't taste like a spy.'

Now it was I who did not reply. The mood of truth was on us both, and it would be a lie to deny that that was why I was here – well, I would have preferred to call myself an emissary; but then so, no doubt, would most spies.

'Are you supposed to try and persuade me to go back?'

'No.'

'What then?'

'Just to see how you are.'

'How I am, who I am . . . does it really matter to anyone but me?'

'It matters to anyone who loves you, I suppose.'

Now he looked at me, as if I had pronounced a command-word. His head lay on its side on the rock on a pillow of salty hair; his eyes were nearly black in this light, and obscured, mysterious.

After a single searching look at me, he turned again to face the sky. 'It isn't me he loves. It's some idea he has of what he thought was promised to him when I was born. Parents shape their children in their own image, like God in Genesis, and then, like God again, are horrified when the unique soul in them pushes their lives and personalities off in a unique direction. But just as God presumably implanted that freebooting quality in Adam, so my father passed it on to me as my inheritance from him. Why is he so appalled that I'm part of my era, that I've gone with my own crowd, doing my own thing? You'd think he might be proud that I lead and don't follow. I've created something original out of my own head which a lot of people like and use as their own personal point of departure in their voyages of self-discovery. He thinks it's stupid and mean-ingless, a form of escape, a failure to take hold of life. Well, that's all right. There was a time when I'd have given anything to have him understand me, but I don't care any more. I see it's not only his privilege to remain shut inside his own conditioning, it's inevitable. If I had a son who wanted to imprison himself in a little shoe-box house and go to business every day, I'd hate him too, and rage against it, and eventually disown him in despair.' He lay quietly for a while, frowning, his hands idling on the white twisted branch. 'Have you ever been out for a walk in the country with my father?' he asked.

'Yes.'

'Have you ever passed a patch of nettles?'

A flash of understanding came over me. I knew what he was going to say and how he was going to interpret it, and my mind raced ahead to counter it.

'Have you noticed what he does? It's his game. He doesn't tread the nettles down, or swipe them with a stick, or, more sensible still, avoid them altogether. He – how does the saying go – he grasps them. On purpose. If he gets stung, the nettle's won the game, and if not, he has. There's always some little thing that people do – they usually call it a game – which is the key to their whole personality and way of life, and that's my father's. He goes out of his way to find challenges and tests, he sets up his own dragons to slay. And he calls me childish and feeble because I believe in floating with the tide. Is a man a coward or a weakling because he leaves the nettles alone?'

'But will they leave you alone?'

He laughed. 'Well, no, of course there are a certain percentage of nettles strewing every path. The fuzz are nettles who actually fling themselves into your way. I don't like going to jug, you know. But on the whole, nettles don't sting you when you're in the water. And here . . .' He broke off, rolled over, and lifted himself on his elbows, so that he faced the invisible sea. He sniffed deeply, like a dog, and suddenly he reached over and grabbed my hand, nearly pulling me over as he lifted it to his mouth and licked the back of it.

'You haven't been in yet!' he said in amazement. 'How long have you been here?'

'About half a day—'

'Unbelievable! What's the matter with you? How can you possibly resist? Come on! Let's go in now!' He leapt to his feet, tugging me.

'*Now?*' I gasped, all my middle age rushing back upon me. It was dark, and the leap from the rocks into the sea terrified me to contemplate.

'Yes, now, this minute! Take your clothes off!'

'Hey, just a minute—'

'Oh, keep your bra and pants on if you must. Just get in the water!' As I stood there, hesitating, chilled and fearful in my youthlessness, he did something extraordinary. He suddenly put his arms round me and kissed my lips with his own soft childish ones. His beard tickled me gently on the cheek, and his hair blew round my face. I felt his slender bony chest pressed against me and his strong, nervy hands on my back. It was not like being kissed by a man; it was not like any kiss of my life. I did something extraordinary too. I didn't pull away.

The kiss didn't last more than a single interminable moment, and then he was smiling at me in the firelight and saying, 'When you're in, you'll understand me better. I want you to understand me.' He took my hand and drew me further down the rocks till we were out of sight of the others on the far side of the fire. We could still see the reflection of the flames, and the billowing smoke, over the bright rim of rock above our heads. Below us, starlit, lay the breathing sea.

Hurriedly, with such an air of practicality that I could not object, Chris began to peel off my dress. He steadied me with one hand while I kicked off my sandals. To tell the truth I seemed to be under some sort of spell. I was reminded of some past time when I had behaved in an entirely uncharacteristic way in alien surroundings – because of them, almost – but I couldn't quite place it. I was hard put to it to place anything in my past at all; this – this moment, this intimacy, this strange childish magic of the boy and the night, the sea and the stars and the scented air, was time out of time; I stood away from my everyday self and watched the familiar figure that was me being embraced, led about and undressed by a stranger, and nothing rebelled or protested, so nothing was done except what he wanted.

The guitar music slid down over the brow of the rocks.

'Now,' said Chris when I stood in my underwear, shivering slightly, before him. 'In you come. I'll taste you again when you come out.'

We stood together on the brink. The sea was not far below us; it swelled up towards us like a beckoning arm. Chris stepped out of his ragged shorts and stood naked in the starlight. Then he took my hand again.

'Jump,' he said quietly.

We jumped together, hand in hand, and the mild, clear water closed over my head. He pulled me down, and I turned my face up and opened my eyes for a second. The surface above me glinted with tiny splinters of reflected starlight.

The hand holding mine released me, and I let myself drift upward. As my face broke out into the night air, I saw the moon's horn lying on the horizon, laying a long luminescent path of ripples straight to me. Below me I could just see Chris's long white shape, broken by refraction, weaving through the transparent water. The first shock of cold had passed; the sea wrapped me round in silky, variable currents, now warm, now chill, as I trod water and moved my arms languidly. I swam slowly out further, and now, looking back, I could see the fire, the firelit figures; I could see John playing, and his guitar-notes came to me in a fine drift, a mist of notes, across the sea-top.

I lay on my back and looked up at the black velvet sky, tasting the salt and the soft night air, and thinking how queer it all was – thinking of the word 'queer' for the first time in years in its original meaning, for truly the events of the night were not merely 'odd' or 'strange' but a little weird, a touch uncanny. When Chris, a naked white sea-ghost, rose at my side and lay gently flapping his fins beside me in the moonlight, and I tried to relate him to the mental picture I had had of him even a single hour ago, I got gooseflesh from the queerness of it.

'There are no words for it, are there?' he asked at last, in what I can only call a reverent tone of voice. There was no need to remind myself that for him this sensual delight had the added dimension of a religious experience, and, incredible as it seems, this realization no longer struck me as in any way comic or infantile or even unlikely. A little longer, floating here, I thought, and I'll find myself sharing his emotions – I'll join his cult if I'm not careful. Because there really was something in the circumstances and in the sensations which could not be explained away in terms of temperature and chemical reactions. There was a strong element of mysticism. Perhaps it was only the proximity of Chris, my sudden vulnerability to his feelings, an empathy I had not expected and could not explain. Lying there at his side in the sea, I thought, 'What is the matter

142

with Andy, that he cannot see this son of his for the gentle, sensitive, genuine and honest creature he seems to me to be?'

We swam and floated together for a long time, until at last the night-breeze began blowing the sea-skin into gooseflesh waves and without consulting each other we swam slowly back to the rocks. Their roughness grazed my legs as he pulled me up, as if the land were punishing me for my infidelity with the water.

We stood together on the ledge just above his deep, sighing sea, and he looked at me for a long time and then said,

'What's so difficult to understand about that? It's beautiful – it's perfect. That's all. Can't you go back and tell him?'

'I don't care what you say, it's different in England.'

He shrugged.

'You can't pretend that sitting in the refuse-filled fountains at Trafalgar Square, or sinking your feet into the muck at the bottom of the Serpentine, or even plunging yourself into that cold grey thing that calls itself the English Channel, can be as readily understood as what we've just been doing.'

He leant his weight on one thin leg and stared out across the puckered surface, frowning.

'Look,' he said. 'Do you like making love? Don't answer, of course you do. Well, some people are harder to make love with than others. Some people resist you, or they don't know by instinct how to caress you, or they do or say something that grates on you right in the middle. But if somebody said to you, which would you rather, make love to all sorts of people including those who are not very good lovers or even unpleasant or violent or ugly, or not make love at all – what would you answer?'

The question was clearly rhetorical, and yet of course I had to answer it truthfully. He was a person whose whole aura seemed to draw the truth and nothing but the truth. A lie, even a temporization, I felt, would bump against something invisible that surrounded him and bounce off before it reached his ears.

'Well, frankly I'd much rather do without.'

His eyes came back to me slowly and incredulously. '*Do without* making love?' he asked.

'Yes. Just as I can understand you feeling a sense of worship for this body of water, but the fountains and the Channel baffle me.

Love isn't love, and worship isn't worth a damn, in my eyes, if they're indiscriminating.'

His expression was baffled now, hurt even. 'But I do discriminate! I discriminate between water and every other element. Worshippers for all the ages of men have gladly put up with shortcomings in their gods. Look at the millions of people who can still accept the Christian god, after all he's been responsible for! It's utterly beyond me how my father, for instance, can still maintain that Christianity is basically good, even divinely inspired, when you consider that it inspired, among other things, the Crusades, the Conquistadors, the witch-hunts and the Inquisition. All those atrocities were carried out, not by outsiders upon Christians, but by Christians in the name of Christ. To me, that, taken with the belief that Christ was divine and all-knowing and therefore knew what he was starting, simply rules out Christianity, however good its original teachings. But my idea is that we love through the senses, and worship through them, too. I think when humanity develops more, we won't need cults, we won't need to worship something other than our own selves. But obviously there aren't many human beings at the moment perfect enough to find anything in themselves worth worshipping. I've always felt a great need to dedicate myself to something – I admit it. I'm not strong enough not to need anything. But to invent some personalized deity and then try to convince myself that he's perfect and omnipotent and omniscient and at the same time capable of perpetrating or even enduring all the horrors and anomalies of this disgusting, *cruel* world—' he lowered his head like a bull and actually stamped his foot on the rock, every muscle taut with a sudden overpowering uprush of revulsion and horror which quite startled me – '*that* I can't do, not even to satisfy my own craven need. So I haven't invented. I've taken something that exists, a life-force, a life-element, in itself positive and pure and combining all the best elements of passiveness and activeness, and capable of giving more simple, unvarnished physical pleasure than anything in life except sex. (And as a matter of fact, even sex is no good if it's dry!) We've embellished it with all sorts of songs and rituals and symbols, but that's more for fun than anything serious. The serious part is that we get, from what you'd call our worship of water, all the comfort that other religious people get, which is, after all, only the comfort of devoting yourself to something great outside yourself which may test you – must test you – but can never fail you. It's always there. It's in our bodies, if nowhere else. Have you ever been truly thirsty and then had a glass of cold water to drink? I bet you've never felt nearer to ecstasy than at that moment. We use that – thirst and quenching – as part of our ritual, to remind us of the whole cycle of want and replenishment that keeps life interesting and at the same time can make it so terrible for so many people. Here, we lie out on the rocks and cook ourselves for two hours before we let ourselves jump into the water. We deny ourselves a drink until our mouths are parched; then we sip iced water drop by drop. Even making love after three days of not, isn't more delicious, more exciting, more calculated to make you happy and grateful and inspired than those first sips of water, that first moment when you plunge your hot, dry body into the beautiful sea.'

We were sitting down by now, he on his shorts, I on my dress, for the rocks here were sharp. I was listening concentratedly and wondering whether it was a side-effect of this magical place which was making this whole diatribe, which Andy would certainly have called bizarre and ridiculous, and which very well might be so, sound perfectly sensible and plausible.

'What are you smiling at?' he asked me suddenly, with suspicion.

'Oh, I don't know! The whole thing is outrageous, just as your father says. And yet tonight it makes sense. Maybe the sea has bewitched us both.'

'If you can think that, even for a moment, you've got to admit it has its own spiritual power. Oh, you're lovely! Being with you is great, and you were beautiful in the water, like a seal or some other sea-creature, so at home and at ease . . . Here, take those things off and let's make love!'

'You're crazy,' I said. 'No, take your hands away. Honestly I can't. It's not in my nature.'

'What on earth do you mean?'

'Well, look. We can meet, and we have met, across the twenty-odd years that separate us; we've been together for two hours now; on terms of intimacy I should have thought unbelievable beforehand. But making love is something else. *You* make love with everybody you like in the least, pretty and ugly, old and young . . . male and female? . . .'

'Sure—'

'H'm. Well, I don't. People of my age, women anyway, don't, and don't start on with this no-difference-between-men-and-women bit, you'll never convince anyone of my generation of the truth or desirability of *that* proposition! My lovers are a very circumscribed lot. They have to be the right age, the right sex, and a lot of other things too. Really, we're so unalike! You parch your bodies so as to enjoy your drinks and swims more, and that accords perfectly with my own philosophy, but "going without" sex for *three days* to work up an appetite makes me wonder if we're of the same species. I take it you don't make love to creatures of other species?' He shook his head. 'Well, that's something! But—'

'But I *would*,' he interrupted vehemently, 'if there were no people around.'

I laughed rather wildly, and couldn't stop for quite a while. He laughed too, but without really knowing why.

'Oh Chris! What *am* I to tell your father?'

'Is he one of your lovers?' he asked abruptly.

I stopped laughing. We looked at each other.

'Yes,' I answered. 'And that's another reason why I couldn't with you.'

'It's the only one so far that strikes me as valid,' he said quietly. 'And I'm not sure why even *that* does. It annoys me rather. It seems he has managed to indoctrinate me to some extent with his constricting values . . .' He stared at me for some moments in the quiet gloom, and then drew a deep sigh. 'No, it's no use,' he said. 'I still like you, but I don't want you any more, not now I know he's had you. Maybe it's just because subconsciously I resent finding out that I have the same taste as him in anything . . .'

Taking my cue, I dragged my wet crumpled dress out from under me and pulled it on. The salt on my skin was beginning to prickle; how John could tolerate, let alone like, this sensation I couldn't imagine . . . All I wanted was to get under a shower. The magic was gone, melted away; ordinary practical reality had crept in and reasserted itself with the drying-off of our bodies.

Chris sat moodily throwing scraps of stone into the sea.

'What's the matter?' I asked.

'Oh, nothing much. I had this terrific feeling of sexiness about you and now it's gone all flat. As you can plainly see,' he added with a graphic gesture. 'Humiliating. Cover it up.' He stood up and pulled on his shorts, keeping his back to me. Again I noticed the thinness of his flanks. Could it be that Andy was disappointed by Chris's failure to grow broad and tough-muscled like him? For the rest, I was bewildered. How was it possible to detest so heartily someone so basically sound and intelligent – albeit promiscuous?

'Chris—'

'Mm?'

'Don't be sad. What about making love to one of the others?'

'Oh . . . Well, I probably will, later. But . . . Oh, hell. I suppose I'm a bit jealous. I wouldn't mind if it were anybody but him.' He sat down beside me again. 'Are you going to tell him about this when you get back?'

'Some of it.'

'This part? Me wanting to screw you?'

I winced. 'Oh, don't talk like that.'

'Why not? That's how we all talk.'

'I thought you said making love is so important to you.'

'Of course it is,' he said in surprise.

'Then why do you use such hideous expressions about it? How would you like it if I called your divine sea a piss-pot?'

He recoiled from me, and uttered a sound of disgust.

'That's what I mean,' I said. 'You shouldn't degrade what you revere with cheap ugly terminology.'

He said nothing, but looked so crushed I put my hand into his and squeezed it.

'Sorry. It's not my business to tell you off.'

After a moment he muttered, 'It is, I suppose, if I offend you.' There was a silence and then he said, in a different tone, 'But you know, the fact is, I don't really *revere* sex. Any more than I *revere* hash. It's great, I mean, I love it, I don't think anyone could enjoy it more than I do, but I do it more or less like – well, eating and sleeping and breathing. It's a pleasure, a joy, it's part of the green salad of life, the sugar on the pill – of course you're right, one shouldn't be casual or crude when one speaks about any of those delights, it's just a bad habit one gets into; but you can't compare it with what I feel about—' He gestured towards the sea, moving his hand slowly outward as if trying to stroke the horizon with his

147

finger-tips. '*That's* what I revere,' he said. 'The rest is just the froth around the edges.'

After another silence, more congenial that time, I squeezed his hand again and said, 'Anyway, I won't tell him.'

'Good. It'd only make him hate me all the more.'

'He doesn't hate you!'

'Despise me, then. Worse.'

'I'm going to try and stop that,' I said.

'You'll have your work cut out.'

We were both beginning to shiver, so we clambered back to the fireside. Several of the hippies had rolled themselves up in their sleeping bags or whatever they had; others were sitting close to John, who was still playing and crooning. Everyone seemed to be smoking . . . The fire had burned low but the embers were still glowing; Chris and I huddled over them, rubbing our hands, and for the first time I began to wonder how on earth John and I would get back to our hotel along that precipitous rock-track in darkness.

'John—'

'Hallo!' he called to me across the fire. He was invisible except for eyes and teeth.

'How shall we get back?'

'We can't now. I stayin' here.'

I looked at Chris.

'We could both get into my sleeping-bag,' he said with a wicked grin.

'Haven't you a spare one?'

'Probably. There's nearly always someone who doesn't get back at night because he's shacking up with someone in the town—' He caught my eye. 'Sorry.' He went over to a pile of something on a far rock and came back with a bag which looked and smelt as if it hadn't been washed for years. I took it gingerly in my hands and wondered if it were within my power to insert my body into it, but the alternatives were too unpleasant to contemplate. 'Thanks,' I said faintly. 'What about John?'

'Don't worry about me,' he said. 'I find someone to share with me.'

I looked at him with astonishment. What sex of a someone, I wondered? If female, and the fawn-faced girl was now lying with

148

her head on his knee looking very much in possession, she was in for a disappointment; if male . . . Well, perhaps it was time John lost his virginity one way or the other; I decided it was none of my business, but I must say I couldn't help feeling concerned. Apart from anything else, for a man as big as John to try to divest himself of his innocence in a small sleeping-bag could lead to complications which hardly bore thinking about.

I looked at my sleeping-bag again, thanked God I did not suffer from over-fastidiousness, scratched myself systematically all over to rid myself of as much salt as possible, and caterpillared my way in. It was warm and snug and, by pushing my face almost into a patch of wood-ash, I managed at least partially to defeat the smell of old hippie-sweat. My eyes were now on level with the fire and I stared into its pearl-grey and vermilion depths, trying to get to grips with the next day's potential and able to think only of the past three hours.

Just as I was dropping off I felt someone kiss me on the cheek, and some soft salty hair fell on to my face.

'It's only me,' whispered Chris. 'I'm putting my bag right next to yours. It's the nearest I'll ever come to sleeping with you . . .' I felt him pressing close to me from behind through the two thick layers of padded cloth. 'Give a bit,' he said. 'Make spoons.' He put one arm over me and after a while he stroked my head. 'Your ears stick out,' he discovered. 'Under your hair.'

'You don't say,' I mumbled.

'Has my father ever noticed?'

'If so he'd be far too polite to mention it.'

'Is he polite in bed?'

'Shut up and go to sleep, will you?'

'Do you love me?'

'*Yes.* Now Sleep!'

'Okay, m'dear.'

What a funny expression for him to use, I thought, as I fell asleep.

At dawn I woke up. He was still cuddled up behind me, one stone-cold arm slung over me. I tucked it into his own bag. I was stiff all over from lying on the rocks, but I had slept wonderfully. I sat up and looked all round, but I couldn't detect which cloth bundle contained John. The sea was certainly beautiful enough to worship; it looked like an endless floor of faintly mottled pink alabaster, lit from below. By God, I thought as I gazed at it, maybe he's right. Maybe it *is* better than sex!

Today I would say goodbye to Chris and we would go back to the mainland, take a train to Athens and get on a plane to Israel. If what awaited me there should prove as strange and unexpected as what I had found on Hydra, there was no knowing if I would ever return to England. Oh, but what nonsense, of course I had to, because of David. Dear me, I hadn't given David more than a passing thought for fully sixteen hours.

I looked down at my other, old-new son. He looked, like all children, incredibly different in sleep, absolutely innocent and without a trace in his features of what he had called 'the freebooting Adam' with which he was so full when awake. I couldn't resist pushing a strand of hair away from his face; the end had stuck to the corner of his mouth and he frowned as I pulled it free. I felt the urge to kiss him as I loved to kiss David, in his sleep. I bent over him and bussed him very gently on the bridge of his nose.

What had he said, last night? 'Okay, m'dear'? Suddenly I laughed. But of course it wasn't 'm'dear'! It was 'Medea.'

PART TWO
TOBY

Chapter 1

THE interlude was over. But it had left its 'queer' taste, strong and tangible, which stayed with me throughout the day, most of which we spent travelling.

On the ferry, on the train from Piraeus, on the bus across Athens and the airport bus, right through the crowded concourse and on to the El Al plane that was to take us on the final stage of our odd journey, I could savour that taste. Its effect was to make me feel light – light-hearted, light-headed, light-bodied. Every time we had a chance to walk, mainly from one form of transport to another, I felt frisky, as if I might break into a caper. I jumped on and off things, threw my suitcase around, and laughed over nothing. I'm deeply inhibited about singing in public, having no proper voice, but once or twice I caught myself humming. I was amazed at myself.

It was love, of course. There are so many different kinds. And it was relief – at much more than just *not* loathing Chris. Poor Andy was so wrong about these kids. I could hardly wait to get back and put him right. As we drove across Athens, I could see the Colonel's men everywhere, even glaring down at us from rooftops, and I remembered the angry, baffled, bovine snicker-snack gestures of the policemen on Hydra. It was awful that so many people didn't understand, saw the hippies as a threat because they refused to conform to the accepted patterns of military manhood. How could men like these soldiers grasp something as simple as the water-cult, the pleasure-principle, the gentle, unaggressive, float-with-the-tide ethic of Chris and his followers? In my sublime mood of this morning my only cause for dismay was that I might be going to marry a man who could apparently only see in it a lack of drive and ambition. Did Andy really consider these so essential that he'd cut himself off from his son because he believed more strongly in them than in him?

My mind was so full that it was some time before I became aware that John's and my silences were incompatible. He had followed me about from early morning with a dog-like air; the only contact between us was physical. In some curious way, the events of the night (whatever they may have been in his case) seemed to have made him feel very vulnerable, because wherever we went I had to lead the way, and whenever we were stationary, either sitting or standing, he would surreptitiously press himself close to me. I had a strange feeling that he wanted to crawl into my arms and hide his face on my lap as he once had in the L-shaped room. On that occasion, I recalled uneasily, he had been feeling desperately ashamed . . .

On the airport bus I was finally overcome by the silent pressure of his feelings and asked what was wrong.

'Boat, train, bus, plane,' muttered John faintly. 'I'm fed up.'

'Is that all it is?'

'Tired of go, go, go all the time,' he said. He sounded peevish and his hands made pointless, nervous movements. He didn't look at me. He hadn't looked at me all day.

'John?'

'What?'

'Want to talk?'

'No.'

'*Is* anything wrong, really?'

'You can't tell that without askin'?'

'Tell me. Maybe it's not so bad.'

'What do you know about bad? You're all right. Nothin' bad for you.'

'That's not true.' I was thinking how I would be feeling this morning if I had let Chris make love to me the night before. It would not, as a matter of fact, have been entirely impossible. But there would have been no feelings of lightness and love this morning, had I done anything so grotesque.

We lapsed into uneasy silence again until suddenly, in the middle of the airport concourse, he asked, 'You did somethin' with that kid that you supposed to be in love with his daddy?'

'No,' I said.

'I seen you down there with no clothes on, both of you,' he said, with a faint note of accusation.

'We went swimming, that's all.'

'That what you say.'

I turned and stared at him. 'Don't you believe me?'

He met my eyes at last, but very briefly.

'I dunno. If you had done something, how could you tell me? You'd *have* to lie about it. The mornin' ain't like the night. You can do things in the night that you just have to lie about in the daytime.'

He looked quite desperate, and I felt suddenly guilty. How could I have been so self-absorbed as not to notice that something was dreadfully wrong for him?

'John, what happened? Was it that boy, the one you held under the water?'

He shook his head. 'He never come back. The others say he was ashamed 'cause of callin' me a black bastard. They supposed to like black people, not be prejudice', but it slip out when he was mad and show that he was, underneath. That was his bag you slept in,' he added drearily.

'So who was it?'

At that moment they announced our flight. We picked up our cases and began hurrying along, two drops in a river of people. It was strange how private we felt among them.

'Come on,' I said, as we were swept along in that half-running gait peculiar to people hurrying in a terminus. 'Tell me.'

John stared ahead. 'Look at that woman.' He indicated, with a tilt of his head, a girl who was hurrying along near us. She was about twenty-five; she wore a white trench-coat and had long red hair tied off her face with a white band. 'You think she's pretty?'

'Yes, quite. Why?'

'Could you do it with her?'

'Do what?' I asked stupidly.

'You know. What we're talkin' about.'

I blinked and almost stopped walking. 'Well, but John—'

'I know. You see, you lucky. Other women don't turn you on. But can you imagine – maybe if you were real high . . . Did you smoke last night?'

153

'Pot, you mean? No. Did you?'

'Sure. We all did. They got good grass, strong. They got great stuff around here.' He sounded bitter and furious, and his words carried a totally reversed meaning from his enthusings of yesterday. 'I was way out, last night. Way, way out.'

We were interrupted by the business of getting aboard the aircraft and settling down in our seats. The third place in our row was taken by the red-haired girl. She had some very pleasant perfume on, and when she took off her trench-coat I could see that she had a nice figure. Every woman has an eye for other women's looks, but I had never looked at a woman in the way that I looked now at that girl. I tried to be entirely objective, for I'd guessed by now, with a quailing sensation of anxiety and pity, what John had been getting at. He wanted me to put myself in his place, as far as possible – the place of a man, by nature homosexual, who has had the misfortune to gain his first sexual experience with a woman.

I kept watching the girl out of the corner of my eye. I had never been high on pot, but I had been drunk. Had I not been drunk one night eight years ago, I would never have started with Toby. In a flash of total recall, I visualized that night in all its bizarre detail – emotions heightened by more than the rum-punches, a misery so deep and raw that nothing but the most drastic therapy could affect it.

Could what happened with Toby by any wild effort of the imagination have happened with another woman?

I set my teeth and forced myself to imagine kissing that pretty girl on the lips, embracing her, stroking her hair . . . I found my face twisted into a grimace. To imagine further took a furious effort of will. To press your breasts against other breasts, to engage in the act of love without the proper means, with some pathetic substitute . . . The thought of it made me shudder. Disgust, and a sense of desecration and disgrace, took hold of me.

I turned to John, who was wriggling about in his small seat like a Great Dane in a Peke's basket.

'No,' I said to him. 'No matter how high I was. It isn't in me.'

'But if you *had*,' he persisted. 'How would you feel?'

'God knows! Unspeakable.'

John threw me one meaning look, and then his head slumped between his shoulders.

I put my hand on him. 'But John,' I said, very quietly so as not possibly to be overheard, 'if that's how it is with you, how – I mean, how were you able to?'

'I don't know,' he said miserably. 'We was so close together. It was dark, and she'd been stroking me, and she smelled good, like the sea . . . Her hair was like a boy's. I just pretended . . . And she did most of it, you know what I mean . . . I didn't hardly know what was happening till it was over, and I even thought I'd enjoyed it, I went to sleep thinking, maybe I *am* just like anybody, maybe I'll be able to find me a girl of my own now and be ordinary and happy. It was only when I woke up in the morning and looked at her, I began to feel so damn dirty . . .'

He turned his head away and stared out of the little window over the wing of the plane. 'Sod that pot,' he mumbled. 'Sod everything I ever done.'

The engines were starting to roar and the plane to vibrate, but I could see his shoulders were shaking. I slipped my arm round him to fish for his safety-belt, fastened it, and kept my arm there. He pressed his own forearm against it, squeezing it against his stomach. I felt I loved him more than ever, but what help or comfort could I give him? Useless to tell him he'd done nothing wrong. There's no balm to be looked for from outside when you've betrayed yourself.

In the end he ran away into sleep, and I furtively dried his eyes while the red-haired girl was standing up to get a pillow from the rack.

As soon as we touched down at Lydda Airport, my lightness and calm abandoned me.

It was almost as if I could *see* a huge, rolling black wave of panic coming towards me, towering over my head, about to engulf and paralyse me. I could scarcely collect my wits sufficiently to get us both off the plane, across the burning hot tarmac through a seering wind that blew dust and dry heat into our faces, and through the blessedly cool, but temporary, oasis of the airport formalities. John seemed helpless, all the strength gone out of him; I had to put things into his hands if I wanted him to carry them, take them out again when it was time to put them down. I suddenly realized that what had happened to John had had an effect on him like a serious accident; instead of my companion and helper of yesterday, I had with me a wounded fellow-creature for whom I had to take responsibility. I had an abrupt change of heart about the hippies, and I'm ashamed to say there was a great deal of self-concern in the vehemence with which I cursed them, their pot and their damned promiscuous love-spreading. It had all seemed so free, happy and innocent last night, in that island world-apart. Even this morning I had been full of foolish admiration. Now I saw the menace in it for any outsider too weak and insecure to hold his integrity against it. I quailed inwardly when I thought how easily I might have fallen victim to it myself. Perhaps there was something to be said for my puritanical conditioning after all, I thought grimly as I led John, shuffling his feet like a cripple, outside again into the blinding, head-rocking downpour of sunlight.

'It's too hot here,' he complained childishly. 'I want to go home.'

'Well, we can't,' I said shortly, turning deaf ears, with difficulty, upon an announcement which trailed out after us of a B.O.A.C. flight to London leaving at any moment.

Jo had booked us into a hotel near the airport, but our booking was for the following day. I only realized this when we got there.

'I am sorry,' said the clerk without a hint of either sorrow or deference. 'We are full up.'

'Even with the crisis?'

He smiled an Oriental smile.

'What crisis?'

'But what can we do for tonight?'

He shrugged.

I'm going to hate this place if I'm not careful, I thought with sudden ferocity.

The obvious thing to do was go straight to the kibbutz, but it was a long way away, it was late afternoon and we were both exhausted. I felt the wall of panic roll closer. I turned to John in desperation.

'What shall we do?'

'Go home,' he said mulishly.

I turned again to the clerk.

'Do you know of any other hotel . . . ?' He turned down his mouth, shook his head slightly, and spread his hands. 'Well, do you know of this place?' I got out Toby's letter and pointed to the address on it. He frowned. 'That is not how you write it. It is a big kibbutz quite close to here.'

'*Close* to here? Are you sure?' I asked in surprise. I had looked it up on a map before I left and it had looked to be about fifty miles south of the airport.

'Do you want to go there? I will arrange for you a taxi.'

'A taxi? Won't that be very expensive?' Another shrug. 'Isn't there any other way?'

'By bus would be difficult – three changes. A lot of waiting, perhaps.'

'Oh, all right.'

While the clerk spoke in rapid Hebrew to the taxi-driver, certainly the most villainous-looking I have ever seen, not excluding those who ply their trade from London Airport, I stood motionless, appalled at the imminence of the meeting with Toby which now, apparently, lay just ahead. I had supposed I would have at least one night of rest and go through the necessary mental scenarios (I've discovered that what I have carefully imagined never happened, so it is a kind of insurance). I had also, of course, planned to ring up and let him know we were coming, as the shock of seeing me when he least expected to was clearly a very unfair imposition. I wondered now what had prevented me from sending him a wire.

The clerk returned to say that it was all arranged, the taxi 'special' would take me to the kibbutz for fifty lira (a sum which meant nothing to me and which I only later realized was over £6). I asked if I might telephone to the kibbutz from the hotel. He smiled again.

'You can try,' he said enigmatically.

I saw what he meant quite soon. Telephoning a kibbutz at five p.m. is like telephoning an abandoned desert outpost. Nobody answered for ages, and when at last somebody did, she spoke only Hebrew. I put the clerk on the line and asked if she could call Toby Cohen to the telephone. They had a jolly conversation, punctuated with bursts of laughter, and then the clerk put the phone back.

'It is impossible,' he said. 'First, she doesn't know him, she was a visitor there who just happened to be near the phone. Second, nobody calls anybody to a phone in a kibbutz, it would mean running for miles and looking for them. You had better just go and give him a nice surprise.'

We piled our scuffed and dusty bits of luggage into the taxi (a vast, ancient American car with extra seats put in) which bounded forward and roared away, seeming to cut a swathe through the heat like a bulldozer cutting through some sort of solid matter.

The temperature was quite incredible. The island and the cool turquoise sea were as the memory of paradise lost. 'Is it always this hot here?' I asked the driver.

'*Sharav*,' he answered. 'Hot desert wind. Blow fifty days a year. Blow now six days, every day get worse. Tomorrow I think I kill my wife. Nobody blame me.'

I sank back and tried to think, to plan, to imagine. The juices of my brain seemed to be drying out. I glanced at John. He was asleep again, his guitar cradled on his knees.

I abandoned my efforts to project myself forward to this terrifying meeting. I no longer either wanted nor dreaded to see Toby; the prospect was quite simply beyond my ability to grasp.

'Is there going to be a war?' I asked the driver.

He shrugged his massive shoulders in their tee-shirt, which oddly enough was not soaked with sweat as one might expect. I, too, was quite dry. It seemed this wind simply evaporated the sweat the second it emerged. Even my hair began to feel brittle.

'If Moshe Dayan takes over, then we will show them something,' he said. 'Now is bad. We sit like ducks and wait for them to start shooting us. I have a son in the army. Two weeks he's waiting. The waiting kills you, special in a *sharav*.'

'Aren't you afraid for your son?'

'You are tourist?'

'Yes.'

'So you can't understand. Is not a matter of be afraid. We are used to be afraid, we don't notice it so much. I fighted in forty-eight, one year, many battles. Since then, no peace, always crisis, crisis, bit of rest, another crisis. True, this time is bigger. But fear is like a pain, you learn to live with it.'

This conversation had the effect of halting the remorseless forward motion of the wall of panic. After all, what the hell had I got to be panicky about? Here was an entire nation on the brink of being wiped out, and this man in front of me was scratching his neck and turning his radio up full-blast and bearing his fear with a shrug. I watched a truckload of young soldiers, armed to the teeth, go roaring by. They were all singing.

I sank back and tried to think about Andy. It didn't help a bit. I seemed to have left him behind on the wharf at Hydra; he was no longer here to help me. John was, of course, a dead loss at this point, and in fact I must spare both time and emotional energy to help *him* as much as I could. I really was alone – entirely alone, thrown on my own resources at this crisis in my own life. It would no doubt be very strengthening for my character. If only it were not so bloody hot! Even with the windows down and the wind blowing in I could hardly breathe, and every inch of my skin was shrivelling from the dryness.

'You want to stop for a drink?' The driver asked.

'How far are we from the kibbutz?'

'Ten kilometres.'

How far was that? I was too hot to work it out.

'Well, let's stop. I don't mind.'

He pulled up at a shabby little kiosk beside the road, jumped out with devastating energy and returned with a bottle of ice-cold lager. It was more delicious than anything I have ever tasted. As the first rivulets forced their way over my tongue through the dust and scum and down my throat, I remembered Chris and his self-imposed thirst-rituals. Next time we met, I would tell him that beer was best.

'What about your friend?'

'I won't wake him. Is this Israeli beer?'

'Yes. Good?'

'Marvellous! How much?'

'No, no. I pay. You are visitor.'

'Thank you.'

'For nothing.'

We set off again. After a while I said, 'It feels as if we're travelling north.'

'North – yes.'

I sat up sharply. 'But the kibbutz is south of Lydda!'

'No—'

'But it is! I looked on a map!'

He screeched to a stop. 'What kibbutz you want?'

Again I got out Toby's letter. He peered at it, and then put his heavy moustached face down on the back of the seat.

'The man at the hotel said it was spelt wrong,' I said.

'I spell *him* wrong, next time I see him,' said the driver, smacking his forehead. '*Tembel!* He is idiot, that fellow! This is not what he tell me. This is a little kibbutz, very far south of here, we are going all opposite direction.'

'Oh my God,' I moaned.

'You want I turn around, take you to this place?'

'I don't know. What do you think? I've nowhere else to go.'

He consulted his watch. 'Is six o'clock now. I get you there by nine o'clock.'

'Three hours! Of this!'

'Be dark by seven. Little cooler. We stop for food and drinks.'

'And the fare?'

'Seventy lira.'

'What? It was fifty to the near place.'

His eyes shifted away from me. 'Did he tell you fifty? I told him twenty.'

Yeah, and besides, since then we've drunk beer together and talked about your son so now I'm getting a fair price, you robber.

I gave him an old-fashioned look which was not lost on him.

'Let's go,' I said.

Chapter 2

THE heat, the jolting and my weariness – not to mention all the beer we had drunk on the way – knocked me out long before we reached the right kibbutz at last. We had been driving through darkness for hours, but the departure of the sun had had depressingly little effect on the *sharav*. I was coated all over with an encrustation of dust, like an old wall smeared with lime; as I woke up and stirred I felt my skin would crack, and my head and eyeballs ached painfully as if from the worst sort of hangover. I began, as I crawled out of the taxi, to wonder if beer was best after all.

I dragged the stuff out, paid the driver, and only then, with a feeling of reluctance, shook John awake. It was cruelty to bring him back to awareness; only when he opened his eyes did I realize the relief, from an empathetic consciousness of his misery, I had felt while he had been asleep.

'Come on,' I said gently. 'We've arrived.'

He got out with an effort, and stood there, blinking and rubbing his forehead.

'Where are we?'

'In Toby's kibbutz. Soon we'll see him.'

He seemed to rouse himself a little at this. The taximan was giving me his card. If I wanted to see something of the country . . . And not to worry about the crisis. 'My son will take care of it,' he said with a grin. 'But if you should want suddenly a ride back to the airport . . . after all, it is not your war. You Jewish? No. Not your war,' he repeated.

I said goodbye to him, he climbed back into his enormous car and roared away, leaving us standing in a little island of familiarity – our luggage – in a great dark sea of strangeness.

We seemed to be in an open space behind a large building. Some steps led on to a kind of platform, cluttered with crates and churns, where there was a light shining, and swing doors. There were a few other lamps, like street-lamps, dotted about, showing various rather ramshackle out-buildings half-hidden by trees and bushes. There was nobody about.

While I stood there, uncertain what to do next, John unexpectedly took the initiative for the first time since morning.

'Come on, let's find him,' he said.

He slung his guitar on his back, picked up most of the luggage, and set off towards the lighted doors. I hurried up the stone steps after him.

'Do you think it's all right just to walk in here?' I asked anxiously.

'Why not?'

He shouldered the doors open and I followed him into a large kitchen, such as you might find in a hotel. The lights were on, but it was obvious that the business of the day was over; all the huge utensils were clean and empty, everything else put away. A few slices of wind-dried bread lay on the bread-slicing machine. John hiked one suitcase under his arm and, grabbing one of these rusks, began to gnaw it. I watched him uneasily. Nobody was there, but still, it seemed a bit of a liberty. John found a huge stainless-steel sink, turned on a tap and put his head under it. He seemed to stay there, sucking the water into his mouth in great noisy gasps, for about five minutes. Then he finished off the bread.

'Funny how you still have to eat,' he said.

'Come on, we'd better try and find somebody.'

We passed through the kitchen into a big, dark hall, full of tables and chairs – clearly the dining-hall. It was empty of people, but there was a glazed double door at the far end, and through that I could see a sort of porch with a notice-board, where two or three people were standing. We hurried between the tables and through the doors. John burst out first. The people outside all gave startled jumps at the sight of his big black figure suddenly leaping out of the darkened dining-hall at them.

'Where's Toby?' he asked in what might well have seemed a menacing fashion to anyone unused to his directness.

They all looked at me.

'We're looking for Toby Cohen,' I explained, and was dismayed to find myself beginning to tremble.

A woman came up to me. She was about my age, not at all good-looking, with lined and shiny skin, soft skimpy hair and very pale, rather bulging blue eyes. She wore a sun-faded sleeveless cotton dress cut away at the neck, and sandals. My first general impression of her was of a comfortable, relaxed ease of manner; a rare quality to find in a plain woman.

'My name is Hava,' she said. We shook hands. Hers was hard and masculine, as I'd expected. 'I'll show you to Toby's room. Is he expecting you?'

'No,' I said, wondering if she had felt, through that hard, muscular arm, how my hand trembled uncontrollably. I thought she had, for she gave me a sharp look.

'You can leave your things here. Are you staying the night?'

'I'm afraid we have nowhere else to go,' I said.

'I will try and find a room for you. Can you share? We are rather full just now.'

'Share?' I thought at first she meant with Toby, but then I realized she meant with John. Her casualness took me unawares. 'Well—'

'There are two beds. It's only for tonight – I thought since you're travelling together—'

'We don't want to give you any trouble.' After all, I had shared a room with John once before, and it hadn't done us any harm. I could almost smile as I thought what Chris would say if he knew how uneasy I felt about it. *You poor old square!*

Hava was leading us through the kibbutz along a broad, well-lit path. Lawns stretched away into the darkness on either side, and there were bushes and trees – it was like walking through a park. The dry wind still blew but it seemed less tormenting now, as if passing through so many leaves had taken the viciousness out of it. Still, it was oddly hard for me to breathe. John was walking beside me. He took my hand, wrapping his huge fingers all round mine so that it lay within his like a child's, curled in a ball.

'Don't be frightened,' he whispered.

Only then did I realize how frightened I was. The shaking had spread to my legs and it was hard to walk in a straight line. Hava was talking to me over her shoulder but I wasn't taking in a word. Memories were rushing in upon me pell-mell as if I were drowning in this dark green wind, which seemed to be whirling me along in a scurry of leaves and dust, snatching at my dress and my hair, pulling me towards this meeting. I saw Toby's face, the beaky, bright-eyed, tender face I had loved so passionately, I saw the black tousled hair and the slight, strong body which could hold me up when I fell or threw myself against it, and yet which had withdrawn and left me to bruise myself with endless falls . . . seven years! What would happen, what would he say and do, how would he look? The wall of panic had become the darkness and the wind and the next bend in the homely path, almost upon me now, making me long to turn and run – away from his need or his lack of it, never to know the outcome of all this suffering I had done, all the wasteful waiting and the regrets and the loneliness. But Hava's broad, sure back led me on, and John's hand enclosed mine like a ball-and-socket joint – I knew it was inevitable, inescapable, that in fact it was what I wanted most.

'Here we are,' said Hava.

It was a door in a low, small building with three other doors; four little windows, four little gardens, four little porch-lights shining in the most prosaic, friendly way. And we were suddenly out of the wind, there was no more tugging; we had arrived at the still vortex, and Hava was knocking briskly on the door to Toby's room.

I thought my legs would refuse to hold me.

'Please,' I said suddenly. 'Would you go away?'

She turned to look at me in surprise. John had released my hand; I glanced round and found him gone, vanished like a headless ghost into the surrounding darkness. I heard footsteps inside and I clutched the door-post with a sharp intake of breath.

'Please!' I said urgently.

She turned and walked quickly away round the side of the house.

The door opened and Toby was there.

The panic-wall crashed down on me and somehow I stood up under its impact and the trembling stopped and I looked at him. How he was changed, I couldn't notice then; I only saw the ways in which he was the same – the shape of the eyes and nose and mouth, the whole look of him that was as much part of my life as a knot in the wood of my own trunk. A warp, perhaps, a blemish which caught the saw of the days and made it screech as it tried to cut through; it was there, he was there, embedded in me, and the more I stared at him the more I thought there was no need to stare, for we were not really separate beings but psychically interlocked. I caught my breath again this time on a sob of despair, for in that moment of seeing him again my first thought was that I would never be free of him, never, and I knew at the same moment that I wanted to be, I did not want to love him any more or be dependent on him, for we were too far apart in all other aspects of ourselves – we were like Siamese twins who are joined at their little fingers only, but who have aberrant bloodstreams – a major artery running through the join – and thus can never be divided, never be released into total individuality even by the most skilful surgery . . .

And now this long, anguished moment was passing and his face began to emerge from its sparkling frame of shock. His arms came up and locked around me and once again I felt that familiar body, ts full length pressed against mine; I felt his ribs heaving and he made strange, incoherent sounds that reverberated through the side of my head. No name, no words at all, just noises of recognition and realization as deep and hopeless as mine. We clung together, not like lovers meeting again, but like victims of some disaster.

At last he let me go, and, without looking at me, walked to the other side of the tiny room which contained a small bed, a plain table and two chairs and a few shelves of books. I, for my part, closed the door behind me and went without invitation and sat down in the armchair nearest to me. He sat down on the bed and we surveyed each other from that distance across a faded rug spread on the tiled floor.

I was horrified, and yet not in the least surprised, to see tears on his face. I didn't realize my own until I found I needed urgently to blow my nose. I fumbled in my pocket, but of course there was nothing there. He saw my need and got up, went to a cupboard by the door, and got a clean handkerchief out of it. He stood near me and held it out; I took it slowly and made use of it. Then I lay back in the chair. I felt too tired to move a muscle. My eyes closed. I forced them open again as I felt him still standing there. We both, simultaneously, gathered breath into our lungs with deep sighs.

'All right,' he said at last. It was half a statement and half a question, which I answered.

'Yes. And you?'

'Yes. But remember, I had no preparation.'

'I'm sorry about that. I don't understand myself why I didn't warn you. I knew I should have done.'

'Of course. Perhaps you wanted me at a disadvantage?'

I sighed again. 'Perhaps.'

'Did you come alone?'

'No. John's here with me.'

'John . . .?' He threw up his eyes and his arms in a gesture of hopeless astonishment and resignation. He didn't ask where John was at that moment. He knew him so well that his delicacy in leaving us alone was something he took for granted.

'You look terribly tired,' he said, and now there was a hint in his voice of the old Toby, the old, tender, protective relationship, which would have unmanned me completely if I had not already been beyond further unmanning. I looked at him again, and now I did see the changes: grey in the hair, lines of anxiety and sadness around the eyes, the mouth grimmer, the jaw more set. Seven years, for him too – not emotionally wasted like mine, but misspent, abused, struggled through, spoilt. I found my head shaking as I looked at him, and he said, 'I know what you're thinking.'

'Do you? I don't know what you're thinking.'

'Then I'll tell you. I might as well . . . No. Better wait a little. Shouldn't say anything committing in my present state of mind.' He looked away from me and around the room, and moved about nervously, trying to calm himself. 'On the other hand,' he muttered as if to himself, 'what else to say? Where else to begin except bang in the middle?'

He sat down on the bed again and lit a cigarette. 'Do you smoke these days?'

'No.'

'Couldn't you have managed to change just a little, to keep me in countenance?'

'I've changed beyond recognition.'

'You haven't changed one iota. Even your hairstyle is the same.'

'I have only one possibility there, because of my ears.'

'Do you remember when I cut your hair and you looked like a cross between a turnip and a feather duster?'

'You said I looked like a little Dutch boy. You never mentioned turnips.'

'I'd done the deed. Why should I malign my own work?'

We stared into each other's eyes. I felt laughter some distance away, but there was so much heaviness in me and in the air that I couldn't reach for it.

'We've got seven years' catching up to do,' I said. 'Are we really going to spend all our time reminiscing about the L-shaped room?'

'I've no intention of trying to catch up. And don't start telling me what you've been doing. If I tried to tell you what these years have really been like, I mean swept clean of metaphors, I'd bore you to tears. Actually they were years of trial and error. And error, and error . . . I can hardly remember one right decision, one praiseworthy action . . . You do the wrong thing for the wrong reason and no right can possibly come out of it. Waste, misery and destruction.'

'But you created, too.'

'You mean my novels?'

'And your children.'

He lay down on the bed, smoking towards the low plaster ceiling of the little room. Every move he made seemed like a picture hung back into a long-empty space in a familiar room. The nails were still there in the wall, and the wall was marked where the pictures had hung, and now they were slowly fitting back into their accustomed places. Just so had he lain on his bed, no narrower or more shabbily-covered than this one, on that Christmas morning when things had begun to go wrong, and his words came back to me. 'I've nothing to give you . . .' How true, and how totally false, they had proved in the event.

'Well,' he said slowly. 'Children are the great exception-makers. Children ratify everything. They underline everything. What's wrong, they make worse; what little is good, they enhance and multiply until one can easily be deceived into feeling everything was justified . . . In the very act of wishing with my whole mind that I had never married my poor little Whistler, it comes to me that, with that thought, I am un-wishing Rachel and Carrie, and the wish instantly loses its dynamic and collapses . . . And yet, to have added two to the legion of children of unhappy marriages and broken homes . . . that is really the ultimate guilt.'

'I'd like to see Rachel.'

He turned his head and stared at me.

'Would you, darling? Then you shall. She's the proudest thing I am of.'

'Toby, isn't she in danger here? Aren't you both in danger?'

'I see Billie's been at you.'

'Not recently. I didn't let her know I was coming.'

'Why was that?'

'Well, in the first place it was all decided in a great rush. But the real reason, I suppose, was that I was afraid she'd impose some monumental responsibility on me.'

'Probably. It's only natural for her to grasp at straws. She must be intolerably anxious.'

'If you understand that, then why don't you send Rachel home?'

After a long time he answered, 'Because I'm a bloody-minded Jew.'

'Does that give you the right to risk her life?'

'Jane—' He stopped, frowned, and went on slowly. 'Look,

you've only just come. I feel instinctively there's very little chance for us, but I'm not about to chuck away the tiny chance there is by launching into a lengthy, helf-jelled credo which you won't understand and which might frighten you off. *If* by some miracle that tiny chance developed into something, we'd have to talk about my Jewishness. It's certainly something fundamental to me now which anyone who – was rash enough to care about me would have to come to terms with. But this is not the moment. My God!' he said suddenly. He swung his legs off the bed and stood up, stubbing out his cigarette in a big, raw-clay ashtray. 'We've forgotten old John!'

He ran to the door and threw it open.

'John! Johnny!' he called into the darkness.

John materialized in the doorway, the tall straight lines of him diagonally crossed by his guitar. His barrel-chest was heaving and his face seemed alight with sudden untrammelled happiness.

'You no-good devil, Toby, I thought you never get around to call me!'

He grabbed Toby and embraced him, rocking him in his great arms and rubbing his hands lovingly all over his hair and face.

Toby hugged him in return.

'Come in, Johnny, you're right, we're monsters! Jane didn't tell me you were here until this moment.'

I winced at the lie, but let it pass, of course. I felt ashamed that we had left him out there so long, but I knew John would rather it had been my fault than Toby's.

John came in and pulled me up and the three of us embraced. We stood like that in a triangle and each had an arm round the other two and we were, for a moment, like one animal with three heads.

'You both! You two people—' said John exultantly. 'I don't care about *nothin'* else now.' He put his head down, first laying his cheek on Toby's head and then on mine, hugging us fiercely until we both gasped.

Chapter 3

AFTER that, things eased a little. The strain between Toby and me softened and buckled in the robust heat generated by John's uncomplicated love for us both, which fanned out on the room like the breath of a blast-furnace.

John sat on the floor between us, his feet crossed and clasped in his hands, rocking back and forth, laughing and shaking his head with delight. We exchanged a few words about nothing, but before any serious discussion could start, John, rocking and heaving as if he might soon explode with the pressure of his feelings, opened his guitar-case and began to pour it all into a sort of orgasm of music. The little room was filled with throbbing from wall to wall; again I had a drowning sensation. I caught Toby's eye over John's thrown-back head, and we exchanged a look which reverberated right through me to my loins. John and his music were generating such an atmosphere of love that the years were struck away. I saw Toby's arms begin to move as if he would cross the room and take me in them. But his face then twitched into a little grimace of realization and his hands corrected themselves, moving unsteadily to take another cigarette.

Someone knocked on the door. John stopped playing abruptly and put his head down between his knees, like someone who has jumped up from sleep too suddenly.

Toby opened the door to Hava.

'Is this a party?' she asked, her plain face modifying towards prettiness as she smiled. 'I've found a room for your friends. Can I take them there now?'

'I'll take them,' said Toby. 'Which is it?'

'Abba Yacov's old room. I've swept it out and put some sheets and blankets on the beds. You won't mind,' she added to me, 'that it's not very grand.'

We all thanked her. 'For nothing,' she said, smiled at us all again, and went out. She left something in the atmosphere behind her which made me frown. She had not looked at Toby especially, nor at me, nor had she said a word which would have led me to suppose she felt anything for him and yet – I felt it. I looked at Toby again, trying to see him through the eyes of another woman. Yes, it was unmistakable, the attractiveness . . . I remembered Billie, Melissa's mother, trampling dents in her office carpet as she paced it, half-hoping I would tell her that her instincts were right and Toby was the wrong husband for her daughter, yet forced by her woman's honesty to admit: 'He *is* attractive, little and thin and all as he is, even I can see that . . .'

'Come on,' Toby said to us.

It was good to get out in the darkness. The air felt radically different, and as soon as we were outside Toby stopped dead and moved his head this way and that. 'The *sharav*'s dropped!' he exclaimed, with the intonation of joyful relief one might use at the cessation of a bombardment. 'Thank God! Six bloody days of it we've had. I began to think it'd never stop.'

'The taxi-driver said if it went on till tomorrow, he'd murder his wife.'

'That's a local joke. On the seventh day of a *sharov*, you're not considered responsible for your actions.'

'Is that the law?'

'I'm not sure . . . It ought to be.'

We walked along the path, John in the middle, still strumming, Toby carrying the luggage.

'It's awfully pleasant here,' I remarked. The absence of that punishing wind was so marvellous I might have turned a kind eye on almost any surroundings, but in fact it *was* pleasant – the heavy grey cloud-cover had begun to show rents crammed with stars, and the little balconies outside the houses were filling up with people, come out of their inner rooms to sit in the new freshness with glasses of tea and their newspapers and radios. Several of them saluted Toby as he passed, and glanced curiously at us.

'Yes,' Toby said. 'It is. You have to live here quite a while to find out just how many advantages it has.'

'You happy here, then, Toby?' John asked.

After a moment, Toby answered 'Yes', but I sensed the qualification in it and so did John.

We came to a building which was much larger and differently shaped from the others. Toby stopped.

'This is where my daughter sleeps,' he said tentatively.

'May we see her?'

He didn't answer, but led us up the steps, across a large open porch and into a big room arranged like a classroom. Several doors led off it, and Toby opened one of them. There was only one light on, but when the door was opened it shone on to one of the three beds in the little room. Toby motioned me to go past him and pointed to this bed.

I stood still and looked down at Toby's daughter. She lay in disorder, her dark curly hair pushed back from her face, short-legged, sleeveless pyjamas crumpled, a single sheet twisted round her feet. One thin brown arm hung over the edge of the little bed; one scabby knee was drawn up almost to her chin.

'She has incredible eyes,' whispered Toby. 'Almost purple. Look at her little nose – poor Carrie inherited mine . . . and her hands . . . She's got the loveliest hands I've ever seen on a child.'

I lifted the limp hand carefully. The long, damp fingers trailed across my own palm like tentacles. They were indeed lovely, with filbert nails and wrists of extraordinary fragility. Yet the skin was rough and brown and the backs were scratched. A tom-boy's hand . . . I held it a moment longer, letting myself sense how easily those tentacle-fingers could get a grip on me . . . Toby's child who should have been mine.

'Isn't she beautiful?' said Toby, gazing at her.

'She is,' I said. 'She really is.'

'Tomorrow you'll meet her.'

He bent to kiss her. Just then from another bed came a whimper. Toby turned quickly, bent over the child, murmured a few words to it, and pulled the sheet up. 'Better cover them all, now the wind's dropped,' he said. He then proceeded to straighten all the sheets, and meticulously tuck them in – not just in Rachel's room, but in all the rooms, one by one.

'How many children sleep here?'

'Fifteen.'

'Is there no one else to cover them up?'

'Oh yes, someone will come and do it, but I'm here, so I might as well.'

'All my sons,' I murmured.

He glanced at me. 'In a way.'

We went out again into the cool night and Toby took us to our room, which was like his, only bare and drab for lack of regular occupancy. Two beds, neatly made up, and a table between them with some fruit on it, a jug of orange squash and two glasses.

'How nice of her,' I remarked.

'She's always like that,' said Toby. 'Thoughtful.'

Or is it just because we're your guests?

'Are you hungrier than this?' Toby asked.

'I'm not,' I said.

'I am,' said John.

We laughed. It was lovely to laugh again. Toby looked at me, a marvelling look which said, 'We can actually laugh!' And I nodded to him, forgetting he hadn't really spoken.

'I'll take you along to the night-watchman's kitchen and find you something. Will you be all right here, darling?'

'Of course.'

They went off together and I was left alone. And very glad to be so. My weariness returned full-force the moment they were out of the room. I looked at my watch, forgetting again that it had stopped, and my eyes fastened themselves to its small, delicate face; the hands pointed to ten minutes past two; it must have stopped just after we arrived at Hydra two days ago. *And why has it stopped, so conveniently symbolizing this hiatus in my life?* Presumably because, for the first time since Andy gave it to me, I neglected to take it off the night before our departure. The night I spent with Andy . . . Lying, as I had, with my head on his shoulder, how could I have dribbled on it? This ludicrous memory suddenly brought Andy back to me, and as he came back into focus I was terrified to realize how completely he had faded, become unsolid and unreal, since I had left him. Twice in three days I had felt some measure of desire – in Toby's case much stronger than I dared admit – for other men. The thought of it appalled me. I sat down abruptly on the hard little bed and tried to force my tired brain to get to grips with it. But I was so exhausted that only fantastic scraps and images, mainly sensual and therefore frightening, floated about behind my eyes. Where was my Puritanism now, in my hour of need? Where my good, defensive wall of middle-class upbringing, which I had so often cursed? My body seemed suddenly to have turned traitor, reaching out covetously towards sensuality and forbidden delights in every direction. I'd imprisoned it in needful chastity for too long and now, the prolonged abstinence broken, it was running wild ... From somewhere far, far back in the past, from that rep in Yorkshire where I had first met Terry, words from a play I had been in came back to me, and I flung myself down on the bed, burying snorts of half-hysterical laughter in the pillow: ''E seems to've woke up somefing inside me that keeps on *gnorrin*' ...'

It was all too much. My mind turned itself off, a relieving darkness flooded over me, and I fell asleep, quite suddenly, fully dressed, with the light on.

For a brief moment I was dragged back some time later. Toby was crouched by the bed, holding my hand.

'John's sleeping in my room,' he said. His face was very close to mine. He laid it sideways on the pillow and our noses bumped as he kissed me softly.

'I can't,' I muttered beseechingly. I felt drugged. Anything could happen; I knew it. He had only to re-enact the first night we had ever spent together – gently take away my clothes and lay himself at my side, and I would be entirely helpless to resist him.

He hesitated, so close to me that his breath, whose male smell I remembered with the deep, griping nostalgia some people feel remembering their mother's perfume, fanned my face. 'You're tired,' he whispered. 'Go to sleep. Let me just stay near you ... dearest. Dearest Jane.'

I closed my eyes. Had he said it, or was it only a memory reflection? 'When you wake up in the morning, the first thing you'll hear will be me telling you that I love you.'

As I dropped again into sleep I could still feel his breath, gentle and rhythmical, coming and going with my own.

Chapter 4

MORNING came.

He was gone.

The other bed had not been slept in. There was a chair drawn up beside my bed, and some cushions on the rug beside it, as if he had tried several positions to get through the night in reasonable comfort; now these attributes of his – what? Devotion? Nostalgia? Simple hunger? – lay abandoned, but clamouring, silent spokesmen for the past and its powerful possessive claims.

I got up. My body was heavy, but my head felt clear, as it had been the previous morning when I'd woken in the sleeping-bag on the rock overlooking the aquamarine sea after a night in the open. Then, I had joined the hippies for another swim, if possible more refreshing and delightful in the opalescent early morning light than in the pouring velvet darkness. I wondered if the salinity was still on my skin from the bathe – I had had no chance to wash it off since. I touched my arm with my tongue; it was there – rubbed off to faintness but still tangible. It tasted not merely of another country but another world, where I had been a stranger to myself, doubly so in a way – Jane Graham past, and present too, linked by the seemingly unbreakable fetter of Toby.

I stood by the little screened window and looked out across a hedge of plumbago, a lawn, past another similar low building, and away across a field of sprouting maize to some abrupt whitish hills shawled in fir-trees. The spell of the night (how powerfully affective upon the morning are the last words and images received before sleep!) was still on me; it was Toby I longed to see, my relationship with him that I felt bound, this bright, hot, clear morning, to continue. Rachel's tousled, oblivious figure was more real and compelling upon my list of compulsions today than Chris or even Andy. Even David stood aside as if to let me find my way unimpeded through this new-old labyrinth.

I stood still a long time, waiting, I think, for Toby to come back and lead me forward to the next, unforeseeable, episode. Then I took another automatic and abortive look at my watch, sighed from my depths, and wandered through the main door on to the small porch.

A tiny passage led me to another door, through which I found a little shower-room and lavatory, made dim by an unpruned jacaranda tree growing outside. I tried both taps. Cold water issued from the shower. There was some kind of oil-fired boiler on the wall, but I didn't feel up to tackling it, and in any case I was so hot and sticky that a cold shower seemed more attractive.

The icy water shocking my skin brought me out of my lethargy. I began to direct my thoughts and feelings, instead of letting them push me where they would. I hadn't brought a towel, but my skin dried by itself in the balmy air, and I put on clean clothes from the skin out. I had washed my hair too, after a fashion, and my scalp drew every breeze blowing through the room, refreshing me immeasurably. I put on some lipstick and eau-de-Cologne and looked at myself in the little mirror over the sink-basin at the end of the passage. It was too dark to see the age-lines, but still, impossible to believe Toby had been honest in saying he could see no change. I had led a quiet life, but it had not been empty of the kind of punishing feelings which age a woman, and without a proper make-up I looked to myself, even in that kindly deceptive gloom, every day of my age.

Yet I must still be desirable. There was still time to make up for the lost years – time to have another man, another relationship, another child. The thought aroused in me an immediate and urgent sexuality, so violent and unexpected that I felt the need to relieve it myself. But I hate that, even more than at the moment I hated and resented this onset of *unspecified* desire, in which, theoretically, I didn't believe. I stood leaning against the wall, pressing my thighs together. Of course everyone accepts this side of their humanity these days; all the naked apemen have done their work well in convincing us that we are what, no doubt, we are, brute beasts scarcely head and shoulders out of the swamps. One may know it; the evidence, at moments like the one I was experiencing in the dark passage, is irrefutable if accepted with honesty. But to acknowledge it is one thing. To *accede* to it, to shrug and clamber on its back and let it carry you off – that is the betrayal. For what was this trip all about, if indeed it were not a complete wild-goose chase? Was it not to discover towards whom I could honestly focus and direct myself? That was what I wanted – not merely a man, but a focus.

When I thought it might be Toby, I felt afraid. But Andy was faint, faint and far-off. The two physical encounters with him, although so recent, so important at the time, had not engaged me to him, 'grappled him to my heart with hoops of steel'. What *does* that, I wondered as I stared at myself, what grapples a man to your heart? Not just sex, not just companionship and respect, and shared laughter and 'things in common', not even an admixture of them all. Not even time. It is – and suddenly it came to me where I had learnt this, from a man now dead, whom I had loved as nearly platonically as possible – it is *pain*, troubles, unhappiness, shared struggles. That is what unites two people. Toby had been with me through the worst time of my life (and John had shared that time, which helped to explain my lasting bond with him). Andy and I had been through nothing together yet. It was an odd proof of this idea that when I *wanted* to feel really bound to Andy, my mind sprang back to one occasion – not our love-making at all, not the pleasure or the happiness, but the time when he had made me crawl away and weep. By the same token, the only moments that seemed, in retrospect, important between me and Terry, David's father, were two – the moment of straight physical pain when he ruptured me and I cried out and pulled back his head by the hair; and once again when he found me bulging with his baby and followed me and wrung his hands till his knuckles cracked, and let Toby beat him up in front of me in an immature attempt at expiation ... I had thought it ludicrous at the time, but now I looked back on it with sympathy, even poignancy. Pain is so horrible, it is the worst thing in the world. Perhaps it is the only currency in which you can buy its antithesis, love and fulfilment and pleasure, simply because it is the last coin you can willingly pay over – the most extreme for the most extreme, the worst for the best. Like childbirth. Like Sally Bowles saying 'It's absolutely right that champagne should be as expensive as it is ...'

At this point I remembered I had forgotten to clean my teeth.

I was just spitting out when Toby stepped on to the porch.

'Charming,' he said, carrying me one step backwards in his seven-year boots.

'Sorry. Very unaesthetic.'

'Oh, I don't mind. I like sharing these little intimacies. When I was a little boy, my parents were so prudish about bathrooms that even the verb "to gargle" was somehow considered rude. From their squeamishness on the subject, I suffered for several years under the supposition that married people made babies by the unthinkable intimacy of seeing each other on the loo.'

'You are funny!'

'Oh, yes. So I'm often told. It's virtually my only virtue.'

'Even if true, that would justify your membership of the human race.'

'Come on, buck me up. Tell me nobody's handed you a really good laugh in seven years.'

Oh, I've laughed, I thought, *but it hasn't been the same.* But that was too dangerous to say. I simply looked at him along the yard of dark passage and then found that was dangerous too, so I emerged as briskly as I could and said, 'I'd laugh heartier with a bite of breakfast inside me.'

'Come on then, I'll take you to our food-factory.'

We walked along the paths.

'What do you think of the place?'

'Pretty,' I said non-committally. I had detected a note of anxiety in the casual question.

'Just a dust-bowl twenty years ago, adorned with rocks and thorn-bushes.'

'And I suppose you wish you'd helped to transform it.'

'I do wish so, very much.'

'But could you have done that, do you think? I mean, is the pioneering bit really you?'

His hands were in his pockets, his head up, looking at the tops of the trees. 'I don't know. That's what I'd have liked to be sure of.'

'Then you'd never have written any books.'

'That's not certain. Some kibbutzniks are creative, I mean they've found time to be. In any case, next to what's going on here, my books all seem a bit—'

'If you dare say "trivial", I'll clout you.'

He stopped walking. 'Will you? Trivial.' He presented his ear to me provocatively.

'Oh, get away.'

Horseplay was more than I dared indulge in with him. I walked on, and he came with me.

'Seriously, that's stupid. I can understand your admiration for all this, even though I know very little about it I can see it represents a great achievement—'

'Not just geographically. Sociologically—'

'Yes, yes, yes, and all the other "allys". But a writer with your talent—'

'If *you* say "—has a responsibility to it", or any such clap-trap, *I* shall clout *you*.'

'Well, isn't it true? You've always known it yourself.'

'Values are different in different places.'

'But not in the same person, surely? I mean, your values are *your* values, in London or here or in Saskatoon, Saskatchewan.'

'Values are not values which alter where they alteration find?'

'Exactly.'

'But one can modify one's values, acquire new ones.'

'Doesn't that entirely invalidate the ones you've based your whole life on up to the time you change them?'

'Not at all. You might as well say the manners and morals of one society, on which you base your conduct when you're living in that society, become invalid if you move to another society and have to behave differently to avoid giving offence to the people there. The manners, and values, in a capitalist, urban society like London *can't* be the same as one finds in a socialist Jewish commune like this. It would be just as laughable to insist on my importance as a producer of English-language novels, which people here have never heard of and couldn't or wouldn't read anyway, as it would be to go on wearing the sort of clothes I wore in London or jingling my money in my pocket when the people here haven't any. I'm not important here because I have a facility for writing stories. My prestige, my place in this little world, if any, is based on my dubious abilities as a teacher of English, a picker of bananas, a layer of irrigation pipes, and a washer-up, once a month when it's my turn, of supper-dishes for three hundred people. Don't get me wrong. If I'd ever been a good doctor or a research scientist involved in some project vital to humanity, they'd respect me here for that as much as they would have in England. But a novelist? *Fui!*' He made a gesture of tossing something away. 'It doesn't rate. And why should it? When you stop to think about it.'

'Don't people here read?'

'Sure they do, more than most people in London. And some of them read novels. But there's no dearth of novels in the world at large, nor here in the kibbutz. Here, there are so few of us that everybody has to fill in where he's needed. Where there is a dearth. And I can see that. I can act on it. That's why I say my values have changed, that they had to change.'

'So leave this "little world", as I was interested to note you yourself call it, and go back to where your rare and special talent will be appreciated.'

'As literary talent is, so noticeably, in philistine, telly-ridden Britain?' he laughed. 'No, I don't suppose I'll go back.'

I stopped walking and stared at him.

'Never?'

'I doubt it.'

'Are you actually telling me you'll never write another book?'

'No, of course not. I'll write again, when I get completely used to the work and not tired by it. I shall write as a hobby.'

'Christ!' I burst out. 'What a waste!'

'Oh, bollocks. You talk as if I were a great writer. No. I'm quite good, at my best; shall we say I'm better than just competent. But it'd be no loss to the world of letters if I never wrote another word.'

'You're only forty. That third novel—'

'Ah, that one! You read that?' He started walking again, and gave me a little sly, nervous smile out of the sides of his eyes. 'Did you notice anything about it?'

I was silenced.

'I see you did. I meant you to. I couldn't openly dedicate it to you, but I did much more. I exploited you.'

After a moment he said, 'Let's not go in to breakfast yet, the dining-hall is so noisy and unprivate. Let's sit here.' We sat on a stone wall. People were passing us, most of them in working clothes, but apart from a few smiles and greetings they didn't impinge. Toby sat quietly, looking out across the main lawn. I noticed a new tranquillity about him; he had always used to be so restless and nervy. After a while he said: 'Please indulge me. Tell me about – your personal feelings about that book.'

I stared at him. Last night, in the first shock of seeing me, he had verged on telling me some fundamental truth about his feelings.

Now I, in the calm of morning, clean and rested, even relaxed, felt some such moment of truth pressing for outlet inside me. But what is the truth, ever, about anything? Every truth bears the seeds of its own antithesis.

'I felt it was a secret message in code.'

I saw his shoulders slump a little; he closed his eyes and smiled. 'I knew it. I knew you'd get it. And did you – decode it?'

'I thought I had. But when you – when I heard about the divorce and you didn't – you know, contact me, I decided I must have been using the wrong cypher.'

'No. You weren't. Something happened to me about the divorce. You know I said to you once – that awful time, the last time I ever saw you, when you came to my flat in Earls Court with John – that one could love two women at once. I did love Whistler. I love her still. She's the sweetest girl, Jane, I swear no one could help loving her, that's why what's happened is so horrible – I'm so afraid that by taking advantage of what she offered me, in her ignorance and innocence, I've damaged her for ever. I feel so appallingly guilty about her. All the time; now, too, when it's supposedly over. I still have dreams of the most primitive kinds, in which all my limbs, my fingers and toes, swell and become heavy and gross and I'm some kind of prehistoric monster, shuffling about and grunting and screeching, catching birds out of the sky and tearing them to pieces, trampling with my great grey ugly feet on little white flowers . . . When she was going to have Rachel she wanted me to be with her, to share it, so we arranged it. She'd done all the preparation and I'd helped her, and she'd believed every word of those lying books and wasn't the least bit frightened – she thought it was going to be a beautiful, elevating experience that we could have together, and she was expecting to sail through it, "breasting the pains like a galleon" she said.' He turned his head away. 'It was ghastly . . . She'd never really been physically hurt before. She tried so hard, but it was too much for her; she started screaming almost at the beginning, and the bloody nurse was so cross with her, telling her briskly to be a brave girl and that there was nothing to make a fuss about yet . . . I tried to help, but it was like holding her hand while she was lying on a rack. I'm not exaggerating. A nightmare . . . She couldn't love me for ages afterwards, and when she did it was never the same.

Carrie was a complete accident. When Whistler realized she was pregnant again she left me and went to Billie. She was hysterical, she said she wouldn't go through that again for anyone. I wanted her to have an abortion but Billie dissuaded her, only by promising to find her a doctor who'd agree to put her out altogether during the birth. In the event she was so tense she had to have a Caesarian anyway. And that was another thing, that scar. She minded so desperately she'd never run around naked after that, the way she used to. The whole business ruined the one thing we had, the physical thing which had been so nearly perfect.' He glanced at me, frowning. 'Do you mind about that?' he asked suddenly.

'That you were happy in bed with some other woman? No, of course not.' Then I realized there was another truth buried in that one, and added, 'I mean, yes, of course. It depends what level I happen to be on.'

He looked at me steadily and shook his head a little. 'You—' he said. 'You really are *the most* extraordinary ...' He broke off. 'What was I talking about?'

'The divorce.'

'Well. By the time it came to the point, I'd felt I'd done her so much damage already that I thought it would be comparatively painless, I mean like letting some poor creature you've broken go free.'

'Really, Toby,' I couldn't help interrupting with some impatience. 'I can't help feeling you're overdoing the *mea-culpa* a bit. Some of it must have been her.'

'I don't think so ...' he said. 'Just *years* are so large a factor in this sort of thing. If one partner is really much older than the other, he's got to accept more responsibility.'

'But if it was simply, even mainly, the business of childbirth, I mean that wasn't your fault at all.'

'Oh, but it was much more than that! It was me writing and me not being patient with her youngness, and – let's face it – me marrying her in the first place when all the time—' He reached out abruptly without looking at me and gripped my wrist, as suddenly taking his hand away. 'It was greed, sheer blind masculine greed, and conceit to think I could overcome everything that was obviously wrong with it and make her happy.'

'Toby, honestly—'

'No, don't try to make me feel better about it. Billie, of all people, has tried, but only I really know. I lived through it, I watched it happen ... Anyway, the divorce. It wasn't the way I'd expected at all. It was as if the prisoner didn't want to be freed. She clung to the bars and had to be dragged out screaming ...'

She seems, I thought grimly, to have done a fair amount of screaming, one way and another. I was having to fight against an ignoble desire to kick Whistler squarely in the pants.

'The whole thing was a mistake, we'd both suffered a great deal, and it was clear to both of us that we had to get divorced. I mean, she did agree to it wholeheartedly, I think it was even her suggestion in the first place, but when it came to it I suppose she was frightened. Lousy husband though I'd been, it was still better than loneliness. And one thing I had been, to do myself justice, was fairly good with the kids, and she was terrified of being left on her own with them. That was why she agreed to let me have Rachel, even to bring her here. She always loved Carrie best, because Carrie didn't torture her getting born.'

The ignobility took another leap forward. Silly babyish little bitch, I thought fiercely. I did try to make myself feel as sorry for her as Toby clearly thought I should, but I couldn't. After all, she was no longer a child-bride exactly, she should have been able to come to terms with some of it. Of course it's sheer nonsense to say you forget about the pangs of childbirth as soon as they've come to a successful end. I still clearly recall how much it hurt having David, but for God's sake you don't blame the baby unless you're a howling neurotic.

'So the divorce, instead of relieving me a little, made me feel worse than ever. She was making reconciliation noises right up until the last moment in court, and I was very tempted; I mean, what can you do when the person you love is holding on to you and crying and pleading with you not to leave her, even when you know perfectly well ...' He groped in his pocket for cigarettes. He was trembling. 'We'll miss breakfast if we don't go in,' he said unsteadily. 'Anyhow, to cut a long story short, I held out because I was so sure it would damage her more in the long run to go on living with me. But that scene in the court was harrowing. I couldn't think about you without a sense of panic; it seemed as if everything I touched emotionally I harmed, and I wasn't going to harm you. But I thought about you, Jane. I thought about you. Did you feel me thinking about you?'

I nodded. His eyes as he looked at me were stark.

'I've always been thinking about you,' he said.

And I of you, my own love, I thought. And why don't I say it now, and put the despair out of your eyes? What is holding me back? Andy is nowhere; here we are, Jane and Toby, looking into each other's minds and memories, feeling the weight of the old love laid on us again, and yet I can't bring words of commitment to my lips . . . Perhaps it's the feeling of a crushing burden, a millstone instead of a blessing, hopeless sadness instead of joy. What is it, what's wrong? It's not what has happened in the intervening years, I'm not afraid any more to tell you I've had other men, for they whirl away into oblivion when I look at you like this; it's the years themselves somehow, the length of time. Our lives have formed an ellipse around that space, and now they are touching again it feels as if the shape of our separation were driving a wedge between us for ever.

And yet I love you, have loved you and will always love you. And you will always love me. I bought my independence, and you your marriage, with an open-ended mortgage upon each other's happiness, which neither one of us will ever quite pay off.

We had breakfast in the big, noisy, bustling dining-hall; we didn't talk much because there were two other people sitting at table with us, one of whom had a lot to say to Toby in Hebrew. John, we were told, had had breakfast hours ago and gone off somewhere.

'Looking for some more noise, I expect,' I said.

'More than in here?'

'How do you manage about that side of it?'

' "My dear, the noise, the people?" Oh, it's not so bad. I quite like noise and people, provided I can shut them out when I want to.'

'And can you? Do you?'

'Yes.'

I noticed several people carried transistors. At eight o'clock (I was astonished it was still only that – the heat must have woken me unwontedly early) a complete hush fell on the room; even the people pushing the serving trolleys stopped wherever they were near a radio and listened as a woman's voice read the news. Through the windows, too, you could see little groups bent over something in their midst. The tension in the air was tangible, and nobody moved for five minutes. Then it was over; as if released from a spell, everything went back to normal.

'What gives?' I asked.

'My Hebrew isn't good enough to understand much,' said Toby. 'Just about enough to know you shouldn't be here.'

'No, seriously – what's happening?'

'Seriously – I think you ought to go home. Later you may not be able to.'

My heart jumped. 'Why not?'

'Ordinary passenger services are usually disrupted by a war.'

'But there's no war yet.'

'There will be.'

'Is that sure?'

He shrugged. 'What's sure? Everyone says so. When two dogs stand growling nose to nose with their hackles up and a bone between them, the chances are they're going to fight.'

'You sound very blasé about it.'

'You know me better than to believe that. I'm scared witless.'

'*Can't* you leave?'

He shook his head. 'I've enough on my conscience without adding cowardice.'

'But Rachel.'

'That reminds me, you haven't seen her awake. Come on, let's go and visit her. It's Saturday, so I don't have to work, and we can take her home.'

We found Rachel playing in her children's-house playroom. She was wearing an unironed sleeveless shirt scooped out on her brown neck, and crumpled blue shorts. Her feet were bare, and her brown hair, very glossy, was caught up in a pony-tail. Her skin was dark brown, her eyes dark blue; as she saw Toby and a smile broke up the smooth lines of her face, one saw that her mouth was in that peculiarly touching stage of vulnerable toothlessness. It marred her looks and made me want to grab her and thrust her behind me, save her from the kicks in those budding teeth she would inevitably receive from life in due course.

Toby hugged her, and she him. Then she said, 'How's the war, Daddy?'

The hug, the name, the sight of her, the sound of her voice, all provided me with one of those classic kicks in the teeth I had just wanted to protect her from. I winced visibly. Luckily no one was looking.

'Not here yet. Have you had a shelter-drill this morning?'

'Yes, right away when we woke up. It's fun down there, but it gets hot when we're all in.'

Toby turned her round to face me, holding her bird-boned shoulders.

'This is Jane. Jane, my daughter, Rachel.'

We looked at each other and I smiled. You little beauty I thought. What would you have looked like if you'd been half mine? I put out my hand and she put her left one into it.

'I hurt my hand for shaking with,' she said.

'How?'

She showed me a bandage.

'Playing with the *patish*.'

'The hammer,' Toby explained. 'Hebrew is beginning to overtake English.'

'Do you want to see what I made?'

She went to a sort of carpentry bench and brought back some bits of wood nailed together into a very creditable boat.

'That's lovely.'

'It's the boat we came to Israel on,' she said. 'Have you any children?'

I looked at Toby over her head. 'A little boy. He's eight.'

'I'm seven. Nearly.'

'Are you?'

'Are you our visitor?'

'Yes.'

'Can we show her the swimming-pool, Daddy?'

'Of course.' He was smiling straight into my eyes, signalling to me: isn't she perfect? The strained look was all gone; his hands on her shoulders were still and sure.

I went back to my room to change, and there I found John, sitting on the grass outside under the jacaranda tree tuning his guitar. He looked up at me and grinned, one-sidedly.

'How's it feel to be back again with Toby?' he asked without preamble.

'I still love him. But it's not simple.'

'Was it ever?'

'How are you feeling?'

He lowered his head. 'A bit more like before. Better, I mean. Toby . . . seein' Toby helped. I still love him too, and that *is* simple. It heals you when you're with a person you love.'

'It didn't help you to be with me.'

'Ah Janie, but you a woman.'

I was silenced by the sudden sadness in his voice. Out of respect for it, and a sense of my own incapacity in this situation, I sat down beside him and we didn't say anything for about five minutes. Only his guitar spoke, a-harmonious, melancholy notes and chords and sometimes weird thin ghostly shrieks as he ran his hard thumb straight up the wires to the keys at the top.

'I decided something,' John said at last. 'I going to find myself a man. Someone who's like me. If you a freak, you need another freak. I'm tired of tryin' to act like anybody. I'm *different*. I can't help it. I tried to, but I can't. I'm goin' to find me a person to love.'

'That makes two of us,' I said. 'Do you want to come swimming?'

The pool, scooped out of the top of a hillock, was like a huge square-cut aquamarine surrounded by a mass of brilliant shrubs that must, from the air, look like a setting of gem-stones. From the air . . . I stared up uneasily into the mysterious unlimited sky. Accustomed as I was to a vision-impeding lid of clouds, this blue infinity called for the deepest focus my eyes were capable of. Lying back like this, staring upwards, one hand cupping the side of my head to hold out the spears of sunlight, I could get lost in that topless blue; it seemed to suck me upwards into itself . . . And strangely, there was a sense of safety in that emptiness, for if there were a bomber, there would be nothing to hide it. But of course this was nonsense. Even as I thought it, a pair of black delta-winged shapes darted from nowhere and tore straight across the sky, followed by

186

an ear-splitting noise between a scream and a roar, as if someone were tearing the very fabric of heaven savagely in half. I glanced round, wincing at the pain in my ears, but no one else seemed to have noticed. Only Toby looked down at me, saw my grimace and said. 'That's our umbrella. It functions twenty-four hours a day.'

'Pretty noisy umbrella,' I commented.

'Better than getting rained on. You've still got a glorious figure.'

'*Me?*' I said, genuinely surprised. If a flat belly and reasonable bust constitute a glorious figure, then I've got one; but I've also got thick legs and duck's disease.

'I don't think I've ever seen you in a bathing suit before.'

'What do you mean, you don't think? Of course you haven't, how could you?' I had been either pregnant or winter-bound (not to mention nursing) every time we had been together.

'Can you swim?' he asked.

'Yes. Can you?'

He looked ashamed. 'No.'

'Lots of men can't.'

'I've never met any. Certainly there's not a male here over the age of four who can't.'

'Would you like me to teach you?'

He was looking at me. 'I want to learn, but . . . no, I'd be embarrassed. There are too many people here.'

'Can't we come up sometime when there's no one here?'

'I might borrow the key from the gardener. Look at my daughter.'

I lifted myself on my elbow. The pool was alive with people. You never saw a scene less easy to reconcile with a country on the brink of a desperate war. I searched for any sign of it, for it seemed incredible to me . . . I knew from old newsreels I'd seen on TV that the British had gone on enjoying themselves in an apparently normal and carefree fashion right up to September 3rd, 1939, but this spectacle of holiday abandon in front of me didn't seem real, somehow. There were transistors, unobtrusively set amid the rumpled bright towels and picnic baskets; the jets ripping overhead from time to time; and, if you looked closely, you noticed a scarcity of young men. But nothing, nothing at all in the atmosphere betrayed the least tension or alarm.

Toby was pointing. I saw Rachel now, in a blue bathing-suit, the straps tied together on her back with a wet hair-ribbon to keep them from slipping off her thin shoulders, poised on the diving-board. Her hair was plastered to her head; she had a seal-look, sleek and dark and so confident that her dive was careless and she side-slipped into the water. I expected her to rise up again with a silver fish in her mouth.

'I love to watch her swimming,' said Toby. 'It's miraculous to me, a child of mine swimming like that, so effortlessly . . . yet she's different here – rougher – she was always so delicate and feminine at home, like a doll . . .'

'Toby . . .'

'H'm?' He was still watching her, and had forgotten me for the moment.

'Let me take her back for you.'

His eyes returned to me slowly. 'Take her back? To Whistler?'

'Or Billie.'

'Darling, Billie's no good with the kids. She's the most un-grandmotherly Jewish grandmother I've ever known. She hasn't the time nor the temperament.'

'Well, to Whistler then.'

He didn't answer at once. His eyes had returned to the black head streaking through the green water. 'I wish she wouldn't yell like that, I always think she's drowning or something. She was such a little mouse in London . . . I think Whistler's got enough on her plate with Carrie. She . . .' He hesitated. 'She was sometimes unkind to Rachel. She favours Carrie, as I told you. When she's got them both together, Rachel gets the scrawny end of the chicken a bit.'

'Just while – I mean, until the trouble here blows over.'

'That may not be for a very long time.'

'Surely you don't mean it'll be a long war?'

'No, I think it'll be over very quickly – one way or the other.'

'Well, then?'

'I meant, there'll always be trouble here, of varying magnitudes. Another thing is that if I send Rachel away now, when none of the others are sending their kids out, I shall be putting myself on a different footing from them.'

'Toby,' I said with the same impatience – almost irritability – I had felt before when he was beating his breast over the Whistler mess, 'I don't understand you. Are you really saying those considerations count for more than her safety?'

Toby lay back on his towel and put his forearm over his eyes. He was silent for a long time; the shouts from the pool seemed to eddy round his silence while I waited for it to end.

'Would *you* take her?' he asked at last.

I couldn't speak for surprise – shock. I had never dreamed of this.

'You can't possibly be serious.'

'Why not?'

'What would her mother feel? What would Billie?'

'I can't answer for Billie, but I should imagine Whistler would be greatly relieved. Naturally she's worried; at the same time, she's frightened by the thought that she might have to have Rachel with her, accept sole responsibility for the two of them. I can't impose that on her. It would be terrible for Rachel. She . . .' He glanced at me darkly from under his arm and then hid his eyes again. 'The plain truth is, she doesn't like her mother very much. As for Billie, her pride might be hurt, but she must realize she can't really undertake it. After all, she works full time, she'd have to get someone in to look after her. And you – well, you're all geared up to look after children. Couldn't she muck in with David for the time being? She's absolutely no trouble as long as she's happy.'

I could hardly believe my ears.

'And what makes you think she *would* be – away from you?'

'Do you see this suggestion in the light of a diabolical liberty?'

'Yes – frankly.'

'Well, I suppose it is. But it's you that keeps pressing me to get her out. And I just can't think of any other solution.'

'When did you think of this one?'

'Last night, as a matter of fact – when I was sitting beside your bed.'

I sat still, trying to think, but the jets going overhead howled down thought.

John, glossy as a sea-lion, rose and waved from the water. I waved back.

'I'm going in,' I said shortly to Toby.

As I stood up, he caught my wrist.

'If you really don't want to, never mind. I'm prepared to keep her here and take a chance. It's up to you.'

Hell's bloody bells, I thought as I pulled free of him and ran down to the pool. Why does it always have to be up to *me*?

Toby came knocking on my door in the heat of the day.

'I've got the key – you promised me a swimming lesson. Come on.'

I didn't want to. My mind and body craved sleep; I was worn out mentally from all the thinking and feeling involved in this situation. At lunch-time I had walked down the hill from the pool hand-in-hand with Rachel, watching her hair jump into curls again as it dried. Her hand had felt different from David's, strong in its grip but still feminine and a little unsure. Once she had left my side to run into a small enclosure we passed, to investigate some ducklings. Returning, she had not taken the initiative, but let her shoulder rub as if incidentally against my arm, waiting to see if I would take her hand again. When I did, she glanced up at me, and although her eyes were so entirely different from Toby's, I saw him in her face for a second, a little shy, a little *sly*, sure and unsure at once, child and woman together, as Toby was child and man.

I had felt suddenly endangered by her, and had made an excuse to break the contact between us. She had instantly run on ahead, seeming not to care, but I sensed a hyper-sensitivity in her which did care quite exaggeratedly about everything touching on people's feelings for her. If it were true that she and her mother . . . But I refused to let my mind stray in that direction, for fear pity might take me in its unbalancing grip.

Despite my unease and the disturbances going on inside me, I had eaten (as indeed I always do, short of some absolute cataclysm) with rapacious appetite, and now I was flaked out on my bed, already half comatose. But Toby was insistent.

'Do please come. There may not be another opportunity.'

I struggled up and put on my bathing-suit (already bone-dry) while he waited outside on the lawn. I slipped on a cotton dress and stepped outside.

The sun was really almost unendurable now, pounding down out of the ruthless sky. The light was as hard on the eyes as the scream of the jets was upon the ears, and there was no respite from it other than passing under the occasional tree.

'The heat's unbearable,' I said, scarcely able to drag my feet along the hot tarmac paths. The tar was liquefying, and my rubber sandals kept sticking to it.

'I like it,' he said. 'It's sort of purifying. You keep pouring water into yourself and almost at once it seems to flow out of all your pores.'

I prickled and sweated and felt a headache coming on. I wished to God I'd got some sun glasses.

'Have you thought any more about – anything?' he asked as we reached the wrought-iron gates of the pool.

'I can't think in this heat,' I said irritably.

But as soon as the water closed over my head, I felt instantly and miraculously better. I swam around awhile, enjoying the sensation of sudden freedom from heat which was the nearest thing to bliss on earth that I could imagine at that moment. My mind went back to Chris, and I blew a kiss to him in my thoughts. If only we were just bodies! Sometimes I felt as if we were. Walking up here, I had been overwhelmed by discomfort, my brain incapable of working; now I was saturated in a contrasting sensation, but still nothing seemed to be moving in my head.

Toby stood in the shallow end waiting.

I squinted down the glittering expanse of turquoise water at him. The top part of his body only was visible. His torso was brown and he had filled out a little since I had known him so intimately that my hands could recreate, even when apart from him, the sensation of touching every part of him. Even now . . . Concealed beneath the water, my hands moved, recovering the feel of his thinly-covered ribs, the elliptical bulge of his shoulder-muscle, the flat planes of his back, and especially the soft teddy-bear fuzz on the back of his neck. And although we were separated by yards of water, I could feel his touch on me . . . I shivered as I trod water, gazing at him with eyes narrowed against the glare, and he gazed back at me.

He raised his arm, and a bright stream of drops caught the sun like a spilling of fire as he beckoned to me.

I swam slowly and luxuriously towards him. An electric-blue dragonfly skittered by across the surface. I could smell the chlorine in the water mixed incongruously with the scent of the flowering shrubs – not a sweet perfume at all, but sharp and startling like carnations. As I drew near to him, Toby suddenly knelt down on the bottom of the pool and putting out his hands, caught mine and pulled me gently towards him. Our limbs floated effortlessly, mindless and sensuous as strands of water-weed, and got entangled with each other.

He kissed me. The sun fell on us. The kiss mingled with the heat and the strong odours and created something like an explosion in my head.

Floating in his arms, drifting, my roots washed free of the earth and nourished by the water, I was content to return to this old, natural, simple haven. The pool water and the water of our tongues mingled, dried in the sun; we put our faces under the surface to renew it, and laughed bubblingly into each other's eyes and mouths through the cool alien element, surfacing in the midst of a kiss.

'Your lesson,' I murmured. But his hands closed firmly on my arms.

'No humiliations,' he answered. 'Let's do something I can do.'

We rose with a cool swishing sound and walked to the broad steps, up them slowly, and then down we came on to our towels on the bank of spiky grass. A young birch-tree dappled our bodies with shadow. I looked around once. Swallows were diving over the water, now glassy smooth. Apart from their cries, and the far-distant purring of a tractor amid a cloud of dust, there was not a sound. The red roofs of the kibbutz lay in the valley below like dolls' houses, uninhabitable by real people who might have to be considered. With all his old tender adroitness, Toby was peeling away my swimsuit. His fingers traced the winding paths that David's milk had stretched on my breasts. Now his lips were fastened where David's had been, with a different, sharper sweetness, and yet – allied, so that I remembered the joy of feeding the baby, just as, while feeding him, I had remembered this.

He lay full length beside me and held me close to him, murmuring to me all the old endearments, some of which I had forgotten. I lay passively, waiting for it to happen, feeling that it was quite inevitable, that here, in this act, lay some kind of magical answer. This accomplished, the nature of all our problems would be clarified; the daily dross would be changed to gold; the snags and tangles would be combed out silky and smooth, like flax, to be woven into a practical, useable length of cloth from which we could cut a brand-new garment, tailor-made to fit our lives and cover up all the old sores.

He stroked and caressed me. We kissed again and again, our hands and eyes and mouths mutually refamiliarizing themselves ... It was lovely. He said so: 'This is so lovely.' It went on like that for a long time. And I began to think, 'Well, when is he going to do it?' And with that thought, I knew, quite suddenly, that he was never going to do it, because he wouldn't ultimately be able to.

Which of us communicated the knowledge to the other, I don't know, but a few seconds later he stopped perfectly still for a moment, began again, half-heartedly, and then abruptly rolled away from me and lay on his back, one arm over his eyes as before, the other hand holding mine. His thumb moved, stiffly, thoughtfully, bemusedly, rubbing back and forth along one bone in my hand.

'What is it?' – although I knew.

'I don't know' – although he did.

We lay like that, still and silent, until it became intolerable. Then he sat up with a sudden, jerky movement, letting go of my hand.

'I don't get this,' he said harshly. 'Am I incapable suddenly, or what?'

'Of course you're not.'

'Then what the hell happened? It all went dead. All of a sudden, I could no more have made love to you than to—'

'To a shadow?' He turned to look at me sharply over his shoulder. His expression was stricken; his eyebrows were raised at the outer ends and strong, hard, angry lines of bewilderment and confusion had appeared on his forehead.

'But I want you!' he almost shouted. 'I do want you! I've wanted you all these years. And now we have it, just look at it – what could be more perfect? And I can't. I can't!' His voice cracked upwards harshly, just as a Mirage wrenched the sky apart over our heads, destroying the illusion of peace.

'It's not only you. I can't either,' I said.

'But *why*?' he demanded.

I couldn't meet his eyes, they were so full of anguish. It was as if he'd begun, very suddenly, to suffer what I suffered seven years ago when I found out I'd lost him. I couldn't bear to think of him having to go through that; I remembered its pain too clearly.

'It's too late.'

'Too late? It can't be too late! Are you in love with someone else?' he asked, in a suddenly altered voice.

'I don't know. There is someone else, but it isn't that, not at this moment. For the past twelve hours I've been expecting this, us, to cancel all that out, I thought it was much stronger. But there's something else against us.'

'What? What is it?'

I sighed heavily. There seemed to be heavy weights of sorrow pressing on my chest.

'Perhaps it's just – time.'

'Fuck that!' he said furiously. 'I love you as much as ever.'

'Me, as I am now? In seven years every cell in one's body is renewed. And a lot changes besides.'

'You haven't changed.'

'It seems I must have. Our bodies know. With our minds we wanted to come together, we were striving to, but when it came to the crunch, we went dead. Both of us. We're – dead to each other.'

With that, something rose in my throat and I began to cry. He held me in his arms like a child and we clung desperately together. I cried in great sobs, as I hadn't cried for many years, and he didn't comfort me but just held me hard until my crying stopped.

Then he let me go.

We sat there, side by side, for what seemed like hours. The swallows swooped for the dragon-flies and the planes periodically raped the stillness; the sun flushed the moisture from our bodies, and the aqua water mirrored the pale blue, the orange, the hibiscus-red of the shrubs. The whole setting was, as he had said, perfection, and we sat in the midst of it like toads in the mud of our misery.

At last he stirred.

'I knew it really,' he said, and in his voice was such a tiredness as one might expect after a long, hard exertion of strength. 'I knew it last night, when I first saw you. I nearly said it to you then, and then I thought, no, give it a chance. Because part of my illusion was true. We have belonged together all these long, blood-stained years, just as I always knew. But you're right. It is too late. Because love's a thread that time draws thinner and thinner. It still carries one's life's blood but after a while it's just not strong enough to do any good any more. Not strong enough to hold two people together, or to support either one of them as an individual.' He turned his face right away from me, towards the hills. 'I held you in my arms just now, and your body was as dear to me as ever, but just the same – it was like holding, not a shadow, but a legend. It's not real, and you're not real to me *in the flesh* any more. Only the dream-Jane that I've created to replace you has any validity in my life.'

And suddenly I knew a truth about him that I had never let myself realize till then. The dream would always be more valid to him than the reality. It had all happened before. His leaving me alone in the L-shaped room because life and its demands were pressing him too hard. His staying in London after David's birth instead of following me, being a stayer, a real, sustaining lover to me, and then later, blaming me for not *insisting*. *He* should have insisted. Then marrying Whistler, when, as he said now, he *knew* ... because Whistler was a dream-girl, young, beautiful, rich, innocent, passionately loving and giving – a changeling, a fairy, a chimera, a will-o'-the-wisp, dancing invitingly before him across the bog. Only through his writing, which is a form of dreaming, had he ever been able to fasten himself to reality. As for me – I and my situation had always been too earthy and too demanding for him. The 'dream-Jane' was the real one to him. No wonder he'd been afraid to come into actual contact with me when at last he was free. He had not been afraid so much of harming me, as of bringing himself once more face-to-face with the need to become fully adult.

It all fitted – even his flight to the kibbutz, supposedly in search of some ephemeral concept of Jewishness and personal integrity, but actually, surely, a simple need to escape into a valley of non-decision. Perhaps Rachel, with her almost angelic beauty, had only begun to seem real to him here – here where she grew brown and tomboyish, scratching her knees and raising her voice and dirtying her clothes, turning into a real child. And now, I thought suddenly, he is trying to wish her off on to me ...

But this moment of harsh revelation did not stop me loving him. I looked at him now, naked and vulnerable, robbed of his dream by that cruel, lie-detecting instrument between his thighs, which, being the essence and symbol of all that is male and human and physical, had refused to perform upon a myth. And I pitied him with my whole heart, and loved him too, if one can love and pity a man at the same time, which till then I'd always doubted. I reached out and touched him, and he turned, and knelt beside me and stroked my hands, gazing into my face.

'You'll never be able to share with me what I've felt these last years,' he said. 'Even if you wanted to, you could never heal over a single one of the wounds I've collected. And I can't heal yours. Least of all the ones I caused . . . That's what separates us for ever.'

He put his head down in my lap in that most touching, because most child-like, posture a man can put himself in, pressing his face into my hands which he gripped tightly with his.

'Jane? Jane?'

His voice was absolutely beyond help, the voice of a man who doesn't even call out loudly any more because he knows he can't be heard, but speaks his plea quietly, for his own ears alone.

INTERLUDE
JOHN

Chapter 1

I FOUND John asleep on the second bed in my room. He lay flat out on his stomach, overlapping the little iron bedstead all round, both hands trailing, legs stretched out beyond the end of the bed from the middle of his shins. Big beads of sweat stood out on his shoulders, and as I looked, one drop joined another and they ran together in a rivulet down the channel in his back.

I touched him and my fingers came away wet.

'John,' I said. 'Can you wake up?'

He grunted and rolled over. 'Ugh, I'm all stickin',' he complained. 'I don't like this heat, 'cept when I swimmin'.'

'Me neither. Shall we go home?'

He sat up, peering at me.

'You all finished here?' he asked sharply.

'Yes.'

He opened his mouth and then shut it again. He stared at me a long time. He wouldn't ask, but I had to answer.

'It's no use, John. We've gone too far away from each other.'

He put his feet on the floor and sat with his head down, looking into the palms of his hands.

'Then it's all over.'

'Yes, in the way you mean.'

He stood up and walked to the window, his enormous shoulders blotting out most of the light.

'You know what I think,' he said suddenly. 'This whole world is just a ball of shit. Nothin' ever goes the way you want it to. Don't matter how you try, how much you hope or deserve the best, it all go wrong just the same. Sometimes I like to just get out of it, run away from the world completely.' He turned round, all in silhouette against the bright afternoon window. 'You don't know how I hoped about you two people. How I was *sure*. Sure it come right in the end. Lucky I ain't got a gun this minute, I think I just shoot myself, have done with it.'

'John, don't talk like that!' I was shocked by the violent despair in his voice. 'It's bad enough without *you* being unhappy about it.'

'Didn't you know I would be?'

I didn't answer. The truth was I hadn't been thinking of him at all.

'To make me better from what happen to me,' he said bitterly, 'I need something good to happen to my friends. But ain't nothin' good ever goin' to happen. I hate this lousy hot place,' he almost shouted with peevish fury. 'Let's get out of here at least and get to where the sweat ain't runnin' in our eyes all the time!'

'Yes,' I said. 'We're going. I've just rung up the airport. All the planes are fully booked, we have to just go there and sit around till there's a free place.'

'You mean, we going to try to get home today?'

'Why not? There's nothing to stay for. Besides, there's a war on its way.'

'But what about all those other things you had to do? The things for your friend and the shop?'

Christ! I'd forgotten. Everything. What indeed about all that lovely leather and filigree and – what else was it Jo had told me to investigate? Silver belts? I could almost have begun to laugh.

'Thanks for reminding me. But it's Saturday. That's the Jewish sabbath. Everything's shut.'

'Then we wait till tomorrow. Hell, we only got here last night!'

'But what about the war?'

'I don't see no signs of no war.'

'And I thought you were in such a hurry to get back?'

'I ain't intendin' to get back to England and then have you turn around and say, how could you let me forget to do all them things I promised? I ain't been much use on this trip so far, I got to do somethin' to help you.'

'Oh God! I can't be bothered. I just can't, John. The shop and all that, it seems so far away . . . besides, imagine tramping the streets of a city in this heat, looking for workshops and trying to make contact with people who only speak this weird language . . . Hell, I can't, I simply cannot do it.'

He came and put his arm round me. His volatile anger seemed to have died away as suddenly as it had blown up. He put his head down to mine tenderly and said, in the almost fatherly tone he sometimes used when he felt I needed it, 'Look, Janie. I sorry for what I said, it was just me being a child who got disappointed. Now you got to forget all that happened on this trip, because this ain't your real life. Your real life is at home, and very soon you be back there, and then it's here, all this, and the island, that will seem far away. You got to do what else you come here for, or later you goin' to be very sorry and ashamed. You got a business, that business keep you and David, and your friend Jo, even if I don't like her so much, she and you is partners and you got to do what you promised. Anyway, it'll help you to feel better about Toby, if you get to work and start thinkin' about your real life you goin' back to. If you start puttin' your eyes ahead of you, instead of behind. It help me too.'

He moved away from me and started to put the few things he'd taken out of his duffle-bag back into it again. I knew he was perfectly right and that soon his words would take effect, giving me back my will and energy; but for the moment I just stood still and stared out of the window at those chalky, pine-clad hills, beginning to go pink in the evening light. There was a hollowness in me that was hard to fill again with saving routine purposefulness and activity. Something very precious to me had gone and would never come back, and the loss of it, barely grasped yet, was as radical to my life as a missing limb or a whole section of my mind deadened by a violent electric shock.

Would Andy fill up that emptiness when I returned? Something would have to, for it was a vacuum which was already sucking at the fullness of my life around it, trying to fill itself up. And as I thought about this, I felt the beginnings of relief. I knew, suddenly, that part of the bill had already been paid. All that suffering I had done when Toby married, that was on account for this moment. I was in credit. One could not go through all that twice for the same person, any more than you can mourn twice for the same death.

I went up to the kibbutz office once again and telephoned a hotel in Tel-Aviv, booking two rooms for the night. All of a sudden, they had plenty. On impulse I rang up the British Embassy in Tel-Aviv. As the number began to ring, I almost hung up, remembering it was Saturday and they would not be open. But they were.

'British Embassy, good afternoon,' said a cool, correct English voice.

'I'm visiting Israel briefly on business. Could you advise me whether to stay a few more days, or—'

'The only advice I can give you is the advice I've been instructed to give all British citizens who telephone. Get out as fast as you can.'

I was taken aback. The cool voice and the terse injunction did not match.

'Is the situation that serious?'

'We can't make any comment on the international situation, Madam. We can only warn you that the Embassy cannot guarantee help to anyone who ignores our advice to leave immediately. If your business obliges you to stay beyond tomorrow, you'll be on your own. Our advice then is to keep your belongings packed, and some food, but you will probably not be able to take more than you can carry, because the transport, if any, will be emergency transport. No scheduled flights can be expected after war breaks out.'

'When is it expected to break out?'

'I can't say, Madam.'

'No, I suppose not . . . Well, thank you very much.'

'A pleasure. Good afternoon.'

I shivered in the sweltering heat of the wooden office. The secretary of the kibbutz, a little fat man with a bald head, smiled at me, shook his head, and lifted his shoulders in a shrug. I took the card my villainous driver had given me and dialled his number.

'Sorry, lady. All that way out there, and back into town? No, not even for a hundred lira. Something could start any time. I want to be near home.'

'You're trying to get a car?' the secretary asked me. I nodded. 'Someone from the kibbutz is driving to town in about one hour. Perhaps he has place. I will ask.'

One hour . . .

I told John, and then went to Toby's room. I stood outside for a long time in the shadow of the open porch. My hand just wouldn't obey me and knock on the door. At last he heard the creak of a board, I suppose, and came out. We stood there looking at each other in the semi-darkness.

'You're leaving,' he said at last.

'Yes.'

'Going straight back?'

'I haven't decided. We'll spend tonight in this Hotel Yarden I've found. Then tomorrow I'll make up my mind. I'd meant to do some business in Tel-Aviv and Jerusalem, but the war-situation looks so threatening, perhaps I ought not to hang around.'

'Of course not,' he said flatly. 'It's not your fight.'

'Is it yours?'

'Something's got to be,' he said oddly. And then: 'What about Rachel?'

I hesitated. 'What about her?'

He straightened away from the door-jamb where he'd been leaning as if tired. 'I wish to God you would take her,' he said unexpectedly.

'But Toby, it's absolute madness! You must know it is. She wouldn't come with me.'

'She'll do what I tell her.'

'But – but – what if anything—'

'What if anything happens to me?' He sounded indifferent to the point of coldness. 'It won't. Unless the country's actually over-run we're not in much danger here. But I want – I'd *like* you to have her. If only for a little while. I want you to know her. In a strange sort of way, you see, she's yours.'

'What on earth do you mean by that?'

His sad eyes were fixed on me through the dimness, and I felt I was seeing him for the last time. 'I'm going to tell you something,' he said in a low, distant voice. 'I said this morning that when Whistler and I were first married, the sex side was perfect. But of course that was a lie. It was perfect – apparently; but only because I imagined, every single time I made love to her, that she was you.'

Of course. How could he have deflowered his dream, his mirage? He would have been as impotent with her as he had been with me beside the pool. The frightening, bitter, deadly irony of all those wasted years struck its final blow at me, and for a second I hated him again, as I had hated him when he had made his first escape from reality and me. To think that he had been vicariously married to me, all the time! Abuse and curses crowded on the tip of my tongue, but I swallowed them, nearly choking with a kind of frustrated angry grief.

'I can't take her,' I said at last. 'I'm not her mother. You'll have to find her somebody who will mother her, somebody you will choose just for Rachel. I don't think she'd be safe with a person you chose for yourself.' And I wonder, I thought, if that isn't equally true of me and David? Could that explain why I am going back to the security of Andy, when impractical sentiment still – despite everything – might hold me here?

'Kiss me before you go,' he said slowly.

Our lips touched across the chasm.

'Good-bye, Toby.'

'Good-bye, Jane.'

His voice was already distant, but his lips were warm, and I loved him still as I stepped off the dark porch into the sunlight and came away.

Chapter 2

'Mees Grey Ham?'

The clerk, sallow and dark and showing signs of irritation, stood in the open doorway leading into the hotel, and craned to look round at all the people crowded on to the patio to catch a breath of sea air and have a pre-lunch drink under the dark shadow of the awning. I didn't realize at first that he meant me. I was tired and my brain wasn't working well enough to identify myself with the grey ham, although it wasn't a bad description. It had been a long, hot, hard morning. We'd walked, bus'd and taxied from one end of Tel-Aviv to the other, locating workshops and talking to craftsmen. I'd placed three orders which I thought would commend themselves to Jo, and was feeling rather satisfied – I'd be able to tell her she'd been dead right about the belts. This afternoon we were due to go to Jerusalem to investigate the Bezalel School and several other possibilities, but first we needed a shower, a change, a drink and a meal. The drink came first, long and cold; as I stared at the congested strip of beach below us I thought longingly of the cold shower which was next on my list of priorities, but for the moment I was satisfied just to sit and savour, not only my lager, but my sense of self-conquest. I had successfully put heart-heaviness aside and done those things which I ought to have done; at the thought of this I put out my hand to John on an impulse of gratitude, and caught his withdrawn look, unseeing eyes fixed on the heat-hazy horizon; his hand felt dead under mine and I wondered where he'd gone.

Then the clerk called again.

'Here—'

He came squeezing between the tables towards me.

'Telegram.'

'For *me*?' How had it found me here? But then I remembered I'd mentioned the name of the hotel to Toby.

I took it from him, a little square envelope made of the cheapest yellow paper. John had come back from his interior distances. As my hands moved to tear it open, he suddenly reached over and snatched it away from me.

'What?' I asked, sharp with fright.

He held the yellow envelope gripped tightly in his fingers.

'Wait. Don't open it till we think what it could be.'

'What do you mean?' I asked in swiftly increasing alarm.

He had his eyes closed. 'What is the worst? Think of the worst first.'

'John, for Christ's sake don't do your witch-doctor act! Give it to me. Nothing we think or prepare for will change it.' But even as the yellow message changed hands, inevitably the words flashed across my mind . . . and were gone, tearing a bit of me away with them because such a terror is never far from the surface in any imaginative mother. And now that I'd paid for it not to be that, I could open it, but it still took an effort to unfold the paper and read the real words.

DAVID HAS DISAPPEARED I THINK RUN AWAY POLICE NOTIFIED PLEASE RETURN IMMEDIATELY

JO.

When my brain cleared I was on my feet, leaning on the balcony rail, which was hot enough to hurt my hands. John had his arm around me and there seemed to be some disturbance at the tables near us, as if I had cried out or in some other way showed what I was feeling. John had the telegram and was reading it.

An American sitting at the adjoining table got to his feet.

'Have you had bad news? Can I do anything?'

'My little boy—' The stranger's face seemed to come and go through a haze of terror.

'Sit down here.'

'No, I must—'

'You just sit right down. Francie, help this lady, she's had some bad news.'

The American's wife was already at my side, pressing me down again into the hard chair, patting my hand with her plump, damp one. The man took John's elbow and edged him away, beckoning the waiter at the same time. I heard him order me a brandy. The wife patted me and made soothing nasal noises. As for me, I was strongly aware of the sun's glare on the sea reflecting straight into my eyes. I kept seeing the clerk's face as he handed me the telegram. Those were my most prominent conscious thoughts. Below, turmoil, and the deep stirrings of the strength to gather myself together, in just another moment, and take action.

When the brandy came, which it did more promptly than anything else I had asked for at the hotel, I took it up and drank it at once, knowing I needed it. It took effect quickly, bracing me and numbing me just enough.

The telegram was lying on the ground. I picked it up and read it again, with the American woman doing the same out of the corners of her eyes.

'Oh, my Gahd, you poor thing! You poor, poor thing!'

I stood up quite steadily and walked into the hotel. It seemed pitch-dark in there; it took me some moments to adjust my eyes and then I could see John and the American standing at the desk. The American was telephoning. He beckoned when he saw me.

'I'm ringing the airport,' he said.

'Thank you. I'll just go upstairs and pack.'

'I'll come and help you, honey,' said the wife, who was fussing about behind me.

'There's no need, thanks. John, will you pay the bill?'

My mind was a merciful blank as I pushed my few things back into the suitcase and went next door to gather up John's belongings. It took me a few moments to find the duffle-bag under the bed. While I was kneeling on the floor I said aloud, with grating emphasis, '*Please*, God.' Later I tried to tell myself that that was not a prayer – how dare one pray at a time like that, when all the rest of the time one abjures belief? But it was.

John came into the room in time to help me down with the things. It was fortunate the American had been on hand, for John was helpless, and in fact in tears. But at least he had hold of himself sufficiently to do the basic things and not actually to impede me.

The American couple were waiting with a taxi.

'The planes are all very crowded, but they might find you something on some flight going out tonight. I think in any case you'll be better off out of here – tomorrow might be too late.'

Only much later, I remembered the war. At the time I thought he meant, too late to find David.

'Do try not to worry. My boy used to run away regularly, but he always came back – at least, until he was nineteen.'

The American woman squeezed my hand in both hers. She had the face of a kindly, bewigged sea lion, with enormous, lustrous black eyes bulging with sympathetic tears. 'I shan't sleep a wink tonight...'

The man disengaged her rather firmly and gave me his card, saying something I didn't listen to. Americans always give you their cards. I took it and put it in my bag.

In the taxi, John broke down completely and I had to console him as well as I could. The worst thing was that he kept saying, aloud, all the things I was trying not to think.

'He's so little – all alone somewhere – he be so frightened – or maybe someone take him—'

At last I lost patience.

'Will you shut up?' I said on a rising note of helpless anger.

We sat in silence for the rest of the journey to Lod. But my imagination was not silent. John's sentimental outpourings were all it had needed to over-activate it to a point where it began to inflict actual tortures on me. What could Jo have meant, 'I think run away'? Running away was clearly preferable to simply disappearing. David, at eight, knew his home address and telephone number and was capable of finding his way around. He knew how to travel, at least on the local buses, though he had never done so alone to my knowledge, and in any case everyone in the neighbourhood knew him by sight. He had no inbuilt reservations about approaching people for help, and he had been thoroughly briefed as to the use of the police-force. The bewildering, the nightmarish question was, why should he run away? From what, to what? David was not given to daring acts of mischief or bravado. Amm, now – Amm might well have gone off for a dare or to pay her mother back for some punishment. But with Amm, one wouldn't worry so much. Or would one? Amm, when all was said and done, was a girl. Yet little boys, too, are attractive prey to the more depraved monsters of this world. Especially when the boys are as beautiful as David.

I shivered and swallowed and put my hand over my eyes as if to shut the horrors out. They played on, visible and tangible as cavorting demons, showing off their obscene caperings behind my eyelids, unstoppably . . .

The airport lounge was like a crazy-house at a fair. Noise, movement, the blurring of many colours and shapes . . . and a feeling, overall, of distortion, timelessness, unreality. There were officials, but they were Kafka-esque beings who seemed to have no real power to effect anything, to solve or clarify or bring any sort of order to the chaos. The multi-coloured fat and thin, tall and short shapes besieged them with a babel of demands, requests and complaints in a dozen languages, and the male and female figures in their uniforms, partially isolated from the hoards of would-be travellers by the stout counter, shrugged and gestured and babbled back, scribbled on scraps of paper, beckoned to each other, occasionally emerging from their little waist-high fortresses to hasten back and forth, exposed to the sleeve-tugging and imprecations of the crowd. All this under bright, hard lights that seemed to make no shadows.

John stood like a tree in the midst of it, swaying a little with the jostle of hurriers-by, and guarded our luggage, while I joined the besiegers and tried to get to grips with some official who might, conceivably, be able to provide me with what I wanted.

Looking back now, I feel I probably exaggerated the chaos because of the chaos within me; in any case, it can't have lasted as long as it seemed to, because eventually I did arrive at the head of some middle-eastern institution only remotely related to a queue, produced our documents – and a miracle happened. As I took the leather pocketbook holding our passports and return tickets out of my bag, a little white card fell out face upwards on to the desk and the weary official before me picked it up and read it. He glanced at me, called somebody else over, and they had a short conference. Suddenly, efficiency, speed and courtesy reasserted themselves. A few scribbles; a brisk, all-conquering thump as an official stamp descended – and the next thing I knew, our luggage was on the scales and we were hurrying out over the bubbling tarmac to a waiting aeroplane.

'What happened?' John asked as we struggled on board and slotted ourselves into our seats. The plane was mercifully air-conditioned.

'I just don't know . . .' Only then I remembered that the card had been handed to me by the kindly American at the hotel. I took out my wallet again and found it.

'It seems that man at the hotel was the Air Attaché at the American Embassy,' I said more than ever bemused. 'He must have done some string-pulling for us over the phone. Funny he didn't tell me to show them his card – it just fell out by accident.'

John leant back and closed his eyes.

'Or maybe I made magic,' he said.

We pulled up and away from the gnome's dagger country and headed back towards our own. There was a feeling of craven relief throughout the plane. I heard one woman behind me crying, and exclaiming in a shrill American voice: 'We shouldn't be leaving – we shouldn't be deserters—' and her husband's soothing mumble, something about having to get back because of the children. I felt a strange pang of conscience myself, which had some connection with Toby and Rachel. But it got submerged in the greater pain of fear for David.

I stared and stared through the small window at the silvery wing. Travelling by air, I always feel suspended – even when there are clouds to prove that one is moving, I tend to interpret the movement the wrong way round, seeing the clouds rushing past the stationary wing, rather than the wing racing through the clouds. Today the sky was empty except for ourselves, and we hung in space, between two worlds of impossibility – the one wherein I had turned my back on Toby, and the one in which David had 'disappeared, I think run away' . . . (If only Amm had run with him – but no, that was wickedness, to desire, even indirectly, that Jo should join me in my wilderness of fear.)

To restore some sense of reality, I occasionally looked downwards. Little movement there, through the heat-haze, but after a while the loudspeaker called our attention to the fact that we were over Rhodes, and soon a plethora of little huts appeared, strewn on the blue floor – the Greek Islands, Hydra among them, and somewhere on Hydra, Chris, the water-boy . . . In some unfathomable fashion, the thought of him and his way of life, detached utterly from the reality I was struggling to grasp, sank a small grapple into me as I hung above him in the glittering infinity of the sky and seemed to pull me gently, uninsistently, but inevitably back to earth. Through Chris to Andy, my thoughts performed two sides of a square, straight down and along the surface of sea and land to England. My heart gave a sudden, tangible leap in my chest and began to beat more persistently, as if to pump my blood faster and give me greater vigour. Andy would have heard; Jo would surely have told him. I would not be arriving back to a vacuum of terror and emptiness; Andy would be there. I was holding John's hand, and I gave it a sudden convulsive squeeze. I loved John, more than ever now that we had shared this strange multi-faceted adventure; but my impulse of love at that moment was born of contrast, of the recognition of Andy as a real man who would know how to help and sustain me in a powerful, practical way, as distinct from John, who was my equal in everything, including, in many ways, womanliness . . .

During our stopover in Athens, we were sitting in the lounge there, an island of strained silence amidst all the bustle and noise, when John suddenly stood up and said, 'I'm not goin' to England.'

I stared at him flabbergasted.

'I goin' back to the island,' he said.

I stood up and faced him. I was on the edge of panic anyway; the thought of being deserted by John knocked the last bit of stuffing right out of me; yet even as I opened my mouth to lash into him, I remembered my thoughts in the plane – disloyal thoughts. Had he picked them up, as he so often did in his uncanny fashion? I shut my mouth again and stared at him speechlessly.

'I know what you thinkin',' he said. 'I leavin' you just when you in trouble. But listen, Jane, I be no help to you at all back there. Look at me, I just got to think of David lost, I begin cryin' straight away. Back there you got Andy, he look after things – he's the sort of man you need, not a half-man thing like me.'

I swallowed and moved my head as if my throat were sore.

'Look,' he went on with difficulty. 'I don't want no England now. You goin' to get married, and not to Toby, and that break something in me that kept me goin' a long, long time. I never be welcome at your house like I been till now. No, don't deny it, you know it's so. Wouldn't matter who you married, exceptin' Toby, I can't be part of you no more after it. As for David, well, it been all right while he's a child, but when he grow up, he soon see what I am and one day I'd have to look at him and see some new idea of me comin' into his face . . . like he'd see I was an old black faggot, and maybe he'd hate me for it. Ain't no future for me with you from now on, Janie. I been thinkin' about it all the time since – oh, since you bust up with Toby, then we heard about David goin' lost and I nearly changed my mind, but now I decided it don't make no difference. You find him okay, and then I'll have come away from my island for nothing and maybe not find the courage to go back and make a new world for myself . . . That's what I want now, Janie.'

'But – but – but – I thought the island was all spoilt for you by what happened to you!'

'I thought about that a whole lot, too. Was my own fault, trying to be what I knew I wasn't. There's boys there that are like me, and nobody thinks they're freaks. I'm older than them, but that's okay, I can be kind of like – I can look after 'em a bit, like I did with you two when we was all together in Fulham. I'd like that. And there's music, and swimmin' . . .' He suddenly grabbed my hand hard in both his big paws, submerging it in a big, hot, black ball of flesh. 'Let me go, Janie. You finished with me. We always keep part of each other. *Please.*'

I nodded slowly, my eyes full of tears. I knew suddenly that, however unacceptable it seemed to me now, he was right.

'And will you still love me?' he said.

'Always.'

'Yes, that's right. You and Toby. Always.'

We stared at each other in silence for a long moment, our hands clenched together in a black-and-white jumble. Then he pulled me against him roughly and kissed me with his thick, soft lips. He had hugged me often, but he had never kissed me before. I threw my arms round him and sobbed once. Then I forced myself to draw back, be English, blow my nose, be practical, even when my life seemed to be tearing apart.

'Come on now,' I said. 'We've got to find out how to get your luggage off the plane.'

The last I saw of him was his tall figure, apparently in silhouette although the sun was full on him, standing on the roof of the airport building. I turned once as I crossed the tarmac, and waved to him; then as I got to the top of the aircraft steps, I turned again. He lifted his guitar above his head with both hands. He looked tremendous beside all the little Greeks, a giant among pygmies. His guitar moved up and down twice, like a signal. That's how I shall always remember him. That, and the strange a-sensual touch of his mouth on mine.

PART THREE
DAVID

Chapter 1

I WAS not tired. I felt, on the contrary, charged with energy, so much of it, so needful of an outlet, that as I hurried through customs I felt it tingling in my wrists and fingers and humming in my ears, bursting to get to grips with this thing that had happened.

As I emerged into the great concourse of the Queen's Building, I saw Jo immediately, with Andy just behind her, waiting in the front of the crowd. Jo reached up and waved, a sharp, almost spastic movement, a jerk of breaking nervous tension. Andy stood perfectly still, his eyes fixed on me as if to read my thoughts as I half-ran up to them. As I got close, I suddenly saw that Amm was there too. This astonished me somehow, until I realized that Jo had probably had no one to leave her with.

When I reached them, there was a full three seconds of complete silence between us, a moment charged with feeling and with unspoken questions. Jo looked at me, and I at her. Her green eyes, as wide open as her swollen eyelids allowed, snapped from one of my eyes to the other, and I thought: she expects me to accuse her, if only in my thoughts. But it wasn't true. I knew Jo, I knew what infinite care she took of her own child and all that belonged to her; I knew her sense of responsibility and how much greater care she would have taken of another woman's child, entrusted to her ... Who can guard against every eventuality, who can prevent a child running away when it is the last thing anyone would expect? I embraced her, swiftly and hard.

'Don't,' I said. 'I don't know anything yet, except one thing – it wasn't your fault.'

Jo made no move to touch me, but I felt her whole body jerk in my arms. 'I'm not sure,' she said in a harsh, low voice. 'I was in charge of him—'

'Come on, I've got the car waiting outside,' said Andy. 'Let's not talk here.'

In the car Amm sat in the front next to Andy, while I sat at the back with Jo.

Jo, although she was by no means a cold-hearted person, was not usually emotional in her behaviour. I had never before known her to cry, except once or twice, very privately, after Ted's death when she and Amm first came to live with us. And she was seldom demonstrative, even to Amm; whereas I am constantly kissing and cuddling David, and Amm too, though she is a rather spikey child. I hardly ever remember seeing Jo really hugging Amm, and she certainly never kissed me, the way Dottie, for instance, quite often used to if she were in an ebullient or affectionate mood. So it was strange and frightening now to see how the tears poured down Jo's face, and even more so when she reached out and gripped my hand with her little hard bony one. It was as if she had forgotten how to manage about crying; the tears just flowed, her nose ran; she did nothing to disguise or minimize it, she only gave great sniffs which obliged her to clear her throat every few moments with a sound like a groan. She even seemed inept at holding hands, for her long nails dug into me. I couldn't look at her; the crying made her look so old and vulnerable, like a miserable, sick, ageing monkey.

I wanted to comfort her, to say, 'It's all right . . .' But it wasn't all right. There was Amm, sitting in front, her neat blonde head next to Andy's dark one, and the sight made me cringe, for that was David's place.

I disengaged my hand and found Jo a Kleenex. She used it inexpertly, like a three-year-old child, mopping and wiping with the thing unfolded like a face-flannel.

'Jo, tell me.'

Another sniff; she put her free hand up to shield her face from me. It trembled. But her voice, though muffled, was her own voice, and under rigid control.

'We were in London,' she began.

I could not conceal a gasp of horrified surprise. Never once had I imagined that he might have got lost *in London*. All my palliatives about how he could find his way home, or be noticed and brought back, in the neighbourhood of the village, fled away. *London!* Its whole amorphous black maze-like monstrousness unrolled before me like some science-fiction horror, a devourer of children . . .

'London—' I whispered. 'What were you doing in London?'

Jo bent over and pressed her face into her hands, almost on her knees.

'They begged and badgered me to take them to see that accursed film, what's it called—'

'*Chitty Chitty Bang Bang*,' supplied Amanda, without turning her head.

'They badgered me. So we went up in the morning—'

'Yesterday?'

'Was it only yesterday? Saturday – yes. I drove them up and we left the car in Hammersmith and took the bus downtown—'

'We rode on top, in the front,' said Amanda. But her voice was without its usual excited lift, and when Andy said, 'Be quiet now, Amanda, let your mother talk,' she subsided at once.

'We went to the zoo and had a sort of picnic in Regent's Park. I can't understand it!' she interrupted herself shrilly. 'If he'd wanted to run away, he had every opportunity earlier – they wandered round in the aquarium, in the dark, by themselves. I wasn't watching them all the time. Anyhow, after lunch we went to the cinema and while we were watching the film, right in the middle David said he wanted to go to the loo . . . I asked if he wanted me to take him, and he said – sort of scornfully, you know – that he didn't want to come to the ladies'; he pointed to the gents' sign and said, "Don't worry if I'm rather long, I have to do big jobs and it takes me ages." ' This was true, he was capable of sitting in there for twenty minutes at a time, singing to himself; but this was not to say he was incapable of hurrying when something interesting was going on. It was inconceivable that he would dawdle long in a cold, un-friendly lavatory when he was missing a film.

'So what happened?'

'After about fifteen minutes I got worried . . . I left Amanda in her seat and went along to the gents and knocked on the door. No one answered, so I went in. It was empty. I asked an attendant if there was another gents, and he showed me one upstairs, but he wasn't in that one either . . . I went to the kiosk in the lobby where they sell sweets and drinks, and they hadn't seen him, then I began to comb the whole cinema. Some ushers flashed their torches along every row in the place in case he hadn't been able to find his seat again and had just sat down somewhere else. By this time the film had ended and the lights came up so I went and got Amanda and we went straight to the office of the manager and he made an announcement over the loudspeaker. If David had still been in the cinema, I know he would have come to me ... Anyway I stood in the foyer for another half-an-hour while every member of the staff combed the place from top to bottom. At the end of that time I was in such a state I could hardly think straight, so the manager gave me a drink and then we decided to call the police.'

All this had come out in a muffled way through her hands; now she straightened up, but with her face turned away from me.

'The police questioned me and all the staff and especially the woman at the box-office as to whether she'd seen him going out alone. But in any case there was a way out right next to the gents which led into an alley beside the building, and *that* led to the main road and the buses.'

'Did he have any money with him?'

'Yes, I gave them five bob each to spend at the zoo, and I know he hadn't spent any of that because I thought it odd at the time, with Amanda scoffing ices and buying bits and pieces; he said he wanted to save it. Then, when the police really started questioning us, Amm remembered that she'd knocked over David's money-box on the Friday night and that it was empty. She even knew how much there'd been in it a few days before, because they were comparing notes. He'd had over a fiver.'

David had developed a passionate interest in money at the age of five and had been hoarding ever since.

'And what have the police done?'

'They're treating it as a case of running away. Of course they can't rule out the possibility that he was lured or – or taken, but really everything points the other way. They want to question you, of course, for instance I wasn't sure how carefully you'd warned him about talking to strangers and so on – if you have, then they're pretty sure he went off by himself, because it's almost unthinkable that someone could have carried him off in broad daylight against his will.'

I racked my brains. Of course I'd warned him about strangers – sometime or other. But I hadn't stressed it as firmly as I would if we'd been living in London. In the village and its environs, one seldom if ever *saw* strangers, and in any case . . . somehow one doesn't worry about such things much in the country. Why alarm him or make him suspicious when there seemed so little danger? David was an outgoing, friendly child. I hadn't ever wanted to inhibit that by putting him in fear of every unfamiliar face. There had not been a serious crime in our village since 1923 . . .

'I'm not sure if . . . Have you warned Amanda?'

'Oh yes. But then I'm such a city person basically, and in the city you have to.'

She couldn't have realized how her words underlined my worst terrors.

'Where are we going now?'

'To the police station where they're dealing with it.'

She hesitated minimally with the 'with', long enough for me to realize that she had nearly said 'with the case'. David's disappearance was a case to them. A newspaper board flashed past the tails of my eyes and I snapped round automatically to look at it . . . Too late, it had gone. Would it, within the next few days, carry David's name in huge cold black print? Would it be another in the unending nose-to-tail series of child-disappearance cases, some of which ended so hideously?

Another newsboard, and this time I looked in time to read 'MIDDLE EAST. On The Brink.' A moment later we passed another: 'Sinai: Nasser's Tanks Move Up.'

'There *is* going to be a war out there,' I said dully.

Nobody said anything. Another few blocks, crawling now through the traffic in Kensington, and then Amanda, who had held her peace far longer than her nature normally permitted, turned her head and said to me, 'David's being very naughty, isn't he?'

'Perhaps,' I said. 'We don't know.' I turned to Jo. 'I suppose Amm doesn't know anything?'

She gave me a strange quick sideways look.

'I've questioned her, Andy's questioned her, the policewoman who's dealing with it has questioned her. If she does know anything, she's keeping it to herself.'

'I don't know anything, Mummy! I've told you I don't!'

Jo looked at her with red-rimmed eyes, and said in a high-pitched voice, almost strangled suddenly with the effort to keep it under control: 'You can't imagine how much I want to believe you. But if I ever find out you've been hiding something—'

She looked and sounded so 'on the brink' herself that I put my hand over hers quickly and said, 'Sh, Jo, of course she's not, why should she?' Again the quick sideways look, a mad look it seemed to me at that moment. It frightened me. I didn't recognize her eyes.

We reached the police station and were shown into an office so familiar from television series that I had a moment of *déjà vu*. Come to that, the whole surrealistic situation somehow had an uncanny underlying familiarity, as if I had lived through it, or something similar, not once but many times before. Even the policewoman, when she came in and shook hands with me, reminded me of someone, or rather several people, I had watched on the set in Jo's living-room going through this self same polite, solemn, yet basically business-like rigmarole in a dozen TV plays.

'We didn't think you'd manage to get back so quickly. Now please do try not to worry too much. We've no reason as yet to suppose that any harm has come to David . . .'

The usual scripted platitudes . . . I felt that I'd been cheated. Television had prepared me in some way for this situation until it was robbed of its reality; it wasn't as true or new or shocking as it ought to be. I was merely wandering in the footsteps of writers and actors who had hacked out the paths through this desperate personal jungle ahead of me. I felt confused and disorientated, struggling helplessly against an illusion of fiction, having to remind myself every moment that we were not acting.

'What's been done so far?'

'David's description has been circulated to all the local police-stations and registered with our central bureau of missing persons at Scotland Yard. We've made enquiries among all the constables who were on duty around Marble Arch yesterday.'

'Have you told the press?'

She smiled faintly. 'You don't have to *tell* the press, as a rule. They just pick it up. If it weren't for the war situation in the Middle East, there'd probably have been something about it in the evenings.'

216

Abruptly my mind turned white and blank in a long flush of fear, because into my mouth had come the automatic telly-question concerning hospitals and I couldn't speak or move for about a minute.

'Mrs Graham, are you all right?'

Andy's hands were holding my shoulders from behind. Somebody moved towards me holding a chair, like a lion-tamer, as if I were dangerous. Everything fragmented and flew off into corners, then coalesced again on to a screen twenty by twenty-two inches, with us all on it in miniature. I wondered if I were losing my mind and gave my head a hard shake which ricked my neck painfully and brought me back to myself.

I sat down and said, 'I'm all right.'

'Can I ask you a few questions?'

'Yes, but I'd like some tea if I possibly could.'

The policewoman ordered some tea and then sat down and asked her questions. They were apparently about David's character, but subtly they swung round to being about our relationship. Had we quarrelled? Was there anyone he liked whom he might want to visit? Someone who for some reason I wouldn't take him to see? I explained that his entire acquaintance, except John, lived in and around the village.

After a lot more questions, not only directed at me but at all the others, the policewoman came round to Amanda.

'Now, young lady,' she said, and the moment she spoke I got the impression that she, like Jo, suspected her in some way. 'Have you remembered anything that might be useful?'

'No.'

Amm was sitting bolt upright on a chair, a prim, well-ordered little figure in her town dress and long white socks, her blonde hair pulled tightly back from a centre parting into two firm, turned-under plaits tied with neat black bows. Her eyes – Ted's eyes, very blue and sharp, unexpectedly piercing between their sandy lashes, were fixed, wide open to the point of staring, at the detective; her hands were pressed together between her knees, the caps of which, I suddenly noticed, were white. She was tense all over; even the corners of her lips were marked with little pale spots of bunched muscle. Something jerked into perfect wakefulness inside me. She did know something. I felt it, knew it, with absolute certainty.

'Amm!'

She was startled into looking at me for the first time. Yes, oh yes, there it was in her eyes, quite unmistakable. Amanda could be sly, like most little girls, she could be secretive; she had an inviolable sense of privacy. But she was not sufficiently devious to hide such a secret completely from people she loved; nor was she, despite the latent toughness of her character, insensitive enough to be able to look at the suffering she *must* be able to see in her mother's face, and mine, implacably.

I found myself crouching beside her, holding her upper arms in a hard commanding grip so that she winced.

'Amm?'

She dropped her eyes and, after a minute pause, shook her head.

'Amanda! You're lying!'

It was a pistol-shot from Jo.

Amm winced under my hands, and then I felt her stiffen.

I stood up. 'Don't,' I said to Jo. It was an urgent signal, and she got it and stopped. I knew, and so did Jo (who better?) Amanda's pride and stubbornness. She would not yield here, in front of a stranger. Nor would she yield anywhere to shouting and threats. I suddenly knew I could get it out of her – at least I knew there was something to get out. And if that were so, then that meant – a plan, some kind of design to the whole mystery, something rational within a child's definition of rationality.

I turned to the policewoman. 'May I have a word with you?'

She motioned me into an adjoining office, and closed the door after us.

'Yes, Mrs Graham?'

'That child knows something.'

'I thought so.'

'It's just not in David's character to do something as – as *big* as this without confiding in someone. I wouldn't have thought it was in him to do it at all.' For just a moment, I had a ludicrous feeling of pride in him, for I had always privately thought him rather a timid, conventional child, and here he had worked out a whole scheme to run away, and had carried it out with obvious success, at the age of barely eight. Clearly I would need to reassess him when I had him back. 'He and Amm are closer than brother and sister. I'm quite convinced, suddenly, that he's cooked this whole thing up with her, and that she's taken a vow of secrecy.'

'Do you think you can get her to break it?'

'I think I might. But just being as sure as I am that she does know what he's up to, relieves me enormously. Clearly he hasn't been kidnapped, anyway.'

'No, well, I never really thought he had. Mrs Graham—'

'Miss,' I said automatically.

The woman sat up in her chair and looked at me in a new way. There was a silence while she thought.

'Miss Graham,' she said slowly, 'Mrs Berkeley mentioned that David was fatherless. She didn't tell me – forgive me, are you unmarried?'

'Yes.'

'So your boy is not fatherless, in the usual meaning of the word?'

I saw her drift immediately; and she saw my face alter. She leaned forward and said, 'Could there be a possibility that he would try to reach his father?'

'I – don't know – it's just possible – but so difficult to imagine! How could he – where would he begin looking for him?'

'We'd better begin by finding out where he actually *is*. How would you begin looking for him?'

My mind raced. David had said he was going to make a film – there was some magazine – what was it he'd said? I strained to remember. At some studios. Something about a tree, there'd been some little joke in my mind, some mistake he'd made – Elm Tree – that was it! He'd said Elm Tree—

'Elstree! Elstree Studios!'

It was odd to see how this little bit of information affected the slow-moving rather phlegmatic woman constable. It quite galvanized her. For ten minutes she had two phones in hand and as many assistants running to and fro to her instructions. She phoned Elstree first, but it was Sunday, so she could only speak to a security officer; but the police have their methods, and several phone numbers were actually given of various people who might know about Terry. None of them did. None of them knew of any picture being made which had him in it. In fact, they'd never heard of him.

By this time one of the assistants, poring over suburban phone directories, had found a Boyden, T., listed with an address in Teddington.

The policewoman phoned the number and I heard a woman's voice answer. The conversation was short and sharp and then the receiver went down; the constable, judging by her expression, had received a flea in her ear.

'He's left there,' she said. 'Six months ago. The woman seemed furious at the mention of him. She said she knew nothing about his whereabouts and cared less.'

'An unpaid landlady, perhaps,' suggested Andy.

She frowned. 'I don't think so. When I told her it was a police matter, she said, "I hope you damn well get him, whatever it's for." But she didn't seem inclined to offer any complaint of her own.'

'It's his wife,' I said with a sudden flash of certainty.

'Yes, probably,' she replied, and gave me a narrow look. 'You might get more out of her than I could. Are you prepared to try?'

I dialled the number, feeling acutely nervous.

'Hallo?' The voice was sharp, tense and high-pitched.

'Is this Mrs Terence Boyden?'

'*No*, this is Mrs *Grace* Boyden. Who are you?'

'My name's Jane Graham, you don't know me. I'm terribly anxious to see your husband. Can you possibly help me?'

'He's not my husband any longer. I haven't seen him for months.' There was a pause, during which I could hear her breathing, and then the breathing stopped for a second and she asked, in a tone still more shrill, 'What did you say your name was?'

I said it again, and then she said: 'Are you the dirty bitch whose brat he's the father of?'

I can hardly describe how horribly these words, contrasting with her supposedly genteel accent, reached me. They seemed to cause a minor explosion in my brain before I could understand that by 'dirty bitch' she meant me, and by 'brat' she meant David. My first impulse was one of fury, but then I thought, no, she can't be normal if she's so angry about this thing that happened long before they met. In any case, I didn't want to make her angrier, if that were possible.

'I'm the person you mean,' I said as quietly as I could.

220

'And what are you after him for? Run away from you now, no doubt. Perhaps you want him to poke another bastard into you?'

I swallowed and said, 'I haven't seen him for eight years.'

'Oh, I'm sure! Very likely.'

'It's true.'

'Don't lie to me. When I turfed him out, he told me he was going straight to you and his bastard.'

In amazement I said, 'But he didn't.'

'You liar,' she said, in a voice low and vibrant with scorn and hatred. 'He must have come to you, where else would he go? He's certainly incapable of living by himself. He was going downhill fast enough even when I was still struggling to keep him on the rails. At least I kept him clean and fed and in work. Naturally as soon as he left me he lost his job. I suppose that was your idea – that he should go back into acting? He said he was going to change his life. He even changed his silly face. Imagine it, spending good money to put his teeth straight just to satisfy his insatiable vanity and get more of you tarts flocking round him . . .' Her voice gathered speed till the words fell over each other. 'Not doing so well with his great film career, I notice, that film he was going to be in was bunged on the shelf and him with it. Was it your idea, the TV commercials? Just about his level, flashing his new teeth at the women and telling them to buy Snow and get their undies whiter . . . Tell me,' she went on conversationally, 'does he bite you on the shoulder and on the breasts? He said women were supposed to like it but how can you *like pain*? It's just a justification men use so they can do what they like with you, and then blame you for being frigid and *sterile* if you don't enjoy it. But perhaps you're a masochist. And how's he making out as a family man? He always bleated for kids. It's a bit of a joke really, bastard father and bastard son . . . You can have him for my part, I don't give a damn—'

I hung up. Jo was watching me.

'Mad?'

'Yes.' I was feeling sick.

The policewoman had been listening in. Now she stirred uneasily. 'Been keeping it bottled up.'

I said nothing. I was thinking about Terry. How long had she been like that, and how long had he stuck it? He'd given me a strong hint, during that phone conversation two years ago, that she was neurotic, but this was something more. I couldn't help wondering if he had not been the cause of part of it. If a woman can't have children, what sort of husband keeps on 'bleating'? If a woman doesn't like being bitten, what kind of man keeps biting her and telling her she's frigid? A nine-year-old memory returned to rouse the heat in my face. Perhaps it was that trick of his that had so effectively put me off, made David's conception such an occasion of non-pleasure . . .

'We're by no means beaten yet,' said the policewoman. 'The wife said something about his making commercials. We'll get on to the people who make Snow and see if we can't trace him through them . . .'

It took an hour just because it was Sunday. Phone call after phone call, and eventually a police car had to be sent out to track down the personnel officer of the commercial film-makers which made the advertising films for Snow.

'I can't see what help this is going to be,' I kept saying. 'If we're having this much trouble finding him, how could David possibly find him all by himself? We're not even sure he's looking for him.'

'It's the only line we've got to follow at the moment,' the policewoman answered soothingly. But I was not soothed. If David had really run away from Jo with the intention of finding Terry, which seemed to me the only reason he could have for doing it, it was almost beyond belief that he would not have asked a policeman how to get to Elstree, or Elm Tree, or wherever he thought Terry was. Perhaps, picking his way at waist-level through the shuffling thousands who swarm along Oxford Street on a Saturday afternoon, he might have failed to find a policeman, and asked passers-by . . . Who might he not have asked? Might it not as easily be some vicious opportunist who would grab him, as an indifferent stranger who would brush past without stopping to notice him? It might, by the same token, have been some kindly, imaginative person who would stop and stoop and listen, and, realizing that something was wrong, have taken him straight to the nearest police station.

But nobody had done this . . . in *twenty-four hours*.

The waiting was terrible. We'd been sitting in the same room now for over three hours. I was watching Amanda, more and more sure she knew something, if only from the way she was avoiding my eyes. Suddenly I said:

'Are we on the right track, Amanda? Surely you can tell us that without breaking your promise – like playing "hot" and "cold". Are we getting warm?'

Everything became very quiet and the full focus of attention fell on Amm. She didn't say anything, and I felt a cruel anger rise up in me. I wanted to grab her and shake her until the secret, lodged in her throat like a half-swallowed bead, flew out. It was in there somewhere, inside that stubborn little body . . . For a moment I hated her.

'Come *on*, Amm! Look at all of us wasting time! Is he looking for his father? Was that the plan?'

But my voice was too peremptory, it made her angry and fearful at once, so that she said 'I don't know' on a note of finality, and clamped her lips shut.

At that moment the phone rang. The policewoman pounced on it. She barked 'Yes – yes—' into it several times and hung up. 'They've got it,' she said. 'It's in Southwood Lane, Highgate. No phone, it's been cut off. Come on, we'd better go out there.'

The imminent terror of facing Terry was dimmed by the sudden jangling of some little, far-off memory-bell. Southwood Lane, Highgate. Highgate . . . I shook my head. I couldn't remember that I'd ever been to Highgate. Yet somehow it was achingly familiar, not a big ache, but a little nagging one, a tiny association connected with a whole chain of events that had followed it.

I was to go in Andy's car. The others climbed into the big police limousine which was waiting at the door, while Andy, after squeezing my hand, walked off to bring his car from its parking place. The police car pulled away, and I was left standing on the pavement. Again, without warning, the sense of unreality seized me. How was it possible that that elusive address to which we were going had become, in my thoughts, part of a sort of molecular pattern? Somewhere I'd heard a theory that time spirals; that one arrives back at the same places but on different levels. There was something *circular* about this journey to that address. I found myself clutching the edges of my coat in sudden panic. The same place, but higher on the spiral, or lower, for of course you could never go back exactly, or the whole thing could be lived again, altered, rearranged . . . I looked round wildly for Andy, but he was out of sight. All around me was a Lob's Wood of concrete, twisting and assuming fierce shapes. I felt as if I might faint, I wanted to, but it was no use – I knew I wouldn't because I never do faint, I never can. I wanted to put back my head and let out long desperate howls, and they would not, at that moment, have been for David or the fear of what might be happening to him, but for myself, only for myself, for the horrifying blankness ahead of me, across which, like some cabalistic symbol, was written that address, Southwood Lane, Highgate . . .

Chapter 2

By the time Andy's car drew up and he jumped out to open the door for me I had passed through some sort of crisis and emerged, cold and shaken but lucid, into something like a rational state. As I passed close to him I looked into his face for the first time since my return, saw it as if at a distance, and marvelled that so much could happen and change in such a very few days. Once that same face had been so dear to me, so intimately familiar; now I knew I would have to strive all over again to reach it.

He felt some of this, too, but his reaction was to close the gap physically, and when we were together in the car, he put his arm round me and pulled me close to him and held my face against his coat. We had no words for each other, and truthfully I had no special feeling for him then – I was too numb with shock and anxiety. But there was something there, something I needed – a purely bodily warmth which enveloped me for a moment and gave me comfort, like a drink of whisky. Shakespeare talks about 'the faint cold fear that almost freezes up the heat of life'. Fear is really like that, and the closeness of another human body can thaw the cold for just a moment, proving that the fear is not invincible.

Then he drew away, and we drove north.

We were not far behind the others, and we caught them up on the way. I could see Amanda sitting in the back and caught myself thinking what a kick David would get out of that, riding in a police-car with the blue light turning on the roof.

We were climbing now, rising out of Kentish Town, up on to the beautiful heights of Highgate Hill. I was looking out at the little shops and elegant cottages, only half aware of them, my mind groping ahead, when I saw a bus pull out in front of us from a bus-stop and suddenly it clicked.

I drew myself together with a sudden startled, shrinking move-ment which caught Andy's eye and made him glance at me sharply.

'What is it, darling?'

'I've remembered. I've been to – this house we're going to – I've walked along this road from that bus-stop – I know the way. You turn right here, then left.' The police driver had missed the turning, or perhaps he knew another way, but Andy silently obeyed my directions. After a few more moments of driving, I pointed. 'There. It's that house, with the yellow door.'

Still the same. The yellow which had been crocus-colour was now faded and peeling, but that was not surprising; the paint had not been quite fresh when I had walked slowly past the house nine years ago. I remembered noticing the colour particularly, it had had some association which escaped me now but which had been significant at the time . . . It had all been significant, how much so I had had no notion of then. Parked now, and sitting motionless looking at that same neglected front garden, the dingy frontage, I was carried straight back to the moment when I had strolled, as if by accident, past that house, glancing at it casually lest he should look out and see me, dreading it and wishing for it at the same time. Terry Boyden, whose ill-planted seed grew into David inside me *because* I had looked at this house nine years ago and decided, sub-consciously, to throw myself in his way again.

'You're so still. What is it? Are you afraid to go and see?' Andy's arm was round me again. 'I'll come with you.'

'No.' I shook my head vehemently. 'You back up and wait for me, and don't let anybody else come. I want to go by myself.'

I got out of the car and walked across the pavement, through a gate left carelessly ajar, up a weed-sprouting path to the yellow front door. The chromium door-knob and letter-box were cor-roded, the knocker hanging off. I stood there. My hand wouldn't move to knock at first, and I thought: this is like with Toby. He's behind there somewhere, and he's not expecting me, and he's been so important in my life. With one small movement I can bring him face to face with me and then we must go forward, unravel it, force our way through our own and each other's and our combined reactions in order somehow to make sense of our connection.

I knocked, and then felt weak and helpless and nearly turned and ran. But the longing I had to recover David kept me rooted, through the approaching footsteps and the click of the inner handle.

The door opened. A man stood there. It wasn't Terry.

Christ, yes, it was.

But how changed! Height and the colour of a man's eyes don't change, but everything else can. His face, which had been grey-hound-thin, had filled out puffily; his hair, which had been fair, was dyed dark brown and hung right down over his eyes, ears and collar. Instead of the rather sporty, ultra-English clothes he had once worn, he now wore a sort of mulberry-coloured shirt open at the neck, with an ornament in the opening, and grubby jeans; his teeth, which I saw at once because he drew his lips back over them in a grimace when he recognized me, were so smooth and white and perfect that they didn't look like human teeth but like a miniature fence covered with high-gloss paint. And there was some other change, too, something which made his face almost a grotesque parody of itself, but somehow I was so shocked I couldn't see what it was.

As soon as I saw him I knew at once that he hadn't seen David. We stared at each other. All likeness to my meeting with Toby was gone, for this man was as much a stranger to me as any man could be. Yet he was *David's father*. He had had me, and despised me for it, and David had come from that mismating. In some horrifying way, that relationship – the physical relationship between David and him – was more obvious than I would have thought possible before. The dark hair, the fatter cheeks, brought about a likeness I had thought didn't exist, and this likeness revolted me further, for Terry now looked not merely rather weak, but almost effeminate – only men of unimpeachably rugged masculinity can get away with really long hair, as only pirates and gypsies can get away with ear-rings. The puzzling, the appalling question was how I had ever found anything solid enough about him to be attracted by, for no man who can alter his appearance, his whole outward persona, as much as this, can have any truly inviolable core.

I felt urgently that I must get it over quickly and be shot of him and of every offensive memory belonging to him. I felt deeply afraid of him and realized for the first time the madness of coming at all.

'I'm sorry to come like this, but I must have a word with you.'

'It can only be,' he said, 'about one thing. Come in.'

He was still staring at me with that rictus of amazement twisting his mouth, but now he gave a shiver, reached out, took my elbow in his thin hand, and pulled me through the door, closing it behind me.

He smelt stale.

We stood together in the dimness of a dusty hall. His tall, no longer perfectly lean body swayed forward a little, and for a moment I thought he might kiss me or do something unbearable, but instead he turned and led me into a pigsty of a living-room.

'Excuse the mess,' he said in a toneless voice.

We sat down facing each other.

'You've hardly changed,' he said in remote surprise.

'You have.'

'What do you mean? Oh, the hair. I had to dye it for a – a film I was doing.'

'What film?'

His eyes wandered and he shrugged. 'It was a telly commercial, actually. I'm doing quite a few now. Pays the gas bill. You'd be amazed at the big names who are doing them these days . . . I met Kenneth More on my last one . . . Why not? You can fit interviews and so on in quite easily, and it's a sort of – shop window, in a way . . .' His voice trailed into silence.

'Terry—'

'Jane.' And now he smiled, and I saw that those awful teeth could be called an improvement, from a telly-commercial point of view; they made him handsome in a way, but I hated them. And what *was* that other, elusive, change? It disturbed me more than the teeth because I couldn't think what it was. It put his whole face out of focus, destroyed the integrity of feature it had had once. More and more incredulously I kept asking myself, how could you have gone to bed with this – this *strange* man? But what did any of that nonsense matter when David was lost?

'Listen. David's lost.'

He leant back in his chair, with both arms limp and hanging, and looked at the ceiling. 'Who is David?' he asked whimsically.

'Our—'

I stopped myself in horror before the single syllable was half-out. 'What are you playing at?' I asked instead, roughly.

'Our son, were you about to say?' He straightened his head and smiled again, narrowing his eyes. 'Your son, you mean. How could he be mine? My seed, but not my son. You denied him to me. You kept him all for yourself.' He put his head back and closed his eyes, his arm still spreadeagled across the arms of the chair in such a silly, affected way that I was suddenly furious. Of course I knew he was doing it on purpose to punish me, perhaps I even deserved it, but it was more than I could take just then.

I got up. 'It's quite obvious you haven't seen him. How could he find you here?' I started to leave, but he was up out of his chair and across the room in a moment, and holding my wrist so tightly that it hurt when I tried to jerk away.

'Find me?' he said in an explosive hiss. 'What do you mean, find me? Is he looking for me?'

I wrenched my wrist away and stood rubbing it, all my pent-up feelings boiling up in anger, glaring at him with pure hatred.

His fair skin had gone a dark, ugly red, a blackish red, dangerously choleric. He'd always seemed to me a rather gentle, indeterminate person; it was a shock now to see him looking, not just angry, but as if he might translate his anger into some kind of physical action.

'Listen to me,' he said in a very low voice, 'eight years ago you had a baby, and I came to the hospital and you let me see it, asleep in that white box-thing beside your bed. I looked at it and I thought "That's mine". And then you went away. I must have phoned your father fifty times, until in the end he stopped putting me off tactfully and roared at me over the phone, "She doesn't want you! Isn't that clear to you by now? She's *ordered* me not to give you her address." And that was it. I thought, well, if that's the way she wants it. So I went back to my own life. I got involved with Grace and she seemed like a nice girl at the time, so we got married, and I remember thinking: "Now I'll have my own kids that nobody can say I'm not entitled to". I kept planning what a first-rate father I was going to be, to prove it to myself, and to you if you ever turned up again, to make you bloody good and sorry you'd been so "who-needs-you?" to me and reduced my ego to a chewed-off stub. You know, I used to watch out for kids, or adults, who'd been brought up by their mothers. I thought, and still think, there's something a bit off about every one of them. They're all off-balance somehow, not quite complete. And I used to think, was I such a rotten sod she'd rather have nothing than me for the boy? Maybe it's hard for you to realize what you did to me by refusing even to let me help you support him. *You robbed me,*' he said, putting his face close to mine. 'And you stole more than I realized for a long time, because for ages I kept hoping that Grace'd produce something. I got so desperate at one point I had her every night for a whole month, in case, twisted and arse-end-up psychologically as she was, she might be twisted physically as well and only able to conceive when you'd least expect it. When that didn't work, she made me go through those fertility tests. Jesus Christ! Do you know what they do? It's like submitting yourself to rape by some a-septic robot. I can still remember those spotless white screens and the lights glaring and the feeling of utter, complete and total humiliation . . . And all the time wanting to yell at them, I'm all right, I've proved it, it's her that can't . . . Grace dares to say I never did anything for her, even after the tests she accused me of being "one of those primitive Englishmen who always blames the woman". We had the results of the tests in front of us, we *knew* it wasn't me, but she still wouldn't accept it. Of course she was already half-way round the bend . . .'

He suddenly drooped at the shoulders. His lank, wig-like hair fell forward like bead-curtains on either side of his face. He turned away from me and slumped into his chair again, bent over, his hands between his knees.

'Trying to avoid self-pity and all that, but you can't imagine what a bloody rotten time I've had since I last saw you,' he muttered.

'I'm sorry,' I said. It wasn't really true, fundamentally. I pitied him, but in an appalled, repelled sort of way, the sort of pity that makes you cringe and want to escape.

He looked up at me again. His eyes were still narrow and full of accusation. 'It could have been so different, if only you'd given me my rights,' he said bitterly.

'What *rights*, Terry?'

'Has a father no rights? And don't you dare say I forfeited them! I asked you to marry me. Now don't deny that. I damn well did ask you! I remember it distinctly—'

'Yes, you asked me, very formally, because you felt you ought to. I remember it distinctly too. I also remember distinctly the look of naked relief on your face when I said no.'

'Well, what did you expect? I was very young, and I wasn't in love with you.'

'Nor I with you.'

'All the more credit to me for asking you.'

'We had no claim on each other. You weren't all that young,' I added as an afterthought. 'You must have been twenty-nine.'

'Very immature for my age,' he said rather primly, so that I could almost have laughed.

'Our ages are irrelevant anyway. I had David without your help or support, what *right* did you have to any share in him?' The old, old arguments I'd used with myself at the time, coming out all pat and neat despite the fact that later events, radical changes in my point of view, had long since invalidated them. I forced myself to look at him again, really at him. 'Gone to seed' was the phrase that came; but how, indeed, might he have looked, how might he have been, if I had acknowledged then what I was secretly obliged to acknowledge now – that he *had* rights, that even an unwilling offer to 'do the decent thing' gives a man a moral claim on his own son; that it was no fault of his that he had not sustained me through my pregnancy, or in fact married me at the beginning of it, for how could he have acted well when I didn't give him the chance? I had never even told him, he had found out only by the merest accident.

And how would David have been now, if I had married Terry – not this horrific version of him with his awful hair and his puffy outlines but the mild, sweet, gentle, inoffensive young man he was then. Weak characters strengthen in the right atmosphere, from the right sort of challenges. We could have lived together and raised David together, the fatal palliatives he had grabbed at he would have been spared . . . No false smile, no telly commercials, no middle-aged-hippie look, which is more pathetic than anything else that can overtake a man . . . Had my pride, my possessiveness, my stiff-necked stubbornness and unwillingness to settle for second best translated Terry into this sad wreck? Had it translated David into a problem-child, a runaway?

I turned away, unable to face him, and myself in him.

'I'm going,' I said.

'No you're not, wait a minute!' He was up and ready to grab me again, but I pulled my arm out of his reach. 'You haven't answered me yet. Is he – David – is he looking for me? Has he run away to look for me?'

We stared into each other's eyes, perhaps the first clear, honest look we had ever exchanged.

'He's run away to look for a father. Not *his*, *any*. He has a dream of you. Even physically, it's nothing like the reality.'

'Do you mean the hair?' he asked again.

Could he really be so unaware? 'It's not just the hair, Terry, you must know that.'

He turned away abruptly.

'I've put on a bit of weight – so what?'

I said nothing. I'd seen that kind of puffy fat on a man's face before – my father's, to be exact, and I knew very well that it is not overeating that puts it there.

He seemed to guess my thoughts, and turned to me.

'All right! It's not against the law. Believe me, most men would have been on hard drugs by now after what I've been through. And living alone here, not working full-time, hasn't helped. What do you *expect*?' he shouted. 'I've never known what you expect of me!'

'The short answer to that is nothing.'

'If you could see yourself. Standing there so calmly, looking so bloody wholesome and clean and above-the-scrum——'

'Oh don't talk such utter rubbish! I haven't had such an easy time myself, you know.'

That stopped him for a moment. I glanced through the window.

There were no cars outside; they must have parked down the road. For the first time I speculated on Andy's state of mind while I was in here talking to David's father . . . I quailed from a sudden sharp pang of real shame and dismay at the realization that I might have to introduce Terry to the others; the only worse horror I could imagine was having to introduce him, at any time now or in the future, to David . . .

I stared speechlessly at Terry, helplessly visualizing the scene of such a meeting, and suddenly I saw what it was – the other alteration. It was his nose. His narrow face had always come to its rather low-key climax in an aquiline nose, which gave it some pretensions to character and distinctiveness; this had been changed, not radically, just the sharpness taken off its crest, so that it now limped down his face from his pale eyebrows in utter ordinariness, effectively removing the last vestige of strength from his features and somehow blurring them until you felt his face could be superimposed on to a million others and just disappear . . .

'Oh my God, Terry,' I said aghast. 'You've had something done to your nose as well.'

'Oh, that . . . I did that ages ago. I couldn't stand that beak I had, it made me look like a bloody kike.'

Many, many times I had unwished my connection with this man. When I was actually in bed with him; the next morning; for weeks afterwards until I finally received his casual, dismissive note; practically the entire period of my pregnancy – and several times subsequently. But never more poignantly than now. My nausea was so sharp that I nearly lost control of myself completely and shouted at him, 'You're revolting! How dare you get like this! How *can* you be David's father?' But I didn't, and I was glad I didn't, because really he was too pitiable to attack.

Nevertheless, I knew suddenly that I couldn't do it. I couldn't show him to Jo, to Andy, I couldn't even show him to W.P.C. whatever her name was. It seemed unavoidable, but I would find some way to avoid it. And without my even having to stop and plan, the right words emerged.

'Look, Terry, I came up here by myself from the police station and I must get back there and tell them you haven't seen David. I want you to stay here just in case he comes—'

'How could he?' he bro[...]
he might just – arrive here [...]

'Well, I found you. Ma[...]
he might, too.' I didn't b[...]
cause he wanted to. Seeing [...]
again, but in the same disgu[...]

'How *did* you find me? I'[...]
address.'

I told him how we'd traced him [...]
live here.'

'How do you know that?'

I had to stop and think. How had I kn[...]
time? 'You must have been listed in the phone [...]
once, because I knew it.'

'Yes, I was. Nine, ten years ago. I bought this pla[...]
married the first time. Then I rented it when my first m[...]
broke up, but I never sold it, and when I left Grace I kicked ou[...]
tenants and came back here.'

'Why did you tell her about – me, and David?' I asked curiously.

'Oh, Christ, how can you go on forever, sparing somebody? I
kept quiet about it just so long as I thought our marriage stood a
dog's chance, but in the end her whining and complaints got me so
livid I just spat it out at her one day to shut her up about not being
able to give her a baby. I must have known it was the end; mentally
I was quite prepared to clear out, even before she threw me out.'

'But did you have to tell her you were coming to me?'

He fixed his blue eyes on me. 'I see you've had a nice long
friendly chat with her,' he said.

'That's one way of putting it.'

'Poor Grace. Being alone probably hasn't helped her any more
than it has me. I think she enjoyed our rows in a way. Some women
need a good all-out screaming match every so often to keep the
bogies away. She was always better after one. Quite sweet and
tender for a while.' He heaved what sounded to me like a faintly
theatrical sigh. His whole manner about everything in his life –
everything, that is, except David – smacked of a sort of languid,
world-weary *je m'en foutisme*. Only when David was in question did
some clear, sharp, genuine feeling seem to come back into his

…is another man who throve
…t David was real enough,
…ld be excused for grabbing
…s a barrier between himself
…ion of body and spirit. I
…nance that David might find
… And yet what could I do to

…y itching to be away, to take some
…nd David and carry him away to
… see what sort of father I had given him.
…s the number of the police-station.' I wrote
…re—' (before he could ask, so that he would not
…(treachery) '—is my number at home.' I wrote down
…umber, a long country number, every digit of which was
…vention.

'I want your address, too,' he said. He was bending over my shoulder, avidly, greedily looking at the figures appearing behind my pencil. I wrote down, 'Fir Top Cottage, Lynch Hill, Wenningham, Suffolk.' This, too, was total invention, and I was amazed at myself for writing it straight off without having to stop and think – it just came. I could only pray he wouldn't check the moment I was out of the house.

At the door I turned, reluctantly, and we touched hands. There was a cold stickiness to both which made their meeting highly unpleasant.

'*A bientôt*,' he said, with a lopsided smile that I remembered from long ago, a caricature now, distorted by the changes around it. Suddenly, just as I was about to withdraw my hand, he gripped it and pulled me close to him. Again I had a horrible feeling he was going to kiss me, though why he should I couldn't imagine; but he only peered into my eyes, holding me by hand and elbow.

'I wouldn't let you out of my sight if I thought you were going to disappear again,' he said gratingly.

'Of course I'm not,' I said airily.

His eyes shifted narrowly from one of mine to the other, trying to read my thoughts, but fortunately he had never known me well enough to be able to. Toby would have known in a moment. I wondered if Andy would.

'David's the only thing of any value left in my life,' he said. 'I'm going to help you find him. And when we do . . .'

He left the rest unsaid, but I knew. He would never let up on his claim to David now. I felt a shiver go up my neck as I forced myself to go on calmly meeting his eyes. They were the eyes of a drunkard, a failure, and a fanatic. I found myself, for one wicked moment, wishing with all my heart that he would – disappear, even from the distant fringes of our lives, that his shadow over us would be lifted for ever; and by that what I was really wishing was that he would die. This wish was very clear, very strong, and quite unequivocal, really, though I dressed it up in my head. I drew my arm out of his hold and said: 'Well, when we do, then'll be the time to talk about the future. You'll ring the police-station if you think of anything, or if . . .? I won't be going home tonight.'

He nodded, still watching me like a hawk watches a snake which is trying to wriggle away. He glanced at the address in his hand, and back at me. He suspected – I knew it.

'Till later, then,' I said, and walked steadily away from him up the weedy path. Then, because I felt my back view must give me away through some communicable wish to break into a run, I turned at the gate and said jokingly, 'Why don't you tidy up your garden?'

'Why don't I tidy up my life? First things first.'

I remembered the L-shaped room.

'Not necessarily.'

'Does David like gardening?'

'Yes.'

'Maybe we could tidy it together.'

Over my dead body.

I raised a false and treacherous smile, waved lightly and walked away.

Chapter 3

THE police car was parked in front of Andy's, so I paused at the window to say to the policewoman, 'Sorry, no good—' before heading for Andy's car, which attracted me like a refuge. But the policewoman called me back.

'I'll just go and have a word with him.'

'No! Please. Don't go. It's pointless.' She frowned, and I gabbled on. 'How *could* David find this address? It's all quite pointless, it always was. Anyway I've left your number. Please, let's get back to the station and see if there's any news.'

'If there had been, I'd have heard on the car radio.'

'Well anyway, let's go.'

She looked at me piercingly. I met her eyes with all the earnest appeal I could muster. Behind her I could see Jo leaning forward anxiously. I realized I'd been in there a long time and that the strain for Jo must have been intense. I managed to smile at her, but not out of pure kindness; I wanted to stop her getting out of the car and going with the policewoman to question Terry.

The policewoman was already on the pavement beside me. 'What is it?' she asked quietly. 'Why don't you want me to speak to him? You never know – it might help in some way—'

I couldn't look her in the face. I just shook my head. She hesitated a moment and then patted my arm briskly. 'Wait in the other car,' she said. 'I won't be long.' Then she walked away.

Without the slightest warning, I burst into tears. Jo jumped out of one car and Andy out of the other, and they enveloped me, and helped me back into Andy's car where they climbed in on either side of me with an instinctive protectiveness which touched me to more tears.

'Oh Christ, oh Christ—' Jo kept saying. She was wringing her hands and banging them against her knees, her face twisted and screwed up childishly. Andy held me silently. At last I put my hand over Jo's rigid ones and said, 'Stop it, Jo, it's not David now, it's Terry, and that's not your fault.' She looked at me piteously. 'He's so awful!' I almost shouted. 'David must never see him – you must never see him,' I added, turning to Andy. 'Promise me you'll never try to see him! – Although I swear he wasn't like that then. I didn't even know him at first. Horrible—'

I shivered. And suddenly I remembered a time, at least twenty-five years ago, when my father, unwontedly convivial and prankish at one of our family Christmas gatherings, had sneaked off with my Great Aunt Addy and got dressed up as an old tramp. She'd used her face-powder to whiten his hair and eyebrows, her mascara to blacken his teeth, her grey eye-shadow to put sick hollows under his cheek-bones and round his eyes. She had displayed a greater talent than she ever had when applying make-up to her own face. When he was all ready, dressed in some terrible old clothes he'd found somewhere and a battered hat, he crept outside and rang the doorbell. Addy came in to the dining-room and announced that a poor old tramp was outside asking for a bite of Christmas dinner and might she bring him in for a drink because he looked quite ill ... Then in he shuffled, and we were all completely fooled, even me; we had him sitting at the table eating the remains of the turkey before something about his ears suddenly caught my attention ... I was only about ten at the time and the shock was like a heavy blow to the heart, because it was him, my daddy, and yet it was a poor toothless seedy-looking old tramp at the same time. I seemed to foresee what might happen to him, or any of us – poverty, illness, destitution, misery ... I remember jumping up from my place and screaming and screaming and screaming. Only Addy's strong arms and soft bosom at last stifled my sobs. She hid my eyes and soothed me with a string of unprintable curses for her own insensitive stupidity, while my uncles and aunts recovered from their amazement and hastily restored my father to normal with crumpled table-napkins and bright cries of 'It's all right, sweetie, look, it's Daddy again, it's only your old Daddy!' But Addy understood, and never forgave herself, as she told me years later ...

And now Terry had given me the same sort of shock, with the same double-image Dorian Gray effect ... Perhaps Andy felt this about Chris, when he despoiled the snapshot in an angry effort to give me his likeness, superimposing another, subjective image ... As Andy held me and stroked my hear, I felt a current of sympathy passing between us. For a moment he was Addy; he was my father,

237

and John, and even Toby, who'd once kissed my tears as Andy was doing now. He was everybody in my life whom I'd ever loved for the comfort they gave. What was it I had thought of, in Israel, about why Andy was not more strongly bound to me? Because we'd never been through any deep troubles together? In that case, this horror we were living through should rectify that if it did nothing else. I put my arms round him and tried to catch my breath against the after-sobs and steady myself.

Andy said, 'We'll find him, darling. We will find him. And never mind that – whatever you found in there, that's over and done with.'

I tried to believe him.

After a short time, the policewoman came out of Terry's house, closing the door and the gate behind her with sharp little bangs echoing the irritation and distaste on her face. She came to the window of our car just as I was putting away my compact after an attempt to blot off some of the damage.

'Nothing to be gained there, as you said,' she remarked. 'Back to the station, then.'

'Could I ride with you?' I asked.

Jo stayed in Andy's car and I got in the back of the police car next to Amanda.

'Wouldn't you rather sit in front?' asked the policewoman.

'No thanks,' I answered. I knew, suddenly, why I had wanted to ride in this car.

The car lurched forward and began to speed downhill. I had my eyes on Amanda. She was staring out of the window fixedly. Her whole body was held taut.

'Amanda,' I said.

She jerked her shoulders but didn't turn round.

'Amm, I'm talking to you.'

I pulled her round to face me sharply and held her by the upper arms.

'I want to ask you something. Have you ever been really frightened? I don't mean now, when you think I might shake you or smack you. I mean *really* frightened.'

'Yes.'

238

'When?'

'It was only for a moment, when I was riding Ant and she was galloping towards a hedge and I thought I wouldn't be able to stop her and she'd jump.'

'Do you remember how it felt, that fear?'

'All my insides were like hot jelly.'

'I have that feeling now. It goes on and on. Your mother has it, only worse in a way because she thinks it was her fault.'

'What was?'

'Don't you know what we're talking about, Amanda?'

'David?' she asked cautiously, after a moment.

'Did you see your mother crying before? Coming from the airport?'

She lowered her head and tried to fiddle with her dress, but I caught her hands quite brutally and held them still.

'I've never seen her cry like that. Have you ever seen her cry like that?'

She shook her head. All I could see of it was the pink clean parting and the straight blonde hair pulled away on either side.

'Don't you love her?'

One nod, the parting arrowing towards her knee.

'Then how can you stand to see her so unhappy when you could stop it?'

Her head came up and her eyes, wide open again but now filled with tears, fixed themselves on mine. She looked quite wild and desperate. She bit her lips together until they disappeared. I wanted to let my hands shake her and shake her; but I stopped them.

'Listen Amanda. I know you promised not to tell. I know you must never break a promise. But some things are even more important. Please, darling! He's only little, he's younger than you and he's not as brave. Maybe he thought he knew what to do and where to go, but do you think you'd like to be lost in London if things didn't go the way you expected? Maybe at this very moment he's thinking to himself somewhere, "If only Amm would tell them so that they could come and find me!" You've seen how big London is, your Mummy's told you how dangerous it is. Can't you imagine being lost in it somewhere and not knowing what to do?'

'But he does know what to do!'

239

The words burst out of her. I let her go. She shrank back in the corner and I sat looking at her, my arms trembling with recent tension. With a fraction of my attention I noticed the policewoman, seated in front beside the driver, leaning avidly over the back of the seat.

'What was the plan, Amanda? Tell me.'

She was crying properly now. How seldom one saw her cry! Not like David, who cried about everything. I turned up her wet red face in my hands, and she gazed at me mutely, her mouth wide open to let the huge jagged sobs out.

'Tell me!' And now I did shake her, and more tears spurted out, shook free of her face and splashed my dress and hers.

It came out in a cataract.

'He's talked about it for ages – how he'd find him when he grew up – and I said, why wait, you could find him any time you liked, only he's a baby and he said you'd never let him – so we made a plan, and he told you to go to Israel, and then we got Mummy to take us to London. He took that picture from the magazine, we'd cut it out and kept it and we used to look at it and make up stories about him ...'

She stopped for breath. The policewoman must have signalled the driver because the car pulled in to the side and everything was still, except for the other traffic tearing past down the hill.

'Go on! How was he going to find him?'

'He was so silly, he thought his Daddy would be in a cinema, or that the studios would be near the cinema somewhere, but I told him someone would have to take him there, so he said he'd go to John's house and John would take him.'

'John!'

'Yes. He copied his address out of your address book. He said he'd get a taxi there, well actually that was my idea, he wanted to go by bus but we didn't know which one went there. So I expect that's what he did.'

'But in God's name, you silly children, did neither of you know that John was going to Israel with me?'

She sat stock-still, staring at me. 'You never told us that,' she said.

Chapter 4

THE house was much as I remembered it, only a bit more dilapi-
dated, if possible. It was one of those big houses in Paddington
which has come down in the world, and will soon, in due order of
Councils and Re-development, come down altogether, presumably
ejecting its nests of occupants from its collapsing ruins, squeezing
them out to scamper desperately in all directions like little creatures
when the last island of the meadow goes under the mower. Certainly
the building was as full of clustered life as any rabbit warren; it
already overflowed on to the steps and pavement in the form of
children (all black) and a few adults who stepped over them as over
inanimate impediments, scarcely glancing down at the small intent
figures playing jacks or chalking on the steps and threshold.

When the police-car arrived, however, there was an immediate
reaction. The children stopped whatever they were doing. Some
merely stared. Others got up and melted away into the dark oblong
of the front door. Still others, either secure in their innocence or in
the covertness of their villainy, came to the edge of the pavement
and crowded up to the car, making it difficult to get out. Their
closest attention was divided between the policewoman, who
seemed to command more nudges and sneers than respect, and
Amanda, who, in her crisp, dressed-up, blonde WASPishness,
formed a focal-point of antagonistic fascination for them. She dried
her final tears hurriedly, sat up straight, and gazed back at them
disdainfully. Out of her haughty eyes I seemed to see Jo's buried
prejudices (which I had never seen a sign of, but which John had
perceived) corkscrewing out like twisted laser-beams – well-
concealed fear behind an assured superiority. Very few of them
stood up to it; the rest withered before it, and by the time we'd got
out and were crossing the pavement, only two little ones were left,
held mainly by curiosity.

Of the row of bells which had once graced the heavy sub-
Regency portico, only one was left; the rest were sockets. We
pressed the survivor, but even through the open door, no peal
sounded. And nobody came. The policewoman banged on the door

with a knocker which actually fell off in her hand; she looked at it in some disgust, laid it carefully on a crumbling ledge, and stepped across the swaybacked stone threshold into the house.

I hadn't been there for some months, but the feel of the house came back to me. It was full of sounds of life so shut-away behind doors that they were little more audible than a pulse, or rather a lot of pulses. The house was still, yet it vibrated with people's movement and breathing and speech. The hall was floored in broken marble tiles, many of which had come out, leaving oblong or diamond-shaped holes which were full of crushed cement and dirt. The walls had been painted orange, and then scratched and drawn on and rubbed. The wide entrance was choked with push-chairs, a pram, two bicycles (one a brand-new Chopper) and several shopping baskets on wheels. The stairs were worn down like the doorstep; as we climbed them, we felt as if we might fall backwards.

The policewoman led the way, followed by me, holding Amanda's hand. We were trailed by two little black whispers, and I felt curious eyes watching us from the stairwell and the porch behind us. I wished Andy were here, but he must have gone straight back to the station. I wished John were here, too, waiting in his great gay shambles of a room up four flights of these concave stairs . . . Then I could be sure of finding David, safe in his protective custody . . .

'Who are you looking for?'

We all stopped, startled. A little coloured woman had suddenly appeared out of a door at the top of the first two flights, and was barring our way with one hand on her bony hip. She wore old-fashioned slimline slacks, the kind with the elastic under the foot, a pink Marks and Spencer's polo-necked sweater, and an overall. She had a scarf tied round her head. There was, despite all this, a look of a fierce little Pygmy warrior defending his village; the broom in her hand took on the aspect of a spear for a moment, and I felt the same atavistic fear of her as I had felt of John, the first time I had seen him.

'We're looking for a child,' said the policewoman.

The casual vibrations of the house seemed to catch like a held breath; through the vaulted darkness of the landing, other doors creaked open a crack, and the house seemed to listen.

The little woman, still taller than we were because of the stairs, glared down at us through fierce yellow eyes. My blood suddenly burned my veins in a flush of renewed panic and terror. In such a house, it couldn't happen that a white child would appear (or disappear) without every inhabitant knowing of it. If this little wiry defender denied knowledge of him, we might go further, get a warrant, search the house from attic to cellar, but we would never find him because the community of the house would have reason to take care that we didn't. What reason? Why was I afraid of them? Had John taught me nothing? But it was *their* antagonism that frightened me, I realized suddenly. They hated us, their children hated our children. 'Whity, whity, lifted her nightie . . .' A cold shiver passed over me, and I felt Amanda clutch my hand in a spasm of echoed disquiet.

'You come for the little boy?'

I, who cannot faint, had to reach out for the greasy banister and hold on to it to steady myself.

'He's here, then?' I heard the policewoman say through a sound-fog that partly blocked my ears.

'He's with Mrs Nelson. You wait there, I go and call her.'

She turned to go further up the stairs, but a voice from above called, 'Okay then, Selma, I heard. I'm bringing him.' And then, fainter: 'David, looks as if your mama's come for you.'

Later we sat in the room where David had spent twenty-four hours. It was at the top of the house, next to John's room, and it belonged to Mrs Nelson and her husband and their baby. The husband was at work, but Mrs Nelson made us tea and gave Amanda a drink of orange. David said nothing. He had sat on my knee and cried until he could cry no more. After that he just sat, with his arms round my waist, and didn't look at anyone or say anything.

I wished we were alone, but we were not, and I had to talk to this woman who had taken him in and been very kind to him but who had not had sense, or courage, or something, enough to get in touch with the police and save us all that misery and anxiety. The policewoman gave her a very restrained, but cutting, telling-off before going to find a telephone. She left me to drink the tea and look after the children until she came back.

Mrs Nelson rocked her baby and smiled at me and said,

'I heard him out on the landing last night, knocking and knocking at the door of John's room. Well now, I knew John was not there, but how do I know where he went? Three days he not been back, anyone else in the house tell his neighbours before he goes off for more than a day, but not John – he's very shut-in, you know, keeps himself to himself, doesn't tell anyone his business. Which is all right, but sometimes you need to know. So I didn't know when he come back, I mean, it could be last night or this morning or anytime soon. Your little boy, he just told me David and no more, said he would wait for John, so what could I do?' She shifted the baby's weight and reached for a feeding bottle of orange-juice. 'It's all very well for *her*—' she indicated the absent policewoman with her head —'to tell me off for not ringing the police. I know my husband, he had enough of them, I didn't even suggest it to him because I know what he'd say. John's room is locked, I can't get in to let him wait in there, and anyway he so little I can't let him be on his own. I think to myself, by tomorrow, if John's not back, I do something. This morning I begin to get a bit frightened, my husband getting angry, we can't keep him here. Of course not, but what can we do? So I say, tonight if John doesn't come, we ring someone. We won't ring no one, he says, I take him to the station and leave him outside. But then David says, I won't go till I find my daddy.' David's arms jerked. His face burrowed closer to my damp shoulder. The woman was shaking her head. 'I must admit I'm glad you got here,' she said.

The policewoman came back without knocking. 'All's well that ends well,' she said with a thin smile which did not seem to include Mrs Nelson, who looked blankly in another direction. I stood up, setting David on his feet. He still clung to me so that I could hardly walk.

'David, say goodbye and thank you to Mrs Nelson.'

He didn't move or speak.

'Don't worry the boy,' said Mrs Nelson comfortably. 'It don't matter.'

'Well, I'm very grateful, anyway,' I said. 'I'm sorry for all your trouble.' I hesitated. Should I offer her some money? I decided to, because obviously David would have eaten something and they were clearly hard up. I pulled out my wallet, but she immediately backed away, waving her light-palmed hands and shaking her head.

'No, no,' she said. 'No, no, no.'

I put the wallet back, feeling ashamed. 'I only thought, for his food—'

'He didn't eat nothing to speak of,' she said.

'Thank you, then.'

We shook hands and I touched the bright-eyed baby with one finger on his satiny cheek and thought, *I'll send some lovely toy.* 'What's his name?' I asked.

'Douglas.'

At the last moment, David recovered enough to wave goodbye to her. Then we walked down the stairs through an underwater silence speckled with anemone eyes, and went out to the car.

'Your friends were at the station when I rang,' said the policewoman. 'They know he's been found.'

I sat with David on one side and Amm on the other. They stared at each other like strangers across me. I put an arm around each, but Amanda disengaged herself quite politely, which freed another hand to hold David, plastered to my side and still faintly trembling.

At the police station we were met outside by Andy and Jo. Jo looked twenty years younger, radiant with relief. She embraced me and David together as we got out of the car.

'Oh darling! I'm so glad, I'm so unspeakably glad! Now I can ask to be forgiven—'

Histrionics were unlike her, actressy as she often was in other ways. I brushed it off almost brusquely. 'Oh, shush, don't be absurd. It's all over.' I squeezed her arm and she briefly pressed her cheek against mine. Then she hugged David. 'You little villain,' she said. 'What you put us through—'

'Not just now,' I said, and she stood up at once.

Andy was beside me. 'Let's separate up and get home now,' he said.

'Of course,' said Jo. 'Come on, Amanda.'

Her voice had taken on a tone I can only call menacing. Amm cast a speaking look of appeal at me.

'I'm sorry, Auntie Jane,' she said in an unwontedly tiny voice.

'Jo,' I said. 'Please don't lean too hard, until we've talked. She was on a fearful spot.'

245

'She's on another one now,' was all Jo would say grimly.

Then David, Andy and I were driving home together.

At first we didn't talk. Andy had to navigate the evening rush out of London. At every red light or other necessary halt, he would take his left hand off the wheel and take hold of mine. David sat on my knee and speedily lapsed into an exhausted sleep.

When we got out of London, we stopped, and laid him on the back seat under a rug. I stared at him in the twilight. I wanted to throw myself on top of him and kiss him until my lips were sore. Nothing else could assuage the feeling of love and gratitude and relief I was suffering from – suffering is not the wrong word, it was real pain. I drew a ragged breath which was almost a sob as I got backwards out of the car, and Andy put his arms round me.

'Cry if you like,' he said.

'I'm all cried out.'

'I think not.'

'Well, not just now. Let's go home.'

'I love you.'

'I love *you*.'

'Are you sure?' he asked.

'As sure as I can be at this moment of loving anyone but David.'

He kissed me and we got back into the car.

'Did you see Chris?' he could, poor devil, no longer keep from asking.

'Oh, God! I'm sorry. I haven't even mentioned him. Yes, I saw him, and we'll talk about him, but Andy, you're quite wrong. I'm crazy about him.'

He looked absolutely aghast with disbelief.

'You can only mean he's got over it,' he said.

'I don't mean that at all. I doubt if he'll ever get over it, in that sense. He's radically different from you and he always will be.'

'But you *liked* him?'

'He's a darling, and sound as a nut. He'll be all right, you'll see.'

We drove on in silence through the dusk. I looked at Andy's profile, and caught an expression of relief mixed with incredulity. Why *is* nature so unreasonable as to implant in us this conviction that our children will or should grow into facsimiles of ourselves?

Yet when I glanced over my shoulder at my sleeping son, the run-away restored, I was struck afresh by the realization that his defection had not merely shocked but staggered me – not by its wickedness at all but because I would never in a million years, at age eight or any other, have been capable of anything like it.

Needing to touch him, I half-turned in my front seat and laid my hand gently on him through the rug. Jo had called him, barely half-jokingly, a little villain, but I was having none of that. David was no villain. If there was a villain in the piece, it was me. I couldn't blame him for trying to get a look at Terry, for trying to get his desperate filial hooks into him; in fact now I thought about it I was quite bemused with admiration for his courage in the doomed enterprise. For my timid, mummy-clinging little cry-baby to plan and execute such an operation, even under Amanda's Machiavellian inspiration, was a feat of daring so astonishing that I could only gape at it, and at him.

'What about your other chap?' Andy suddenly asked.

'Over,' I said.

'Finally?'

'Oh yes.'

He drew a deep, ragged breath.

'Still,' he said, 'I'm glad he's three thousand miles away.'

I tried to be utterly sure it didn't make the slightest difference, but I couldn't be, so I said nothing.

'Was it the sort of affair you wish afterwards hadn't happened?'

Not for the first time, the essence of Terry-and-me, and Toby-and-me, sprang up side by side, offering their wild contrast for instant comparison. The first had taken on new and sombre tones, with several added warps and twists, since what I profoundly hoped would be my final encounter with him that afternoon. What a man becomes is what he essentially was all the time, and to have loved, or even only lain with, a man like Terry, could only be regarded as a signal blot on any woman's escutcheon. As for Toby, our combined love-image was also not undamaged, but it still stood tall beside the other, head and shoulders above every other relationship in my life so far. But there was room for a greater to follow, something to be built unashamedly out of need, David's, Andy's, and – at last I could look at it straight in the eye – my own. I seemed to see the three of us, drawing together as if a suture-thread around the open wound of loneliness were closing the natural gaps in a healing bond.

'Well?'

'Sorry, what did you say?'

'I asked if you regretted your affair with him.'

'No, I don't.'

'That's good.'

The headlights fanned round the dark bends ahead.

'Are we away then? – You and me?'

'Yes.'

David stirred under my hand and I felt a light-wave of love and excitement strike through me as a spear strikes through a fish, impaling it. For a moment I gasped and writhed; even to be impaled by a happy fate makes you jerk against the knowledge of inevitability, a final commitment. But I wanted it really, as I had wanted the impalement of David, pinning me to life for ever. I put my free hand on Andy's arm as the car swerved and began to bump over the first ruts on the lane leading home.

THE END

Postscript

EXCEPT that of course it wasn't the end.

On arriving at the cottage that same night we found a cable from Toby, very terse, saying Rachel was being put on a plane which would be landing at London Airport in the early hours of the following morning. There are either no words, or at least two thousand, to describe the discussions of the night . . . I met the plane with a sense of numbed inevitability. She has been with us ever since.

Now it's 1973. David is nearly fourteen. Rachel, my unadopted daughter, is thirteen. And my second son, Andy's and mine, Guy, is five. We live in Andy's house-in-the-field, enlarged now to hold our curiously-constituted family.

It would be pleasant to be able to say that Chris, on his return from his wanderings, settled down with us and married Georgie, but he didn't. True, he lived with her for a bit, but then took off again, to the Far East this time, after a series of shattering rows with his father. The last we heard of him he was living with a stone-age tribe in Borneo. Andy still can't speak of him calmly and I still love him. So, more oddly, does Georgie, who with her three-year-old daughter, lives with us, though officially she's supposed to be renting Andy's cottage. For me it's like watching history – my history – repeat itself. She also refused an abortion, and wouldn't allow us to locate Chris and tell him . . . Well, but at least she had us. And one day Chris will turn up . . .

For the rest: Whistler has married again. I've met her several times. She's very sweet, as John said, not a ha'poth of harm in her. But although basically antagonistic to me, she was, when it came to the crunch, glad enough to let me keep Rachel, though I've never been given any legal security. Impossible for me to understand . . . We could never be friends.

When I married I sold out my share of the shop to Jo, and she moved herself and it to London, leaving the original as a branch with Georgie nominally in charge. Amanda is at boarding school and we see her every holiday, except when they go off to glamorous foreign parts. She is highly sophisticated and David finds her far too much to handle. He may catch up later, but at the moment all his brotherly devotion is for Rachel. He is what Toby would call quite a little *mensch* these days – my queer-fears have long since melted away, thanks largely to Andy.

Andy remains to some extent a mystery to me. Perhaps that's the secret of our success. Closed doors have opened one by one, but not all of them by any means, and those remaining closed continue to intrigue me. The open ones have revealed a man whom I was entirely right to entrust myself to.

Terry died. He actually did die . . . It was poor mad Grace who wrote to tell me, through the police . . . Her strange letter struck an astonishing note of grief, a grief she apparently expected me to share. But for my part, instinctive relief mingled thickly with guilt, for hadn't I ill-wished him? Andy pooh-poohed my unease, but years later, when I told John, he said matter-of-factly: 'Yes, you probably helped to kill him. Happens all the time. Can't be helped. Anyway, everybody better off now, specially him.'

John has become a name to conjure with. He roamed about the world with his dwindling hippie band (he took over their leadership when Chris left) picking up folk-songs all over the place, and suddenly burst upon the pop world from San Francisco . . . I believe he even had his budding entourage of groupies before he firmly shook them off. Somehow he has managed to remain a loner, even in that claustrophobic world, and basically I found him unchanged. Of course the look of contempt he feared in David's eyes has not appeared; rather there is a gleam of devoted admiration. David is only too delighted to brag at school that John is his friend.

David is normal, as normal as any fourteen-year-old can be in these peculiar times. Even Rachel's ill-timed advent and Guy's a year later, didn't unduly upset him – I think because he was too absorbed at the time in coming to terms with his adventure, which was traumatic for him and for us. It really is tempting to go on at length about the children, all so different and so exciting . . . Guy promises to be the cleverest, Rachel is the strongest, the most beautiful and the most temperamental; but David and I went through most together and for me he will always be the one I am closest to.

And Toby? Toby is still in the kibbutz. He writes occasionally, I mean he writes to me, but of novels there has been only one in six years, a strange introverted book with a kibbutz setting which I think hardly anyone read except me. It was not very good; it was as if his mind had been on something else when he wrote it – irrigation, perhaps . . . That novel freed me as nothing had until then, and I can view his proposed visit next year to see his daughters (Rachel has been annually to see him) with reasonable equanimity, or at least, I could, were it not for the appalling fear that he will have grown up and want to take her from me . . .

But that's another story.

MORE ABOUT PENGUINS, PELICANS
AND PUFFINS

For further information about books available from Penguins please write to Dept EP, Penguin Books Ltd, Harmondsworth, Middlesex UB7 0DA.

In the U.S.A.: For a complete list of books available from Penguins in the United States write to Dept DG, Penguin Books, 299 Murray Hill Parkway, East Rutherford, New Jersey 07073.

In Canada: For a complete list of books available from Penguins in Canada write to Penguin Books Canada Ltd, 2801 John Street, Markham, Ontario L3R 1B4.

In Australia: For a complete list of books available from Penguins in Australia write to the Marketing Department, Penguin Books Australia Ltd, P.O. Box 257, Ringwood, Victoria 3134.

In New Zealand: For a complete list of books available from Penguins in New Zealand write to the Marketing Department, Penguin Books (N.Z.) Ltd, Private Bag, Takapuna, Auckland 9.

In India: For a complete list of books available from Penguins in India write to Penguin Overseas Ltd, 706 Eros Apartments, 56 Nehru Place, New Delhi 110019.

The earlier volumes of
Lynne Reid Banks's trilogy

THE L-SHAPED ROOM

Unmarried and pregnant, Jane Graham is cast out of her suburban home. Lighting dejectedly on a bug-ridden room in a squalid house in Fulham, she gradually comes to find a new and positive faith in life.

THE BACKWARD SHADOW

After the birth of her son, Jane exchanges the L-shaped room for a remote country cottage. She is joined by Dottie, and together they embark upon an enterprise that is to change both their lives.

and

CHILDREN AT THE GATE

Gerda is a Jewish-Canadian divorcee alone in a miserable room in the Arab quarter of Acre. It is the only home she has left.

Her sole comforts are drink and an Arab friend, Kofi, about whom there is considerable mystery. And Gerda is gradually sliding downhill. She is thirty-nine but looks far older; emotionally her life is a shambles.

But Kofi has three solutions to her problems, solutions that have an amazing ability to create more. But then, children do . . . Gerda's rediscovery of her former self through these children, and the happiness she is able to bring into their lives, form the core of this impassioned novel by the celebrated author of *The L-Shaped Room*.

AN END TO RUNNING

Seeking refuge from the domination of his sister and from his own Jewishness, Aaron Franks turns to Martha, his secretary. Together they travel to Israel and a kibbutz – Martha with strong misgivings, Aaron full of anticipation.

A CHOICE OF PENGUINS

☐ **The Englishman's Daughter** Peter Evans.   £1.95

From London and Venice to Moscow, Peter Evans's brilliant, surprising thriller traces a grey landscape of treason and sexual duplicity. 'Stunningly plotted' – *Guardian*. 'As fast-moving as *Gorky Park*' – Len Deighton

☐ **A Dark and Distant Shore** Reay Tannahill   £3.50

Vilia is the unforgettable heroine, Kinveil Castle is her destiny, in this full-blooded saga spanning a century of Victoriana, empire, hatreds and love affairs. 'A marvellous blend of *Gone with the Wind* and *The Thorn Birds*. You will enjoy every page' – *Daily Mirror*

☐ **Death in Zanzibar** M. M. Kaye   £1.95

Holidaying on the beautiful 'Isle of Cloves', Dany Ashton is caught up in a plot whirling round buried gold, blossoming romance, and murder ... 'I recommend it wholeheartedly to those who fancy the idea of Agatha Christie with a touch of romantic suspense' – *Standard*

☐ **Running Time** Gavin Lambert   £1.95

From child starlet to screen goddess, this is the story of the meteoric rise of Baby Jewel, propelled through the star system by her glamorous, calculating mother. A Hollywood bestseller, and 'a funny, dazzling showstopper' – *Good Housekeeping*

☐ **The Best of Roald Dahl**   £4.95

Twenty ingenious and blood-curdling tales chosen from Dahl's bestselling volumes – *Over to You*, *Someone Like You*, *Kiss Kiss* and *Switch Bitch*.

A CHOICE OF PENGUINS

☐ **The Far Pavilions** M. M. Kaye £4.95

Exotic with all the romance and high adventure of nineteenth-century India, M. M. Kaye's magnificent – now famous – story holds at its heart the passionate love of an Englishman for Juli, his Indian princess. 'Wildly exciting' – *Daily Telegraph*

☐ **Rumpole and the Golden Thread** John Mortimer £1.95

Here Horace Rumpole continues to deftly juggle the vagaries of law, taking on the con-o-sewers of the art world, dabbling in some female politics and, unfortunately, incurring the wrath of Hilda . . . 'A fruity, foxy masterpiece' – *Sunday Times*

☐ **The Sunne in Splendour** Sharon Penman £3.95

A soaring historical novel that re-creates the passions, the treacheries and the rich Gothic tapestry of medieval England during the Wars of the Roses. 'A very fine book' – Rosemary Sutcliff

☐ **The Watcher** Charles Maclean £1.95

The compulsive thriller about Martin Gregory, who used to regard himself as a fairly ordinary man . . . '*Not* a book for bedtime' – Piers Paul Read. 'I'm something of an insomniac. I read *The Watcher* and stopped sleeping altogether' – Paul Newman

☐ **19 Purchase Street** Gerald A. Browne £1.95

By the author of *11 Harrowhouse*; the international bestseller about 'a dazzling billion-dollar heist so daring and elaborate that it makes most episodes in *Mission Impossible* seem like fraternity pranks' – *The New York Times Book Review*

A CHOICE OF PENGUINS

☐ *Lace* **Shirley Conran** £2.95

Lace is, quite simply, a publishing sensation: the story of Judy, Kate, Pagan and Maxine; the bestselling novel that teaches men about women – and women about themselves. 'Riches, bitches, sex and jetsetters' locations – they're all there' – *Sunday Express*

☐ *Castaway* **Lucy Irvine** £2.50

'Writer seeks "wife" for a year on tropical island.' This is the extraordinary, candid, sometimes shocking account of what happened when Lucy Irvine answered the advertisement and went off to discover for herself the realities of such a 'marriage' – and all our desert island dreams. 'Fascinating' – *Daily Mail*